HOUSE ARETOLI

A NOVEL OF MEDIEVAL VENICE

K.M. BUTLER

First Firsthand Account Press Edition, October 2023
Philadelphia, PA

Library of Congress Control Number: 2023907812

ISBN 978-1-7376391-4-5 (paperback)
ISBN 978-1-7376391-5-2 (ebook)

Cover design by Cutting Edge Studios

Printed in the United States of America
10 9 8 7 6 5 4 3 2 1

For my wife Shelby,
who has patiently awaited seeing this,
her favorite novel, in print for more than a decade

HOUSE
ARETOLI

Mediterranean Sea
AD 1365

CHAPTER ONE

August 8, 1363

NICCOLO

A FAINT BREEZE CARRIED the scent of pine to Niccolo Aretoli atop the battlement. He would never grow used to being surrounded by so much land. The unending shadows of the Cretan wilderness beyond the walls of Candia seemed menacing, dangerous. He shivered at the thought of what could be lurking in that vast darkness.

He longed for the comfort of moonlight reflecting off the water. He longed for home, his Venetian lagoon.

Up ahead, a sentry slumped against his pike and kicked the mortar from a loose stone with his boot.

Niccolo sighed. A careful watch wasn't essential on the island of Crete, alone in the middle of the Mediterranean; the Venetian fleet and its merchants in every port throughout the known world would provide ample warning of any threats. But duty was still duty.

"Look sharp, sentry."

The man jumped and gripped his eight-foot pole tighter. "Captain Aretoli?"

Niccolo raised his chin and arched an eyebrow. "Anything to report?"

"There's never anything to report, sir."

He was right, of course. The governor may fret after arguments with the island's Cretan and Venetian residents, but there hadn't been trouble in months.

A giggle sounded from the patchwork of buildings encircled by the walls. Illuminated by the light of a torch, a fiery redhead sashayed and hiked her dress up to reveal a bare ankle. Even from this distance, Niccolo could read the invitation in her eyes.

Pulse quickening and cheeks flushing, he forced himself to turn back to the sentry.

Hungry desire burned shamelessly in the other man's expression.

Niccolo could sympathize with him. In a month, the prostitutes of Candia would be busy with the many lonely sailors returning with the convoy from the Black Sea. A simple sentry wouldn't be able to afford their time.

Time. Niccolo had almost finished his term of service. Then, he could return to Venice and his dear Rosalia.

He shook his head, banishing the thought before longing overwhelmed him. Instead, he focused on the sentry. "What's your name?"

The man tore his gaze from the redhead. "Eduardo Gallozi, sir."

Niccolo offered a reassuring squeeze of the man's shoulder. "I'm sure you can find her when your watch is over."

"I'm on duty until dawn." The words spilled out as a whine.

"I rather prefer that to my night." Dinner at the governor's house involved dishes far too exotic for Niccolo's simple tastes.

"Sir?"

"Nothing." He couldn't avoid his responsibilities, even if they cost him a night of indigestion. If he delayed any longer, he'd be late.

With a salute, Niccolo descended the stairs and disappeared into the depths of the city. A few moments later, the sentry succumbed to his desire and abandoned the wall for the redhead's beckoning arms.

Neither of them witnessed the three-pronged hook sail over the battlement and bite into the stone of the embrasure.

NICCOLO

"Oysters are the finest delicacy of the sea. Don't you agree?" Governor Dandolo purred with eyes closed. As he slowly chewed, his fingers stroked the lacquered Dalmatian wood of the dining table.

Only a lifetime of senatorial feasting kept Niccolo from gagging as the slimy mollusk slid down his throat. He concealed a grimace with his palm as he pushed a stray lock of his chestnut hair back into place.

The third diner, his friend and fellow captain Giovanni Sabarelli, grinned at Niccolo's discomfort. He scooped up the contents of the last remaining shell. "They are delicious, Governor. I'm sure House Sabarelli could help you acquire more at a very reasonable price."

Eyes opening, the governor barked a laugh. "I'm sure it would." He waved a finger at Giovanni. "Your father would be proud of your efforts to profit from your position, captain."

"If I did otherwise, I would not be Venetian."

The exchange bought Niccolo enough time to drown the urge to vomit with a long draught of wine. He offered his friend an appreciative smile for rendering it unnecessary to share his own opinion.

Dandolo raised his goblet. "To the finest merchants in the world. *La Serenissima.*"

Niccolo and Giovanni joined him and drank deeply.

The dining room provided ample evidence to justify that boast. Byzantine-style tapestries stretched from the ceiling to the floor depicting scenes from the foundation of the first Venetian settlement on Crete. Their deep crimson, cerulean, and purple hues came from ports throughout the Mediterranean and Black Seas. Midway between the Doric columns in the corners hung four large oil lanterns constructed of Venetian glass ringed in delicate Castilian silver. The pride of Venice, those beautiful glass panes—six on each lantern—amplified the light and cast the flames' glow on the finest goods from across Europe and Asia.

A shadow traced beneath the ash doors at the far end of the room and interrupted Niccolo's moment of admiration.

His eyes narrowed. "Governor, are you expecting another course?"

"Not to my knowledge."

Niccolo studied the crack beneath the doors. A scraping sound slid down the other side of the wall and ended in a thump.

He knew that sound.

"Giovanni?"

His friend stiffened. "I heard."

Dandolo frowned at his captains. "What's the matter?"

Upon seeing the second shadow, Niccolo sprang to his feet and reached for Dandolo. "Governor, do as—"

Four men burst through the doors with a violent crash. Two of them raised crossbows and fired. Niccolo shoved Dandolo to the side an instant before the bolts embedded themselves into the governor's chair with solid *thunks*.

Niccolo stepped between the attackers and the governor and drew his sword. The reassuring weight of the hilt in his hand calmed his nerves. Beside him, Giovanni did the same.

Two of the intruders charged with swords drawn as the others reloaded. Niccolo ducked to avoid the first and shoved him into his companion, sending them both crashing into the wall.

"Yours," he called back to Giovanni.

Niccolo charged the two crossbowmen, a swarthy Cretan and a man with a jagged scar on his cheek. Eyes widening, they abandoned the half-cocked crossbows and reached for their swords. Niccolo jabbed again and again until his blade met resistance. He pushed with all his weight, driving the tip deep into the chest of the scarred man.

The scar danced as the man screamed. After collapsing, he scurried into the corner, clutching at the fresh wound.

The swarthy Cretan slashed at Niccolo's throat, but Niccolo

deflected it up and away. With a quick flick of his wrist, he drew his dagger and thrust it between the man's ribs. The Cretan collapsed with an abrupt thud.

Heart hammering in his chest, Niccolo glanced backward. Giovanni had dispatched the others and now knelt beside the wide-eyed governor, checking him for injuries.

"Dandolo is unharmed," his friend reported.

Approaching the wounded crossbowman, Niccolo asked in Greek, "Why did you attack us?"

A spasm of pain contorted the man's face. Already he looked deathly pale, and a damp red stain had spread across the bottom half of his tunic. He responded not in Greek, but in Italian with a distinct Venetian accent. "We will be"—he gasped and winced—"we will be free of Venice's tyranny." He inhaled a raspy breath. His voice had faded to a mere whisper. "Hear our liberation."

Niccolo paused to listen to the faint shouts in the distance. "A revolt?"

"Impossible," the governor blurted.

Niccolo returned his attention to the wounded man only to find him lying motionless.

Giovanni stood. "Nico, it's not safe here. The barracks?"

He nodded. "Governor?"

Dandolo held a hand against his stomach and inhaled a long breath. The color returned to his face. "Lead on, captain."

On their way down the hall, they passed the bodies of the governor's servants. Both had had their throats slit.

It wasn't fair. They had been innocents, simply trying to earn their keep. Niccolo hadn't realized Cretan sentiment against Venice had gotten this bad.

Giovanni opened the outer door a crack and peered into the night. Thankfully, the hinges did not squeak. "The Heights are burning."

Even the Venetians who lived in the city resented those gaudy estates and large gardens built by senatorial families. The Cretans viewed the neighborhood as a constant reminder of their subjugation by a lagoon city a thousand miles away.

"Don't these fools know we're their only protection from the Turk?" Dandolo's voice burst with disbelief. "We were working with them, improving their industry. I don't understand why—"

"Answers can come later," Niccolo interrupted. Dandolo could pontificate for hours about colonial policy. "We must save the city if we can and protect our citizens if we cannot."

Giovanni's worried expression suggested he shared Niccolo's doubts about their prospects, but his friend simply reported, "It's clear outside. Let's move."

They kept close to the buildings as they traveled to avoid drawing the attention of any rebels whose path they might cross. The barracks were only a few streets away, intentionally close to the governor's palace in case of a crisis.

A crash sounded in the distance. Flames peeked out from beyond the buildings. Behind them, the cries of a mob filled the air.

"Hurry," Niccolo hissed. "We don't have much time."

The imposing edifice of the barracks appeared around the next corner. Members of the garrison stood in the square before it, goaded to dress quickly by lieutenants buzzing around them. Pikes rested against their shoulders as they strapped on breastplates and straightened helmets.

Giovanni led them toward one of the other captains. "What happened?"

The man saluted the governor before answering. "Armed men scaled the walls and opened the gates. Hundreds are inside the city now, and they're headed for us."

Groups of frightened residents, holding their children close, were streaming into the square toward the barracks. This was their home. On fire.

Niccolo swallowed to still the flutter in his chest. "We saw the Heights burning. Did they come from that direction?"

The captain shook his head. "We think those fires were set by people already in the city."

"What does that mean?" the governor demanded.

Niccolo drew his lips tight. "The city is lost."

Dandolo gasped. "Impossible."

"If they're attacking your palace and burning the Heights, they've already spread throughout the city. They know our strength. They wouldn't risk so much if they didn't have the numbers to overcome us."

The square was filling quickly now. They would be facing a mob of desperate people before long.

The governor lowered his gaze. "We must save as many as we can. I may have lost Crete, but I won't see our people massacred."

Niccolo turned to his fellow captains. "Ten galleys are in port."

"Will it be enough?" Giovanni asked.

"It'll have to be."

"My company can get the citizens to the port," the other captain offered.

Niccolo nodded. "Have some men dismantle the barracks. Leave nothing for them to use against us when we return."

"I'll go with him." The governor had recovered his poise. "I've spoken to the old women in the Senate. I can calm our citizens."

"Thank you, Governor. We'll delay the rebels as long as possible."

"Gentlemen…" Dandolo cleared his throat. "I don't want *any* of our people to die. Don't waste your lives." With a nod, he departed to address the civilians.

Niccolo pulled Giovanni aside. "What do you think?"

"We'll never hold them." Giovanni shook his head. "Too many intersections."

"Delay them, then fall back?"

"Agreed." Giovanni offered one of his smiles, but it didn't quite reach the corners of his mouth. "Be smart."

Niccolo clasped his friend's arm. "You too."

The men of the fourth division piled cots, blankets, and leather armor onto a bonfire in the center of the square. The rebels likely wouldn't notice one more fire, but burning the supplies might make reclaiming the island easier when the Venetians returned.

Niccolo agreed with the governor; the Venetian navy was the only force capable of preventing the Turks from sweeping across the sea and conquering every Christian island. Venetian protection was surely better than Muslim rule. Venice was hardly oppressive; while it had appointed a senatorial governor, the island's residents could conduct their affairs as they wished, so long as they sent their taxes and obeyed Venetian trade policies. Every Mediterranean power expected that of its subjects.

Niccolo hurried his troops a few hundred yards into the city and split his fifty men into groups on either side of the street leading to the main bazaar. Safely hidden, they waited in a silence broken only by the occasional cough or clink of a pike on a breastplate.

The sounds of shattering glass and splintering wood rolled closer. Each crash made Niccolo want to rush for the docks, to flee for the safety of Rosalia's embrace. Only the eyes of the men around him steadied him. They needed him to be confident now, even if he didn't feel it himself.

Swallowing, he narrowed his eyes and tightened his grip on his pike.

Only when it seemed as if the noise would overwhelm them did the Cretan rebels turn the corner and stream into view. Swords, hammers, and axes waved in the air as they advanced.

"Form squares!" Niccolo shouted.

His pikemen poured out from the side streets and formed two adjacent squares five men deep, blocking the mob's path.

"Present!"

Down came the pikes to form a layered grid of needles.

The flood of angry Cretans crashed into the Venetian pikes. Impaled, the front ranks of the mob fell amid shrieks of pain. Incensed, the second wave charged, seeking to dive under or knock aside individual spears, but Niccolo's men slashed at the rebels mercilessly.

The wave of rebels continued to advance, but their rear ranks were struggling to find footing among the swiftly pooling blood and squirming sea of their injured comrades. Eventually, the mob ground to a halt.

Satisfied at the delay, Niccolo called for the retreat while the rebels recovered and tended to their injured. His soldiers had done what they could. He had lost four men but left no wounded behind for the Cretans to abuse.

They reached the docks out of breath. Giovanni's division had already arrived. His friend was still alive, tending a wounded soldier.

"Giovanni?"

"We met the main force. They had armor, Nico." Giovanni gestured to his arm, slashed but not dangerously so. "They almost overwhelmed us."

"Where's the governor?"

"Already at sea." Giovanni looked grim. "Nico, I've seen some of those men at council meetings. Venetian natives are joining them."

Niccolo drew in a slow breath. "Are you certain?"

"Yes."

This was far worse than a simple colonial revolt.

Three ships remained. Sailors loaded men as fast as they could, but the thundering of the approaching mob continued to increase. His and Giovanni's men had bought time, but only a little.

Niccolo bit at his lip. "How many of your men can still fight?"

Giovanni swept his gaze over them. "Maybe thirty."

"I could use them to guard our retreat."

"Take who you need. I'll get the wounded aboard."

A soldier ran up, panting heavily, and saluted smartly. His clothing, although disheveled, showed no evidence of dirt or bloodstains.

Niccolo recognized him as the sentry from the wall. "Eduardo Gallozi. Glad to see you made it."

Eduardo blurted, "I was cut off, sir. People kept flooding over the walls. They filled the streets so fast." He gripped his pike tightly enough to make it shake.

Niccolo rested a hand on his shoulder. "Did you see any civilians that way?"

Eduardo shook his head. "I didn't mean…I can't believe I let this happen—"

"There was nothing you could do about this." Niccolo's words had no effect on Eduardo's growing panic, though. Grasping Eduardo's other shoulder, he squared to face him. "Eduardo, your fellow Venetians need your help." He met the man's gaze. "Can I count on you?"

The man's posture relaxed. "Yes, sir."

Niccolo smiled, both out of pride and to reassure him. "Good man."

The shouting of the mob intensified. Sailors were helping injured men aboard the three ships moored alongside long piers stretching into the dark sea.

Niccolo mounted an overturned crate and waved his hands to attract the remaining garrison's attention. "Soldiers of Venice, we must defend these ships. Once you board, use your crossbows to support those still on the piers. Do you hear me?"

The Venetians gave a rousing shout that vibrated the crate beneath him.

Niccolo drew his sword and thrust it skyward. "For the republic!"

The Venetians arranged themselves into defensive lines guarding the three remaining piers. The front of the mob spilled out from the side streets, first from the south and then the west. Without pausing, they surged into the solid rows of pikes.

The militia absorbed the impact but gave ground slowly while the loading continued behind them. As soldiers boarded and their ships pulled away, they began firing their crossbows. The intensifying rain of bolts relieved the pressure on the remaining defenders.

Niccolo boarded the same galley as Giovanni. Their ship launched second. "Support them!" He pointed to the final ship between cranks of his crossbow.

Hails of projectiles held the mob at bay as the last three Venetian soldiers cut a wide swath with their pikes and rushed for the departing ship. Two made it across the gangplank before it collapsed into the water. The last soldier leaped for the railing. He caught a trailing rope and dangled from the side precariously until his companions hauled him up to the deck.

Left in possession of the city, the mob broke into cheers as they watched the Venetians sail away.

NICCOLO

A strong easterly breeze let the Venetian fleet unfurl its sails and spare the rowers. They passed Corfu at the mouth of the Adriatic without the usual stopover and quickly skirted Dalmatia, which had been captured by the Hungarians only a few decades earlier. The comparison between that loss and their present situation soured the mood aboard even further. Venice had lost too many battles in recent decades.

Despite the circumstances, Niccolo looked forward to returning home. He could still remember that last, moonlit night in Venice with Rosalia. The cool air had tickled his skin as they had spent the fleeting hours before high tide together where the Grand Canal met open water.

In that stolen moment, she had gazed into his eyes. "But Crete is so far, Nico."

"Not far at all, Rosa." Time had slowed as he had placed her hand against his chest. "You'll be right here, with me."

What a fool he'd been. He should have kissed her under the moonlight, taken her in his arms, and petitioned the bishop to marry them. He had squandered that moment. Finally, he'd have a chance to correct that mistake.

Seven days out of Crete, the convoy reached the Venetian lagoon. The tolling of bells spread through the city as the lead ship unfurled its banners. By the time Niccolo's and the governor's ships had docked, three dozen senators and many of the soldiers' families had clustered around the piers. Disembarking, individual men disappeared into their mothers' and wives' embraces while Dandolo outlined the situation to the senators.

Recognizing his father's blue and silver coat in the crowd, Niccolo tugged on Giovanni's doublet. "Let me introduce you to my family."

As they approached, the crowd parted to reveal a young blonde woman charging toward them. Giovanni jumped back, narrowly avoiding flailing limbs as she leaped onto Niccolo.

"Camilla!"

He squeezed his youngest sister before stepping back to recover his breath. Prior to his leaving for Crete, she had still been a girl with a too-long nose and puffy cheeks. But the beautiful woman smiling at him now had grown into that nose, and her eyes looked confident rather than petulant.

His other sister, Asparia, approached with a graceful smoothness. She had the same high cheeks and dark, nearly black hair as their mother. But gone was the severe and lecturing look she had worn since their mother's death. Instead, her face showed only joy.

She had locked onto Giovanni's gaze and hadn't let go.

Niccolo suppressed a grin. "Where are my manners? Please let me introduce my dear friend, one of my fellow captains on Crete—"

"Giovanni Sabarelli." He stepped past Niccolo and flourished his hand as he bowed to Asparia alone.

"Asparia Aretoli, Signor Sabarelli." Niccolo had never before heard her use such a husky tone.

"It is my most ardent pleasure to meet you, lady."

Face reddening, Asparia extended her hand delicately. Giovanni stroked it gently with his fingertips before kissing it. She returned the furtive caress with a curl of her fingers.

Niccolo had never dreamed she would act so boldly!

Behind her, his father's eyes danced with obvious delight. Who would have imagined steady Asparia losing her head over a man? Of course, it would be a favorable match; Giovanni's father had very nearly been elected as doge, the republic's ceremonial ruler.

Angelo Aretoli stepped past the besotted couple and clasped Niccolo's arms. "My son, I am relieved you're safe. I feared…" He shook his head.

Niccolo now understood the composition of this greeting party. While Camilla had come for the excitement of an unexpected convoy, Asparia had come to support her father in case Niccolo had been killed.

He forced a smile. "I am, Father. Flavio's training helped immensely."

The mention of his brother's name cast a shadow over Angelo's face.

Niccolo's heart began to hammer. "Has something happened to Flavio?"

"He…" Angelo swallowed.

His sisters' smiles had faded, too. Even Asparia had turned from Giovanni to look piteously at Niccolo.

"He is married, Niccolo."

"Married?" He looked to his sisters, then back to his father. "But that's wonderful news!" A new thought made him frown. "Was it the result of a scandal?"

"They're our most important partners, Niccolo. Their enemies called in their debts, and we needed to quickly demonstrate our support."

No. Knees weakening, he reached out helplessly. Giovanni cast supportive arms beneath Niccolo's shoulders a moment later.

Our most important partners.

"Who did he marry?" The question was a mere whisper.

No, his father couldn't be referring to the Cornaros. Aretoli interests must have shifted since he'd left for Crete. Such things happened all the time. Surely, he'd misinterpreted his family's sympathy.

Yes, it had to be someone else.

"Rosalia Cornaro."

The pronouncement battered Niccolo as if he'd been physically struck. "Rosalia." Anguish poured out with her hushed name. Dreams of being with her again, caressing her hand, had sustained him during his time in Crete.

This had to be a mistake. "When?"

"Not but a week ago, son." As an afterthought, Angelo hastily added, "Had we known about the rebellion, we could have delayed until—"

"No." Legs strengthening again, Niccolo flung his hands out, pushing aside the terrible thought. He couldn't endure his father saying he'd lost Rosalia forever for want of a week. "Don't say it." He covered his mouth, suppressing the scream that threatened to rip free.

They would be as close as kin but forever separated. This was worse than losing her to some other man.

His own brother.

"Oh, Nico," Camilla lamented.

Rosalia had comforted him after his mother had died. That year, the plague had taken many, including Asparia's intended. Only being in her arms had given him joy in those days. He had cried then, ashamed of his weakness but unable to stop himself. Yet when he had finally summoned the courage to meet her eyes, he had found only compassion and acceptance.

He remembered stolen caresses during *Balla d'Oro* and Christmastide feasts. The feel of her against him even then, long before they truly knew how a man and woman loved, had filled a hole in him he hadn't even guessed existed.

That hole had just become a chasm.

"Signor Sabarelli, would you please see my daughters home safely?" Angelo spoke without shifting his gaze from his son.

Giovanni bowed graciously and offered each an arm. Asparia spared a glance for her poor brother before accepting. When Giovanni winced at the pressure on his wounded arm, she promptly shifted her attention to fussing over him.

Turning to face the nearest galley, Niccolo watched the dockhands stack cargo from one of the galleys in neat piles on the nearby boardwalk.

"Did…" His voice faltered. "Was this really necessary?"

His father sighed. "Cornaro's brother is still a prisoner in Hungary. His ships hadn't arrived with his profits, so when we heard of pirate attacks in the Aegean, his enemies pressed the moneylenders to call in his debts. Marrying Flavio to Rosalia demonstrated our support and bought him time for the ships to arrive. It saved him."

"But did they…consummate?" The word felt ugly on his lips. "Maybe it can still be undone, and she and I—"

"I'm sorry, Nico. Only a real marriage would avoid his ruin."

Niccolo closed his eyes, but that only allowed his imagination to populate visions of the newlyweds' bodies pressed together, writhing in delight. He rubbed his eyes fiercely and instead focused on the water beneath him, rippling softly against the poles thrust into the lagoon to form the dock's foundation. Watching that calming rhythm eased the sorrow of a stolen life.

But only for a moment.

He had lost more than he had thought on the docks of Candia. He had lost his Rosa, and unlike Crete, she was lost to him forever.

CHAPTER TWO

MARCH 24, 1365

NICCOLO

NICCOLO LEANED OVER the deck railing as far as he could, watching the white waves crash against the galley's prow. The foam danced along the surface momentarily before dissipating into the flowing current. Good Venetian craftsmanship and Mediterranean water rocked together in a rhythmic dance.

The last time he danced was with Rosalia more than three years earlier.

He had managed to avoid seeing her and Flavio until he could escape with the expedition to recover Crete. In the first few weeks of the campaign, he had single-handedly saved a division when the rebels had retaliated after the Venetians recovered Candia. His men had called him a hero.

In truth, he felt more like a coward for avoiding news from home. Letters from his family containing words of sympathy about Rosalia had done nothing to banish the emptiness. Once he had shared enough news of Crete to invest his family with apprehension for his safety, the sympathy turned to worry, and reading their letters had at least become bearable.

While Niccolo had dreaded letters from the Aretoli, Giovanni had delighted in them. Each ship had carried a sweet-smelling opus from Asparia. His dear friend had never shared the contents, but Giovanni would invariably return with an unshakeable smile after privately reading them.

Once, Niccolo had commented, "You look as pleased as a pampered sultan, Gio."

"You're just jealous." Giovanni's eyes had filled with regret the moment the words had left his mouth.

Niccolo had forced himself to keep his tone casual. His friend hadn't meant offense. "Jealous of the man who has to deal with my sister? Oh, my dear friend, I pity you."

His mood had worsened when a lucky Cretan landed a glancing blow off Giovanni's ribs. Watching him sail away with the other injured Venetians and mercenaries, Niccolo honestly hadn't known whether his friend would survive.

Giovanni's first letter after returning home had proved his concern unfounded. Asparia hadn't left his side during his recovery. Only two weeks after he could stand, they had married. Yet again, Niccolo had missed another important family event.

Giovanni's second letter had announced Asparia's pregnancy.

Niccolo had had little to occupy his time except bolstering the defenses of Candia while the *condottiere* companies searched out pockets of resistance. It had been slow work, but the tide had turned, and Governor Dandolo had left at the close of the year. His replacement, Michele Steno, had recognized that the republic couldn't employ mercenaries indefinitely and had offered amnesty to the remaining rebels. Most had jumped at the chance. The Cretan resistance, and Niccolo's excuse for remaining abroad so long, had come to an end.

It was time to come home.

By the mast, a sailor hummed softly as he expertly unwound and retied the knots anchoring the mainsail. He was solidly built but smaller than the average Venetian, with several scars winding along his forearms. The way his fingers nimbly wove a new, more complex knot identified him as a Venetian more surely than his accent could.

"How long have you been at sea?" Niccolo asked the man.

He flashed a broad smile that was missing a few teeth. "Ten years. I started on the western routes to England and the Dutch."

Niccolo nodded. "Running silk?"

The man nodded eagerly. "Aye, sir. I've never seen so much soft cloth in my life." He glanced around nervously before whispering, "Sometimes I'd sneak into the hold and feel it. Mighty fine material." Blinking, the man looked as if he had only now realized his admission. He shifted his weight to his other foot. "You won't tell no one, will you?"

Niccolo grinned. "My lips are sealed."

With a relieved smile, the man returned to his work.

Left with no further distractions, Niccolo turned back to the water, wishing it could wash away the troubles he would face at home.

And then, Venice rose like a mirage out of the waters of the lagoon, sunlight glistening off the gold and painted frescos on the roofs and domes of the great buildings, illuminating the horizon in a riot of color.

The *laguna viva* danced in the light. Hundreds of ships—from tiny skiffs shuttling residents between the various islands to laden galleys returning from exotic ports—glided across the water. On the shore, merchants, crewmen, warehouse workers, and dockhands shuffled back and forth in their endless handling of the republic's goods.

And everywhere were the domes and statues built and beautified over nearly seven hundred years.

Joy filled Niccolo's heart. Home. This time, he returned to *La Serenissima* not as a refugee but as a hero.

In the distance, a lagoon officer waved a black flag with a light blue stripe toward the shore, then pointed a second flag, a smooth field of the same light blue, toward the southeastern end of the island. In response, the captain shouted orders to bring the ship about and the crew snapped into action.

Niccolo crossed the deck. "Is everything well, captain?"

The captain, a round, older man with a slight limp, grinned. "Not to worry, lad. We just missed a bad storm. Looks to have sent wash pouring into the lagoon, so the western approach is closed till either they clear it or the current takes it away. We'll have to circle around La Giudecca."

On the horizon, dark clouds puffing an angry last look at the city confirmed the captain's pronouncement. They would have to pass the length of the city before they reached the merchant wharves on the western side of the Rialto.

"Must we take such a long route?"

Eyebrows hardening, the captain glared at him. "We can't disobey a lagoon officer."

The vessel passed by the looming Rialto Island, the bustling center of the capital. To the east, smoke rose in massive plumes, marking the shipyards of the Arsenal, the mailed fist of Venice that produced the fastest and strongest ships in the Mediterranean. Beyond would be the Murano glassworks. It and the high-grade silk that only Venice produced provided the city with unimaginably profitable monopolies. The Aretoli used to hold an interest in both silk and glass, but their glass contracts had been stolen a few years ago by the Feratollos, who had then promptly lost them to others.

The galley turned west to enter the Grand Canal and the city proper. After two years of the squat, functional structures of Crete, the splendor of the buildings ringing the square caught Niccolo's breath. The great layered arches and columns of the ducal palace fronting the square dwarfed all else. Its white-washed edifice faced the watery entry to the city like a sentinel. Coming into view behind it, the second jewel of Venice, St. Mark's Basilica, was its only rival. Peaked by pinnacles and massive stone and gold crosses across its summit, even this beautiful dedication to God contained a truly Venetian stamp: the *Quadriga*, a bronze sculpture of four horses looted from Constantinople during the Fourth Crusade.

The ship continued its course further into the city. The curve of the lagoon took the plaza out of view, but it also brought the rising scent of bread cooking in the city's bakeries and the bitter odor of the saltworks.

Niccolo had missed that smell.

With a final few, careful maneuvers, the galley drifted into an open berth along the southern wing of the merchant docks. The sailors tossed docking ropes to the waiting dockhands while the crew lowered the planks of the loading ramp.

As Niccolo's feet touched the ground, the subtle sounds of home replaced the calls and creaks of the ship. The soft slap of water against the side of the galley. Far in the distance, toward the center of the island, the dull chant of monks making their daily rounds. The tinkling strikes indicating the delicate work of craftsmen.

A nearby watchman lowered his gaze to Niccolo's hand. "Welcome back, senator."

Niccolo twisted the ring on his finger. Three years ago, he'd shocked his family by winning the *Balla d'Oro* and a Senate seat. They hadn't had the money to assure the result with a bribe; fortune alone had allowed him to pick the golden ball that gained him early admission to the Venetian elite. He had left for Crete before he could even take his seat.

"It's good to be back."

He had been cowardly to stay away so long because of Rosalia. Arranged marriages happened. Something as foolish as sentiment couldn't stand in the way of a family's well-being. The Aretoli had to be protected. The alliance with House Cornaro had kept them secure for generations.

He passed over a small wooden bridge straddling a *ria*, one of the watery canals separating the tightly packed districts. The sliver of water was so small that the bridge had to incline sharply at both ends to allow gondolas to pass beneath it. A brief ray of sunlight sneaked through the opening in the packed structures on either side, bathing

Niccolo in a sudden warmth that made him pause. Closing his eyes, Niccolo savored the rare pleasure. A cold breeze normally rolled across the lagoon this time of year.

A gondola drifted lazily across the path of a canal fronting one of the side streets. Down that path lay the Grand Canal and the main, waterborne entrance to the Aretoli apartments. He hastened his pace down a cramped and dirty walkway running parallel to the canal and followed it—dodging the occasional puddle of some malodorous liquid—to its end.

Stepping out of the alley, Niccolo joined the throng of pedestrians on the main walkway. Before him lay the Aretoli home, a large, two-storied structure that had been in the family for generations. It was old, old enough that stains and discolorations had soaked into the very stone. Indeed, that mottled appearance gave the residence its claim to veneration.

Exhaling, Niccolo pushed open the doors and stepped inside.

"Nico!" A bookish man—no longer a boy—with soft, round eyes and an even softer smile halted halfway up the stairs and approached with outstretched arms.

"Marco!" Niccolo embraced his younger brother. When Marco kissed him on the cheek, he returned the gesture.

"You're finally back."

"Don't you start too," Niccolo warned. "Asparia ends every letter by asking when I'm going to meet my nephew. Pacifying Candia took time."

Marco narrowed his eyes, and his expression morphed into a look of pity. "How are you?"

Niccolo shrugged. "Oh, fine."

"No…" Marco placed a hand on Niccolo's elbow. "How are you?"

"I'm…" A hot sigh escaped his lips. He'd have to get used to answering that question over the next few days. "I won't know until I see them."

Marco's lips drew tight. "Nico, I'm sorry, I know you loved Rosalia, but there truly was nothing to be done. Father said we needed to preserve our relationship with the Cornaros. Even Flavio spoke against the match. Please don't blame them."

Flavio's reluctance surprised him, even as Niccolo regretted the thought. He could always trust Flavio to cover for him with their father or help when Niccolo got in over his head fighting the other boys. Of course Flavio wouldn't intentionally steal the woman he loved. To think otherwise unfairly maligned his brother.

"Truly, I don't, Marco." He changed the subject before it shifted to Rosalia. "Are you still painting?"

Marco scoffed. "Yes, and Flavio lectures me endlessly about how I should be spending my time preparing for the *Balla d'Oro*."

He spoke with just enough despair to discourage Niccolo's planned rebuke. One brother haranguing him was sufficient. "You really don't want to be in the Senate, do you?"

Marco lowered his gaze. "If my family needs me there, how can I refuse?" More quietly, he asked, "Why must I give up everything I love?"

The question pulled at Niccolo's heart. He didn't have an answer, or at least not one Marco wanted to hear. Even someone as secure as Governor Dandolo still had to devote time to maintaining his influence. Power left little time for other vocations.

"I wish I could tell you everything will be fine." He paused. "Where would you study if you had the chance?"

His brother's expression brightened. "Florence has maestros who employ many apprentices. I could learn so much." Though Venice had skilled artists, the very finest resided in the city-states to the south.

"Can I make a suggestion, then?"

Marco cocked his head, and Niccolo had to suppress a laugh. He looked so much like Camilla.

"Has Father given you any of our interests to manage?"

Marco shook his head. "That all sounds like a lot of work."

"Some, yes. But Father would let you keep the profits. You could save enough to study in Florence."

"He'd never let me go abroad."

Niccolo shrugged lightly. "Perhaps not yet, but if we can convince him, you'll have the money to afford the trip. If he doesn't, you'll need to know how to manage your finances."

"I hadn't thought of it that way." Eyes widening, he clasped Niccolo's shoulder. "Thank you, Nico. I…I don't know what to say."

"Just show me your paintings." He gestured down the hall. "Is father home? How is he?"

Marco shrugged. "A couple of months ago, we feared he was dying when he only had indigestion." He smiled again. "You'll see. He's his usual self."

They walked a few paces down the hall, stopping before the great carved door that had always instilled terror in the hearts of misbehaving Aretoli sons. This door had represented both their last hope and the final harbinger of their father's anger. Every time Niccolo had approached it after some transgression, he had hoped it would jam, granting him a reprieve.

But, of course, it never had.

"Speaking of which," Marco asked, "Do you like surprises?"

Niccolo shrugged. "It depends." The last surprise had cost him Rosalia. "Why?"

Marco grinned mischievously. "We're expecting a guest. His ship should arrive any time now."

"Who?"

His face brightened. "Francesco Petrarch."

"Really?" Petrarch was famed across Europe for his diplomatic skill. He also purportedly wrote poetry.

Marco beamed, more excited than Niccolo had ever seen him. "Look, he wrote me this." Retrieving a well-handled parchment from within a fold of his doublet, Marco presented it the way the doge might bestow a formal commission. "He says he has a new composition to show me."

Niccolo studied the letter. "He must think very highly of you."

Marco carefully folded and returned the letter to its home. "I can just imagine Father's reaction when he meets him."

"Instant friends, I wager," Niccolo said with a grin.

Marco studied the door and shuddered. The brothers shared a chuckle before Marco waved and mouthed a quick, "Good luck."

Niccolo inhaled a calming breath and knocked on the door.

"Enter," came the call from beyond.

Niccolo pushed open the door and stepped inside. His father was sitting at his *tavola*, the carved table that held his ink pot, ledgers, papers, and correspondence.

Angelo Aretoli had aged ten years since Niccolo had left to recapture Crete. He had lost enough weight that he seemed to swim in his coat, and the worry lines on his face had deepened.

Yet upon seeing Niccolo, the elder Aretoli cried out in delight. "This is good. Yes, yes, very good." He rose and circled his *tavola* with a grin of genuine joy. "My dear boy." He squeezed Niccolo with surprising strength. "I was so worried. You've been gone for so long." Releasing him, he gestured for Niccolo to sit. But rather than resuming his seat on the other side of the table, he sat beside his son. Never before had Angelo greeted his son as an equal. "You look well."

"I am, Father."

"The Senate read Governor Dandolo's reports of your accomplishments. He spoke very highly of you."

His eyes widened. "Did he?"

"Oh, yes. You have many senatorial admirers for one so young."

As tenderly as he could, Niccolo asked, "How have you been feeling, Father?"

"Never better," came the quick reply. "Old wounds ache before bad weather, but that's true of every man my age. Marco insists I'm slowing down, but I've never missed a festival or Senate meeting, and I'm not about to start now."

Niccolo smiled softly, relieved at the news.

"How was your journey?"

He shrugged. "Better than my last two, certainly."

"Well, you made good time. You received my letter?"

"Letter?" Niccolo shook his head. "We had to rely on foreign ships for correspondence, and pirates seized a few. Some rogue named Bolando Colmiera. We've had no news from home in three months."

"Three months? Then you don't know." Angelo's forehead wrinkled in tension. "Your timing is fortunate, then."

He tensed. "What now?"

"The doge called a meeting of the Senate for the morning after tomorrow."

Niccolo leaned forward to cover his sudden release of a worried breath. "A ducal meeting?" Normally, the Council of Ten called Senate meetings. Much of the doge's power had eroded in the last century. Gone were the days when defying the doge was dangerous, but he still had influence.

"Our diplomats haven't fared well lately, I'm afraid. Our neighbors believe us weak. Some in the Senate want to commission a standing army to recover Dalmatia, even conquer Padua or Verona to show our strength. We can't do that with galleys alone, even the finest on the seas."

Niccolo straightened. "That's not our way." Conquest involved enormous defense and administrative costs. Profit came from trade. For centuries, Venice's weapon had been its merchant quarters in the major cities throughout the Mediterranean, and its spoils were reduced prices, tariff waivers, and exclusive rights. "What happens when our aggression causes another papal interdiction?"

"You see the danger." Angelo gave a weak smile. "You always see the truth of things."

"Flavio does as well." Niccolo wished he didn't have to single out only Flavio, but Asparia was too passionate and Camilla and Marco too flighty.

Angelo shook his head. "Flavio and I rarely agree. He obeys me because I'm his father." Rising, Angelo crossed to a large chest in the corner. "He is brave and honorable. But you share my love of learning."

Raising the lid, Angelo rooted around the base of the chest before removing a scroll. When Niccolo had hidden in that trunk as a child, crumpling those scrolls, his father had made him read every one aloud before forgiving him. "Some would say this is our failing, but I disagree." Returning to his seat, Angelo passed the scroll to Niccolo, who accepted it gingerly. "Do you remember this?"

Opening it, Niccolo translated the Latin. "Aristotle's definition of happiness." He grinned broadly. "I still have the bruises from you rapping me on the knuckles for forgetting it." Closing it delicately, he handed the treasure back to his father. Each of those scrolls was worth a fortune.

Angelo caressed the paper with a finger. "Marco and Camilla would call this text heresy. Flavio and Asparia would just as happily use it as kindling. But you and I, Niccolo, we understand how precious it is."

"I wouldn't say that too loudly, Father, or too close to the bishop."

He waved his hand. "Yes, yes, but it's just us here." Placing the scroll on the *tavola*, Angelo stared at it. "I'm very proud of you, son. All you've accomplished...the great joy of my life is seeing you grow. I can see so much of myself in you."

"Father..."

Angelo reached over and squeezed his son's arm, eyes glistening with unshed tears. His father had never spoken to him with such affection. When had that changed?

Of course, he knew. It had changed when he'd arranged Flavio's marriage to the woman Niccolo loved.

He swallowed. He needed to face this now. "How is Flavio?"

Pain surged across his father's face. "He and his wife are both well." He lowered his gaze. "They do not have children yet."

Conflicting emotions tugged at Niccolo. An ember of hope rekindled even as his mind told him the marriage could not be undone. Yet he still felt a degree of regret. While the Sabarelli line would continue, the Aretoli still hadn't expanded to the next generation.

"I've invited them to dinner tomorrow, on the eve of the Senate meeting. We need to plan. I hope you'll attend?"

Niccolo managed a faint smile. "Of course, Father." He would have to face the new couple eventually; better to have it over with sooner than later. Two years had been too long already. "As always, you have my support."

NICCOLO

Custom demanded that every senator maintain his own residence, a vestige from when only heads of households could hold the position. Niccolo hadn't had time to buy a home before he'd left for Crete, but now that he'd returned, he would have to remedy that deficiency.

With limited options, he decided on a modest two-story corner house with a bedroom, office, reception room, kitchen, and three rooms for servants. It sat beside a *ria* too narrow for a gondola to turn around in, three canals deep from the Grand Canal. Yet, even so, he still had to agree to a criminal rate of interest.

Nonetheless, it possessed something precious: a wooden pole with a hollow tube at its end extending above the water over the canal-side door. By placing a flag into the slot facing either end, he could signify to any passing gondolas that he wanted to travel upstream or downstream. For most citizens, flagging down a gondola was merely an expression, not an actual strategy.

Niccolo had already arranged for his few possessions to be sent ahead while he lodged the deed with the record office. But as he returned to his new home, his father's steward—a man with crinkled, squinting eyes that somehow observed everything—was directing a retinue of servants carrying furniture.

Pietro Corsici had been Angelo's steward since fleeing Corsica nearly twenty years earlier. He had never given his real surname, and Angelo had never pursued the topic. Though Niccolo's parents had both been stern with their children, Pietro had been a true friend within the Aretoli home. There wasn't a man alive—Giovanni included—whom he trusted more.

The old steward offered a mischievous smile as Niccolo approached. The steward's golden curls had faded to gray. Once again, Niccolo reflected on all he had missed. He'd been gone too long.

"Pietro, I don't understand. This isn't from my room at the house. Where—"

"Your father thought you deserved a home worthy of an Aretoli and a senator of Venice."

Niccolo studied the activity around him. Two servants carried an oak dining table with intricate carvings along the legs. A chair sitting beside a nearby wagon had a velvet cushion and a wooden lace back. Angelo had spent a small fortune.

Pietro followed Niccolo's gaze and grinned. "He didn't limit how much I could buy."

"You?"

By way of answer, Pietro winked and tapped his nose. "I've arranged for some of our men to stay on until you find your own people."

Glancing around, Niccolo studied the faces of the people filing in and out of his home. "Pietro, I don't recognize these people."

"There are servants, and then there are our *people*," The old steward started to chuckle at Niccolo's widened eyes. "Let us take care of you, Master Niccolo."

Every powerful senator had ways of keeping tabs on his peers, but Angelo had never shared the names of his contacts with his sons. Pietro evidently knew, though.

How many times had he been in real danger without knowing it? His father had enemies and had served through the terrible events when Doge Marino Faliero had tried to overthrow the government.

Everyone had suspected everyone, and several senators had been killed in the months leading up to his fall.

Now, he realized that his father had prepared well for such dangers. Niccolo remembered Pietro suddenly gathering the children in the kitchen during that year, even pulling Camilla away from her evening grooming. Someone had knocked on the door several times, but the steward had continued telling them stories as if he hadn't heard. There had been a faint tinkling noise in the hall that had confused Niccolo at the time. But now, he recognized the sound as plate armor flexing with movement.

His father had been protecting them all their lives in a very real and tangible way.

Pietro stalked off toward a servant who had bumped into the door frame with a chair. His departure left Niccolo alone, forgotten. His presence was hardly necessary here, not with Pietro organizing the effort.

In one of their last letters, Asparia and Giovanni had invited Niccolo to see their new home, so Niccolo followed the snaking path of the Grand Canal toward it. As he ascended the steep incline over the *ria* leading to their neighborhood, the quality of the buildings changed. This district seemed bright and cheerful, with gold and bronze filigree accenting the ledges and statues built into the higher floors.

Giovanni's home dwarfed his own, both in size and the intricacy of the carvings along the exterior. He felt a momentary pang of envy for his friend. While Niccolo had been hiding from Rosalia in Crete for two years, Giovanni had been expanding his holdings. And with no brothers, he had inherited everything from his father, while Niccolo would only receive a third of the *fraterna*.

The price of that inheritance had been steep, though. Niccolo wouldn't trade places with his friend if it meant losing his father as Giovanni had.

Niccolo swung the knocker against the door several times, summoning a well-perfumed servant who ushered him into the reception room on the ground floor.

He was absently studying the filigree on a porcelain vase containing a score of roses when a familiar voice said, "I see you lounged around Candia instead of keeping your instincts sharp, eh, Nico?"

Niccolo smiled at the dark, rugged face and dancing eyes he knew so well. Crossing the short distance, he clasped his friend in a tight embrace and joined him in laughter. Pulling away, he placed a kiss on each of Giovanni's cheeks. His friend had been bedridden and pale the last time he'd seen him. "You look well."

Giovanni shrugged. "Married life agrees with me."

"It certainly better had!" Asparia turned the corner and joined her husband.

Niccolo crossed to his sister, taking her hands lightly in a polite embrace. "Dear sister."

"Oh, Nico, I've missed you so much. I was so worried about you, and now you're finally here. This whole sordid business is over."

Niccolo waved her off. "Come now, 'Ria, the mercenaries did most of the hard work in the wilderness. The biggest threat I faced after the first few weeks was cutting myself at dinner."

All three of them chuckled, but the laughter had an undertone of released nervousness.

He sighed. "Gio, you can't imagine how many oysters I had to eat with Dandolo."

"And I'm sure they were dreadful, too." Giovanni's eyes darkened for a mere instant; Dandolo hadn't taken Giovanni up on his offer to supply him with oysters. "Well, you've picked an excellent time to return"—he turned to Asparia, who nodded as a smile tugged at the corners of her mouth—"since you're going to be an uncle again."

Niccolo blinked. "Again? Already?"

Asparia beamed and nodded with fresh excitement. She looked more like Camilla than the dignified, responsible woman he remembered.

"I'm–I'm shocked, honestly. Congratulations to both of you." He grinned as he shook his brother-in-law's hand vehemently. "Can I see young Alessandro?"

"He's in the nursery. He's finally sleeping more than half an hour at a time." Though Asparia had paid for the easy birth with a difficult infant, Niccolo prayed that that pattern would repeat. Even Camilla had commented about how silly she'd felt for fearing pregnancy if young Alessandro's birth was typical. No one in the family had the heart to correct her.

"My God, I've missed so much. Too much, I fear. Our family is growing so quickly."

Giovanni grinned. "I've had plenty of time to devote to my dear wife: I want a whole army of little brats."

"Oh, and will you bear them, as well?" Asparia poked Giovanni in the stomach. "I don't remember seeing a womb under your tunic the last time we—"

"'Ria!" Niccolo didn't want that particular image in his mind.

Her face brightened in a shameless expression of glee that matched her husband's. If he did nothing else with his life, he would be content with having introduced them.

Giovanni released a light sigh. "I wish my father could have lived to see this little one." He patted his wife on the belly.

"I'm sorry I wasn't here for the funeral," Niccolo offered.

Giovanni's eyes darkened. Clearly, the grief still lingered.

"But he lived to see young Alessandro," he continued. "That had to please him."

Asparia rubbed Giovanni's arm, and her smile roused him. "Did you have fair winds on the voyage in?"

"Overabundant, if fair. We had some nasty gusts, and during one, some rigging came loose and struck one of the crewmen."

Giovanni patted his wife's arm. "No pirates, though?"

He shrugged. "A few sails on the horizon, but nothing catches an Arsenal galley."

"Too true." The other man nodded.

"Oh, I'm so sorry, 'Ria." Niccolo flailed his arms. "I forgot to bring you something from Candia. I owe you a few presents, I imagine. For the wedding, the baby…" He grunted. "Babies."

"That's quite alright." She offered a sweet smile. "Venice has markets if you really want to make it up to me."

"And I'm sure you have something in mind," Niccolo added.

"I could think of *something*." She twirled a lock of hair around her finger. "Perhaps a pair of Tyrian purple silk pillows in the back right corner of Rafael Corrodina's stall in the lacework district?" Smiling innocently, she glanced off to the right. "It's the set with the gold satin lace edging. I put it on hold this morning."

Niccolo laughed heartily enough to bring tears to his eyes. "Oh, I've missed you, 'Ria."

But Giovanni wore a sincere look of horror that sent Niccolo into further hysterics. Asparia performed admirably; her expression never changed.

"I swear by God almighty," Giovanni mumbled, "I'll never forget a gift again. Tyrian purple, 'Ria?"

Asparia smirked. "Good husband."

The awkwardness of their easy intimacy sobered Niccolo. His sister laughed more easily and seemed so much happier since her marriage. Had Rosalia changed that much, too?

Infusing as much humor into his voice as possible, he asked, "And would you have any suggestions for Camilla? I'm sure she'll expect something."

"Buy her a mirror." Asparia waved her hand dismissively. "If she looks up, she'll thank you for giving her what she loves most."

"Too cruel," Giovanni defended. "Your sister's just young. She's a sweet girl."

Asparia offered Niccolo a knowing expression before patting her husband on the arm. "Of course, dear. You're right."

The light mood lingered, none of them wanting to ruin the atmosphere. But their easy affection focused his thoughts on his own challenges. "I only hope I can satisfy my dear sisters' exotic tastes, between the costs of buying a home and two years of neglect."

Giovanni frowned. "Don't tell me you haven't tended to your interests since leaving for Crete."

"Be glad you returned," Niccolo said, meaning it. "Crete offered plenty of easy distractions."

Asparia chuckled lightly, some of the tension dissipating. "Especially when she bats her eyes—"

"Don't you start," Niccolo chided. "I meant the rebellion."

Asparia offered an unsettled smirk that indicated she had another purpose in mind.

"Asparia…" Niccolo narrowed his eyes. "Are you worried Giovanni and I spent all our time with the women of Crete?"

She opened her mouth to protest but paused. Her gaze dropped. Giovanni rounded on his wife. "'Ria, are you jealous?"

Pouting, Asparia crossed her arms and inhaled to respond when Niccolo interrupted. "Sister, let me ease your mind. Giovanni was more worried about establishing oyster monopolies than diving for pearls."

Asparia frowned. "That isn't a denial."

Niccolo had hoped she wouldn't notice the ambiguity. Of course they had visited brothels, though they had tired of them quickly. But that had been long before Giovanni had met her. Not that it would matter, of course. He knew she would obsess over the thought of her husband in the arms of another woman, no matter how long ago.

"Giovanni didn't patronize the women of Crete, Asparia."

His sister brightened. "Oh, Gio, I wouldn't have minded, just so long as it wasn't after you met me." She draped her arms around Giovanni.

Over his wife's shoulder, he glanced pensively at Niccolo, who shook his head firmly at the unspoken question. He knew his sister too well.

They loved each other, honorably and passionately. He had to know that kind of love could endure. Too often, the world brushed it aside. He wouldn't allow anything to risk destroying it.

Though his thoughts turned to Rosalia, the familiar pain did not come. As a girl, Asparia had grown to love her betrothed only to lose him to the plague. And yet, here she stood, delighted with a man she hadn't even known back then.

He had lost Rosalia, but he would eventually give his heart to someone else. He may even already know her. Would he pine for Rosalia until then? Of course not.

For the first time in years, Niccolo could imagine a world of possibilities. Turning his attention back to his sister and brother-in-law, he smiled with genuine affection. They had unknowingly melted his icy heart, and Niccolo swore to remember that gift forever.

CHAPTER THREE

NICCOLO

THE NEXT AFTERNOON, one of his father's servants brought a summons to a dinner in honor of Francesco Petrarch, who had arrived that morning. Genuinely curious about the famous diplomat, Niccolo changed into a more elegant, lace doublet.

When he arrived at the side door of his father's home, a servant in formal attire ushered him into the reception room. Angelo and Emilio Cornaro, Rosalia's father, sat in high-backed wooden chairs, flanked by Marco and their guest, an elderly man with thinning white hair.

Petrarch had chosen to remain standing beside a vacant chair. He favored his right leg, but he hid the fact well. Only the occasional movement revealed the delicacy with which he kept his balance. He was proud, then, or at least self-reliant.

In the other corner, Giovanni and Asparia were losing their patience with Camilla, who fluttered around them like a butterfly. When Niccolo had left for Crete, his younger sister had been too young to attend formal dinners. From her excitement, he concluded she had only recently earned the right.

Flavio and Rosalia hadn't arrived. He offered silent thanks for the chance to greet the others first.

Cornaro had been saying something, but he stopped abruptly upon Niccolo's arrival. He, at least, understood the consequences his fiscal irresponsibility had had on the lives around him.

"Father." Niccolo knelt beside Angelo and kissed each of his father's cheeks.

"Ah, Niccolo." Angelo's smile had the appearance of cheer, but his eyes carried tension. Niccolo suspected he had worried how his son might react. "We've been blessed by our guests today." He gestured to Emilio Cornaro.

Niccolo took the cue. "Signor Cornaro, please accept my apologies for my tardiness. I would like to place myself at your service, should you require anything."

Blinking, Cornaro gasped at the old form of respect, now rarely used. Recovering after a moment, he bowed his head. "I am honored by your courtesy, young Aretoli."

"I quite agree." Petrarch stepped forward as Niccolo rose again. "You'd be surprised how infrequent proper courtesy is throughout Italy. One must look to the ancient Greeks for such a display of hospitality."

"Greeks…" Cornaro scoffed and shook his head.

Angelo ignored the outburst. "Allow me to introduce the Florentine diplomat, Francesco Petrarch, lately from Rome. Signor Petrarch, this is my second son, Niccolo."

Niccolo expected a scholar and poet to stoop and squint from years of writing, but Petrarch stood straight. His air of nobility emanated from something other than his age, which Niccolo put at about sixty. He looked much like Angelo, but not larger than life as Marco had described him.

Petrarch bowed with surprising agility, considering his leg.

Niccolo returned the gesture. "I'm quite fond of the Greeks. I can't count the number of times I fell asleep with my nose in Aristotle, only to wake up with ink on my face." He smiled at the memory.

Petrarch barked out a laugh. "Right here." The scholar pointed to the tip of his nose. "I could never quite get it clean."

Niccolo laughed lightly, warming to the man. "They say learning is a mental exercise, but cleaning up afterward is most certainly physical." The poet cackled in the easy habit of a man accustomed to laughing often.

Cornaro added, "Your father was recounting the good service you gave on Crete. It comforted me that you remained on the island until the job was finished."

Niccolo appreciated Cornaro's courtesy in framing his absence as a virtue when they both knew the real reason. Such a man didn't deserve rudeness for acting to preserve his family, no matter how much it had wounded Niccolo.

"I thank you for your kind words, but I can hardly take credit for the governor's solid strategy."

Marco pounced on an opening in the conversation to change the subject. "Master Petrarch, what did you think of Rome?"

Cornaro subsided, exchanging a glance with Angelo.

Petrarch sighed. "I imagined the Colosseum and Forum. Instead, I found refuse in the great arena and sheep grazing on the Palatine." He clutched at the air dramatically. "Oh, where are the Caesars and Agrippas of our age?"

"Would you really wish such men on Italy?" Angelo asked.

"Oh, signor, absolutely. Europe hasn't had a truly gifted statesman in two hundred years, and he was a Plantagenet." His mouth soured. "Then again, considering how Venice derailed an entire crusade, perhaps I spoke too soon."

Marco grinned without remorse. "Perhaps when you're settled, we can visit the *Quadriga*." Venice displayed that prize specifically to mock the Byzantines, from whom they looted it.

"Rascal," Petrarch charged.

"When the discussion turns to the crusades, I must take my leave. I should greet my dear brother-in-law." With a bow of his head, Niccolo departed for the other cluster of guests.

Mid-stride, he turned to the doorway and his leg buckled. He caught himself awkwardly by clenching his hand around a nearby chair.

Flavio stood within the door frame, staring at his brother with a look of anguish. His widened eyes carried none of their usual charm or appeal, only a haunted quality.

Niccolo believed Marco's claims now: Flavio had truly suffered for these past years, no doubt prolonged by Niccolo's long absence. Of all the emotions he'd imagined for this moment, he hadn't anticipated feeling pity.

Yet, this man had still married and bedded Niccolo's beloved. Images of their coupling filled his mind unbidden.

"Hello, Flavio."

Flavio managed a faint nod. "I'm glad you arrived safely. Welcome home." In a hushed voice meant only for him, he quickly added, "I'm sorry, Nico."

Niccolo swallowed. His brother's expression pleaded for forgiveness. "It's not your fault." He couldn't hate this man for an unwanted marriage. He'd had no choice but to obey. "Just treat her as she deserves."

Flavio nodded and took a deep, calming breath. "I half expected you to challenge me to a duel."

That brought a grin. "You're the better swordsman." But the smile faded quickly. "You're my brother. I would never turn on you."

Rosalia entered as he finished his sentence.

Niccolo noticed her hair first. When he had left, she had worn that flowing chestnut hair long and free, swept slightly to the side but unbound. Now, though, she styled it as a married woman, worn high in braids that coiled around the crown of her head. It testified, as no words ever could, that his Rosa wasn't his anymore.

Married.

A few tendrils hung down in loose curls, though, framing the graceful slopes of her chin and cheeks. Her face still held that same firmness that used to make her smile tug on her earlobes. She was as beautiful as he remembered.

Her eyes, two shining pools of pale blue that he had drowned in more than once, swirled with panic. She picked at the folds of her dress with shaking fingers.

Dimly, Niccolo recognized the other conversations had stopped. They were all watching him.

His resolve wavered as her expensive floral perfume tickled his senses. She had worn that same perfume the last time he'd seen her, the last time he'd held her.

"Rosalia."

"Niccolo." Her voice sounded flat, empty of life.

The burning desire ignited again, and he fought to smother it. Formality would help. "Dear lady, I greet you as a sister and offer my congratulations on your late marriage."

Resolve weakening, he had to touch her, no matter the cost. Extending his hand, Niccolo fought to control the flush in his cheeks. She clasped it, eyes offering only the slightest reservation.

For a moment, his mind reeled with memories: a hand threaded through his arm, a gentle stroke of his shoulder as she sang with laughter, a stolen caress of her cheek in the darkness of midwinter.

He recalled Asparia's daring gesture when she'd first met Giovanni. It was selfish, but he couldn't resist. Flourishing his free hand and bowing as a distraction, he gently stroked Rosalia's palm with his index finger.

No one seemed to notice the subtle motion. Though her hand tensed at the furtive gesture, she did not pull away.

This was his brother's wife. What was he doing?

No, this was Rosalia, and they shared an unbreakable bond.

And then, just before releasing his hand, she squeezed it.

The moment passed, and the conversations began again with a fresh edge of excitement. "Thank you, Niccolo," Rosalia said. "I know

Flavio has fretted over this business for the past two years, though I tell him God moves us where he will."

Having spent his passion on a single stroke of his finger, he had nothing left for wit. But he still needed to convince Flavio of his good intentions to put this behind them. He couldn't endure more of these conversations.

"We are Aretoli."

It had the desired effect. Flavio nodded solemnly, his eyes containing understanding and the memory of their father's lesson. *Your family will always stand with you, my sons. We are Aretoli. That bond is stronger than all else.*

"Thank you, brother. You've set my mind at ease as it has not been these past two years."

Swallowing, Niccolo turned and approached his sisters. Camilla was giving a diatribe about the dreadful fashions this year. After a few excruciating exchanges, Niccolo excused himself for the privy. But as he crossed the room, he caught Rosalia's gaze and halted.

"That's a story I'd like to hear." Petrarch had sidled up surreptitiously.

Surprised, Niccolo managed a gruff, "What?"

He gestured to Flavio and Rosalia. "They're a strange couple."

"She's my brother's wife," he replied flatly.

"How long have they been together?"

"Why do you care?" He forced the irritation down; Petrarch didn't know their history. "Two years."

"Can I assume you don't want to discuss them?"

"No, I don't."

"Ah." He leaned closer and whispered, "Then I recommend not staring so amorously."

Niccolo gasped at the man's audacity. Before he could reply, Petrarch laid a hand on his shoulder. "I know how you feel, son. Her name was Laura."

"Laura?"

Petrarch's gaze shifted. "She was everything I ever wanted. She

could quote any Bible verse and had the voice of an angel. Her skin…"
A faint smile twisted into a scowl. "But she was married to some oaf
twice her age. I never saw her again." He swallowed the last of his wine.
"I suppose that was better than watching her with another man. But
I know I'd have wanted someone to warn me if they saw me about to
do something irrevocable."

Niccolo swallowed, understanding his meaning. "I took your
words for an insult. I apologize. It's no way for a host to treat a guest."

Petrarch patted Niccolo on the shoulder. "Had I meant an insult,
it would be no way for a guest to treat a host." Without another word,
he shuffled off to rejoin Marco.

Niccolo studied his drink absently. The exchange had quieted the
ache in his heart, and Petrarch had done it artfully. If his guest had
survived his loss, Niccolo could endure his.

When a young servant announced the first course, Angelo ushered
everyone through the carved double doors leading to the dining room.
Fresh flowers adorned a series of three vases spaced evenly along the
length of the table, a beautiful, carved monster of dark oak capable
of seating sixteen. To fill out all that room, the guests would be far
enough away from each other that, without conversation, dinner could
feel almost private.

As they settled in their seats, Rosalia said, "You have such a lovely
home, Signor Aretoli. The flowers are beautiful. Don't you think so,
Father?"

A flock of servants entered carrying trays of sliced fruits arranged
on colored glass plates.

Cornaro smiled. "My daughter has more sense than I in such
matters, I'm afraid. They are lovely, now that I look at them." He turned
to Flavio. "I'm grateful you could spare her for my Easter celebration."

Organizing that event would require a massive amount of time.
Niccolo wondered why Rosalia would commit to it with her own
household to run. And she and Flavio still had no children.

The thought caused him to lose track of the discussion until Flavio reached out to pour himself a glass of unwatered wine from one of the jugs in the center of the table.

"Signor Aretoli." Petrarch raised his glass. "History may have made Florence and Venice adversaries, but we are united in the generosity we extend to our guests. I offer my warmest thanks for your and your son Marco's kindness."

Angelo raised his own glass. "You are most welcome, Master Petrarch. We are honored to have such an esteemed visitor." The room fell silent as the diners sipped their wine. Flavio took a deep draught. "Are you finding Venice to your liking?"

"Venice is more than I imagined." The poet popped a slice of plum into his mouth and chewed. "I grew up hearing stories of a corrupt republic that undermined its neighbors. I met my first Venetian in Avignon, a young priest translating Muslim texts for the pope. To my surprise, he did not have horns or breathe fire."

Rosalia and Camilla giggled. Asparia met Niccolo's gaze and, waiting until he took a sip of his wine, rolled her eyes. A bubble of laughter sent some dribbling down his chin.

They turned toward him in surprise.

Eyes widening, he muttered, "I apologize. I imagined a demon casually thumbing through a manuscript in the papal curia." His gaze darted toward his sister.

The troublemaker merely grinned.

Emilio Cornaro frowned. "I hardly think that prospect worthy of mirth."

Unable to help himself, Niccolo glanced at Rosalia. Her eyes carried laughter she dared not release. The devout Emilio Cornaro held genuine concern about the souls of the Aretoli. Educating their daughters and indulging in pagan texts, the Aretoli were good partners but a little odd.

"In any case," Petrarch resumed, "I realized Florentine tales were much like the tales told about every city's enemies."

"Indeed so," Angelo agreed. "We told quite a few during the last war, and I suspect Niccolo could enlighten us with a few passed around the barracks about Cretans."

Across the table, Flavio stiffened. "Yes, let us hear stories of the Cretan Fox." His tone held more than a hint of bitterness.

"Cretan Fox?" Emilio Cornaro asked.

"That's the militia's name for Niccolo, Father," Rosalia explained. "They mean it as a compliment."

Niccolo shook his head. "No truth to them. They hardly even mention Giovanni here."

Giovanni raised both of his hands. "No, no. If I'm known as a hero of Venice, I can kiss my shady smuggler contracts goodbye. I was careful to only implicate you."

"What!" Niccolo shouted louder than intended. A reputation of any sort attracted jealousy.

"Your sister said you deserved to be embarrassed. Something about chasing her with shears as a child?"

Asparia smirked and raised a single eyebrow. "No doubt, it will take as long for you to quash those stories as it took me to grow my hair back."

Niccolo cursed, triggering another round of laughter.

But not from Flavio. Before his brother looked away, Niccolo caught a flash of something dangerous in his eyes. If the revolt had happened one year earlier, Flavio would have gained the accolades and Niccolo would have married Rosalia.

Then, the cause of Flavio's jealousy dawned on him. Rosalia had known all about Niccolo's reputation. She must have followed the stories about him.

Flavio leaned forward. "Master Petrarch, what do you think causes such rumors?"

Between bites, Petrarch asked, "About young Aretoli?"

"No, we know the truth about that." Again, his voice carried an edge of hostility. "I refer to vile stories about one's enemies. Why do you think we invent such tales?"

Petrarch leaned back and rested his hands on his belly in scholarly reflection. A moment later, Marco reproduced the maneuver with an ease that made Niccolo grin. What a joy it must be to sit with his hero!

"It's only natural to make one's adversary appear monstrous. God preaches against murder, even the murder of one's enemies, but allows the culling of wild animals. The more we label our enemies the latter, the less we feel the guilt of the former." The poet beamed in appreciation for his wit.

"Well said." Emilio Cornaro drummed his goblet on the table.

Flavio pressed, "So we use such stories to justify murder?"

"Oh, not just murder, all sorts of crimes."

"Then such stories are corrupting influences. They distort reality and corrupt our souls."

"They can, yes." Petrarch narrowed his eyes. "In certain circumstances."

Nodding, Flavio sipped from his goblet. "Then why do we permit them? Why not ban them—and the storytellers—outright." He gestured to Niccolo. "Does it serve the republic to paint a humble young senator as the greatest warrior of our time?"

The comment struck the table like a thunderclap, stilling everyone except Emilio Cornaro, who nodded thoughtfully as if unaware of the undercurrents.

Rosalia stared daggers at her husband. Only because Niccolo knew her so well did he recognize the shame hiding beneath her anger.

But his father's glare outshone even Rosalia's. Niccolo could almost feel the fury radiating from him.

Petrarch responded before Angelo could erupt. "That's an interesting opinion." His expression indicated quite the opposite. "Tell me, what do you think of *The Iliad*? Marco says you've all studied it."

His barb not having the desired effect, Flavio looked cautious now. "It's a fine story, I suppose." He nodded to his father-in-law. "Though, it contains pagan heresy."

"Ah, indeed." Petrarch leaned forward. "So *The Iliad* distorts reality? There is only one God, and a single soldier cannot kill fifty men. Nor will Ares or Athena save a favorite hero, yes?"

Flavio narrowed his eyes. "Of course not."

"And nor did Alexander the Great conquer Persia?"

Niccolo restrained a laugh as his mind grasped the poet's argument. Flavio frowned. "What does that have to do with it?"

Petrarch shrugged. "You claim tales offer false expectations and corrupt the soul. Yet, Alexander, inspired by the tale of Achilles, conquered Persia. Now, we can debate whether that conquest was noble since it wasn't in the service of the one true God." The comment dripped with a sarcasm Niccolo hadn't expected; this papal scholar was full of surprises. "But we can reasonably claim *The Iliad* influenced the conquest of Persia. So, I repeat my question. Are you saying Alexander didn't conquer Persia?"

Scowling, Flavio drank again from his goblet. "Of course not."

"No, of course not." Petrarch spoke slowly, as if to a child. "Stories and tales do what we wish them to, not the other way around. Whether a man will be corrupted or inspired is up to him." He took the last bite of his fruit as one of the servants came by to remove his dish. "If you ask me, poor logic has caused more horror throughout history than any story. Take your brother, for instance. The stories about him will likely inspire his fellow Venetians in some future battle. Only if he allows arrogance to take hold will it lead to suffering."

A profound silence filled the room. Very neatly, Petrarch had put Flavio in his place without forcing either Niccolo or his father to react to Flavio's dreadful behavior. By defending his profession, he had nonetheless done them a very great favor.

Angelo had recovered his control. "Your words are wise, Master Petrarch. Enough harm has come from faulty judgment, I warrant." He pinned Flavio with a scathing stare.

Flavio continued to fume while the servants brought in the guinea fowl. Marco, on the other hand, doted on the poet with abject adulation. As the diners picked at their meals, Niccolo secretly studied Petrarch, only to find him returning the favor.

He liked this man immensely.

Unsurprisingly, Asparia and Giovanni returned to their meals with enthusiasm. He willed himself not to glance at Rosalia; he suspected she had an unpleasant night ahead of her. At least they would all return to separate homes after this dinner.

As the servants cleared the plates, Giovanni turned to Petrarch. "I imagine it's a fascinating business, distributing poems and the like." He swirled the wine in his goblet. "Is there much profit in it?"

Niccolo bellowed a deep laugh. "Oysters, now poems? You never stop."

"I can't," he replied quickly. "My wife has excellent taste. Excellent, expensive taste."

The rest joined in, welcoming the change in topic. Asparia simply raised her chin and continued to enjoy her meal, but Niccolo observed a distinct twinkle in her eye. He suspected some kind of collusion between her and her husband in changing the topic.

Angelo suggested that Marco show their guest around the city, but the poet politely declined, claiming exhaustion, and instead limped off to bed with Marco leading the way.

A lightning-quick glance from Angelo brought Camilla to her feet. "Well, ladies, I fear the men will begin discussing politics. Shall we leave them to it and find some trouble?"

Rosalia rose gracefully, gathering the folds of her dress neatly as she stepped away from her chair. Turning to Flavio, she gave a stiff bow, keeping her eyes fixed on his until he broke the gaze.

Niccolo could remember that look well enough. Poor Flavio.

When Asparia rose, she did so elegantly. Giovanni did the same, embracing her in a scandalous display of affection. Kissing her husband lightly, she leaned in and whispered something in his ear that turned his face bright red. Circling the table, she threaded her arm through her sister-in-law's before marching off after Camilla.

The phenomenon of Rosalia and Asparia brought a smile to Angelo's face, but Flavio and Giovanni simply turned to each other and shared a knowing expression.

Regret and a hint of jealousy washed over Niccolo at being excluded from that moment, but he managed to calm it before his father began speaking.

"My dear Camilla could have been an Oracle at Delphi had we lived in a different age. She is correct. Tomorrow, the Senate will vote on the measure to create a standing army."

"A *costly* standing army," Giovanni amended.

At his words, the mood in the room hardened. The night had been building to this point.

"Where do we stand?" Flavio clenched his fists around the now-empty goblet. Niccolo pushed the decanter over to his brother, who nodded his appreciation. He relaxed slightly; there would be no grudges from tonight.

"The doge supports us, as do three of the Council of Ten," Angelo explained. "But as you know, many senators would like nothing more than a Venetian Empire."

"The doge surprises me," Niccolo offered.

"Perhaps he wants to distance himself from recent history," Flavio said. "I wouldn't want to follow in Marino Faliero's footsteps." The former doge's effort to overthrow the government had resulted in his immediate execution.

"In any case, Lorenzo Celsi is with us, and he brings many with him." Angelo added, "They think him humble and view his stance as a denial of ducal powers."

"You have my support," Giovanni added. "My father's name still holds influence."

Angelo frowned. "He was a noble man and would have made an excellent doge."

Giovanni offered an endearingly awkward nod of appreciation. "Flavio has the ear of the younger noblemen."

Niccolo's brother badly needed that particular salve.

"And we must not forget the Dandolos," Flavio added with confidence. "They look on us favorably, and Niccolo in particular." He met his brother's eyes, smiling uncertainly. All was forgiven, then.

"You give me too much credit," Niccolo warned. "I doubt the governor would vote against a standing army. He believes mercenaries are a waste of money and thinks militia isn't effective enough."

Flavio snorted. "I've been saying that for years."

"Nonetheless, we will vote against this measure." Angelo peered at his eldest son. This obviously wasn't the first time they had disagreed on policy. "Our republic is defended by the love of its citizens. We've gone seven hundred years without an insurrection in the city."

Niccolo licked his lips. "Who opposes?"

"The Feratollos, of course." The Aretoli feud with that family had started when young Lucia Dandolo had chosen Angelo from among her many suitors. Guiseppe Feratollo had hounded the Dandolos for her hand until she had pledged to publicly surrender her virginity to the *arsenalotti* before marrying him. Overnight, he had become a joke. Niccolo suspected his father regretted Giuseppe's embarrassment, but the damage could not be undone. Though most of the Feratollo family had died in the plague ten years ago, his eldest son Umberto had adopted the feud with vigor. "Also, Alvero Madina."

"Of course," Flavio muttered. "Those two broods of villains are joined at the hip."

Angelo reluctantly added, "I suppose it helps that I haven't made enemies as a councillor yet." It had wounded his father's pride that he'd never achieved that position, considering how the Senate chose ten councillors every six months. "My inoffensiveness is why the doge asked me to lead this effort."

"What will Doge Celsi say tomorrow?" Cornaro asked.

Angelo shook his head. "His support is well-known, but he believes it unwise for him to speak."

"Why?" Flavio asked.

"If he supports the creation of a professional army, many will charge him with designs on tyranny, just like the other Italian dukes. If he defeats it, others will question whether a doge should be able to influence the Senate so strongly."

"And if he speaks against it and fails, he looks like a fool," Giovanni said.

"Exactly. Among us, Niccolo is best equipped to influence the Senate."

Flavio stiffened. "Why do you say that?"

Emilio leaned forward. "Forgive me, Niccolo, but are you truly the best choice? You've never spoken before and don't know what to expect. It should be you, Angelo."

Angelo shook his head. "His war record speaks well of him, as much due to Giovanni's tales as to the glowing reports from the governor. And this is his first speech. The floor will be intrigued to hear his style. They'll give him a chance."

No one replied, letting the truth of Angelo's summary hang in the air.

Niccolo broke the silence. "Father apprised me of the situation. I have a good idea what I'm going to say."

"And what should I do throughout this little speech?" Flavio asked hotly.

His father's eyes hardened again, exposing the strain within them. Flavio had definitely become more hostile over the previous two years.

"If what was true two years ago is true today, you're admired for giving Alvero Madina the thrashing he so rightly deserved. If you speak first, your passion will set the right tone."

Flavio's expression became unreadable for a few moments. "Very well."

Niccolo briefly wondered which Flavio would show up for the morrow's meeting—the brother who sought his brother's forgiveness or the poorly behaved dinner guest.

No, that was unfair. Niccolo's pain of loss was still fresh, but how much worse must it be for Flavio, whose marriage had inflicted that pain? His guilt must have been terrible.

NICCOLO

The morning brought a thick blanket of mist, the lingering effect of a terrible storm the night before. Lightning had struck the Orseolo house, one of the oldest buildings in the city, and set it aflame. Torrents of rain doused the blaze before it could spread to the adjacent buildings, but by daybreak, the old landmark had been reduced to a ruin. It was a bad omen.

Niccolo hoped God had reckoned without the benefit of his pending speech.

A crowd had already gathered by the time his gondola reached the ducal palace, and he wearily picked his way through it. Senators had gathered in groups with their families and friends around the colonnade surrounding the palace. Niccolo had almost reached the entrance when he witnessed the dark-haired Umberto Feratollo slide up to another senator. After a few whispered words, the blood drained from the other senator's face. Umberto met the man's gaze quickly before patting him lightly on the cheek and leaving him in motionless shock.

Niccolo clenched his teeth. Issuing threats mere steps from the Senate? The Aretoli couldn't leave the republic to men like Feratollo.

He passed beneath the marble angels carved into the entrance archway leading to the great chamber. The chamber itself was massive, capable of comfortably fitting hundreds of senators. Seats flanked either side of a central aisle, in rows of ascending height. The result was a central clearing nearly the length of the hall with space for the doge, his advisors, and Council of Ten all arrayed at the end opposite the entrance.

He was entering this room for only the second time in his life. Excitement and apprehension battled in the pit of Niccolo's stomach.

Off to the right, Flavio joked with some of the younger senators inducted over the past few years. Laughing, he demonstrated his dueling pose, directing some of the younger men in their stances. His brother had a definite charisma about him, but if last night's erratic behavior was typical, he'd never build a following.

Emilio and Marco Cornaro, the latter recently returned from Hungary, sat with their backs completely straight, gazing ahead with dignity. Niccolo almost laughed aloud. Senators admired the Cornaro name. Despite their recent troubles, they needed only to look admirable to accumulate support.

At the far end of the hall, the doge took his place. Tendrils of gray hair with flecks of white poked out from beneath his pentagonal silk hat. His stiff robes and flared boots were inlaid with fine gold. The weight must have been immense, but he held himself erect nonetheless. Though he was elderly, his alert gaze found each member of the assembly in turn.

Shuffling feet replaced chatter as the senators took their seats. To the left of the doge, the Council of Ten settled behind a long oak table. Another similar table remained empty across from them. Matteo Vellini, the finance minister, casually reclined with his family across the aisle.

"Father, why doesn't the doge have his ministers by him?" Niccolo asked.

"I'm guessing they don't all share his opinions," his father explained. "Distributed among the house, they can vote as they choose without insulting the doge."

"Why would he do that?" Niccolo settled next to Flavio, behind his father's chair. His brother leaned forward to listen to the answer.

"It would harm his influence if his ministers didn't vote with him." Angelo gestured to the head table. "We're about to begin."

Antonio Galli rose and rapped his knuckle on the table. His grandfather had entered the Senate after pioneering the Egyptian silk trade. While most of Europe had refused to trade with the sultanate, he had quadrupled Galli wealth almost overnight.

"Gentlemen." His voice thundered over the remaining conversation. "Our session is now open. I wish to welcome those newly returned to our fair ranks, particularly Gandolfo Ventisi, lately returned from a diplomatic endeavor among the Rus, and Niccolo Aretoli"—Niccolo grimaced as Galli placed the accent on the second syllable of his given name—"finally returned from Crete. Every son of Venice appreciates your contributions to our great republic."

Niccolo, surprised by this special acknowledgment, only rose when Flavio jabbed him in the side. He offered a deep bow. Ventisi, an elderly man, merely inclined his head to acknowledge the praise. Having served the republic for years, he'd earned the right to remain seated.

"Now, gentlemen," the councillor began. "As we've already discussed this topic at length, we'll limit the summation to one hour per side before voting." Unlike earlier stages of the debate, the formal summation would involve fewer interruptions. Niccolo and his father had developed their strategy specifically for the summation; otherwise, others would drown out Niccolo's words.

Galli turned. "Doge Celsi, does this meet with your approval?"

The doge flashed a silent question to Angelo, who nodded quickly. "Conduct your meeting as you see fit, Signor Councillor."

"Who will speak in support of this proposal?"

"I will." Across the room, Leonardo Dandolo rose and descended the tiers of seats to stand in the center of the well. Niccolo watched his former governor with sinking spirits. He didn't relish the prospect of refuting a man he admired. The governor likely wouldn't take a hard stance, but if he did, Niccolo would need to tear his argument to pieces.

"My fellow senators," Dandolo began in his easy tenor. "The past thirty years have been the hardest in our republic's history. I've served in two armed campaigns and have seen many kinds of forces arrayed both for and against our republic. I tell you, we are at a dangerous crossroads."

He sauntered toward the main tables. "In the last two years, our citizens on Crete revolted against our rule. Reclaiming the island fell to our militia, temporary levies called up as a garrison. It fought valiantly, but their pike walls failed. We needed to hire mercenaries, *condottiere* companies, to crush this rebellion. Foreigners who practiced their skills on the blood of our subjects."

He swept his hands out before him. "What sense does this make? Why should we rely on foreigners who conspire against us? We won the latest war at the expense of the next one. The Viennese or Paduan mercenaries we hire today will surely come back as aggressors tomorrow. Have we forgotten Dalmatia?"

Niccolo grimaced. Dandolo was doing well. Merely mentioning Dalmatia could often incite a crowd.

"The only way to maintain our self-sufficiency is to train our own soldiers and hire them out as *condottiere* in foreign wars to gain experience. They'll fight the very neighbors we'll face in battle and will learn not to fear them. No foreigner will develop a taste for Venetian blood or learn the secrets of our cities. With a standing army, Venetians will win our victories, and Venetians will earn the respect of our people."

He licked his lips once. "There is one more thing. Recent discoveries reveal that the Cretan rebellion received support from outside forces."

The pronouncement caught the room unprepared and triggered a chorus of startled chatter.

"Signor Dandolo, you have been warned in the past about passing speculation off as fact," the doge warned.

"With the Muslims stirring, we've kept a vigilant watch on our sea," Dandolo said. "There are very few who could slip past our patrols. And yet, someone must have, for the Cretans wore breastplates and wielded swords. With a standing army, we would not have lost Crete. That, gentlemen, is the simple truth."

Dandolo confidently strode back to his seat. The speech had suggested a conspiracy, whereas pirates and smugglers had most likely provided the armaments. The governor's comments also brought the events of that night into clarity. Dandolo's sluggishness the night of the attack had resulted from his overconfidence in the sea patrols.

The next speaker was a poor choice to follow the governor's staggering claim. Niccolo took the opportunity to reconsider the order of his speech to refute Dandolo's arguments. Lost in his thoughts, he didn't notice Umberto Feratollo rise to speak next.

"I challenge anyone here to give a good reason why we shouldn't replace our citizen militia with a professional army." His harsh and unforgiving voice surprised Niccolo to attention. "We need soldiers who can compete against Genoa and Austria. Where will they come from if not a standing army? Our possessions have expanded these past hundred years, and if we want to keep them, we need more than our navy. Faster production in the Arsenal won't cut it. Hand over the money to preserve our possessions now or lose them tomorrow."

He stomped back toward his chair and plopped into it heavily, leaving the Senate shocked by the short tirade. A few more speakers rose and echoed the same arguments as Dandolo, but Niccolo's attention turned to Umberto, who glared a challenge at the Aretoli.

When Cornaro rose to speak, that fury shifted to the old man. Only then did Niccolo realize Umberto's glare hadn't been about the debate at all, but rather had been directed at Flavio, who had saved the Cornaros through his marriage. The Feratollos had almost certainly arranged the attempt to ruin them.

A gasp caught in his throat. This man had cost him Rosalia.

On the floor, Emilio Cornaro stood motionless. "My family has served this republic for centuries. I have spent my life serving my people. Young Feratollo may extol an army for the violence it unleashes upon an enemy. However, I've seen the violence armies can unleash upon their own people.

"What is the difference between a militia and an army?" He allowed the question to hang in the air like the first stirrings of a storm on the wind. "Militiamen come when mustered then return to their occupations. But a soldier's occupation is warfare. Without a war, they are idle. Such idleness has ruined governments. Our fathers knew this. It seems we've neglected to teach our sons the reasons for our traditions."

As he sat, Marco Cornaro stood but didn't bother to move to the center of the room. "During my imprisonment in Hungary, I observed a standing army up close. They harass women and quarrel unendingly. Those of you who received letters from me during that time have the proof of it."

Now Flavio stood and sauntered into the center of the chamber. "Martial matters are of particular interest to me, ever since my youth. I read everything I could find about the great soldiers of the past. I spent much of my youth training to become a skilled warrior like Caesar, Agrippa, and Belisarius. Yet for all I admire their skill, I am also aware of the ugly side. Signor Cornaro is wise to warn you of the plague you'd unleash. Consider Padua and Milan. Do you want to lead our republic down the road of civil strife?"

As Flavio seated himself, Niccolo studied the effect of his words. Some of the more moderate senators rubbed their chins and lowered their gaze to the floor in encouraging signs of doubt.

Niccolo delayed until the soft murmur of growing expectation filled the room. Only then did he stand. The murmur became a surprised outcry, followed by an excited chatter. As he descended row by row, clusters of men pointed. One senator in the closest row shook his elder kinsman awake and whispered in his ear. Nothing stirred the Senate to action like novelty, and the thought of Niccolo offering up the first taste of his oratory skill was a tantalizing treat.

Niccolo held the attention of the sitting officials as he took his place at the center of the room. He clenched his hands at his side to hide their shaking. He wasn't ready for this after all.

Umberto glared in hungry anticipation, no doubt waiting for Niccolo to embarrass himself. Somewhere in the sea of faces, Alvero Madina would be wishing for the same.

But his father had trusted him with this task, and he would see it done. He decided to abandon his intended opening. He needed a flourish.

"A reckless man only sees the edge of the cliff after he has fallen off. Staring up at the ledge, he cries, 'Let me go back, let me choose again.' But he cannot. His fate is sealed. The moment before he strikes the ground, he remembers all the signs he missed. But his doom is already sealed. I doubt anyone here wishes for death, so I must assume you don't see the cliff we're racing toward."

Only a few senators met his gaze as he swept it around the room. Most turned away.

"No one here seeks a weakened republic. Why, then, do we disagree so sharply? I intend to reconcile the misunderstanding that divides us."

He gestured vaguely toward Dandolo. "Some have said that only a permanent army can defend the republic. Where does this belief come from? Perhaps we want the power of the French knight or the discipline of German men-at-arms." He paused to let the question sink in. When he continued, he shaded his tone with pride. "Why? When properly trained, our pikemen can withstand a cavalry charge and our crossbowmen can devastate infantry. Our navy is unmatched throughout the world. Why should we abandon these strengths for untried foreign advantages?" He raised his hands in resignation. "Perhaps I am mistaken, though. I invite the man who has charged mounted knights into a line of pikemen to correct me."

Of course, no voices rose to challenge him. That form of warfare wasn't the Venetian way. He had broken through their natural arrogance.

"Why should we abandon our natural skills for unfamiliar tactics? Have we fully considered what such an army would do to our republic? Where are the Venetian vassal lords to provide knights and men-at-arms for us? Who, exactly, will pay for all these men?"

Flavio and his father were both grinning openly. He had started strong.

"You've heard about the danger of idleness. But what of subversion? How long will it be until someone subverts our army with the promise of more money, land, or spoils? Milan, Ferrara, and Padua were once republics as we are, yet they're now held hostage by brutal tyrants. Would Carrara sit on Padua's throne without a ready military force?"

The dark murmurs began at once. Almost since the day Francesco da Carrara had claimed the Paduan throne, he had proven himself deceitful and tyrannical. If Carrara had been here, the chamber would've torn him to pieces.

Angelo had been right to insist upon this particular tactic.

"But at heart, I am a merchant. My commercial soul finds a far worse condemnation of this army business." Niccolo turned to the finance minister across the aisle. "Signor Vellini, what did the militia cost us on Crete before the rebellion?"

Sitting with his family, the minister hadn't the space to lay out his reports in an organized manner. It took him some time to find the figures. "Provisioning a full division for a month cost approximately eight hundred ducats."

"Thank you, Signor Vellini." He raised his voice. "Eight hundred ducats for a single division. We had four divisions on Crete. A year's service cost us nearly forty thousand ducats. That's almost how much Genoa paid us in reparations after the last war. And that's just for a single garrison. Four hundred men. A professional army would also require us to buy weapons and armor, whereas the militia largely provides its own. A field army requires wagons and animals to carry supplies, siege equipment to invest towns, and money to hire local guides, translators, factors, and facilitators."

He paused to allow the senators to finish their calculations. "Austria can field tens of thousands of soldiers, as can Hungary or France. How many soldiers would we need to defend against such a force? Maintaining such an army is a huge expense. In comparison, our navy pays for itself through its seasonal trade runs."

He had given them the facts. Now, he would speak from his heart. He wouldn't let the Senate castigate the garrison he had proudly led. "And don't forget the intangible costs. Currently, every Venetian male must attend military maneuvers throughout the year to improve with the sword and crossbow. Our entire citizenry is capable of serving his republic when the need arises. How many Venetians would bother to hone their skills if our defense relied on a professional army? There is no surer way to weaken the loyalty of the common man than to relieve him of responsibility for his own defense."

His words resonated in their expressions. "If you mandate a professional army, our defense will rely upon the goodwill of those who practice no trade worth defending. Let our descendants celebrate our wisdom, not condemn our folly."

With a short bow, Niccolo turned toward his seat.

Several members of the house rose and began to applaud. The rest of the house joined them a few moments later. Even his opponents participated, albeit reluctantly.

He had quite forgotten. This was his first formal speech, and they wanted to welcome him. Smiling uncertainly, Niccolo raised a hand to acknowledge the praise before sitting down.

As the final senators quieted, Galli announced, "The debate is closed."

The doge rose. "Let us proceed with voting."

"Signor Doge?" In front of him, Niccolo's father rose, conspicuous among so many seated senators.

Murmurs arose, matching Niccolo's own surprise. This wasn't part of their plan.

"Signor Aretoli, you wish to add your comments to the debate?" the doge asked.

"No!" Alvero Madina shot upright.

"You are not recognized, Signor Madina."

"I don't care if I'm recognized. The debate was closed. If he wanted to speak, he should have done so earlier. Sit down Aretoli."

Councillor Galli cleared his throat. "The senator is correct. The doge has closed the debate. Signor Aretoli may not speak regarding the issue of the army."

"My comment does not relate to the impending vote," Angelo said, "but to another emergency matter."

Galli hesitated before waving Angelo to proceed. Alvero sat down heavily and continued to fume.

"A deficit exists in our militia. The effectiveness of our garrison could be vastly improved by more opportunities to work together before it is called to action. I propose that we double the number of training musters required for every city, quarter, and colony. Our citizens will then improve their abilities at very little additional expense. I call for an immediate vote on this emergency measure."

The doge narrowed his eyes. "I don't see how this is an emergency, Signor Aretoli."

Niccolo swallowed. Why did the doge hesitate to act on this proposal? If it passed, some senators might consider a full army unnecessary.

Across the aisle, Emilio Cornaro grinned. "Every moment we do nothing, we're risking our future. I would consider that an emergency." He shrugged. "And it costs us nothing."

Murmurs of agreement rippled through the chamber.

The doge surveyed the chattering assembly for a long time. Biting back a response, he instead sat down.

Galli met Celsi's gaze for a long while before shrugging. "Then let us vote. All those in favor will stand."

The shuffling of feet began slowly. The Aretoli led the procession, but soon four councillors and most of the house stood. After some time, the doge joined them.

Assessing the room, Galli nodded. "The militia will gather on an increased schedule. We'll appoint a committee to announce the applicable days within the week." As the senators took their seats again, Galli continued, "Now, we will vote on the creation of a standing army. We will not tolerate ambiguity. All those senators approving of the measure will step to my left, and all those denouncing it will step to my right. Stand and be counted."

The supporters crossed as a group, with Umberto glaring at each senator he passed. The man he had spoken to outside quietly rose and joined him, soon followed by his family members, whispering in confusion as they did.

The rest of the body began to divide. Angelo and Flavio had already moved to the other side of the room. As Niccolo crossed, almost two dozen senators rose and joined him.

A burst of pride lightened his steps. Was this the beginning of his own faction?

The doge joined their side but, curiously, did not stand with Angelo even though he had personally requested that he lead the opposition.

Heads twisted and bobbed as several senators, including his father, made their own counts of the roughly equal sides.

Galli's count, however, was the one that mattered. "The vote is tallied and will be entered into the registers. By a margin of twelve, the measure is defeated."

Cheers erupted from the Aretoli side, soon matched by outrage from the other. Around Niccolo, senators clapped him on the back, whispering praise he didn't hear.

They had done it, and in so doing had paid back Umberto Feratollo for creating the crisis that had made Rosalia his sister-in-law.

CHAPTER FOUR

Niccolo

FOR THE NEXT few days, winners and losers met in the local pleasure houses, forgetting the source of their disagreement after a few cups of wine. While some taverns hosted thinly clothed dancers to entice patrons, most abandoned any pretense and offered bare, exotic flesh for the sampling.

Marco pleaded with Niccolo to celebrate his success with a night's festivities. Niccolo only agreed because Giovanni would be coming too. However, Asparia wasn't pleased when she discovered their plans. Only her poor aim saved Giovanni from a flying hairbrush. He wouldn't have done more than a little gambling and some light entertainment. But recalling his sister's concerns about Crete, Niccolo supposed her outrage wasn't unexpected.

No one blamed Giovanni when he sent word declining Marco's offer.

Petrarch chose the night's activity. "This is my first time in Venice, and I intend to enjoy myself."

It would have been impolite for Niccolo to ask what the poet's wife thought of his chosen form of entertainment, so he kept his peace as they walked. Most pedestrians had already chosen their revels, and the streets were nearly deserted. Traveling from the Aretoli's upscale—and wholesome—neighborhood to one of the finer establishments of dubious industry took perhaps half an hour.

When they reached the door, Marco knocked three times. A young man in a fine cotton doublet opened it a crack and studied them curiously.

"May I help you, sir?"

Niccolo straightened his doublet with his right hand, making a great show of his gold ring.

"Thank you, senator." The greeter opened the door the rest of the way and stepped back to allow them entry.

Niccolo entered into a haze of incense thick enough to make his eyes water. By the time his vision had cleared, they had turned the corner and entered a large sitting lounge occupying most of the ground floor. Beautiful women were everywhere. They lounged on fainting couches and adorned the knees of the men playing dice at the few tables sprinkled about. Some of their dresses were modest enough for the most conservative courts in Europe, but more than a few had opened their bodices. One of the younger ones was fully naked, encouraging her client's hands to stroke her soft skin.

The cloud of incense was even thicker here, smudging the flames of low candles into halos of diffused light. Someone played the harp. Tinkling music danced over the room, broken by occasional laughter.

A middle-aged woman in a spidery black silk gown approached with a broad grin. She stroked Marco's and Petrarch's arms. "Gentlemen, welcome to the Garden of Eve. I am Lucretia de Ferro, your hostess." She extended her hand, palm up.

Fingers trembling, Marco fumbled for his money and handed Madame de Ferro several gold ducats.

"Don't be nervous, young man. Here, you will find the appreciation you deserve." She glanced down, and her grin broadened. "Particularly when you carry such a pouch."

Petrarch whooped with glee.

"Have any of you been to the Garden before?"

Before Niccolo could reply, a beautiful blonde on a nearby couch beckoned invitingly. Adjusting a pillow on her lap, she revealed a shocking amount of inner thigh. He shifted at the sudden tightening beneath his codpiece.

Petrarch answered, "My lady, I heard the women of Venice were beautiful, but I see the rumors don't do them justice."

"A visitor to the city? From where do you come?"

He bowed slightly. "Florence, Rome, Milan. You could call me a son of Italy, my lady. Francesco Petrarch, at your service."

Her eyes brightened. "The poet." She leaned forward and brushed her hand over his chest. "I have enjoyed such pleasure while reading your work, sir."

"Well, I…um…" He cleared his throat, and Niccolo delighted in seeing the great man blush. "I'm always glad to meet the people I've… touched with my work."

Laughing, de Ferro swept a hand over the room. "We welcome you to sample any pleasure we offer, be it in the form of game, libation, or sensual delight. We have one strict rule, however." Her tone hardened. "Within this room, you are among gentle company and should act accordingly. Should you wish for a more private experience, we have separate rooms upstairs." Her smile faded. "Our servants are well-trained with sword and knife, for the safety of all."

"Of course, of course." Petrarch licked his lips. "Would you be agreeable to sharing some of your…passion for poetry?"

"Such a discussion warrants a little privacy, wouldn't you agree?" Her eyes shifted to something behind them.

"Absolutely."

She returned her gaze to Petrarch. "Nothing would please me more. But first, allow me to attend to something."

She departed for the corner that had drawn her attention. Niccolo turned to follow her passage, only to discover that Marco had already disappeared into the crowd. Their hostess slid up beside a young man entwined with a black-haired woman who had shed nearly all of her clothing. After a few quick exchanges with the hostess, the man and woman made a quick exit.

Petrarch waved limply at Niccolo before meeting de Ferro halfway toward the stairs. Once arm-in-arm, they ascended toward a private room.

Left alone, Niccolo sighed. How did one begin? He'd never visited a proper Venetian brothel before, only those on Crete.

He needn't have worried. The blonde who had met his gaze earlier tossed her pillow aside and approached, the soft silk gown barely containing her breasts as they bounced with her graceful movements. "What may I do to help you feel welcome?" she asked. Her directness surprised him, but her perfume and the curves of her body forgave much.

He swallowed, unable to focus on anything but the way her skin glistened in the soft candlelight. "What would you suggest?"

A beautiful redhead with clear blue eyes strode up behind the blonde. The black lace of her gown clung to her, guiding Niccolo's gaze to her hips and legs while still covering them. "I would suggest," she began in a thick northern Italian accent, "that you let me minister to the dear senator. You lack the skill to properly care for him."

"Get your own," the blonde hissed, face frozen in outrage.

But the redhead merely threaded her arm through Niccolo's and pulled him aside. "These Venetian women think they need only spread their legs to receive the praise of the world."

She was undeniably beautiful. Her eyes held an ageless quality that intrigued him. Those crystal irises suggested more worldly knowledge than the most experienced traveler or the finest of courtesans.

She differed from Rosalia in every possible way.

He raised his hand to stroke her cheek. Rather than resist him, she moaned softly without breaking her gaze. Continuing the motion, he traced the line of her throat down to the edge of her dress, following his fingers with his gaze. Her white skin was so exotic, framed by that fiery hair.

She raked her fingertips along his chest, easily navigating over the layers of clothing. The potency of her tingling touch forced a gasp and sent his body wild.

"You are Niccolo Aretoli, the Cretan Fox."

He had gone deaf to any other sound in the room beyond the rhythm of her breathing. "I am."

She lowered her hand to his hip. The touch sent shivers up the back of his neck. "Will you permit me to show my respect?"

Fame had its benefits.

He pulled her close to him. He suddenly felt very warm. "But you said you're not Venetian."

"Did I say that?" Her breasts rose and fell with her breathing. "Tonight, I wish to show an impressive man what I think of him."

She turned to the side and lifted Niccolo's hand to cup her breast. His fingers instinctively curled to caress her. Grinning, she stepped back, threading her fingers through his, leading him up the stairs. He neither felt the grain of the wooden railing nor heard the creaking of the steps as they made their way toward a vacant room on the second floor.

She backed against the door, turning her head toward the room's interior. Candlelight from within washed across her body, concealing the curve of her chin and casting a deep shadow between her breasts.

Niccolo leaned in, touching her lips with a feather of a kiss. She was close enough that her breasts brushed against his chest with each of her breaths. Lowering his hand, he stroked her thigh.

Stumbling backward, she fumbled with the bindings of her corset. Niccolo tossed his doublet to the side. Down went her corset, then the outer layer of her gown. Forced to step away from her to remove his shoes, he grunted in frustration. Even the small distance between them rebelled against his instincts to hold her.

He stood brazenly nude as she ran her gaze across his body.

Lips curling in delight, she murmured, "A *very* impressive man."

Meeting his eyes, she brushed her chemise off her shoulders to pool at her feet.

Closing the distance quickly, Niccolo took her into his arms and kissed her neck. She led him toward the bed and pushed him onto it. Slinking down, she teased him with her tongue.

The riot of sensual delight shocked him. Unable to wait, he pulled her up on top of him. She guided him into her, sending ripples of pleasure through his body. They began to flow together naturally, slowly at first, as they matched each other's rhythm.

Fingernails pressed hard against his back, sending spikes of pain. She gasped and leaned forward, showering him in a red river of hair as she clenched tighter. He held her close, and only her faster rocking told him he wasn't hurting her. His muscles no longer obeyed him.

Finally, the tingling waves burst through, and he exhaled, a mix between a breath and a moan, as he began to pulsate. She screamed in response and clenched tightly. Her rocking turned into a slow grinding. A flow of warm liquid dampened him as she collapsed into his arms, breathing heavily.

Struggling for breath, Niccolo watched her for a long while, but she didn't look up. The moment of passion was over. Their business was concluded. She would probably return downstairs for another client.

The bile rose in his throat at the thought of what he'd done. In place of pleasure, he felt only deep confusion and shame. What made Giovanni and Flavio so special that they could enjoy the real thing while he had to buy an imitation?

Her chest rose and fell evenly. Only after watching her for a time did he realize she was asleep, lying draped across him, unapologetic in her nakedness. Any other woman who had shared his bed had immediately covered herself.

She moaned, turning to rest her head in the crook of his arm, and he saw her face more clearly. She looked peaceful, content. Should he leave her be, or did she mean for him to stay the night?

His muscles ached, and a wave of fatigue started in his eyes. A moment before he surrendered himself to sleep in the embrace of the exotic redhead, he realized he didn't even know her name.

UMBERTO

The light had burned low by the time the others arrived. Umberto began to worry he'd have to change the candle. That simple chore always gave him a momentary panic that the wick would fail before he could transfer the flame, leaving him in the terrifying dark. Why had he dismissed the servant? He kept his gaze on the candle, holding his breath with every flicker.

No, no servants tonight. They were notoriously loose-lipped, even *his* servants.

The candle flickered again as the door swiveled open. With a quick motion, he drew a knife from its concealed sheath.

The figure began to chuckle. "You look a-fright, Umberto."

He audibly exhaled. "Next time, say something." He revealed the knife. "I almost gutted you."

Alvero Madina grinned wolfishly. They both knew Umberto was clumsy on the attack. "Is that any way to greet a childhood friend?"

"Apologies." Muttering, Umberto rose and clasped Alvero's thick shoulders. "Did anyone see you? Where are the others?"

"They're downstairs. I think they misunderstood our suggestion about disguises. Forget poor, some look downright diseased."

Umberto grinned. "Does Galli look like a beggar? They say he never wears the same boots twice."

"He looks like an *arrogant* beggar," Alvero replied. "By Jesus, this Old Guard doesn't understand intrigue. They're too noticeable."

"Are they a liability?"

Alvero laughed. The sound bounced off the walls like thunder in the quiet. "I doubt we'd let that happen. Besides, some of us can't afford for this to fail."

"You're referring to—"

"Yes." Using certain names, even in private, was dangerous.

"I hope he's ready to act, not just scheme."

"We could always proceed without his approval," Alvero suggested.

"Don't even think it," Umberto warned. "We'll need protection if something goes wrong. Why else would we have delayed this long?"

"Delaying is the point." His friend leaned against the table, grinning dangerously. "Delay distances us from blame when we achieve our revenge."

The door opened, and the first person entered. With him came an odor of such magnitude that Umberto had to hold his nose. "I'm surprised to see you, Antonio, after you allowed that 'emergency measure' travesty."

Galli dismissed the barb with a wave of his hand. "I had no choice but to follow the forms. It won't matter, though."

Before Umberto could respond, half a dozen more men filtered into the room, shunning the candle's light by arranging themselves along the walls. Cowering nervously while waiting for their final guest, they looked timid, hardly as committed to the cause as they'd claimed.

They stood a little straighter as two more guests entered. The first, a man, wore a magnificent shimmering gray silk cloak that concealed his face. Gold thread running through the material reflected the candlelight, consuming him in a net of glowing lines. He exuded an unmistakable authority.

The other visitor interested Umberto far more, though. Concealed within a thin cloak, this figure was smaller. It must be the 'Lucia' he had heard about. She was some kind of courier, though he couldn't imagine who would trust a woman with important messages. She'd be too easy to overpower without bodyguards.

Her hood drooped loosely over her head, folding far enough forward to conceal her face. A few patches of auburn hair peeked out of the darkness, providing a frame of reference for her features.

"Let's have some more light, Alvero," the newcomer in the magnificent cloak said in a solid baritone. He still hadn't removed his hood.

The woman placed her hand on his arm in a surprisingly confident gesture.

"No?" the man asked her. "Very well." He turned slowly, facing each of them in turn from beneath the cloak. "You all look terrible. What's so important to bring everyone out here in rags?"

"It's time you made a decision, signor," Alvero piped. "He's starting to get in our way. You need to let us do what we have to."

The newcomer turned to study him. This one didn't fear Alvero. That thought unsettled Umberto; no one stood up to Alvero.

"What do you have in mind?"

"A length of Spanish steel inserted right about here." Alvero gestured to his side about halfway up his torso.

A few of the others shifted their weight. These disgruntled patricians lacked the will to carry out their ambitions. But every coalition needed financiers.

The man in the gold-threaded cloak remained still. "That's a brutish way to handle the situation."

Alvero pressed, "Can I interpret that as your consent?"

"If we murder him openly, his family will declare *vendetta*," the man said. "They'll pursue whichever of us they can implicate. We don't need that scrutiny."

"So, what do you suggest?" Alvero wore a mask of wounded betrayal. This was his opportunity to exact some well-deserved revenge.

"I suggest something easily concealable. Something indirect. Something subtle."

"You mean poison," Umberto supplied. "A coward's method of murder."

"Do you believe our victim prefers to be stabbed?" the man countered.

Alvero ignored the question. "How do you suggest we do it?"

"Something targeted. We can't have droves of people dropping dead," the man continued. "Other than that, it's probably best I don't know."

Umberto clenched his fists. No one reduced him to a lackey. They were partners in this venture. Other than Alvero, whose eyes flared with a rage that usually presaged murder, no one seemed perturbed by such condescension. Sycophants, all of them.

"I have just the thing." Alvero's voice held a surprising calm, betraying none of the fury in his eyes. The hooded man clearly meant to put them in their places, but Alvero had chosen not to take offense…for now.

"Something painful, I trust?" Umberto asked, following his friend's lead.

Behind him, the cloaked woman scoffed.

Alvero turned to her. "Do I offend your sensibilities, my lady?"

The light encroached a little further into her hood, but Umberto still couldn't distinguish her eyes. Nonetheless, a chill rolled down his back as she turned her invisible face toward his friend. This woman frightened him.

"My sensibilities are in no danger of being offended, signor," she began coolly. "Kill this man as you will. I simply disapprove of amateurs."

"Amateurs?" Alvero scoffed. "I've killed more men than you can imagine, madam."

"You would be surprised at the extent of my imagination."

Alvero's expression assumed an unnatural and uncharacteristic stillness.

"Murder is not an emotional action," she continued. "This man must die without raising suspicion. If you let your passions rule you, you'll be discovered. If that happens, there will be consequences." A silence fell across the room. No one dared to turn his eyes to that empty hood. "Anyone who believes this is about your petty rivalries is mistaken. This is about restoring the Venetian Empire to strength and security."

The word "empire" struck the room like an anchor. His whole life, Umberto had been taught the republic was an island against the despotic madness infecting the mainland. To hear someone call his city an empire unsettled him. Yet, upon considering further what they hoped to achieve with this cabal, he couldn't deny the word's accuracy.

"Thank you, my dear." Her companion spoke as if she'd offered him wine. "Now, if there's nothing else, I suggest we disperse. We all have places to be." He looked around, but no one else spoke. "God keep you all."

The others began to shuffle out. When only the two newcomers, Alvero, and Umberto were alone, the man placed a hand on his shoulder. Umberto had witnessed him use that same gesture many times over the past few days, to both friend and enemy alike. The observation unsettled him.

"Do be careful, Umberto. You and Alvero are both too important. I can't afford to lose you at a time like this."

Umberto glanced at Alvero and saw the same suspicion. "We won't disappoint, signor."

"I know you won't. Fortunately, this annoying man isn't an important senator. It isn't like I asked you to kill poor Galli, is it?" He laughed lightly, but something about the comment seemed too natural. "Well, if you need help, let me know." He strode toward the door but turned before reaching it. "But I'm certain you won't, yes?" With a smile, he departed, followed by the woman.

"That man is a snake." Alvero straightened. "Does he ever speak the truth?"

"We should prepare in case he decides to betray us. I'm sure one of your boys can slip a knife under his ribs."

"Oh, Umberto." Alvero flashed that bright grin. "I saw to that a month ago."

Umberto couldn't help but bark a laugh. He never could resist his dear Alvero.

FLAVIO

Flavio adjusted his doublet for the fourth time and studied his reflection. With a free hand, he shifted his dagger to sit lower on his hip. Rosalia was right. It looked silly slung so far back.

"How's this?" he asked over his shoulder.

She had been braiding her hair in an intricate pattern. After shifting the strands around to fit into a single hand, she removed the brush from her mouth. "It looks better sitting forward. I'm told it's more comfortable that way, too."

Flavio tried it and took a few steps. Normally, his sword sat on his left hip, but they were forbidden tonight. While the Cornaro residence was large, it was still indoors. A few hundred men wearing swords would be bumping into each other all night.

"Wherever did you learn that?"

Her fingers, brushing the unbraided side of her hair, hesitated. "I don't recall."

If he asked Niccolo about the positioning of the dagger, he'd probably receive the same answer.

Part of him wished his brother had never returned from Crete. He could have easily decided to stay on the island. He didn't wish for Niccolo to die, of course; that would be terrible of him.

He hadn't asked his wife her feelings about seeing Niccolo again. The Senate had kept him busy, while Rosalia had spent much of her time at her father's house, preparing for tonight. He'd been watching for signs that her old feelings were re-emerging, but so far, only his outburst at dinner had roused her. And that had been his fault, not hers. For his part, Niccolo had acted with perfect decorum.

The anxiety of the past two years was finally beginning to drift away.

"You look…"

Rosalia looked at him with curiosity.

The words had to be something meaningful. "You look very nice, my dear." *I sound like a fool.*

Rosalia's smile filled him with delight. "Thank you, husband." She ran her gaze across him. "You look quite handsome, as well." She didn't regard him with the lusty gaze women had given him in the past, but she did offer a genuine smile, empty of regret.

Had they been carrying the same worry all this time? They hadn't shared a bed in months, let alone be properly man and wife. She barely responded when they had lain with each other. Maybe now that they knew Niccolo wouldn't stand between them… Did he dare hope for children?

"Could you help me?" Her eyes carried a longing that mirrored his own.

Smiling, Flavio crossed to her. She fumbled for a moment, trying to find his fingers, before pressing a few strands of hair between them. "Yes, like that. Do you have it?"

"Yes." He held the silky hair as still as he could. After a few moments, his fingers began to ache from the unfamiliar tension.

She tilted her head down, looking for something in her lap. The hair pulled taut in his hand.

"Are you alright?" he cried.

She laughed lightly. The sound soothed his bruised heart. He hadn't heard her laugh like that before.

"You should see what my ladies do to my hair."

He would have words with her ladies to be more careful.

She took the strands from him and began to weave them together, fingers dancing nimbly back and forth, faster than he thought possible.

"I was thinking we could visit Milan next month," he blurted. "Would you like that? I hear the best French fashions come through there."

"Can we do that?" Excitement carried her voice higher than usual. "Don't your duties keep you in the city?"

"I can take some time away. There are other captains."

"If you like, yes." Her smile reflected in the mirror. "I've never been to Milan."

"Then it's settled." Now, he had to leave before he ruined the day's progress. "I should tell the servants we're ready." He turned to the door but halted. "Are you ready?"

Her gaze lingered on him. "Yes, I shouldn't be long."

Smiling, Flavio stepped out of the room, thoughts occupied with planning the details of this new trip.

NICCOLO

Niccolo meant to arrive at the Cornaro Easter celebration early but couldn't decide what to wear. He first chose his best doublet, made of gold and blue brocaded silk. However, following his first speech in the Senate, several fathers had extended dinner invitations to meet their eligible daughters. He wasn't yet ready to field those conversations, and wearing such a fine garment would only increase the number of polite rejections he'd have to give. Opting for modesty, he instead chose a simple dark green doublet with broad slashes to reveal the shimmering silver tunic beneath.

An older couple sat within the gondola that responded to the flag he'd placed outside his door. Niccolo boarded, and the gondolier began pushing them along the *ria*.

The wife asked her husband, "Did you hear the latest rumor?"

The husband let his gaze drift lazily at the passing buildings. "Mmm?"

"A ship arrived a few days ago carrying a Paduan diplomat."

A woman's laugh on the shore distracted the husband. "There's a new Paduan embassy, is there?"

"That's just it. There isn't. No one seems to know anything."

"I'll keep my eyes open for a diplomat," he added absently.

She whispered, "Maybe it's a spy. Wouldn't that be exciting?"

Niccolo suppressed a grin at her idea of excitement as the gondola docked in front of Emilio Cornaro's home. Small stuffed birds that looked real in the pale light perched within the ivy coiled around the lantern posts on either side of the door.

A servant he didn't recognize led him down the main hallway and past the kitchen. Nose tingling from a panoply of delicious scents, he peeked inside. Dozens of chefs scrambled from table to table. A cook stirred a trio of large pots of soup. Servants busily piled cut fruit and vegetables in front of an apprentice who arranged them on a large, wheeled table. A cluster of cooks stood like guards by the fires, slowly roasting boar, lamb, and several whole chickens.

A master baker waved his hands at his apprentices. "No, no, they must be rounder to catch the light from any angle. The glaze isn't just for taste, it must make our guests salivate!"

And salivate, Niccolo did. Rosalia had probably instructed the servants to lead her father's guests on this roundabout route to build anticipation before entering the main chamber. She really did have a flair for this sort of thing.

He caught up with the servant as he opened the large doors to the main chamber. Tables covered with enticing dishes encircled each of the room's columns. Around the stone pillars in the center, colorful floral displays filled the empty spaces between the plates. Coils of ivy reached up and encircled each one, seamlessly blending both table and column. Such a riot of floral color would have cost a fortune, but the display's classical simplicity suited the occasion better than some of the gaudy jewel-and-gold displays he had seen in prior years.

If he felt particularly brave, he might even steal a private word and give her his compliments.

His host was chatting with Angelo while Flavio hovered protectively nearby. With a deep breath, Niccolo maneuvered past a group eagerly discussing an upcoming tournament in Verona.

"Niccolo." His father clasped his shoulder before presenting a plate. "You really must try some of this."

He eyed the plate dubiously. "Apple slices?"

"I mean the powder on top. Emilio brings it in from Alexandria just for me. Isn't that right, Emilio?"

Cornaro patted Angelo on the arm. "Cinnamon. Something special for my dear friend."

"Don't eat too many, Father, or you'll have a sick stomach," Flavio cautioned.

His father defiantly popped another piece into his mouth. "Delicious, Emilio."

"It's the least I could do to show appreciation for your support while my brother was imprisoned." Cornaro met Niccolo's gaze for a moment before looking away. "I should check on my brother." Without another word, he wandered off into the thickening crowd.

Angelo sniffed the apple slice and smiled with obvious delight. "A decade ago, Emilio and I visited the east and discovered this spice." He took another bite. "Now, he prepares some for me when I dine with him in memory of our travels together." He raised the plate for Niccolo. "This batch isn't as good as usual, but it's still a taste you'll never forget. Try it."

Niccolo eyed the tray suspiciously. The last time he tried something exotic was on Crete. Suppressing a shudder at the memory of those shells, he politely declined.

Flavio offered Niccolo his hand. "It's good to see you at one of these celebrations again. I was beginning to worry you weren't going to make it."

He took it in a good, strong clasp. "I wanted to arrive earlier, but haven't had to dress for a formal occasion in years."

Flavio laughed lightly. The sound soothed Niccolo's ears. "You should have asked me. Let's see… If I remember correctly, the style was broad slits and tight hose when you left." He stroked his chin. "Yes, I dueled a foppish lad from House Colletti around then." He must have been foppish indeed for Flavio to consider him so; his brother followed every fashion. "He ripped his pants when he lunged and spent the remainder keeping his cheeks together."

Niccolo laughed at the image, but he wondered how many duels his brother had fought. "I'm guessing he lost?"

Flavio grinned, "I slit his hose the rest of the way. He had an embarrassing walk home."

Angelo barked a laugh, nearly choking on his treat as a result. Flavio typically didn't discuss his duels with Father.

"I wish you'd come to me, Niccolo," Flavio continued. "The style is more subtle. See?"

He reached up, fingering the small slits in his doublet. Rather than Niccolo's tighter hose and codpiece, Flavio wore breeches ending at the knee with hose beneath.

Niccolo suddenly felt naked and very exposed. "Do I have time to change?"

"I'm afraid you've attracted too much attention." Flavio spun him around to face a young woman watching them. Caught, she blushed deeply enough to match her crimson dress but nonetheless stole another look at Niccolo's codpiece.

Niccolo turned around quickly.

"No luck there. She'll just get a look at the other side," Flavio joked.

He shoved Flavio while their father cackled in genuine pleasure.

"I see the Aretoli brothers have finally turned on each other," a voice behind them said. "It was only a matter of time, what with Flavio's marriage."

They whirled and assumed identical defensive stances.

Umberto Feratollo grinned at them like a cat discovering mice for the first time. Niccolo wanted to knock that smug expression off his face.

He restrained himself only because Umberto desired exactly that reaction. Houses were supposed to halt feuding during church festivals in honor of God and the dignity of the republic. Any who violated the peace would be ejected from the celebration.

Beside him, Flavio went rigid. The last time Niccolo had seen his brother like this, he had crippled a man with a flawless thrust through the shoulder. It was the closest Flavio had ever come to killing one of his opponents.

Angelo responded first. "I'm sorry that my son's happy union foiled your shameful schemes."

Umberto whirled around to face the older man.

Angelo craned his ear toward the other man. "Exactly how much did your bribes to ruin the Cornaros cost you?"

"Where does such slanderous speech come from?" Umberto extended his hands, feigning offense. "I've always held House Aretoli close to my heart."

"Whereas I've always rubbed House Feratollo against my arse," Flavio countered.

Umberto's mouth quirked subtly. He turned to Niccolo. "I was concerned about Rosalia when you left for Crete, but I'm glad Flavio took such good care of her for you."

In a flash, Flavio extended his hand and slapped the villain across the face.

Umberto recoiled and raised his hand to his face. When he removed it, a thin red line ran down his cheek. Niccolo caught the glint of a broken blade in Umberto's hand.

He had cut himself!

The altercation drew angry murmurs. More than a few looked toward Emilio Cornaro expectantly.

"You strike me, sir?" The triumph in Umberto's eyes belied the wounded inflection of his voice.

"If my intention was unclear, allow me to repeat myself." His brother made a fist.

"Flavio!" The authority in Angelo's voice silenced the room.

"Will no one save me from this abuse?" Umberto asked a little too loudly.

Was this a distraction, a signal for something worse? Niccolo searched the crowd for additional threats.

"If you want salvation, I can lead you to it tomorrow morning with the weapon of your choice," Flavio replied coldly.

Emilio Cornaro strode forward and offered Flavio a piteous look.

He inhaled a long, slow breath before saying, loudly enough for everyone to hear, "My friends, I beg your pardon for this discord." Turning to Flavio, Emilio sighed. As host, Cornaro had no choice in his next words. "Signor Aretoli, I know you've taken some drink, so we will forget these ill-considered words."

Flavio hadn't had a drop all night.

Then, he turned to a triumphant Umberto, who didn't bother to hide his glee. "We will likewise forget your mortal insult against Signor Aretoli." He raised an eyebrow. "Perhaps tomorrow, our memory will return, and the two of you will be called to account for tonight's actions."

Niccolo felt a momentary satisfaction when Umberto's eyes widened in recognition that he may not have evaded a duel, after all.

"But tonight, we celebrate the enduring dignity of Venice, and those who tarnish that purpose are not welcome." Cornaro turned from Flavio to Umberto. "For violating the peace tonight, I banish you both from these festivities."

Satisfied that Cornaro had fulfilled his obligations, the crowd returned to their previous conversations. They had gotten their entertainment.

"But you can't… I didn't…" Umberto scoffed. "You'll pay for this, Cornaro."

"That attitude brought you here, Umberto. Shut your mouth before you make it worse," Angelo warned.

"I don't have to take that from a filthy Aretoli." Muttering a string of curses, Umberto spared a glance for the apple slice in Angelo's hand before storming out.

Swallowing his embarrassment, Flavio offered a stiff yet graceful bow. "Signor Cornaro, allow me to apologize for my reaction. I wish you and your lovely daughter a fine night." He turned on his heel and strode to the exit.

Emilio let out a heavy sigh as he approached the remaining Aretoli.

"The devil of it is, if Flavio hadn't said it, I would have. He insulted my daughter, as well."

Angelo patted his friend on the shoulder. "I'm sure that wasn't easy for you, but the forms must be obeyed."

Emilio nodded and sighed. "I should speak to Rosalia before she hears about this from some gossiping old man." He turned to walk through the crowd. Several senators bowed as he passed. The night may have become a personal sorrow, but it may yet become a political success.

Niccolo noticed his father watching him with the same worried expression as back on the docks when he had returned from Crete. "You knew this would happen, didn't you?"

Angelo lowered his gaze grimly.

Niccolo bit his lip. "How many duels has Flavio fought over his marriage?"

His father's shoulders sagged. "I don't know. If they occurred, I did not observe any injuries from them."

"How would you? He has his own home to go back to now," Niccolo retorted with more force than he intended.

"Indeed." Angelo pressed his lips together. "At least Cornaro had the quick thinking to banish Umberto, too."

Niccolo shrugged. "The poor man thought only physical violence could break the peace."

"Sympathy for an enemy?" His father swallowed his slice of apple and took another.

"Perhaps," he conceded, "but pity doesn't require mercy. I still hope Flavio presses his challenge tomorrow."

His thoughts returned to Rosalia. It was unfair for her to suffer insults for something beyond her control. Every time Umberto or some other fool mocked her marriage, he'd want to reach over and choke the bastard. "I can't help him with it, you know." Surrendering to that urge would only prove the truth of the insinuation.

Angelo sighed. "I know."

Niccolo suppressed a sudden chill. What if Flavio challenged someone too skilled for him? If he died, wouldn't he be obliged to offer to care for Rosalia? The thought nagged tantalizingly at his mind, even as he was ashamed of its terrible consequences. But the more he tried to banish the traitorous image of himself cradling her, the stronger it became. He could smell her hair again, could see her smile with prophetic clarity.

The usual crowd murmurings died down, replaced with an eerie silence. Had he inadvertently revealed his clandestine thoughts? He looked around apprehensively. A few women in the crowd were studying something critically, and Niccolo followed their gaze.

On a platform raised slightly from the rest of the room, Rosalia stood serenely, waiting for silence. She looked magnificent in a beautiful emerald dress embroidered with rows of golden leaves at the cuffs, waist, and neckline. The sleeves flared out, making her upper body look much bulkier than usual. Niccolo had always thought that type of dress looked terrible, but he now understood how wrong he had been. She looked majestic, far from the victim of circumstance he had lamented.

His tongue darted out to lick his lips before he realized it. *That's Flavio's wife.*

Angelo shifted uncomfortably next to him. Chastened, Niccolo quickly reached for one of the cinnamon apples on the tray in his father's hands. Angelo looked away, feigning interest in something in the distance.

Niccolo popped the fruit into his mouth. The hint of bitterness surprised him. As the juice began to roll down his throat, he almost gagged but managed to keep it down with some effort.

On the dais, Rosalia addressed the assembly. "Senators, patricians, and dear friends, welcome. This home has served the Cornaro family since the foundation of our city. There is no more fitting site to commemorate our enduring love for the Most Serene Republic." Her lips twisted into a wry grin. "Indeed, I fear this famed serenity has proven too much for some of us. My dear husband already had to escort one of our guests out to recover his wits."

A few bursts of laughter bubbled out from among the crowd.

Niccolo started to bristle that she would make light of the altercation, but a gentle touch of his father's hand stilled him.

Of course. Her casual dismissal of the argument also cleanly dismissed the implication. Compared to her family, the Feratollos were peasants. A shrug and a jest had done more for her honor than a hundred challenges.

Rosalia was more cunning than he remembered.

She continued, "I should like to introduce a troupe of players who hail from Padua. By divine will, they were passing through the city on their way to Constantinople. They have agreed to honor us with some light entertainment commemorating the Senate and people of Venice."

She stepped down, and a flurry of servants positioned stools, chairs, and tables around the dais before departing. Four musicians approached, carrying a lute, a dulcimer, a gittern, and a flute. As they moved, threads of real gold woven into the brocade edging of their identical royal blue tunics caught the light.

Evidently, the gossip had been wrong. Musicians, not spies, had arrived on the mysterious ship.

They began to play a slow resonant piece as the audience returned to their conversations. Rosalia joined a circle of young women, both married and unmarried, based on their hairstyles. As they chattered and shifted, Niccolo identified the distinctive facial structures of at least one Dandolo, a Morosini, and a few other ancient patrician houses.

Nervously, Niccolo picked at the hem of his doublet. "I suspect you'll receive inquiries."

"Hmm?"

Niccolo gestured to a few of the young ladies eyeing him appraisingly.

Angelo grinned. "What are your instructions?"

"Instructions?"

"I won't force you to marry someone you don't care for. Not after…" He lowered his gaze.

The sentiment touched Niccolo, even as he struggled not to turn to the woman it referenced. But she was already married, and Niccolo could not wish ill upon her husband. "Be vague. There might be a charming young woman out there, and I wouldn't want to close any doors I may one day wish to walk through."

His father's eyes widened.

Rosalia was now a respected wife with her own household. Pining for her would not change that fact. He had to make peace with it.

He regarded the girl in the crimson dress. He let his gaze wander down to the curve of her breasts poking ever so slightly out of the neck of her dress. Perhaps she was destined to become his wife.

But a young woman and her father were striding toward him, and Niccolo's courage failed him. Fathers may be ready for those conversations, but he wasn't. He patted Angelo on the shoulder and ducked into the crowd.

Before the surrounding chatter overtook him, he heard, "Signor Aretoli, allow me to present my daughter…"

NICCOLO

Niccolo sought solace in the old nursery where he'd play when his family visited the Cornaros during his youth. Lifting a commandeered candlestick, he studied the room, replete with dust and cobwebs. It probably hadn't been used since Rosalia outgrew it.

Their fathers had always intended for them to marry, but after the death of Asparia's betrothed, Angelo had refused to sign any more underage marriage contracts. They would still visit often, though, and Niccolo had spent much time here. This room had contained his and Rosalia's mischief in their youth and had been their sanctuary when their bond grew beyond simple companionship.

Now, crates filled the space, and deep scratches marred the smooth oak floor. An ugly black smear, the remnant of an ancient abortive fire, ran along the far wall. Most of the original paint had chipped off, collecting in the corners and along the walls.

This wasn't the room of his memory. It, too, was lost to him. The thought left him feeling empty. He sat on the nearest crate.

"I didn't realize the servants had done so much damage until just this week," a voice behind him said.

Rosalia.

She stood in the doorway with the light of her golden candelabra reflecting off her eerily, as if she were a fantasy of his mind. Only the emerald dress he remembered from earlier convinced him she was real.

He gazed at her for a long while, soaking up her face. "It seems a shame." In this light, her features seemed harsher, like the faces of his men after leaving Crete. The comparison unsettled him.

Pain flashed in her eyes. "I can leave you alone if you prefer. I never meant to cause you discomfort." She turned to go.

"No, don't!"

Halting, she offered a quick look down the hall before stepping inside and closing the door.

At the click of the latch, his pulse raced. They were alone.

"Do you remember when I pleaded for my father to give me a cup of wine?" she asked. "I was only twelve, but I suppose I wanted to be more mature."

"If I recall, you hated it and tossed it across the room."

She smiled faintly. "Right onto the silk scarf my mother had given me." They laughed together for a moment, but the casual ease of it abruptly silenced them. "I also remember you taking the blame. It was very noble."

His father had whipped him when they'd returned home. He'd take a thousand beatings to save Rosalia from harm.

"Looking at you now"—she took a step closer—"I see that same noble, young man."

The light glistened on her skin again. Only the thinnest margin of control kept him from proving her wrong.

"I'm not as noble as you think, Rosa." His delicate control made his voice waver. His will was fading, but he had to speak now. Flavio was gone for the night. He couldn't let the opportunity pass. "Two years, Rosa. Every day in Crete, I thought of us standing next to the canal or our stolen caresses. Of every time you touched my hand behind a pillar…" He took a deep breath. "Or the first time I kissed you. Do you remember?"

"Nico." She took a single step toward him before reasserting control. She ran her hands along her stomach, smoothing her dress. "Yes, I remember. Every touch, every time you held me in your arms." She lowered her gaze. They carried a fresh pain when she raised them again. "And the promises. You never came back for me."

She was right. He had chosen to succeed Flavio on Crete. He had abandoned her.

His eyes widened. "I'm sorry, Rosa, I was too late. I couldn't have known." He rose from the crate. "If I had, I'd have never left. If it meant things could be different…"

"I don't blame you, Nico. Or Flavio. It was the only way to keep my family safe." She crossed to the cold fireplace, refusing to meet his gaze. "Did you ever blame me?"

"No." He pursed his lips. He could not lie to her. "Yes. At first, I couldn't believe you and Flavio could betray me." She remained silent. "Then I realized you had no choice. My father feels so guilty."

"So does mine," she added. "He tries to hide it, but when he told me, papa just kept repeating how sorry he was."

They fell silent. Every breath she took, each shift of her weight, urged him to reach out to her. He closed his eyes. "Do you still love me?"

She turned. A hand rose to caress him, but she caught herself and lowered it again. "Nico, you have no idea how hard it is for me to stand here with you now."

"I'm sorry."

"No, you don't understand." She clenched her fists. "I can barely restrain myself from begging you to run away with me." She huffed and raised her voice. "Damn you, Nico, why did you wear a codpiece? Didn't you know every bratty girl would be eyeing you up?"

"This, from the woman who beds my brother?" Even despite the low light of the candlestick, he saw her face redden. "Oh, Rosa, I'm sorry. That was terrible of me. I shouldn't... I'm so—"

"It's you every time, Nico."

"What?"

"Every time, I imagine it's you inside me." She lowered her gaze to his lips.

"We could..." Having conceived the thought, he had to give it voice. "We could have an affair."

Her expression hardened. "Would you put me on the level of the woman you visited last night?"

He turned to hide his flush of embarrassment. Memories of his shame in the moments after his collision with that redhead returned.

"Asparia told me. Marco invited Giovanni, if you can believe it."

"I'm sorry, Rosa."

"Oh, stop apologizing. I can hardly lay claim to your chastity." She took a deep breath. "You've been gone, but I've been here. I hear the gossip. Affairs only lead to pain. Either we'll tire of each other, or Flavio will discover us and be forced to challenge you to a duel. Can you imagine what that would mean?"

They fell silent again. A giggling couple ambled down the corridor before he spoke again. "Do you truly love me?"

Pain tugged at the corners of her eyes when she smiled. "I do, Nico. But Flavio has been polite and patient with me. He suffers as we do."

"I'd hardly call marriage to you suffering."

"He knows how much we cared for each other. Do you truly think he'd take pleasure in this?"

He sighed. "No, not Flavio."

"As boys, did you ever betray him to save yourself, or he you?"

"You're right," he admitted. "It's easier to think of him as a monster, but that's not fair."

"He's a good husband."

Niccolo replied before he could stop himself. "Be careful, Rosa. He's jealous, too. Did you see the daggers he shot at me during dinner?"

"He was quite drunk."

"And when did that start?"

"It was the first time," she said. "He's usually so restrained."

Niccolo knew the reason, of course. Hopefully, time would heal that wound as well.

"What are you thinking?" Rosalia asked.

He shrugged. "How am I going to live without talking with you like this?"

She remained silent for so long that Niccolo wondered whether she would reply. "I dreaded seeing you again. I feared we would have jumped on each other by now."

The image formed, and he found himself admiring the curves under her dress. She blushed, and he realized she'd followed his gaze back to their thoughts.

"But I also looked forward to it. To seeing you again. Not jumping on each other. Well, that...no..." She shook her head. "I mean I wanted you to come back so we could get these first few days out of the way. If we don't arouse... raise any suspicion..." She reddened further and rubbed her chest lightly at the word. "Eventually, everyone will forget about this whole affair...situation."

He sighed. "I suppose a few years should do it."

"A few years!"

He nodded. "Flavio will be the hardest to convince. After a few years without us causing a scandal, he'll realize we aren't plotting behind his back."

"You've obviously thought about this more than I have."

"I've had a lot of cold nights since that day," he said without strength.

"Where does that leave us?" Her voice carried a touch of desperation.

"I love you more than I'll ever love anyone else. That will never change. But you are my sister now." The words pained him. "I'd rather have your friendship and company than nothing of you at all."

She stared at him. "Will you grant me one favor?"

"Anything."

She moved closer and gazed into his eyes. "Kiss me. I need at least one more to keep with me."

"Rosa…" He leaned toward her but halted when he imagined them lying naked in a tangle on this floor. "Could we stop at just one kiss?"

She pulled back and nibbled her lip. "Oh, Nico." She leaned into him, but instead of kissing him, she rested her head on his shoulder.

"My rose." He cradled her gently so her hair didn't fall loose. They would never live down the rumors if they returned looking disheveled.

"You're a better man than he is. You resisted, and he didn't."

"That's not fair, my love." Despite his words, he felt the tug of doubt.

"No, it's not." She rose and began straightening her clothes. "It isn't fair at all."

NICCOLO

Niccolo agreed to leave first, so he casually strolled back to the main chamber. The musicians had taken a break, leaving their instruments under the watch of a servant who showed little interest in the precious possessions.

Angelo had drifted a little from where Niccolo had left him, speaking with another father-daughter team. Niccolo grinned, wondering how many eligible young women Niccolo had missed.

His father jerked suddenly and held his side in pain, cutting his conversationalists off mid-sentence.

Niccolo crossed the distance and grasped Angelo before he could topple over. "Father, what is it?"

Angelo clenched his arm. "S…sharp pain…can't…can't breathe."

The worry in Asparia's letters came flooding back. Niccolo guided his father toward the entrance. A canny gondolier was waiting to transport senators leaving the Cornaros' dinner, and Niccolo ushered his father into the boat.

"It's passing. I'm fine," Angelo insisted. "We should support Emilio."

Niccolo restrained his father when he tried to stand. "Gian Jacopo will judge whether we can go back."

At the mention of the Cornaros, his mind returned to the precious few minutes when he'd thought things might turn out well.

He should have known better.

CHAPTER FIVE

NICCOLO

NICCOLO SENT FOR the family doctor, Gian Jacopo de Villa, the most knowledgeable man in the city. If he had been Christian, even a great house would have struggled to afford his services. But few in the city would trust their lives to a Moor.

The old doctor had been at evening prayers. But upon hearing of Angelo's affliction, he had quickly muttered a summation and slid his feet into his boots.

Crouching over his patient, Gian Jacopo prodded Angelo's stomach, occasionally asking a question in his heavily accented Italian. "Have you had any indigestion in the past few days? Any unusual bowel movements?"

"That isn't any of your business," Flavio shouted.

Angelo flicked his gaze to Niccolo helplessly before clenching his teeth at another wave of discomfort.

"Flavio, let the man do his job," Niccolo said.

"I'm not about to let an Arab insult my family," he insisted dangerously.

"I'm a Moor," Gian Jacopo protested.

"No," Niccolo agreed, "but you will let a doctor inquire after the health of his patient."

"It's a completely different ethnicity," the doctor muttered sullenly.

"None," Angelo panted, answering the original question.

"Then it's unlikely to be a serious affliction," the physician concluded. "Did you eat anything unusual recently?"

Niccolo laughed suddenly, his concern evaporating. "Did he eat anything? Only a whole plate of cinnamon apples tonight."

"Did either of you eat any?"

"Good Lord, no." Flavio's anger subsided.

"I had one," Niccolo said.

Nodding, the doctor gave his verdict. "Perhaps, Signor Aretoli, you should limit your consumption next time. Drink a good deal of milk to settle your stomach. The type matters not. You should be fine in a day or two."

Visible relief washed over Angelo's face.

Flavio shook the doctor's hand vigorously. "Thank you, Master de Villa."

Niccolo escorted the man out, offering an apology once they reached the hall. Over the last hundred years, Venice had had more to fear from fellow Christians than Muslims, excepting, of course, the Turks.

"I've dealt with such things all my life, Signor Aretoli."

"Is there anything else you can do?" Niccolo gestured back toward his father.

"Anything else would simply add cost without benefit. Of course, I would understand if you desired a second opinion—"

Niccolo placed his hand on the physician's shoulder. "No, no, your judgment has always been enough."

Straightening with pride, Gian Jacopo smiled. "Please call me if there is any change in your father's condition. I will come immediately."

By the time Niccolo had returned, Angelo had settled into a

comfortable sleep. Flavio rose and gestured for his brother to follow him outside.

Flavio spoke as soon as he'd closed their father's door. "Do you think he'll recover?"

The fact of his father's mortality terrified him. "Yes. Yes, I'm sure he'll be fine. As Gian Jacopo said, it was the apples."

"You had some of those apples. How are *you* feeling?" Niccolo couldn't tell whether the question was intended to assess his brother's health or their father's chances of survival.

"I'm fine." Niccolo paused. "Well, no. To be honest, I do feel some pressure in my stomach. I should have asked the doctor about that."

"That's another thing." Flavio's tone darkened. "Why did you summon that heathen? We hardly need him learning everything about our personal lives. For all we know, he's a spy for the Turks."

"He's cared for us for the past twenty years."

"Yes, and mother died under his supervision."

"He's a doctor, not a prophet."

"Oh, he's not Mohammed? He looked just like him." Flavio scowled. "For all we know, he poisoned Father."

That was too much. "Don't claim a religious fervor with me. You're about as religious as an average cat." Softening when Flavio gave no response, Niccolo sighed. "We should tell our sisters what happened."

"You go. I'll wait here with Father. Besides, Asparia would prefer hearing it from you."

"I'll send Camilla back with a hefty supply of milk when I find her."

"Until then, brother." Flavio hugged him tightly.

Niccolo returned the embrace. A feeling of security flowed through him. Why did it take hardship to muster this affection? He prayed that, in time, he wouldn't need a crisis to restore his relationship with his brother.

NICCOLO

Satisfied at the improvement in his father's condition over the next three days, Niccolo returned his attention to his sorry financial state. He was visiting Giovanni for advice about some investments when one of Angelo's servants arrived with an urgent summons for the whole family.

When they arrived at their father's home, Pietro's drawn expression nearly broke Niccolo's heart. "I'm sorry, I should have realized. God knows I've seen enough of poison."

"Gio!" Asparia raised her hand to her mouth.

Giovanni steadied her with an arm and turned sympathetically to his friend.

But Niccolo was already running, charging through the hallway to his father's room. Poison. The very word chilled his bones. It was a terrible way to kill someone, employed only by cowards.

He pushed open his father's door. The bed was empty. Frantically, he searched the room. Petrarch was consoling Marco by the far wall. Camilla wept in the corner. But he could not see his father anywhere.

He had missed his chance to say goodbye.

Muffled voices bled through the door to the antechamber. After a moment of confusion, he recognized Gian Jacopo's thick accent, followed by his father's voice. The cadence was calm.

Relieved, he rubbed his face, glancing at Marco through his fingers. His poor brother looked absolutely pale. Niccolo crossed to him and embraced him.

Petrarch met Niccolo's gaze with a look of silent relief.

"Oh, Nico…" Camilla rushed over and buried her head in his chest.

Feeling a knot tighten in his stomach, he wrapped his arms around her. He'd have to make an effort to be patient with her. They would only have each other now.

He blinked away tears before they could fall. "Brother, Pietro said—"

"It's true." Marco glanced furtively at the antechamber before whispering, "But the doctor said it was caused by overeating. How could this happen?"

Niccolo intended to find out. Gian Jacopo had always been a skilled healer, but now he wondered if perhaps the Muslim had been guessing all this time. Had his father been wrong to trust him?

No, the doctor deserved a chance to explain. Besides, an Italian would have prattled on about the humors and bled Angelo to death.

Giovanni and a shaken Asparia entered. Niccolo crossed to her and placed his hands on her shoulders. Terror filled the eyes staring back at him. First, she had ministered to a dying mother, and now this.

Clenching her close to him, Niccolo let the tears fall. He couldn't endure the sight of his sister, usually so strong, on the verge of collapse. He hardly felt Giovanni wrap his arms around both of them.

"You all make me so proud." Angelo stood by the door under his own power, though Gian Jacopo stood a pace behind, ready to assist if he faltered. Perhaps Pietro had exaggerated the danger.

"Father!" Camilla ran to him.

Angelo held out his arms and stopped her before she could entirely envelop him. Niccolo's trained eye saw the slight teetering in his balance. Though he remained upright, the panic on his face revealed the seriousness of his condition.

Shaken, Niccolo lowered himself onto a nearby chair and closed his eyes. *This has to be a dream.* He hadn't expected this to happen for years, decades even.

He opened his eyes when Asparia said something in a shaken voice beside him.

Angelo lowered himself into his bed. "I don't think so, no. From the sound of it, it's very slow-moving. Our best guess is I was exposed to it at Easter."

Could Niccolo have prevented this if he hadn't been with Rosalia? Then, he remembered the plate of aromatic treats. "The apple slices."

"The apple slices," his father agreed. "Not many senators have a passion for cinnamon, and I'm the only one on intimate enough terms to impose on Emilio's hospitality by devouring his entire supply."

"Based on the progression, a single dose would likely have done no lasting harm, thank Allah," Gian Jacopo explained. Far from providing comfort, the unspoken implication gave Niccolo a chill; more than one dose was fatal. "Your father is strong, and it is possible he will recover. The situation is grave but not hopeless." Gian Jacopo's tone wavered, but Niccolo's siblings didn't seem to notice the catch, for the tension drained from their shoulders. Only Giovanni eyed the physician with narrowed eyes. "However, your father will require much rest."

The door burst open as Flavio rushed into the room and knelt at Angelo's bedside. "I'm here, Father."

"Oh, do stop fussing, everyone. Poison or no, I won't be clucked over." Angelo shouted with surprising force. But the effort drained him, and he leaned back against his pillow. "Just seeing you all here, I feel better already."

Petrarch coughed. "We must allow Signor Aretoli to rest."

"For at least a few hours," Gian Jacopo agreed.

"I'll be back to myself in no time, making mischief for you all." Angelo laughed, but the sound sputtered out unevenly.

Gian Jacopo's eyes flashed with concern.

Asparia clutched Camilla and led her back toward the kitchen. Petrarch whispered something as he led Marco out. Niccolo appreciated the poet's presence.

Lingering, Giovanni glanced furtively at Angelo. It was terrible enough to lose one father. Now, he would lose another.

Tugging at Flavio's sleeve, Niccolo gestured toward his friend.

Nodding his understanding, Flavio crossed to Giovanni and draped an arm around his shoulder. "Come. I have some gossip for you. Do you know Katerina Rossi? Well…" He led Giovanni through the door.

"Niccolo?" Angelo called once they were alone. "Come here, son."

Settling on the edge of his father's bed, he rearranged the blankets, tucking in the sides tightly. He felt like a little boy again, watching a parent die.

"Look at me."

He obeyed, facing those dark eyes encircled by shadows. The nose between them looked stark in contrast, and his father's mouth, usually curled into a smile, drew tight. Seeing a strange face staring back at him somehow made this easier.

"You don't believe Gian Jacopo's reassurances." He lifted his hand and grazed it against Niccolo's chin. "I can see it in your eyes."

Niccolo lowered his gaze. "It was the pitch of his voice." He turned to the doctor. "You care about my father too much."

"I should have caught it earlier," the doctor muttered.

Angelo waved his hand weakly. "You aren't infallible, my friend. In any case, you could do nothing."

Gian Jacopo nodded. "Your fate was sealed the moment you'd ingested enough poison."

"Then there's nothing to regret, but that I failed to heed God's warning against gluttony." He released a strained chuckle that ended in a wince. He turned to his son. "I spoke the truth when I said I'm proud of you all. But I'm most proud of you, Niccolo."

Gian Jacopo backed up and slipped out the door, closing it behind him.

"How can you say that?" Niccolo shook his head. "I'm not married. I haven't even given my holdings the attention they deserve."

"All meaningless," Angelo dismissed with a wave.

"What?"

"So you're not married. That is my fault. That you didn't rush into the next woman's arms shows your steadiness. And you made me so proud on Crete—"

"Flavio did as well. And he's fought more duels to defend our honor."

"Isn't that telling?" Angelo replied sharply. "Flavio is not a wise man, my son. You are. Safeguarding our family will fall to you when I'm gone. Whether they realize it or not, they'll look to you to lead them."

Niccolo frowned. "How can you say this?"

"Because I'm dying and don't have the luxury of letting time calm Flavio or ground Marco or sober Camilla. And that temper of Asparia's..."

"She always takes care of her family, and Giovanni has soothed her so much," Niccolo defended.

"Yes, they're a good match. I'm glad you found a friend like Giovanni. People like us need loyal companions." He smiled faintly. "Like Pietro has been to me. He helped me build House Aretoli into what we are now. Not the wealth, but the power."

"I know you trusted him with things you didn't trust us with," Niccolo said. "Special tasks."

"Pietro wasn't just a servant, Niccolo. He developed my network of informants. The *avogadori*, the people who watch the guilds, even a few agents in senatorial households... They all answer to him."

Niccolo gasped. He hadn't thought anyone but Angelo would manage those informants. All those years, Niccolo hadn't suspected the depth of Pietro's importance to their family. "Does Flavio know?"

"No." He coughed again. "Like me, you can't do it all yourself. You'll have to find the right people to trust. Giovanni is one of those people. He's a true and loyal friend, like Emilio is to me."

"That's why you risked so much to defend him."

Angelo lowered his gaze. "Yes."

He nodded slowly. "Giovanni will make his father proud."

"As will you, son," he replied. "Already, you rise to defend your family."

Niccolo considered his siblings. Asparia was a force of nature, but she didn't have a vote in the Senate or the authority behind her to muscle in on a competitor. Camilla's attention seemed limited to whoever complimented her, but age might settle her. Poor Marco only wanted to escape his obligations. And Flavio... Flavio confounded Niccolo. He could seem supremely confident one moment, then morose, then uncertain. His brother was capable of anything.

"You see the sense in my words. You won't turn away from the truth because it's too painful. Not anymore."

He was right. Losing Rosalia had shattered his dreams, but it had also hardened him. Nothing seemed too terrible to face, even this. "Rosalia and Flavio...you didn't do that to teach me a lesson, did you?"

"No, no." His eyes widened. "I lost the love of my life when your mother died. I wouldn't inflict that pain on anyone. But I did observe how you handled it. Your letters from Crete were so restrained. I feared you would withdraw into yourself and would never come back. I saw it happening to one son and couldn't bear to see it happen to another because of a single decision."

"What do you mean?" He wasn't sure he was ready for the answer, but they had no more time.

"Flavio argued with me. He insisted we could wait. But Umberto did his work well. Cornaro would have been ruined, and we would have soon followed." He swallowed and reached for the glass. "To this day, he and Rosalia do not have a...normal married life."

His heart leaped at the news, but he dared not show it. He couldn't allow his father to die thinking one son would betray another. "I didn't realize it was so bad."

"Yes you did," his father chided. "I think you realized it when you came to dinner."

"How can you possibly know that?" Niccolo didn't bother to deny the truth of the insight.

"Because of all my children, you react as I would."

A hollow sensation filled his chest. "What?"

His father's voice became gruffer. "Niccolo, when I look at you, I see the man I used to be before..." He drew in an unsteady breath.

"Before your mother was taken from me. You're a thinker, Niccolo. And a brooder."

He had tried so hard to follow his father's example. His heart swelled. "Why didn't you tell me this earlier?"

"Because I hoped it wasn't true."

Niccolo's eyes widened.

"I saw your pain when you saw Rosalia. Yet you restrained yourself. I don't know if I could have done the same if I'd felt what you feel for her."

Niccolo leaned back. How could he discuss this with the man who had set this all into motion? He felt exposed. Only one thought sought to cover the wound stripped bare. "Does Flavio know?"

Angelo smiled. "Flavio has his strengths, but insight is not one of them." He cleared his throat. "You didn't ask whether I thought Rosalia knew. Can I assume you've already discussed this with her?"

Niccolo looked away, unable to meet his father's gaze.

"I see."

If Angelo inquired further, he might learn how close he had been to betraying his brother. "What did you mean, you hoped it wasn't true? That I wasn't like you?"

"I hoped you might be spared the pain of that curse."

"What curse?"

"The curse of wanting to do the right thing, but always choosing the necessary thing, even knowing the cost." Angelo's voice began to rasp, and he paused to take a few breaths. "It's a lonely path. God's wounds, it's been so hard. Ever since Lucia…" He rubbed his eyes to banish the unshed tears. "She was so wise. She knew the toll it took on me."

Niccolo rested his hand on his father's shoulder but had no sympathy to give. He could not deny the truth of his father's words. In similar circumstances, would he deny his own son the love of his life? For the sake of his family, he would. By God, he would.

"I'm sorry, Nico. I'm so sorry."

"Don't be sorry, Father." He wanted desperately to reassure him, to save his father from facing death with regrets. "If you truly did what was necessary, then you have no need for grief. What you really wish is that the world was better than it is." He smiled faintly. "Doesn't everyone?"

Angelo laughed lightly. "I suppose you're right."

The action brought about another round of coughing, this one far worse than before. Niccolo helped his father to a handkerchief beside his bed. Angelo raised it to his mouth. When he removed it, it was stained red.

His father didn't seem to notice; he looked only at his son. "Have I done well for myself?"

This plea of a dying man seeking comfort broke Niccolo's heart.

"You have five loving children, had the love of a good woman, and saw your family rise higher than ever before. I'd say you did well." He embraced his father.

As his son leaned close, Angelo whispered, "Thank you, Nico. Thank you."

NICCOLO

Niccolo left his father's room after Angelo fell into an uneasy sleep. All the while, his anger remained. His father may never rise again. He would find whoever was responsible and make them pay.

Flavio descended upon him the moment he emerged, but Niccolo already knew what he would ask. "He wanted to know if I blamed him."

"For?" Flavio prompted.

But Niccolo couldn't speak the words, not to the man who had married his Rosalia.

"What did you say?" Flavio couldn't quite mask the apprehension in his voice.

"I told him I'd learned to live with it long ago."

Flavio smiled faintly, but he quickly directed his attention elsewhere.

Cornaro had sent word that he would interrogate everyone who worked during the Easter celebration—both the household staff and the temporary workers—but it would take hours before they received any news.

Asparia rallied to oversee her sister, but her grief returned within a few minutes. Giovanni took her into a back room to rest. Asparia re-emerged an hour after sundown, having restored a tenuous control. Her husband, however, hovered nearby with a look of concern.

Petrarch took Marco for a short walk, hoping fresh air would cleanse his spirit. Niccolo didn't have the heart to tell him that, in a city surrounded by canals carrying away human waste, the air was fresher within houses warmed by fireplaces and scented with incense.

Even Camilla had Flavio and Rosalia to calm her. Seeing everyone support each other only made Niccolo feel more alone. The Aretoli he held most dear lay in the other room, dying.

Left by himself, Niccolo turned his mind to the question of his father's assassin.

The poison itself had been almost unnoticeable; only Gian Jacopo's exotic experience had revealed it. The assassin had probably counted on the symptoms being mistaken for a natural affliction. Sometime before or during the party, someone would have mixed it with either the apples or the cinnamon. Poisoning the apples would require saturating them, which would likely make them absorb too much poison. The dosage had to be small enough to harm only someone who ate several, or else many guests could have died. That meant it had to have been in the cinnamon.

Had some Arabic trader wanted to make a few faceless Christians suffer? No. What trader would sabotage his own trade routes?

Niccolo turned to Flavio, who was chatting quietly with Marco and Petrarch. He and Flavio would need to discover the murderer. Marco wasn't made for such work, and if his sisters became involved, they would lose the protection of their gender.

What if they couldn't find enough proof to expose the assassin? The Aretoli hadn't undertaken a true *vendetta* for a hundred years, and there were clear rules. While the Senate would look the other way for a grieved family, if Niccolo and Flavio started attacking people in the streets, the Senate would have to intervene. They needed subtlety, something Flavio lacked.

Niccolo would have to manage his brother carefully, or this could see the end of the family.

Later that evening, Emilio Cornaro arrived wearing a mask of grief and the fatigue from hours of investigation. Angelo had saved his family, and now he would die from something that had happened at the Cornaro home.

Niccolo could think of only one reason for his visit. "You've discovered something."

Cornaro nodded. "One of my servants remembered a stranger with a snake-like scar on his cheek. When I described it to my men, one remembered seeing him around the docks."

"What's his name?" Flavio asked.

"Alberto Brattori."

"Why do you suspect him?" Niccolo said.

"He was near the kitchens. My man didn't see him go inside. He thought it strange that Brattori stood there so long, seeming to do nothing."

Alberto Brattori. "Thank you, Signor Cornaro. Most sincerely."

Flavio eyed his brother. "What are you thinking?"

"We need to speak to this Brattori."

"Yes, speak." Flavio gave a cruel grin.

"Now see here," Cornaro bristled. "I didn't tell you this just to have you kill this man."

"What did you expect us to do?" Flavio cried.

Niccolo placed a hand on Flavio's shoulder. "We can't kill him."

Flavio brushed him aside. "Why the devil not?"

"Because he probably didn't act alone, and I want the person responsible. We need him to talk."

"Agreed." Cornaro spoke as if his opinion mattered when this was a family matter.

Niccolo restrained himself from correcting the old man; they may need his help later. He had a deep friendship with Angelo, but whether that friendship continued with his sons depended on how they treated him in the coming days.

"Fine." Flavio subsided. "We won't kill him yet."

Only their father had been able to control Flavio. Niccolo would need to learn that skill to keep the family intact, but this was a good start.

But the mood in the room soured. Cornaro shuffled off to check on his daughter, and Flavio, frustration now roused, stalked to the back of the house to fume.

Niccolo fell silent, debating his next steps. When he emerged from his thoughts, Camilla was standing beside him. She had wiped away her tears, but the puffiness around her eyes remained.

He, Asparia, and Flavio had their own households now, and Marco would inherit a third of their father's money. But what about Camilla? They all dreaded the day a courier would arrive to announce his younger sister's sudden marriage. Would Camilla use the same sense in choosing her husband as Asparia had? Niccolo doubted it.

With genuine pity, Niccolo placed a hand on her shoulder.

To his relief, she leaned her head against him without breaking into fresh tears. "Why did this happen, Niccolo?" Her tone lacked its normal bouncing quality.

He could go over all the possible plots, accidents, and reasons, or that their father could have died years ago in war, but none of that would ease her pain. No words came to mind that might comfort her. He felt woefully inadequate for the simple task of comforting his sister. How did his father expect him to guide his family?

Evidently, Camilla hadn't expected an answer. She kept her head against him and closed her eyes. He removed his hand from her shoulder and draped his arm around her instead.

Together, they waited for the inevitable.

NICCOLO

Around mid-day, Angelo began to cough up more than a little blood at a time. Niccolo wasn't alone in praying for a quick end to his father's suffering now that it was upon them.

Niccolo joined his siblings in filing into Angelo's room. The smell of death filled his nostrils. Camilla flinched at the same moment Niccolo noticed the odor. He squeezed her shoulder and tugged her forward.

Once they had filed inside, an elderly priest made a discrete exit. Gian Jacopo had thought to arrange for Last Rights. Though natural enough for a Christian to consider, it meant even more that the Moor had remembered. Any man would want consolation when facing death.

The poison had taken a terrible toll on his father's body. He had retreated into the bed itself, a far cry from the solid man of only thirty-six hours earlier. Sweat saturated his clothes, and his cheeks looked ashen. Niccolo repeated his prayer for a merciful end.

Angelo's eyes fluttered open. He tried to lift a hand. They encircled the bed cautiously, as if fearing to disturb him.

"Don't be sad for me." A grimace of discomfort spread across his face. Even the simple gesture of licking his lips appeared sluggish and desperate. "I go to see your mother."

"Father!" Tears fell down Camilla's cheeks in streaks.

He coughed again, a spasm of movement that shook his bones and filled his eyes with panic. Marco steadied him while Gian Jacopo lifted a cloth to collect the phlegm. Though the doctor tried to conceal as splash of blood on the cloth, Niccolo noticed it.

Angelo rasped, "Things to say." He struggled to speak on each exhale, but he formed the words clearly. "None of you is alone, even when I am gone."

Camilla lowered her head against Niccolo's shoulder.

A spasm caused the vein at his neck to bulge. "Blood is the

strongest bond of all." A drop of blood ran from his nose. "Trust in each other, always."

He began to shudder. Like a man desperate to cling to these last moments, Angelo clenched his teeth, willing the convulsions to subside. He met Niccolo's gaze. "I'm so sorry." He exhaled the words in a mere whisper with his last breath.

Niccolo buried his anguish and forced himself to smile, desperate to convince his father of his forgiveness in his last living moment.

Angelo's chest never rose again. A thin trail of blood escaped from his nose as his head slumped to the side. Angelo Aretoli, the man who had protected and nurtured them for their entire lives, was dead.

Behind them, Petrarch blessed himself. *"Requiescat in pace, in nomine Patris et Filii et Spiritus Sancti. Amen."*

CHAPTER SIX

NICCOLO

NICCOLO BARRELED THROUGH the door with grim determination. They had much to do before word of Angelo's passing spread. The priest had stopped to find Pietro for payment and hadn't yet left the house. Niccolo corralled the man with the pledge of a generous donation if he would remain within.

A bewildered Marco stepped into the hall as Niccolo returned with the priest. "Where are you going?"

Niccolo spoke to Pietro behind his brother. "It's time."

With a nod, the steward retreated down the hall.

Placing a hand on Marco's shoulder, he continued, "I need you to do something for me."

"What? Where are you going? Father—"

"This is for Father, Marco."

"How can you just leave him? What's so important?"

"I need you to keep the priest here until Flavio or I returns." Over his head, Niccolo shouted, "Flavio?"

Marco grasped Niccolo's doublet. "Return? Where are you going?"

His older brother emerged and braced himself against the door frame. Upon meeting Niccolo's gaze, he nodded and strode down the hallway.

Niccolo shouted after the swiftly departing form of his brother. "Daggers only. And get one for Pietro."

"He's coming?" Flavio asked.

Niccolo nodded. "He's earned the right."

"Answer me!" Marco pushed Niccolo against the wall. "What's happening? How can you leave Father?" His voice rose near the end, drawing Camilla out, too.

Giovanni and Asparia remained inside. His friend, at least, would understand what needed to happen.

"Flavio and I are going to confront the man who administered the poison."

The response silenced him, and he needed a few moments to recover. "Right now?" Marco made the mistake of glancing inside his father's room unprepared, and the color drained from his face.

"Yes, now." He turned Marco away from Angelo's body. "We have to get to him before it's too late."

Flavio returned with a few daggers in sheaths, handing one of Father's militia daggers to Niccolo. But it wasn't Angelo's best; that gold-encrusted one sat at his brother's hip.

He wove his belt through the slots on the sheath. "The assassin wouldn't discard the rest of the poison until he was certain the job was done. Between the priests and Cornaro's servants, all of Venice probably knows Father was ill, but they don't know…" He swallowed. "We have to reach him before he discards the evidence."

"How do you know how he'd behave?" Marco asked.

"It's what I'd do," Flavio answered.

Niccolo nodded in agreement.

"How can you even think that?" Marco demanded.

"Because we must, to discover who ordered his murder."

"And what then? What happens when you find him?" The steadiness of his tone tapered as he met Niccolo's gaze.

"We'll bring them to justice."

"You mean kill them?" Camilla gasped.

"If that's what it takes." Flavio's voice carried a dangerous edge.

Marco had a good heart; he would not easily accept the need to track down and kill anyone, even his father's murderer. But Niccolo didn't have time to reconcile his brother to the need right now.

Niccolo turned to Flavio. "Ready?"

He nodded.

Niccolo met Marco's gaze. "Will you keep the priest here until we return?"

Marco's head bobbed up and down the faintest amount. "You can't just ransack someone's home. You need proof."

"Pietro is summoning one of the guards Father bribes." He swallowed. "Used to bribe. He'll be waiting for us." He rested a hand on Marco's shoulder. "Stay with him, please?"

Niccolo swept through the door an instant later, his elder brother a step behind him.

NICCOLO

They met Pietro and an officer of the republic a block away from Brattori's building. The city guard was as conspicuous as Niccolo had feared; his bright steel breastplate reflected every scrap of light in the area. With an inward groan, Niccolo approached. He'd rather do this by himself, but he needed someone to vouch for any evidence he found.

"Captain." The guard bowed deeply to Flavio, then offered Niccolo a perfunctory bow. "Signor. What is the purpose of this meeting? Your man wasn't particularly informative." He scowled at Pietro, who weathered it dispassionately.

"We require you to witness a search of the home of a man who we believe assassinated our father," Niccolo answered.

"Jesus Christ!" The officer blessed himself. "When did this happen? I hadn't heard anything."

"Less than an hour ago, of poison. We thought it best to keep it quiet until we could conduct this search," Flavio replied.

Irritation tugged at Niccolo that Flavio would take credit for this strategy despite objecting to delaying vengeance even this long.

"I'll testify truly. Angelo Aretoli was a good man." He didn't mention the daggers at their hips. That discretion put Niccolo's mind at ease.

Flavio led them through the walkways along the canal, a knife-like slit of water barely sufficing as a *ria*. The streets were deserted except for a couple seeking the solace of dark corners. It was that kind of neighborhood, Niccolo realized belatedly. He cursed under his breath. His father taught him to be more aware of his surroundings than this.

"What was that?" Flavio's tone carried the same suspicion as when he had emerged from his father's room.

"Nothing." Niccolo would have to watch how much he shared with his brother now that…now that Father was dead.

They arrived at a two-story structure with peeling paint and several split timbers. An odor of foul water emanated from somewhere nearby.

"Here we are." Flavio frowned at the façade.

"We will have to announce our presence," the guard said.

"We'd prefer not to," Pietro interrupted.

"On what grounds?"

"The risk of obstruction," the steward explained. "If we announce ourselves, the assassin will destroy any evidence linking him to the murder before we enter."

"Very well. We'll enter by force." He took a few quick steps and forced his shoulder into the door. Unlocked, it gave way on the first try.

Flavio and Pietro charged up the stairs to the second floor, followed by the guard. Coolly, Niccolo turned and closed the door. It wouldn't do for anyone to hear screaming or the sound of a struggle; an open door revealed much.

As an afterthought, he slid the lock into place. Pulling his dagger out of the sheath, he placed it against the door frame and pulled hard, tearing the latch from the wall.

It would appear as if they had broken the lock. No one could have possibly tampered with the room—or any evidence within—before they had arrived.

With a vault, Niccolo followed the others. The house, if it could be called such, was small. As he ascended the steps, his thighs burned; they were steeper than he was used to. The top floor had a small landing but only one room. Skin tingling, he studied the contours of each shadow in the darkness.

"No one," Pietro hissed, disappointed.

"And nothing, it seems," added Flavio.

This was too simple. Cornaro had found their conspirator so easily, and they hadn't even faced a struggle when entering. Perhaps they wouldn't find anything after all.

"Don't be so certain," the guard cautioned. "No one would leave poison sitting in the open. Everyone stay where you are. I'll conduct a search." He stared pointedly at Flavio. "You must not disturb anything."

"I won't," he growled.

The guard moved from area to area. A couple of times, he tapped the floor and the walls, checking for hidden compartments. His hands prodded every imperfection on the walls, every hole in the floor.

After perhaps fifteen minutes, he announced, "I found something."

"What?" Niccolo rushed beside him.

The guard had his back to him, but Flavio wore a look of disgust mingled with shock. Circling to the right, Niccolo cleared the man's shoulder and saw a tiny bottle made of thick Venetian glass. It looked inconspicuous.

"Is that—?" Flavio began.

"Don't know." Niccolo pulled a packet out of his pouch and unfolded it, revealing a pinch of pure, untainted cinnamon. Taking a deep breath, Niccolo noted the scent of the pure spice. "The bottle?"

The guard handed it over, and Niccolo gently opened the stopper. Half-full, they had more than enough for an experiment. Tipping it over, he splashed a few drops into the cinnamon and inhaled. He could smell a hint of the acrid odor now, just as at Easter. "This is it."

A hush descended upon the four men for several heartbeats. Niccolo stared at the liquid, sloshing ever so slightly because of his shaking hand. The contents of this bottle had murdered his father.

The guard broke the silence. "I'll faithfully report everything I've seen here."

"We'll keep the evidence." Flavio raised a hand. "Our enemies surely have contacts among the guards."

The man nodded. "Nothing in the procedures prevents that." He took the bottle and inhaled. Nodding, he handed it back. "I've got the scent of it and can attest if it's the same liquid."

"Gather a group to look for the owner of this"—Flavio scowled as he looked around—"lodging. We must question this assassin."

Even now, the word seemed dirty, like an unworthy end to a senator. The thought of it made Niccolo cringe: Angelo Aretoli had been assassinated. A finished deed: the implications struck home yet again.

"We'll find him." With a nod, the guard departed down the stairs.

Niccolo eyed his brother with growing respect. "Nicely done."

"Yes, well…"

A noise at the door interrupted them both.

"What's that?" Niccolo whispered.

"The guard?" Flavio's tone matched his brother's.

"He'd already gone."

The sound of a key scratched in the lock.

"It's the assassin." Softly, Niccolo mouthed, "He doesn't know we're here."

A door shut, and a pair of feet shuffled erratically up the stairs. From the cadence, Niccolo suspected he was drunk, or at least well on his way. The casual pace suggested he hadn't noticed the damage to the lock.

Flavio primed his legs, shifting for a better position for quick action.

The man's head and shoulders came into view. Flavio leaped around the railing, jumping across the open chasm to the lower floor. He grasped the man as he landed, dragging the figure into the center of the room. Pietro drew and held his dagger against the newcomer's neck.

Wide eyes filled with terrified clarity searched each of them in turn.

"Are you Alberto Brattori?" Flavio demanded.

"What?"

"Tell me!"

"Y-yes, yes," he stammered.

Niccolo stepped forward. "I am Niccolo Aretoli, and this is my brother, Flavio Aretoli. You murdered our father."

The assassin's gaze darted to the place where he'd hidden the poison.

This is too easy. But, then again, many things are easy when you hold a knife to someone's throat. "It's not there anymore." Niccolo revealed the bottle in his hand.

Brattori lunged for it, but Pietro slashed his dagger along the man's thigh. A choked cry of anguish spilled out before he fell to the floor, cradling the wound.

"Try that again, and I'll tear your fingers off one by one." The hiss of Pietro's scratchy voice sent chills down Niccolo's spine. He had never seen this side of the steward.

Brattori stilled. "What do you want?"

The steward glanced at Niccolo, who nodded for him to continue; Pietro likely had more experience in this kind of thing.

Flavio interrupted first. "What do we want? How about my dagger thrust into your chest?"

"Flavio, easy." Niccolo patted his brother's shoulder in a rebuke, but a mild one. Terror had its uses. "Did you know who your target was when you planted this poison?"

"Poison?" Brattori licked his lips and gave an awkward shrug.

"It's just a flavoring. I wanted to see if people enjoyed it before I acquired more."

"That's a pity," Niccolo began easily. "If you could offer us some reason to keep you alive, our conversation would be much longer. Pietro?"

Baring his teeth, Pietro adjusted his grip and pressed the knife harder against Brattori's throat.

"Wait, wait!" Brattori leaned his head back, away from the knife. "Fine. I knew it was poison."

"Did you know *who* you were supposed to poison?" Niccolo pressed.

"They just told me to mix it with that spice."

"*They?*"

His eyes widened.

"You're working for someone."

"I... No one told me—"

"Don't be a fool, Brattori. If you were only following someone's orders, I doubt the Senate will order your death."

He gasped. "You'll let me live?"

"If you start talking. Otherwise, I'll tear everything I need to know from you before I dispose of what's left of your body." The threat didn't have the intended effect, so Niccolo improvised. "Then, I'll track down your family and ask them the same questions. Perhaps a sister noticed you hanging around someone suspicious?"

Panic flowed into Brattori's eyes.

"Niccolo!" Flavio cried.

"I've hit the mark, haven't I, Alberto?" Niccolo put iron into his voice as a feral smile curled across his lips. "Which will it be?"

"You can't do that. She's innocent!"

Niccolo closed the distance and wrapped his hand around the man's neck. "You took my father's life." Tortured anguish spilled out with the words. "You don't get to lecture me on innocence."

The assassin's face had drained of its color. "If I tell you what you want to know, they'll kill me."

Niccolo leaned closer, pinning him with a stare. "I'll kill you right here if you don't start talking."

Brattori's eyes widened.

Satisfied, Niccolo repeated, "What were your instructions?"

The man darted a glance at Pietro. The blood dripped from Brattori's thigh to pool on the floor beneath him, but he made no attempt to stop the bleeding.

"I was told to mix the poison with the cinnamon. I was worried it would hurt too many people. They told me the food was prepared especially for only one person, but the dosage wouldn't harm someone who had just a taste."

"Who told you to do this?"

His gaze again darted to Pietro's blade. "Umberto Feratollo and Alvero Madina."

Niccolo released a tense breath. They had exploited Father's tastes. How long had they been waiting to use that knowledge against him?

At least, with both of them involved, Niccolo could put an end to his family's two worst enemies at once.

But he had to be certain. "Why did they want to kill my father?"

"They only told me what I was supposed to do."

"How well do you know them?"

"I do odd jobs for Signor Madina." His voice steadied as he spoke. "Moving crates, mostly."

Niccolo had hoped for a stronger link, but it should be enough. A dockworker couldn't find or pay for such an exotic poison by himself.

"I was loading some casks and crates." He spoke with more confidence now. Niccolo suspected he realized his chances of survival grew with every word. Alvero had probably chosen him because he had some sense. "For a ship he had going to Constantinople later this week. Big shipment, lots of good work. He called me over and offered me a hundred ducats, just to mix a liquid in with a spice."

"Don't be a fool," Pietro interrupted. "You knew what he was paying you for. You knew someone would die because of you."

The man lowered his gaze.

"So, Madina recruited you." If Niccolo had his way, both vipers would lose their heads. "How do you know Umberto was involved?"

"He handed me the poison."

"When did they approach you?" Flavio asked.

Niccolo nodded his appreciation at the good question.

"The night before the party."

Niccolo stroked his chin. That was why they could track this man down so easily; everything had been planned hastily. With more time, they'd have planted a more skilled assassin among Cornaro's staff weeks ago. Such a man would have never seemed out of place, and Niccolo and his brother wouldn't be here now.

But they were.

Niccolo took a step back. "You've taken my father away from me. For that, I should kill you where you sit." Niccolo continued speaking over Brattori's protests. "But I'll let you make up for your sin and save yourself from eternal damnation. Do you hear me?"

Brattori drew in a breath. "Damnation?"

"You coldly and senselessly killed one of your betters. Angelo Aretoli did more good in life than you ever will."

The assassin remained silent for a long while. When he finally spoke, he sighed with resignation. "What do you want of me?"

Religion was a beautiful weapon.

"You will testify when we bring charges against Alberto Madina and Umberto Feratollo." He nodded. "You'll go with my man here. He'll take care of you until you explain to the Senate exactly what happened."

"And afterward?"

"You'll likely spend your life in prison." Remembering the effect religion could have, Niccolo added, "Perhaps you may work off your sin in God's service at a monastery."

"What if Senator Madina—"

"He won't be a senator for very long."

Brattori swallowed. "What if Madina and Feratollo escape the city?"

"I hope they're that stupid," Flavio cried. "I'd enjoy hunting them down."

"I mean, what if they try to find me?"

"They won't be around to find anyone," Flavio answered.

"One more thing," Niccolo added. "They've already killed a senator. I doubt they'd hesitate to kill a dockworker. If you were to escape, both of us would be searching the city for you with the same goal. Do we understand each other?"

Brattori lowered his head into his hands. From beneath them came heavy sobbing. Niccolo nodded, and Pietro reached for a cloth on a nearby table and tied off the man's bleeding thigh. Task completed, he hauled Brattori down the stairs.

Flavio wheeled on him once they were alone. "What's wrong with you? Would you have really tortured his sister?"

"If I had to." At Flavio's shocked expression, Niccolo lost his temper. "This isn't a game. They murdered our father. Who says they'll stop there? What if they mean to wipe us out? I'd do anything to protect Asparia or Camilla from being the next to suffer."

"I suppose you're right." Flavio's frown creased his forehead. "I've just never seen this side of you. I remember my little brother, fighting over a pear from the kitchen."

Niccolo smiled and received an encouraging smile in return.

Flavio sighed. "It's hard to realize the people around you have changed."

Niccolo had seen the truth of it every day since he'd returned. "This isn't a new side to me, though. When I fought over pears, did I ever let go?"

"No," he replied slowly, "No, you didn't."

"And I'm not letting go now."

They had one more thing to do, a tradition they could not afford to overlook. As much as he thought of Pietro as a member of House

Aretoli, he wasn't a blood relative. He could not participate in this ceremony.

He drew his dagger and traced a thin line along the meat of his palm, drawing a few drops. "We now know who killed our father. We have a responsibility to see justice done by any necessary means." He handed the blade to Flavio.

With a quick movement, Flavio pricked his finger, drawing a drop of blood. "We will not rest until our father is vindicated."

Only one thing could avenge their father's death and bring peace to his memory. A promise honored no matter the cost.

"*Vendetta.*"

NICCOLO

Pietro secured Brattori before visiting the doge's palace to insist on an audience. Unfortunately, Celsi was taking the sacraments and couldn't be disturbed.

"He's getting his ducal dick sanctified, they mean," Flavio grumbled. He shook his head to Pietro. "Go back and get the soonest audience you can. Say it's an issue of extreme importance."

A couple of tense hours after nightfall, they finally received their ducal audience. Whether he intended to honor his friend or to exact retribution against those who had tried to ruin him, Cornaro accompanied the brothers. Niccolo welcomed his support, given what they would reveal.

Celsi hadn't yet changed after his excursion. Water saturated his boots, and his doublet, cast over a chair back, bore heavy wrinkles. Off to the side, a beautiful gray silk cloak of the highest quality lay draped over a couch. Tendrils of pure gold that seemed to radiate light ran throughout its length. Niccolo wondered how he could discreetly visit a brothel in a cloak as noticeable as that.

They had agreed to let Niccolo do the talking. Charging senators with murder bore risks, and Niccolo's performance in the Senate had proven his oratory.

Niccolo began as the doge took a sip of his wine. "Doge Celsi, this morning, after a brief struggle, our father passed into the loving embrace of our Savior." Somehow, the formal report hurt more than the blunt announcement to the assassin.

The doge coughed, dripping a little wine down his shirt. The deep purple liquid quickly soaked through, leaving dark splotches. "What? He's dead?" He dabbed at the stains. "I didn't know he was ill."

"He wasn't."

"Then how—?"

"The cinnamon on the apple slices at Signor Cornaro's feast was poisoned."

The doge swallowed as if his wine disagreed with him. "If that's true, many more may be ill."

"We doubt that. The assassins chose their method well. Signor Cornaro prepares a cinnamon delicacy every time he sees my father. The murderers knew he would consume the most, but they used a small enough dosage that a single taste wouldn't kill."

"What if they'd been wrong?" the doge asked, visibly shaken.

"Anyone who had ingested enough of the poison would be beyond help."

"Thank you for warning me of this, even if you waited so long to do it." He scowled. "I'll make sure no one else is ill. You've done a service to your fellow Venetians."

Niccolo clenched his hand behind him. "That isn't why we came. If you haven't heard of anyone else falling ill, there won't be any further deaths."

"Then, why? Oh, of course." He nodded slowly. "Your father was a war hero and noble senator. Of course, he'll receive a full state funeral."

How could this man think they wanted a spectacle when their father had been murdered? "We want those responsible to be punished."

"Of course, of course. I'll have the guards investigate."

"That won't be necessary," Niccolo explained patiently. He was finding it difficult to show the respect due to a doge. "We know who's responsible." This was the careful part. They couldn't be swayed out of pursuing the matter, even if it meant the public shaming of senators. Yet, they couldn't risk offending the doge by circumventing him. "We're here tonight as a courtesy to inform you we'll be bringing formal charges against the murderers."

A curious mix of expressions passed over the doge's face, many of which Niccolo couldn't identify. "How did you discover their identities?"

Niccolo furrowed his forehead. He would have expected the first question to be who the assassin was, not how he'd discovered them. "Signor Cornaro's servants identified a man named Alberto Brattori hanging around the kitchens that day. We found his home and discovered this." Niccolo withdrew the bottle from a pouch hanging at his waist and held it at a distance.

"You entered this man's house?" He shook his head. "Flavio, you may be a captain of the guards, but how do you expect me to hold this man responsible on the evidence of that bottle?"

Flavio stiffened. "Isn't my word good enough?"

"One of the city guards accompanied us," Niccolo interrupted. "He met us a block away and observed our search. In fact, it was he who discovered the bottle. We even mixed some of the contents with a sample of cinnamon, and the smell was the same as the night of the festival."

Panic flashed in the doge's expression before disappearing again. Niccolo almost missed it. "Excellent. I'm glad you took that precaution. It'll make my task easier."

"Will you help us bring those responsible to justice?" Niccolo asked.

"Of course, my son." He produced an easy smile.

Niccolo released a silent breath. He had the doge's promise. "He did not work alone. He followed the orders of Alvero Madina and Umberto Feratollo."

The color drained from the older man's face.

Such charges could easily erupt into open hostility between patrician houses. Not fifteen years earlier, a particularly violent feud had rocked the city, killing several members of each of the feuding houses.

"That's a very serious charge."

The hair on the back of Niccolo's neck stood up. Such a statement did not presage support.

"No more or less serious than a moment ago," Cornaro reminded.

"You know that's not true, Emilio. Madina and Feratollo are senators. We'll have pandemonium if we discuss this openly in the Senate."

"If?" A dangerous inflection crept into Flavio's voice.

"Well, I'll need to talk to them first."

"Your Excellency, they won't simply admit their guilt," Niccolo said.

"But the way they deny it will tell me much." The pitch of his voice had increased.

"With respect, Signor Celsi, that will only give them time to concoct a lie. There's no reason to warn them before announcing charges. Nothing in our law requires it."

"It's a courtesy we extend to senators," Celsi explained.

"To murderers, you mean?" Flavio said under his breath.

Celsi pierced him with a glare. "That hasn't been proven yet. Until it is, you will treat them with respect due to their positions."

Niccolo met the doge's gaze. "Do you doubt our word?"

"You are all honorable men." The calm reaction only heightened Niccolo's apprehension. "You must understand how this will look, though. Two Aretoli and a Cornaro charging a Feratollo and a Madina. Everyone knows the, ah…animosity…over your mother. Signor Cornaro here nearly suffered a financial catastrophe, rumored to be instigated by Feratollo. Do you think the Senate will believe these charges?"

Niccolo couldn't believe his ears. "But our witness—"

"Had better have a reputation as clean as a senator's."

"That depends," Cornaro replied with hostility, "on whether we can rub enough pig shit on him for the odor to match a Feratollo."

"Emilio!" Celsi shouted, as shocked as Niccolo. "That's exactly the attitude I'm referring to." As an afterthought, he asked, "Who is this witness?"

"A dockworker named Alberto Brattori administered the poison."

"And in exchange for testifying, you promised him safety, yes?" the doge asked.

"He has nothing to gain by lying. He expects to spend the rest of his life in prison."

"Well, at least there's that." Celsi rubbed his chin. "No one will doubt him if speaking costs him his freedom." He didn't sound very glad of that fact, though.

Niccolo had hoped for the doge's support, but the man clearly feared to disrupt the balance of power in the Senate by accusing the murderers publicly. The reason, though, eluded him.

One thing was certain: this conversation no longer had a purpose. "We thank you for your time and your advice, Signor Celsi. We did not want to jeopardize our family's recent relationship with you by pursuing the murderers without the courtesy of informing you."

He rose. Beside him, Cornaro and Flavio exchanged a confused glance. The doge may have little power compared with European princes, but one simply did not abruptly end an audience with him.

Far from taking offense, Celsi smiled and politely extended his hand for Niccolo to kiss.

Once safely outside, Cornaro shook his head. "You should show him more respect, Niccolo. Interrupting? Walking out? Your father should have taught you better."

"What about his insults?" Flavio faced his father-in-law. "He has no intention of supporting our cause. He, who was so quick to ask Father for help. But, then again, I suppose Father can't be of any more use to him."

"I will not listen to this." Cornaro shook his head and began to descend the marble stairs leading to the ground floor.

"Signor Cornaro." Niccolo halted him with a hand on his shoulder.

"Celsi didn't offer sympathy for our father's passing and undermined every point we raised. Do you doubt that Feratollo and Madina killed your friend?"

"Of course they killed him," Cornaro said. "They couldn't destroy my business, and your father's interests were too diverse, so they resorted to the only remaining option."

"The doge clearly doesn't agree. I doubt even a signed confession would convince him. And we both know senators have been strung up for less."

"Regardless, he's the doge. What does it benefit you to anger him?"

You. He had already begun to distance himself from their cause. If the doge's cold reception could frighten their closest ally, they would need to use extra caution when presenting their evidence to the Senate.

Cornaro shook his head and walked away, the lines on his forehead drawn tight.

Niccolo sighed. "It's clear the doge doesn't want a formal trial."

"To hell with what the doge wants," Flavio muttered.

"My thoughts exactly."

NICCOLO

Niccolo had tossed and turned for much of the night, trying to banish the memory of his meeting with the doge. The next morning, he felt drained, both from exhaustion and the certainty that the day's activities would bring no relief.

Strangely, he wished his father's funeral would last as long as possible. Once it was over, the only person who had truly understood him would be gone. An inheritance would provide no comfort for Angelo's passing.

A few drops of water had splashed against his cotton robe. Tears? It seemed a shame to spare only a few for his father when he had cried a sea for his mother. It felt like a betrayal.

A rustle behind him caused him to stir. Niccolo's new manservant, still a few years away from adulthood, bowed self-consciously.

"You don't need to bow each time you see me, Joseph. You'll forever be bumping into walls."

The young man looked up. "Yes, sir."

"Is everything ready?"

The young man nodded. He had prepared a thin black silk doublet, solid, without slashes, and a pair of breeches cut large. Beside them lay a simple black silk shirt with a tie at the neck and a leather belt with a dagger and sheath threaded into it.

"Did Pietro help you?"

"Yes, Signor Aretoli," he admitted. "He also provided this." He crossed to a trunk in the corner and returned holding Angelo's coat.

The beautifully made silver-on-blue brocade coat had hung to his father's knees. Rather than just a thin layer along the edges, white rabbit fur lined the entire interior. It had cost his mother a fortune. After her death, Angelo had desperately clung to it, his final memento of her.

Despite last night's succession of realizations that his father was truly dead, this coat, sitting in his home, broke his control. Niccolo sunk to the bed and let the tears flow freely, burying his head in his hands.

"Master, was I wrong in bringing this?"

Wiping his eyes, Niccolo recovered enough to answer between sniffles, "No, you did well."

Instinctively, Niccolo reached for his clothes, proceeding by habit more than by conscious will. More than once, Joseph adjusted a fold to make them lay properly. But his gaze never left the coat, and his mind lingered on the man who had arranged for him to have it.

Flavio would probably claim the Aretoli house, but he'd bring the staff he had depended on for the past two years. Angelo's staff would have nowhere to go.

And that would include Pietro, the man who had built Angelo's network of informants. Flavio couldn't possibly know the old steward's value. It didn't make sense to let it go to waste, particularly when the Aretoli were under assault.

He would convince Pietro to join him here. He couldn't abandon such a treasure.

Resolutely, he retrieved the coat from the bedpost and headed downstairs.

NICCOLO

A hundred years earlier, an Aretoli ancestor had established a small monastery to tend a family graveyard on the mainland. Only a short boat ride away, it nonetheless avoided the usual marching routes for armies traversing the region.

Pietro's informants had announced Angelo's death and funeral plans, so more than fifty senators and their families met Angelo's procession at the monastery. Niccolo, Flavio, and Marco, each riding a rented chestnut stallion, crested the hill and came into view of a sizeable crowd in fine wool, cotton, and silk.

The size of the gathering warmed Niccolo's heart. It was a fitting tribute to a loyal son of Venice and a good man.

A few feet behind them traveled the cart carrying Angelo's coffin, accompanied by Giovanni and the Cornaros. In the rear, Pietro drove the carriage containing Rosalia, Asparia, and Camilla. It was a good collection of loved ones for a man to leave behind.

It would also send the right message to their enemies.

As they approached, the mourners separated to allow the procession through. The crowd included several familiar faces, including Leonardo Dandolo leading a contingent of his kinsmen. Niccolo nodded in passing and received a sorrowful smile in response. No hard feelings for the Senate meeting, then.

More than a few senators seemed to notice his father's coat. When he could, Niccolo met their gazes until they looked away, determined to show them that Angelo's death hadn't left the Aretoli helpless.

A priest stood behind Angelo's plot with dozens of monks clustering around either side. His father, hardly a steadfast believer, would have appreciated the spectacle.

They dismounted and handed the reins to a collection of young pages who led the horses off to the stables. The servants withdrew the coffin and set it next to the grave as Rosalia helped Asparia, who was now feeling the effects of her pregnancy, disembark.

On the other side of the carriage, Camilla took the hand of a young man Niccolo didn't recognize. As soon as her delicate foot touched the ground, she swooned into his arms. Several women rushed to her side, waving fresh air toward her with their scarves. The young man ran a hand across her face, at which point she stirred and smiled up at him. Then, as if remembering where she was, she burst into tears, burying her head in his shoulder.

Niccolo couldn't decide whether he had witnessed a contrived or genuine display of grief. Asparia, making no secret of her feelings, glared icily at her sister. If Camilla was toying with the situation, her older sister would have words with her.

The young man, probably a Braccati or an Erizzo by the look of his straight, flat nose, guided Camilla to her brothers and offered a pained expression that served as an apology. Niccolo nodded his thanks. Even at her father's funeral, it would be unseemly for Camilla to muddy her clothes.

When the priest finished his sermon, Niccolo and his brothers maneuvered the coffin onto thick ropes lying over a pair of well-polished poles straddling the grave and stood back as the gravediggers quickly lowered it.

That was it, then. In less than a quarter hour, they had put their father in his grave. Niccolo had lost his mother, his father, and even Rosalia's gentle embrace.

Wanting to do the good thing, you will always choose the necessary thing. Angelo had entrusted the family's future to him. Flavio would act out of anger. But he would act out of necessity, no matter the cost.

Marco rested a hand on Niccolo's shoulder. His eyes held grief, but also concern.

Niccolo managed a faint smile. "It's up to us now, brother."

"Back-to-back," Marco replied with hollow cheer.

Niccolo surveyed the crowd. He should say something to the many who had gathered.

Flavio acted first. "I thank you for coming today. On behalf of the Aretoli, I invite you to say your final goodbyes to my venerable father."

Niccolo's temper flared at his brother's presumption even though he had intended the same. This wasn't France, where the eldest child inherited a father's rank and wealth. In Venice, all sons shared equally in both wealth and influence.

He tried to meet his brother's gaze, but Flavio simply stared at Niccolo's coat until the approaching mourners drew his attention. That icy jealousy had returned.

Niccolo frowned. Why shouldn't he wear his father's coat? He was more like Angelo than any of his siblings. Flavio had viewed their father as an old man with antiquated ideals. Wasn't Rosalia enough? Did he need everything?

With an effort, he restrained his anger. He wouldn't argue with his brother, not today, of all days.

A few of his father's close friends expressed their regrets, gaze lingering on the coat. Pietro Morelli, Calvino Morosini, Antonio Pillo… These men would be important allies in the coming years.

Thinking quickly, he slid his left foot slightly forward and pulled back the left side of the coat to put his fist on his hip. It was the stance his father had often used.

Angelo's death would not destroy his legacy or his house.

CHAPTER SEVEN

NICCOLO

NICCOLO AND HIS family didn't return to the city until the evening. The quiet morning service they had expected turned into a chain of conversations celebrating Angelo's life. Petrarch offered a tender sonnet expressing his regrets to the family that had hosted his visit these past few weeks. It charmed everyone in attendance and even managed to soothe Flavio, if only for a few moments.

"What are you smiling about?" Flavio demanded as they returned to the city. His mood had noticeably frayed as the day progressed.

Yet again, Niccolo wondered how his brother would build a following. The image of Flavio grabbing a senator by the collar and striking him came to mind.

"It meant a lot that so many came to see him buried."

Flavio grunted. "Probably to be sure he was really dead. I heard more than a little laughter today."

A person couldn't wear grief for too long before having to lay it down. "Maybe," Niccolo replied with a shrug. He had no strength for an argument, not when other matters required discussion. "I was thinking of asking Pietro to stay on as my steward."

Flavio turned to glare at him. "Moving into Father's house already?"

"Not at all," he replied easily. "I rather expected you to take it since you have a family to care for."

Flavio nodded, but the suspicion lingered in his expression. "That's right."

"I just thought, since you already have a steward who knows your habits and I don't, I could take him off your hands. He's getting older, and though I'd be responsible for his care when he retires, he can train a replacement for me."

Flavio shrugged. "I suppose that's a good idea."

Niccolo faced ahead lest his brother notice the triumph in his eyes. When they divided the *fraterna*, each brother would receive an equal share of Angelo's possessions and contracts. Fighting for the Aretoli house would have required Niccolo to sacrifice one of the family contracts. However, servants weren't property and weren't factored into the division.

Satisfied, he fell back to share the news with Pietro, who accepted eagerly. They may eventually quibble over the *fraterna*, but Niccolo had made the best acquisition of all. With Pietro came his father's informants.

The party broke up at the docks and headed wearily to their beds. Pietro continued on to the Aretoli home. Niccolo gave him enough money to hire a good carter and the authority to extend an offer to any of Angelo's servants he thought were particularly loyal. He probably wouldn't be back before nightfall.

His stomach growled. Realizing he hadn't eaten anything all day, he stopped at a tavern on his way home. The food had enough spice to make an Alexandrian merchant squeal, but he resolved to at least taste the soup put in front of him. It wasn't as fishy as he'd feared.

Satiated, Niccolo ambled home, where Joseph greeted him with a pained expression.

"What is it? Has Pietro returned yet?"

He shook his head. "He sent word that something needed to be done, and he would stay the night." He glanced behind him, though.

"Is someone here?"

"Your brother, Master Aretoli."

"Marco?"

"Your older brother, sir."

Niccolo frowned. Flavio should be home with his wife. He couldn't possibly have thought to move into their father's home tonight.

"The reception room?"

Joseph nodded and preceded him in. True enough, Flavio's doublet flashed past the slit of the partially open door as he paced. He descended upon Niccolo the moment Joseph opened the door.

"I can't believe it. Filthy *fica!*"

Niccolo instinctively slid into a defensive stance. The Flavio he knew rarely flew into a rage of this severity, and the list of possible causes began and ended with his forbidden chat with Rosalia. "What is it?" He gauged the angle of his exit and the location of the furniture, just in case he needed an obstruction…or a weapon.

Flavio snatched a rolled parchment from the table and thrust it into his brother's hands. Niccolo unrolled it carefully. The high quality of the paper sent a wash of relief over him. This wasn't about Rosalia, after all.

"Who's it from?"

"The doge." Flavio scowled and jutted his chin forward. "Read."

Signor Flavio Aretoli, loyal son of Venice and captain of the city guard,

I had heard the name Alberto Brattori before. After our conversation, I searched my records and discovered that Alvero Madina employed this man until a recent dispute over his stipend. The conversation apparently ended in a disagreement, since Alvero Madina lodged a complaint that Brattori had threatened to stain the Madina name. Brattori did not specify his threat, but it appears as if his claim to be working on Signor Madina's behalf in the matter of your father's death is false. I spoke with

Signor Madina, who confirmed he had no part in its planning or execution.

Niccolo gave a cry of shock. Why would the doge do such a thing? A little more remained, probably just the meaningless salutation that ended every patrician letter. Flavio was watching him carefully, though, and Niccolo wasn't so sure.

Due to these false claims, my men attempted to acquire Brattori from the home of your agent. Unfortunately, he died from injuries sustained during an escape attempt.

Since the murderer of your father has been brought to justice, Signor Madina has declined to charge House Aretoli with slander. He understands your grief. I offer my deepest regrets about your father and wish only for our continued friendship.

Sincerely,
Lorenzo Celsi, his most serene...

He cast the paper aside as if it burned his fingers. "The doge was involved in Father's death."

Flavio gasped. "It isn't Celsi's fault Alvero planned this all so carefully."

"You don't believe this, do you?" Niccolo asked harshly. "The man we accuse just happened to be threatened by the assassin? It's an obvious lie. And Alvero would never pass on a chance to charge us with slander." He shook his head. "The doge wants this whole matter dropped. He must be involved."

Flavio's mouth fell open.

Niccolo crossed to the discarded letter and picked up the parchment. "Charging us with slander... We made no public accusations. He's trying to frighten us into silence. I just don't understand why."

"He wants to protect the peace." Flavio's voice carried more than a little doubt.

"How could he arrange all this so quickly unless he was complicit? He already knew what he would do if Brattori were to be discovered." Now, fury kindled in Flavio's eyes. "And, he knew to strike while we were burying Father."

Niccolo scowled. "He killed the assassin to silence him." A few coins dangled before the right people would reveal where they had stashed Brattori. Niccolo couldn't even blame his people for letting the city guards have him; they would have assumed the Aretoli had succeeded in charging the murderers. Who would imagine that the doge would have a man killed?

"He acted like he truly cared when we went to him." Flavio shook his head, his previous anger utterly spent. "All the while, he planned to betray us."

Justice had seemed so close.

This was conspiracy, including at least the doge, Umberto, and Alvero. Celsi had to be certain Brattori would be killed during arrest, as well. "Do you know of any guards the doge personally recommended?"

Flavio crossed his arms. "Not that I know of."

Niccolo pressed his lips together. "Celsi would need men he could trust."

"It's strange that Feratollo and Madina would use poison. They aren't cowards."

"Secrecy would be important if the doge was involved. If the Senate hears of this, he'd lose his head, not just his position."

"Are we sure he's involved? What if he just wanted to keep a senator from being charged with murder?"

"And risk open violence between patrician houses?" Niccolo shook his head. "If it ever came out that he could have stopped it, the Senate would be appalled."

Flavio nodded, conceding the point.

Niccolo lowered himself onto one of his new oak chairs and threaded his fingers through his hair. "We only have one choice."

"We can't prosecute without Brattori."

"Mentioning the poison would only implicate the man who administered it, anyways," Niccolo agreed. "The doge's solution is a clever one. The story of a disagreement severs the tie between the assassin and House Madina."

"Then what can we do? Attack his family's holdings?" Flavio asked.

"A man without money is like a shark without teeth."

"What else is there to take?" Niccolo asked. "The Madinas have one trade route to Constantinople, buying silk and selling wine, but it'd take months to position ourselves well enough to threaten that. And the Feratollos have long-standing arms contracts we could never dislodge."

"Then what can we do?" Flavio met Niccolo's gaze with a seriousness that made Niccolo proud. His brother was a warrior, through and through.

"Do you remember your Caesar?" Niccolo asked.

Flavio scowled. "Why?"

"Father read it to us. *When the law ceases to be just, a man must make his own justice.*" Niccolo leaned forward. "We have to take matters into our own hands."

"You're not suggesting—"

"Did you or did you not stand in the street outside Brattori's house and declare *vendetta* with me?" Niccolo had accepted that it might come to this the moment his father died.

But Flavio clearly hadn't expected their evidence to fail. "I can't believe you're proposing that we—"

"We must hunt them down ourselves. What did you think I meant by *vendetta*?"

Flavio rose and began to pace. "The brother I remember wouldn't suggest such a thing."

"The brother you remember never saw captured enemies be granted release only to show up a month later raiding Candia," Niccolo countered. "That brother hadn't lost a father to a wasting poison that filled his last days with suffering. Poison!" He had never personally said an unkind word to any Feratollo or Madina, yet they had killed his father in the most painful way imaginable.

"I saw Umberto's hate in the Senate and at Easter. Hate doesn't stop. It consumes. What if Marco suffers next?" Niccolo leaned back on the chair and rubbed his temple. "I won't let that happen."

"You're right." Flavio lowered his gaze. "I suppose…"

Niccolo waited for him. He needed to know what resided in his brother's heart.

"It's one thing to kill a man in self-defense. You forget I served on Crete before you did." He chewed his lip. "But this is a sin."

The admission shocked Niccolo. Never before had Flavio expressed such faith. He could do little to soothe his brother's soul, but he could address the necessity of their situation.

"Umberto and Alvero killed our father. Maybe they didn't administer the poison, but they ordered it. The law has been corrupted by a deceitful doge, and our father's murderers will go unpunished. Do you want to see that happen?"

"Of course not." Flavio's reply carried some of his old strength. "Don't talk to me like I'm a child, Niccolo."

"Then stop acting like one. We tried to prosecute them, and now our only evidence is dead. If that doesn't tell you all you need to know, what will? What's to stop them from killing all of us if we don't respond to this? We have to stop them now."

"No matter what we have to do, you mean."

"I'd kill a hundred murderers to avenge one of the republic's noblest senators."

"You may have to if this conspiracy grows any larger." Flavio resumed his pacing.

They could not take the legal path if the doge refused to cooperate. In the face of hatred capable of killing, the Aretoli needed to react with the same degree of finality. "If you give them time, they'll hire every thug they can, vandalize our property, and strike our trade routes. They know where we make our money. The Feratollos used to control many of them. Every day we delay makes it less likely we can end this cleanly."

"You almost sound eager to commit murder," Flavio observed.

Murder had no justification. This was a reckoning. "I'm eager to end it."

"Do you understand the consequences of killing a doge?"

"For now, let's focus on Umberto and Alvero. We'll have to move quickly. If either learns what happened to the other, getting to the survivor will be much harder. A quick cut."

"You talk like you're sewing pants."

"I'm quite aware of what I face." He swallowed. "Even if we succeed, we'll get sidelong looks for years, and I doubt people will ever forget. But it needs to be done if we want to be safe. This isn't an emotional decision."

"Don't tell me you wouldn't take satisfaction from the death of Father's murderer."

"That's not why I'm doing it. Are you going to back out of *vendetta* because you may get your hands dirty?"

"I just want the chance to find a way out of this before we do something rash."

Their relationship had changed completely in just a few years. They were no longer the same men they had been. A gulf now separated them.

"Then look for one." Niccolo doubted another viable option existed, but he had to give his brother the chance to accept this decision willingly. An extra day might help Flavio see reason.

And Niccolo would need time to arrange his plans.

FLAVIO

Flavio left Niccolo's home in distress, his thoughts jumbled. He had watched Father do so many things he hadn't agreed with, and now his brother was doing the same. The tightness around his chest returned.

If someone found out, he'd lose his appointment as guard captain and the Aretoli would be ruined. By rights, he should turn his brother in.

Where was the old Niccolo who had explored the city with him? Something had happened on Crete to destroy that innocence. He didn't understand his brother anymore.

So how could he consider this crazy plan himself, when he didn't agree with it and couldn't understand why his brother had suggested it?

Of course, Flavio knew why. Niccolo had exploited the grief of his father's death to force an oath on him. Had Niccolo ever fought a duel? For God's sake, he had only spoken in the Senate once. As the eldest brother, he, not Niccolo, would have to carry out this *vendetta*.

At the time, he'd thought they'd only need a bit of oratory in the Senate. The other senators hated the Feratollos and feared the Madinas. The evidence would condemn them. But the doge had to stick his nose in and ruin everything.

Or did he just fear the prospect of getting his hands dirty, as Niccolo had said?

No. He hadn't faced a full-scale uprising on Crete, but he had led his contingent against more than his share of bandits and insurgents. He was no coward.

A sensible man would be nervous about murdering three senators, one of them the doge. Any attack on the ducal house would have terrible ramifications. Lorenzo Celsi had powerful allies; he could not have won election as doge otherwise. This could lead to civil war.

Flavio swallowed. The republic hadn't suffered a civil war throughout its almost thousand-year history. He didn't want to be the cause of one.

As he walked home along the *ria*, a shadowy figure concealed by a cloak separated from the wall and halted before him. He stared in disbelief. It had moved so fast. A moment ago, he had been alone in the alley.

The figure threw back the hood, revealing a cascade of dark auburn hair, a bemused smile, and deep blue pools for eyes.

A woman.

He should have made another sweep of the area around him. He should have kept on his guard in case she was merely a distraction for something else. Instead, he simply watched in open-mouthed disbelief.

"I come as an emissary of Doge Lorenzo Celsi." Her lack of fidgeting and careful control gave her an eerie presence.

He took a breath, using the extra time to gather his bearings. "How long have you been following me?"

"I delivered the letter for His Excellency." She must have been following him even before he had spoken with Niccolo, all without being seen. How had she gotten in front of him without being noticed?

"You've been watching me this whole time? Why?"

Her lips dimpled into a smirk. "You were in a furor when you arrived at your brother's home. When you left, you appeared to be reserved, pensive. I found that interesting."

"Did you?" Flavio's mind raced. She obviously wished him to know she was no mere servant. "And what does that tell you?"

He thought about seizing this woman and calling for Niccolo, though she had done nothing to warrant such treatment. Her controlled bearing screamed at him that she was dangerous. His instincts urged him to plunge his dagger into her chest.

"It tells me you care what your brother thinks. You didn't seek out your father-in-law or your sisters." Her eyes danced. "You wanted his approval. Yes, now I see. But you didn't get it. The two of you disagreed."

"You know what was in the letter?" Flavio asked, uncertain what to make of her insight.

"Of course. I wrote it."

An interesting fact, but Flavio couldn't decide why. "Then you know how to threaten and insult someone with delicacy."

"One could say that," she replied demurely.

"You don't deny it?"

"Anyone with eyes can understand the letter's intent."

"Then why disguise its meaning at all if it won't fool anyone?"

She pressed her lips together. "Courtesy is not meant to spare feelings, young Aretoli, but to show others the care we give to our words. Sweet words reassure us no harm is intended, despite their meaning."

"Young?" He was no child to be lectured. "We're much of an age."

Her lips formed a humorless grin. "I would reconsider your judgment that we are equals." She delivered the simple sentence with an ocean of confidence but not a trace of hostility.

Flavio swallowed. "So, you craft a pretty letter and follow me"—he elected not to dwell on how long she'd remained hidden—"only to reveal yourself now. Why?"

Her eyes danced. "As I said, I noticed your reaction."

"You didn't say that."

She shrugged. "In so many words."

That simple statement disturbed Flavio more than any other. She credited his ability to interpret her answers, yet he had utterly failed to do so. "And what does my reaction tell you?"

"It tells me you should speak to Doge Celsi."

"Your master?" he asked.

A faint dimpling of her mouth preceded her answer. "The doge."

The opportunity suited him, even if the manner of its offering unsettled him. Only by speaking to Celsi could he find another way out of this crisis. If they'd wanted him dead, he suspected he would be.

With a nod, Flavio fell into step behind her, following at a safe distance of a few strides. From the way her clothing moved and caught at unusual places, she had to be carrying at least three hidden weapons.

They took a winding route to the ducal palace, clearly chosen for discretion, not speed. After perhaps half an hour, they emerged into St. Mark's Square from an obscure side street. She clearly knew her way around the city.

Flavio recognized the men on duty outside the palace and was about to shout a greeting when she snapped a hand out to stay him. "Do not greet them. Someone may overhear."

Against reflexes like those, he doubted he could defend himself in a fight. The thought only deepened his apprehension. He swallowed and nodded meekly.

She led him deep into the building, behind the main reception hall. They seemed to descend forever, passing through a succession of hallways that grew ever darker. The massive ducal palace had always awed him. But now, the great building seemed oppressive.

Flavio's guide stopped outside a small door that seemed fit for nothing but storage. But after corridors dark enough to belong in a dungeon, he'd appreciate even a table and chair. When the woman swung open the door, Flavio simply stared.

The light came from so many candles that his eyes hurt, not only adorning the tables and mantles but also suspended from the ceiling on large chandeliers. Overlapping fur rugs covered the floors. Portraits of some of the most recent doges and tapestries of Venice's greatest victories hung on the walls. Two chairs flanked one of two large fireplaces warming the chamber.

They hadn't traveled beneath the palace at all; this was one of the doge's private chambers.

"Milord?"

Lorenzo Celsi and Antonio Galli twisted in their chairs. If it included Galli, this conspiracy was larger than even Niccolo had believed.

"Ah, Lucia, it's good to see you." His expression shifted to surprise when he met Flavio's gaze. The doge obviously hadn't been expecting him. He must have great trust in this woman for her to feel comfortable bringing a guest here on her own initiative.

Abruptly, Celsi stood. "I'm pleased to see you're well, young Aretoli. I trust you received word of the good news?" He extended his hand to Flavio.

Flavio forced himself to focus on the doge and not the room. This man was involved in his father's murder. Celsi's hand remained suspended unshaken.

"I received your letter, if that's what you mean."

"I trust this matter can be settled without further complication." Celsi lowered his hand.

"I doubt that."

The doge blinked and glanced at Lucia again. She offered a discrete nod.

"What do you mean?"

"Umberto Feratollo and Alvero Madina murdered my father. Do you think me simple enough to believe otherwise, based only on your letter? Alberto Brattori spoke the truth."

Celsi slowly circled to a table off to the side that held a bottle of dark red wine. Lifting a goblet, he began to pour himself a cup. "What will you do, if I may ask?"

Flavio edged closer to the door without turning his back on the woman beside him. How would she react if he admitted he and Niccolo would take matters into their own hands? Why had he agreed to this meeting before he had an alternative in mind?

Lucia answered for him. "I suspect the Aretoli brothers don't agree on that topic."

"Oh?" The doge gestured with the hand holding the goblet. A flash of light reflected off a pair of gold rings. "Let me hazard a guess. One of you suggested assassination, and the other found the idea repulsive?"

Galli snorted, making his presence known for the first time. "I told you young Niccolo had no stomach for this sort of thing." He subsided when Lucia shot him an icy glare.

Flavio wouldn't correct them about which brother had advocated murder. "So, you did kill my father." Flavio spoke calmly, belying the fury building in the pit of his stomach.

Celsi, rather than Galli, responded. "Yes, with the support of Umberto Feratollo and Alvero Madina."

"You don't deny it?" Such an easy admission!

"You knew as much before you walked through the door. The question is, will you take compensation for the wrong we've done to you, or do you prefer to be destroyed?"

"A knife in the back as I leave the ducal palace, is it?" He backed up toward the door. "Is that the reward I get for properly declaring my grievance?"

"Oh, no." The doge took a sip and gestured limply with his free hand. "You're free to leave tonight. But if you strike at us, we will destroy your family."

"Not before we expose you and your collaborators," Flavio retorted.

"Perhaps, but you stand to lose far more than we do," the doge countered.

Lucia added, "Naturally, you discussed this with your brother. You know what we say is true."

Damn her perception. Now the Aretoli would have to face House Galli as well. How could they defeat four families at once? If only he could avoid the disaster that would follow…

He straightened. "What sort of compensation would you possibly offer?"

Celsi smiled. Even persuading Flavio to discuss the possibility was a victory. "How about any appointment you desire? Within reason, of course. If I remember correctly, you've been a captain on Crete and of the guards here. Perhaps something different next? A provincial finance minister, perhaps of Modone or Istria?"

Flavio rolled his eyes. "That much would come to me without this mess." But he could see the possibilities now. "You stole my father from me. He'll never see any but one of his grandchildren, and my poor sister, Camilla, has nowhere to go now. This isn't a case of slander."

"What if I purchased a house for her, as a consolation for her suffering?"

"She would probably appreciate that."

After a lengthening silence, the doge pressed, "What will it take to call off your fury, young…Signor Aretoli?"

At the doge's correction, Flavio's eyes widened. He was no longer one of the young Aretoli sons; he was the eldest member of House Aretoli. Didn't that make him its leader? With that position came the responsibility to see his family prosper. Throwing themselves against the might of the doge, a councillor, and two other enemies would only extract a terrible toll, if they survived at all.

Angelo had tried to rise politically without success for so many years. Wasn't the best way to honor his father to pursue those dreams as his own? Angelo had never supported mindless violence; he'd be ashamed of his sons contemplating it on his behalf.

"My father had a dream. He imagined House Aretoli as powerful, important. What better way than a position on the Council of Ten?"

The doge fell back a step at the extent of Flavio's reach. On their own, the Aretoli would never rise so high in this generation. Even the Celsis hadn't earned a council position before Lorenzo had become doge. Though ten councillors were elected every six months, most appointees served one term on, one off. The Dandolos alone held two positions.

Of course, Flavio knew what he asked. To arrange for enough votes for him to win an election even for one term would displace another senator and make the doge a new enemy.

"You can have anything but that," the doge finally pronounced.

A chill crawled down Flavio's spine at the way Celsi dispensed offices that weren't his to give.

"I want a seat on the Council of Ten," he repeated. "Anything less would dishonor my father's memory. He strove for a council seat above all things. It's either that or a public battle among us." Even a whisper about a conspiracy involving the doge would likely galvanize the Senate against him. The subsequent investigation would reveal his involvement in the murder of a senator, and he'd be forced to resign, perhaps even exiled from the republic. "How many powers will the Senate take away this time?"

Galli rose and approached Flavio menacingly, murder in his eyes. Part of him wished for the man to strike him. The other part wondered how Lucia would react. Flavio shifted his weight in preparation for an attack, but Galli reconsidered his advance.

A low chuckle emanating from the doge's throat became a full-bellied laugh. Even Lucia tensed in surprise.

"My boy, it takes something rare to speak thusly to a doge!" He approached and draped an arm around him. "I like you immensely, Flavio. With that kind of spirit, you'll go far." He straightened. "I do have some conditions, of course."

"Name them." He had come too far to worry about the obligations of patronage.

"If we are to truly end this feud, we should look at this as a partnership, not a bribe for silence. Yes?"

"That seems reasonable." If the doge needed him, treachery would be less likely.

"You will support my efforts?"

Flavio frowned. "Which efforts?"

"Mostly diplomatic solutions to some of the hostility we've experienced in the past decade or so. I hope to prevent further bloodshed with our neighbors until we're stronger."

It seemed reasonable. "Anything else?"

"I need to know everything the council discusses and the opinions and motivations of its members. Galli is doing that for me now, but his term is coming to an end. You'll do the same during yours."

The Senate explicitly forbade such ducal oversight of the council. Accepting this offer would cause trouble in the future. "For that, I'll need something more in return."

"Oh?"

He raised his chin. "I must always hold a position superior to the Feratollos and Madinas."

The doge barked a laugh. "Done!"

Flavio blinked at the quickness of the doge's assent. In one conversation, he had hamstrung his family's two worst enemies, provided for his unwed sister, and achieved his father's greatest dream. He, Flavio Aretoli, would catapult his family to the ranks of the most powerful patricians in Venice.

Let's see you beat that in your lifetime, Niccolo. Taking the doge's hands to seal the pledge, he struggled to restrain his delight. He would accomplish great things. The doge was already tapping him to help secure long-term peace in the republic. Their success would be his testament to his father, instead of the murder his brother would deliver.

He had found a way out of this mess.

NICCOLO

"Have you completely lost your mind?"

Flavio's smile rapidly faded under the onslaught of Niccolo's barely contained fury.

At first, Niccolo had thought his brother's tale about the mysterious Lucia and his secret meeting in the ducal palace was a bad joke. But as he listened in growing horror, the cold truth of Flavio's utter betrayal began to sink in. Not even when his thoughts turned their darkest had Niccolo imagined his brother following such a course of action.

This wasn't the kind and generous Flavio who had protected his family. This was the jealous Flavio who had embarrassed himself at dinner. This was the Flavio who had disagreed with their father's every decision. This was the Flavio who had agreed to marry the only woman his brother had ever loved.

"Only a fool would trust these people."

Flavio's eyes went wide. "I've saved us from a feud that could see our family destroyed."

"There wouldn't have been a feud if you'd simply let me kill them."

"You would have me sit back while you start a war with four senatorial families?" He scoffed. "What kind of man do you take me for?"

"The kind of man who has fought more duels than I can count. But now I see you're just a man who protects his father's murderers."

"I'm protecting my family," he insisted. "If I let you kill Alvero and Umberto, what sort of retaliation would we face from their kin or their allies?"

"None!" Niccolo shouted. "The Feratollos and Madinas are nothing without those two. And even if they were, no one would know who killed them or why they died. Their secrecy is our security."

"My arrangement with the doge is our security," Flavio countered. "My deal saves us from the risk of a feud. You would threaten our very survival."

"No." Niccolo took a step forward. "I'd punish those who threaten us. You've doomed us."

"How have I doomed us? Everything I've done strengthens us."

"What will people say if they learn we did nothing about this?" He paused for only a moment. "They'll say we're *castrati*." He swept his hand sharply across his body. "Any respect our family has gathered over the generations will be wiped out by this…this impotence. What's to prevent Umberto and Alvero from killing you or me like they did our father?"

"They wouldn't dare while the doge defends us."

Niccolo stepped back and pointed at his brother. "And there you are. You've turned us into his vassals. And we all know what he does with supposed allies, don't we?" The image of his father's coffin came unbidden. Niccolo turned his back on his brother. "Why couldn't you keep your mouth shut?"

"The Dandolos or Orseolos would never have people killed."

"Do you think the Dandolos and Orseolos got to where they are through forgiveness? Their feuds are simply too far in the past for you to remember them."

Flavio crossed his arms. "Comforting words, but the doge would still be our enemy. I've forged an alliance with him."

"You've forged a collar around our necks," Niccolo shouted. "What happens when we disagree with him? Father was a senator and his ally, yet Celsi killed him. What about Alvero and Umberto?"

"What of them?"

"They were Celsi's co-conspirators and he happily brushed them aside in favor of you. Don't you think they made a similar deal with him? If he didn't honor his word with them, why would he honor it with you? I trust him about as much as I'd trust Francesco da Carrara." He paused as another thought occurred to him. "I start to wonder if the rumors about Celsi's miraculous escape all those years ago were true after all."

Celsi had always decried the rumors he had conspired with the Austrians and Hungarians in his bid to become doge. Yet, of the three men who had gone to the Hungarian court so many years ago, only Celsi had received an invitation to stay behind. On the way back, the others, including Rosalia's uncle Marco, had run into Austrians and spent the next two years in prison.

"Don't be absurd," Flavio said. "Our father trusted him enough to work with him."

Niccolo's patience snapped. "How can you cite our father one moment and abandon his memory the next? He isn't even cold in his grave, and you've already forgotten him."

"Everything I've done is for his memory."

"He'd never consent to this," Niccolo shot back. "You'll be on the council and rise in office, yes, but if I were you, I'd hope the doge doesn't realize he can wiggle out of his commitments if you wind up face-down in your stew." He wrung his hands in the air. "Why couldn't you just let me handle this?"

"Because I won't take orders from my younger brother!" Flavio took a step back, eyes widening. Niccolo suspected he had never intended to reveal that.

The last barriers of civility had fallen.

"I've been in the Senate all these years, but our father let *you* anchor our faction for the debate." Flavio's voice lowered into an eerie calm. "Why did he call you into his room before he died, Niccolo? What did you do, poison him against me when I wasn't there? Is this because I married Rosalia? Is this your way of getting revenge?"

Niccolo stood in stunned silence. Flavio's cool demeanor at the family dinner had just been a thin veneer. Only now did he realize his brother's pettiness. Flavio had been first in everything; the first to marry, the first to serve in Crete, the first to stand in the Senate. But, for all his advantages, his brother hadn't accomplished nearly as much. Flavio wasn't a great man, only a jealous one.

Had Angelo understood this? Was that what they had really been discussing that night, while his father had slowly slipped away?

Flavio could never be trusted to lead the Aretoli. In less than a week, Niccolo had lost both his father and brother. The first may have fallen to poison, but Flavio had fallen to his greed and jealousy. In his brother's place now stood a traitor to everything Angelo had represented.

The ache in his heart quickly faded into something sharper, more dangerous.

"I have neither the time nor inclination to reassure you of your worth. I've never diminished your accomplishments. If you question yourself, that's your burden. But I have to deal with this madness you've thrust upon us." He raised his chin. "Will you denounce this agreement you've made?"

"I will not."

Niccolo swallowed. So be it, then. "I refuse to recognize your pact with the doge. You're my older brother, but this is Venice, not France. We are equal in our inheritance."

He still needed to insert one further dagger, one that would shatter Flavio and ruin his confidence. Niccolo couldn't confront four houses and face the full measure of his brother's skill and ability at the same time. To save his family from the deadly ramifications of this pact, he had to destroy his brother.

Wishing to do the right thing, you will always do the necessary thing.

Niccolo swallowed. "We may be brothers, Flavio, but we are not equals. I'm the better man by far. Otherwise, you wouldn't have sold your family into vassalage to the doge. Father realized this when he asked to see me. He pitied me, you know. He knew I had the strength to protect our family and you didn't. You want to be the head of our family? You aren't worthy. You aren't half the man Father was, and he knew it."

The sheer brutality of the words, wrapped in such a calm delivery, left Flavio speechless. They were words for a traitor, not a brother, and he could not misunderstand them.

When Flavio finally responded, his voice lacked the bravado he normally exuded. "I won't let you endanger us."

"But you seem willing enough to endanger us yourself. I would have thought that you, of all people, would know that the wicked cannot be reasoned with." He rose. "We're done. Leave my house."

Eyes burning with fury, Flavio hastily turned and left the room, his movements sudden and clumsy. As the door shut behind him, Niccolo sank into a nearby chair.

He had lost his brother. Never again would "House Aretoli" mean what it once had. A low scream began deep in his throat and bubbled to the surface in a shrill cry of agony.

His heart was broken.

The terrible sound subsided, his spirit drifting away with the final echoes. Niccolo lowered his head into his hands. Flavio had shaken hands in peace with men who had orchestrated the death of his father. He had skulked back home like a dog kicked between the legs. His betrayal was total, complete.

Niccolo straightened his doublet. Flavio had told the doge of his intentions. He would have to act tonight, before Madina and Feratollo could be warned.

"Joseph!" He crossed the room and withdrew a thin dagger from a chest in the corner. "Bring me my cloak."

The boy popped his head into the room. "Which cloak, Master?"

The boy's eyes held the same innocence Niccolo had just lost. Had those been his eyes when Pietro had ushered them all into that back room so many years ago? Oddly, the thought comforted him. They had survived then and would survive now.

"The black one."

He would need clothes that could conceal the stain of blood.

UMBERTO

The sound of Umberto Feratollo's laughter reverberated off the walls of the small room. Everything was going so well. Now that he had dealt with Angelo Aretoli, he could direct his attention to that bastard Emilio Cornaro.

It was strange to think that Aretoli, who had fought like a lion so many years ago, would die so easily. He had saved Cornaro but couldn't save himself.

What did it matter now? His enemies were broken and had more to fear than ever before. In a few months, the doge would grant him the judicial seat he so richly deserved. Then, he could finish off those damned Cornaros and the rest of the Aretoli.

In a mood to celebrate, he wandered to a seedy tavern not far from one of the worst parts of town. The air was damp, with an odor like an army camp. It carried the delightful smell of desperation.

Best of all were the young girls from the local neighborhoods. Some were beauties. Besides, why should he pay for what everyone else had enjoyed when he could take a girl for the first time? He'd enjoy watching the tears streaming down her face, pleased to have saved her from a life of impossible dreams. Best they learn how the world works now rather than later.

Sometimes, their fathers would take one look at his fine silk clothing and start haggling away their daughters' purity. People would sacrifice almost anything for the right price.

With a shower of gold, he bought a few rounds of drinks for the other customers and basked in their adoration. Someone began playing the lute. Soon, everyone was clapping and drinking freely. Why couldn't those senatorial parties be more like this?

Ah, yes…because of stuffy Cornaro and his prude of a daughter.

The cheap wine began to go to his head after only a dozen cups. The owner's best vintage, indeed. It tasted like canal water.

With surprise, he noticed a few men laughing and joking at his table. Where had they come from?

Peering to steady himself, he saw a barmaid arrive to remove some of the cups. He put a hand under her skirt and grabbed her hip, hauling her down on his lap. She squirmed and screamed as he wiggled his hand between her legs.

"Come, now, m'dear. Le' see what ya got." Louder, he asked, "Who owns this one? Whatcha want for 'er?"

One of her flailing arms struck him squarely in the temple and a thunderclap of pain filled his already aching head. He shoved her to the floor and cradled his head.

"Damn woman," he barked. "Lemme s-slap some s-sense into ya!"

"Is there a problem?"

An older man stood over him with a cup in his hands, muscles tensed.

"Whassit to you?" A father or uncle, ready to teach him a lesson?

"It concerns me any time a customer doesn't enjoy himself in my tavern." Instead of offering a good brawl, the man crossed behind the bar and retrieved a bottle from somewhere underneath. "I don't normally do this, but let me offer some of my private supply as an apology for this trouble." He took a quick sip of the contents, nodded his approval, and extended the cup to Umberto.

Now this was how a man should treat a customer! Umberto hazily remembered being upset about something but couldn't recall what. Taking the cup, he hungrily swallowed a few large gulps. Its quality was much better than the swill he'd been drinking.

When he next looked up, the candle on his table had burned low. His vision had cleared, along with the worst of his intoxication. Several people had left. A few of the tables had overturned chairs resting on top of them. Someone should be clearing this cheap earthenware from his table.

Across the room, the tavern owner was stacking his dishes. The loud clanging of the cups and bowls hitting each other stabbed pain into Umberto's temples. He rose to say something about ceasing the racket.

Two hands clamped on his shoulders and forced him back down.

"What?"

He tried to turn his head, but fingers halted the movement by grabbing his hair.

"Don't you know who I am?" It was probably some local thug. He could use a fight.

The man behind him yanked hard, tilting back his head. A black hood hung low over the figure's face, but at this angle, Umberto recognized the features. Blinking a couple of times to clear his vision, he looked again. Those eyes chilled him to the bone. They were the eyes of a demon, terrifying in their calmness.

Niccolo Aretoli.

Umberto fumbled at his belt, looking for the dagger he always carried. Gone.

He tried to wiggle out of his chair but couldn't break Aretoli's iron grip. Niccolo didn't even smile.

"What do you want?" His voice quavered.

This was not the proper form of a challenge.

In response, Niccolo's other hand moved with a fluid motion. The stroke across his neck was surprisingly painless. Umberto only realized what had happened when warm liquid gushed down his shirt. A moment later, Niccolo let him go, and his head snapped back down. Try as he might, he couldn't raise it again.

Then he saw the dagger in Niccolo's other hand, covered in blood. His blood.

He tried to scream but only produced a gurgling that sent more liquid surging down his chest. Only when his sight began to fade did the pain finally come. Like a sharp tear, he felt as if the dagger had drawn across his neck again.

It screamed at him in darkness for a brief moment before it, too, faded into oblivion.

NICCOLO

Circling to avoid the rapidly growing pool of blood, Niccolo quietly wiped the blade on the corpse's sleeve and casually made his way to the bar. Alvero had already left for Constantinople on his galley, but at least one of his father's murderers had paid for his crime.

His hood still covered his face. A few patrons watched him with frightened respect, but no one confronted him. Their terror made him sick. How could people like Umberto enjoy this feeling?

The deed hadn't brought him any satisfaction, and he hadn't expected any. But that corpse would eventually be found. The doge would realize—but would never be able to prove—what had happened here. He would understand the true nature of Aretoli will.

He turned to the tavern owner and the young girl who sheltered in the crook of his arm. Her clothes bore stains of spilled ale and frequent mending. He doubted she owned another set.

"I apologize for the mess." He masked his voice with a wheeze.

The man clutched the young girl beside him protectively. She didn't seem to notice, only glare at the mess that had been Umberto.

She reminded Niccolo of his sister, Asparia.

"I'll take care of this," the tavern owner said. "Tell your master I thank him, for my own reasons."

Niccolo's mouth quirked upwards, but he didn't correct the man. It would help if they sought a brute, not a senator.

Without another word, he stepped out into the night.

CHAPTER EIGHT

NICCOLO

N ICCOLO SLEPT WELL that night. He would have more work to do when Alvero returned, but he had done all he could for the moment. No. He amended that thought. He had done all he could without his brother's help.

In the morning, he decided to consult with his family. He had needed to act quickly last night, but now that he had time, they deserved to know what he'd done.

He was writing invitations for them to gather at his home when he heard Flavio's voice at the front door. With a quick motion, Niccolo hid the half-finished papers beneath a ledger on his *tavola*.

Flavio stormed in a moment later with Joseph and Pietro in tow. "What have you done?"

"I'm sorry, signor," Pietro said brusquely as he interposed himself between the brothers.

"It's fine." Niccolo couldn't imagine that his brother intended him any harm; that would be unconscionable. "We have much to discuss."

Flavio kept his peace until Pietro ushered Joseph out and closed the door. "I thought I was clear that the doge and I had already settled this matter."

Niccolo grunted. "And I was equally clear that your agreement had no hold over me."

"You've murdered a man."

"Has something happened?" He gasped in feigned ignorance. "I've been home all night and haven't yet heard this morning's gossip."

His brother crossed his arms. "Do you expect the doge to believe that?"

"I hold it worth a pile of horse shit what the doge believes. He's responsible for our father's death."

"Why can't you see the sense of this?" Flavio clutched the air like a man catching butterflies. "You'll doom us all."

"We've been through this already." He sighed. "I'm assuming one of the assassins died yesterday. How did you hear?"

"The whole city's talking! That tends to happen when they find a senator dead in a tavern."

"I'd rather think it worthy of gossip if a senator died in his wife's bed, for the sheer novelty of it."

It was exactly the type of comment he ought to make, but this time, his brother's strained expression warned of a temper barely held in check.

"Well, the doge certainly wasn't in *his* bed this morning," Flavio growled. "He came by personally to share the latest gossip. I told him we'd abandoned our plans for revenge. That, surely, my brother would inform me before taking such a reckless action."

"An interesting assumption. Didn't you consider that I might make some unilateral decisions of my own?"

"I had to make my choice right then." Flavio's arms fell to his sides. "I didn't have time to discuss it."

"Nor did I, not if I wanted to preserve any chance to surprise our enemies after you betrayed us to them."

"Oh, give that complaint a rest."

"I will not!" The *tavola* and papers upon it vibrated with the strength of his shout. "How can I trust you, Flavio? Will you avenge me if I'm killed? What if Asparia or Camilla was merely raped? Would that be enough to rouse you from your delusion?"

The muscles of Flavio's neck tightened. "I will protect my family."

"No, you'll just profit from their ruin. And you dare to question me when I take matters into my own hands? No, I won't give it a rest. You have to decide: will you stand with your brother as he avenges our father, or will you stand with the men who murdered him?"

"I'm not going to answer that."

"Why not?" Niccolo spread his arms. "You've had a night to think about it. That's longer than it took you to climb into bed with the doge."

"I won't break my word once I've given it."

"But you will stand against the family who never required a formal pledge? Perhaps Father should have made us each sign contracts of fealty to be lodged in the Ministry of Records. Then again, he was a fool, wasn't he? He assumed his sons were men of character."

"You will treat me with the respect I deserve."

"Of course." Niccolo sneered. "Come back after I've had some more to drink. You'll serve well as a chamber pot."

Flavio's eyes widened. "You dirty piece of…" He cocked his fist. "By refusing to honor an agreement made by your older brother, you've betrayed everything our father ever taught us."

It was an asinine statement. Why did he fixate on birth order when that had never mattered in Venice? They had no primogeniture laws designed to secure the power of inbred noblemen. Only ability and talent mattered here, and Flavio evidently lacked both.

He briefly considered responding with Angelo's dying words, but cruelty hadn't worked as well as Niccolo had hoped during their last conversation. Instead, he merely waved a dismissal. "Do what you will. I don't care anymore. You'll wear the dishonor when I alone dispense the justice they deserve."

"Never speak to me again," Flavio pronounced. "Never speak to our sister Camilla or our brother Marco. I can't speak for Asparia, but never again come near my home. You are no Aretoli. I will expect you to return all the servants from my household."

What an arrogant request!

When he responded, Niccolo surprised even himself with the calmness of his voice. "You don't want to speak to me again? Fine. Live what remains of your life in peace. Take our father's house with my compliments. *Fraterna* requires an even division of Father's property. Not even your new allies can change that fact. Clearly, you haven't realized the house will come out of your share."

Flavio inhaled to speak, but Niccolo continued over him. "But don't presume to tell me who I can and cannot visit. You've already betrayed us, and I won't let you destroy us in your madness."

He began to turn from Flavio, unable to watch the anguish playing over his brother's face. Dismissing him after playing on his brother's jealousy and feelings of inadequacy was the worst way Niccolo could imagine to punish Flavio.

He halted when he remembered Flavio's last, equally unreasonable demand. "Oh, and the staff decided to join my household freely. I'll have Pietro give them the choice to return, but I'll make sure they know they're welcome to stay. We'll see what they decide."

The rage did not flow. Instead, Flavio simply narrowed his eyes. "You always planned to cheat me out of my share."

"I haven't cheated you of anything but your presumption. I had my doubts you had the strength to see Father properly honored. I only regret that my prediction proved to be so accurate."

"You're a scoundrel, Niccolo." It carried the same malice as his words to Umberto Feratollo at Easter. That night seemed so long ago now. A week ago, he'd had a living father and a loyal brother.

Niccolo shrugged. "Relentless, cunning, vindictive, perhaps. But not a scoundrel. I'm honoring those whom I have a sacred duty to defend while you've betrayed your family's interests and safety."

Flavio stared at his brother, his lip curling into a snarl. Niccolo's mind reeled. Would he actually attack his own brother? Flavio was always the stronger. Neither of them wore a weapon, but even if he had one, could he raise it against a brother, even one who had betrayed their father?

The crisis ended as quickly as it arose. Flavio turned on his heel, split the door with a vicious kick, and stepped over the wreckage with a flurry of his cloak. He didn't bother asking Niccolo's servants to join him on his way out. Evidently, he had realized there was no point.

Niccolo clenched his fists behind him, trying to slow his heartbeat. What would he have done if Flavio had attacked him? This was his brother. What had happened to him?

Pietro rushed into the room and studied the damaged door frame. "I see that didn't go well."

Niccolo shook his head. "No, it did not." Niccolo had told Pietro about the doge's letter, but he knew nothing about Flavio's decision. How would he react? The old man was the last link with his father, and he didn't want to disappoint him.

"You disagree on what you must do?"

Niccolo chuckled lightly, remembering a few hours ago when that had been his most serious problem. "Rather, on what's already been done."

"I don't understand."

He had best state it plainly. "Flavio sealed an agreement with the doge. In exchange for not retaliating after my father's death, he'll be given a seat on the Council of Ten."

"What?" Pietro grasped a nearby chair to remain upright. "Is he mad?"

Relief. "I said very nearly the same thing. He genuinely believes his decision will keep us from further harm."

Pietro was of old Italian stock, not Venetian. In the south, many still carried that wild blood that had seen entire families eradicated for honor's sake. His eyes became distant, filling with a strange sorrow.

Angelo had worn the same look when Niccolo had discussed Flavio with him.

"Did we fail in our care for him? He was always so bright, but this…" Pietro shook his head.

"You do know I can't let this go, right?"

Pietro regained some of his composure. A hint of some other emotion shone in those eyes. Pride? "This agreement is a betrayal of us all. We'll have to avenge—"

"Be still, Pietro." He placed a hand on Pietro's shoulder. "I've already taken steps, but I'm more concerned about Flavio."

"He's gone too far."

"I agree."

"This agreement has to be repudiated."

Niccolo nodded. "I told him as much."

"Alvero and Umberto must be killed. The sooner, the better."

"Umberto is already dead."

"What?" The word carried only surprise.

He reached into a chest and handed Pietro the dagger he'd used. "With this dagger, as a matter of fact."

Instead of recoiling, Pietro took it and studied it closely. "It's been cleaned, but not very well. There's still blood in the corners." He frowned. "I'll have someone melt it down. Can you spare a chest?"

"I suppose. Why?" Niccolo asked, confused.

"I'll strip the metal bands and send them with it. A pile of scrap will arouse less suspicion than a lone dagger, particularly the day after one of your enemies is found dead." He lowered the blade. "Who did you use?"

"I went myself."

Pietro scowled.

"I didn't have time to go through one of your people, Pietro."

The old steward showed no reaction when Niccolo referenced his informants. Had he and Angelo talked about this before his death?

"What if you'd been seen?" Pietro spoke with urgency. "The doge would manufacture evidence if he could find even one man to claim he recognized you. When these things are done, you must be seen elsewhere to reinforce your innocence. Do you understand?"

Niccolo blinked, surprised at his vehemence. "Yes, Pietro. I'm sorry."

"Don't apologize." Pietro's voice had softened. "The beast deserved what he got." He placed a hand on Niccolo's shoulder. "You aren't alone, Niccolo."

The words contrasted sharply with his own thoughts. He had to turn away so Pietro wouldn't see the tears forming in his eyes. "Thank you, old friend."

"And your loyal man, signor."

Niccolo needed a moment to fully comprehend the meaning of that simple statement. Pietro had sworn oaths to his father as the only male Aretoli alive at the time. The distinction between his loyalty to the family and to the person hadn't been an issue. But now, with more than one Aretoli male to claim that loyalty, it couldn't be taken for granted.

"You are House Aretoli, my boy." Pietro offered a reassuring smile. "What comes next?"

Niccolo wanted to embrace this man as a true treasure, but he had precious little time. Even after they settled on the final distribution of their father's possessions and contracts, what would prevent Flavio from seizing them by force? Niccolo would need to solidify his relationship with the factors of their trade routes and the managers of Aretoli possessions before the *fraterna* if he hoped to keep them.

"I need to speak with my sisters and Marco as soon as possible. If Flavio reaches them first, who knows what lies he'll tell."

He spoke with his father's confidence and voice of authority. Perhaps Pietro's words had unlocked something within him, something that had been cultivated by years of listening to and watching his father.

Angelo may have died, but he would never truly be gone.

Pietro nodded and ducked through the splintered remnants of the door. Flavio's kick had struck it solidly and split it down the middle. The pieces had shattered; they would never fit back together again.

NICCOLO

Whether they were still shaken by the loss of their beloved father or interested to hear about the investigation, the remaining Aretoli wasted no time gathering at Niccolo's home upon receiving his summons.

Confronted by Camilla and Marco's sorrow and Giovanni and Asparia's patience, doubt began to gnaw at Niccolo. What if they didn't agree with him? If his entire family turned against him, what was the point in defending their honor?

"Is this related to Father?" Marco's question broke him out of his thoughts.

"It is. There are a few things the family should know." He cleared his throat to draw the attention of the rest. "I love you all dearly. Including you, Giovanni. But Flavio and I decided to keep some things from you until they developed further."

Asparia sat up at this prelude and glanced at her husband.

"Please believe we did this to protect you and for no other reason," Niccolo continued.

"Shouldn't Flavio be here?" Camilla asked.

"Let Niccolo explain," Giovanni said gently. "I'm sure that's part of it."

Niccolo nodded slowly. "As you know, Flavio and I left our father's bedside after he died. We went to find the man who poisoned Father."

The room fell silent; Camilla even stopped playing with the embroidery on the hem of her dress. Not even Asparia ventured to break the stillness. The soft rustle of Giovanni reaching out for his wife's hand resonated loudly.

He recounted the events of the previous night, including the discovery of the poison and the doge's murder of Brattori. Camilla's face turned ashen at the news of another death, and Niccolo's heart softened. Perhaps their father's death had affected her more than he had thought.

Asparia began to clench her fists early in Niccolo's tale. She nearly sputtered with rage by the end. Beside her, Giovanni had risen and turned his back to them, staring out the front window.

Marco's face was a mask. What he thought, Niccolo couldn't guess.

Giovanni turned. "To think, the doge deceived us for all that time."

Asparia was studying Niccolo with narrowed eyes. "That's not all, is it?"

"No." Circling one of his wooden chairs, Niccolo lowered himself into it. "When we received the letter, Flavio and I disagreed on what should be done."

"Which of you suggested assassination?" Marco asked.

"I did," Niccolo admitted. "Of Feratollo and Madina."

"And Flavio?" Marco leaned against the wall with his arms crossed.

The phrasing disturbed Niccolo deeply, even though he understood Marco's meaning.

"He decided on another course of action." He lowered his gaze. "After we spoke—argued, actually—Flavio met with the doge, who offered him a Council of Ten position, a house for Camilla as the only unmarried Aretoli daughter, and ascendancy over the Feratollos and Madinas on the condition that he take no further action against them."

"He has no right to offer that position!" Giovanni cried.

"To murder a man, then insult his relatives with such an offer," Asparia breathed.

Niccolo ran his tongue along the inside of his gums. "Flavio accepted."

Asparia scoffed and clenched her fists. The revelation apparently bothered even Marco, who uncrossed his hands and pushed himself away from the wall. All eyes were on Niccolo except for Camilla's. Her lips curled into a faint but distinct smile for a moment before the mask of concern returned.

He had expected more of her.

Niccolo continued, "Flavio pledged that none of us would seek justice for our father's murder. He had no right to make that decision, and I refused to acknowledge it."

The room fell silent. Niccolo had considered how to respond to this moment for a long time, but he had ultimately rejected persuading his family to support him. For him to know he could rely on them, they needed to feel the horror of Flavio's actions for themselves.

Only Giovanni met his gaze. Within his friend's eyes, Niccolo saw determination and unwavering support. He was a loyal son who genuinely mourned his father. Most young men would delight at the prospect of inheritance. Niccolo loved him specifically because he had not.

Once he saw that Niccolo understood, Giovanni shifted his attention to his wife and draped an arm over her shoulders. Asparia shrugged it off and rose, storming across the room.

When it came, her response was both gentler and more brutal than Niccolo had expected.

She composed herself with a deep breath. Returning to her seat, she meticulously arranged the folders of her dress. "I cannot abide a man who forgets my father. Never again will I entertain Flavio in my home." She nodded to Giovanni. "With my husband's agreement, of course."

Giovanni glanced from his wife to his friend before finally nodding.

Camilla raised her chin. "Well, I will. It sounds like he just wanted to keep us all safe." She spoke with a finality brokering no argument. "In fact, I'm going to tell him what you're doing here. I can't believe you'd discuss this when he's not here to defend himself." With that, she gathered up her dress and stormed out of the room.

The sight of his sister's indignant exit left Niccolo speechless.

Asparia also watched her go with a slack-jawed look of surprise. "She's just happy with her new house," she finally managed long after Camilla was gone.

"She's right about one thing, Niccolo." Marco stepped closer. "He is still our brother. Think carefully about what it means if you turn your back on him completely."

"I don't have a choice, Marco. He already declared he would shun me."

"And just what does that tell you?" Asparia asked.

Niccolo hadn't considered that aspect. That simple comment seemed to throw Flavio into the wrong as nothing else could. If he had thought of it himself, perhaps Camilla wouldn't have run off. But it was too late now.

"We haven't addressed what to do about those responsible," Marco said.

"They must die," Giovanni said.

"Dear!" Asparia gaped at her husband.

"He's right." Marco looked away. This had to be painful for him to discuss. He had never wanted the responsibility of matters such as these.

"Umberto Feratollo is already dead." They looked at him with surprise. "I had to act quickly because Flavio revealed our intentions to the doge. It was either last night or not at all. I apologize that I did not inform you beforehand."

"So, it's only Alvero left?" Marco asked.

"And the doge. And Galli, since the doge spoke so freely in front of him."

"But you have no proof of that," Marco warned. "It's one thing to punish the guilty, but quite another to kill a doge and a councillor based on suspicion alone."

"Do you doubt they were involved?" Giovanni asked. Now that his wife had willingly committed them to this path, he could freely advise them. "You heard what the doge did."

"I'm certain they were involved, but that isn't enough."

"Marco is right." Niccolo's words drew more than one look of surprise. "Without proof, we risk condemning the innocent with the guilty." Not that he thought they could strike at the doge, in any case. "Can I interpret your comments to mean you also reject capitulation to the doge?"

He had carefully chosen to exclude mentioning Flavio. He refused to force them to choose one brother over the other, merely to commit to a course of action.

Marco nodded. "No one deserves Father's fate. We can't let his murderers go unpunished."

His brother's eyes contained all his love for their father and the pain of his loss. Niccolo crossed the distance and clasped Marco about the shoulders. If gentle Marco could see the sense in what he proposed, then it was worthwhile, after all.

Niccolo had his support for the moment, but without some incentive to keep Marco moving forward, that righteous fervor would diminish.

Marco released him. "But Niccolo, I can't give up on Flavio. He's our brother. We must help him see the madness of this pact."

The last time he had given someone the luxury to indulge their feelings, Flavio had turned around and betrayed his family. He stood to lose so much if Flavio somehow turned Marco to his cause.

No, he refused to doubt all his siblings because of one brother's decisions. "If you can open Flavio's eyes, Marco, I will praise you as a saint. But he won't speak with me."

"And I won't speak with him," Asparia repeated.

"What do we do?" Deep lines formed on Marco's harrowed forehead. "I…I don't know what comes next."

Niccolo squeezed his shoulder. "The best thing you can do is remind Flavio how important family is. Let me worry about the rest. I have some help."

"And a loyal friend," Giovanni said. "I have several dozen men and a good network of informants who would jump at the chance to hone their skills."

Asparia crossed the room to her husband's embrace. Placing a hand on his chest, she laid her head against his shoulder. He smiled down at her and kissed the top of her head.

The tender exchange made Niccolo think of Rosalia. This rift would tear her apart. Only respect for Flavio had stopped him from kissing her in the storage room. He could still feel the softness of her skin underneath his fingers. If he had known what would happen, he'd have taken her in his arms and never let go. It hadn't been long enough, that time alone.

No, it had been too much. Now, he'd probably never see her again.

What would Emilio Cornaro do? Niccolo had already wiped away one of his family's most obstinate enemies. Could he really act against Niccolo after the service he'd done for him? Flavio may have bought him time two years ago, but Niccolo had eliminated the threat entirely.

"The *fraterna* may grant Flavio, Marco, and I each a third of Father's estate, but nothing prevents Flavio from underbidding us like he would a rival," Niccolo said.

Giovanni sucked in a breath. "Would Flavio stoop that low? If he sets the precedent of bidding against his own brothers, your partners won't ever stop playing you off against each other."

Even Marco chipped in, "The relationships Father built would be destroyed."

"There's little I'd put past an angry Flavio. I need to firm up my share of the *fraterna* now so he can't dispossess me later."

"Just your share?" Asparia raised an eyebrow.

"Just my share. I won't ruin my own brother."

"Should I do the same thing?" Marco may not have shown much interest in his inheritance before, but Father wasn't around to take care of him anymore.

"I don't think so. His quarrel is with me, not you. He believes you're harmless. You also haven't declared *vendetta*."

"Besides which," Asparia explained, "If Flavio dispossesses Niccolo, you can funnel him money to continue the fight."

Giovanni grinned at his wife. "I should put you in charge of my finances."

"I've been saying that for years." She smiled. "Then I'll know you aren't sneaking out with my brothers in the middle of the night."

Evidently, the brothel argument wasn't quite over yet.

"What was that?" Giovanni craned an ear toward his wife.

"Nothing." She gave another of her innocent smiles.

Niccolo and Marco each released an uncommonly loud laugh fueled by tension.

Sobering, Niccolo asked, "Will you be there for me if I need help?"

"Yes." Marco and Giovanni answered simultaneously.

"Let's just resolve this quickly." Asparia cradled her belly. "I don't know how much more worrying I can take."

"I just have Madina left, for the moment. If Galli and the doge don't move to protect him, they're unlikely to retaliate against us."

"Where is Alvero now?" Giovanni asked.

"He left for the east early this morning. I was too late."

Giovanni pressed his lips together. "How long will he be gone?"

"Hard to say. His man said he would go to Negroponte, then Chios, and then to his main buyer in Constantinople. After that, I think he said Acre and Alexandria."

He released a short whistle of surprise. "That'll take months. A lot can happen by then."

He was right, of course. With Umberto, Niccolo had had surprise on his side. That wouldn't be the case next time, and Alvero was far more deadly. But Niccolo had accepted the potential consequences when he'd declared *vendetta* with Flavio. To end the threat Alvero posed, he would gladly endure a little hardship.

NICCOLO

The rain picked up again later that morning, bathing the city in an eerie fog. As he walked toward the silk district, Niccolo hoped the weather would keep most people indoors, especially his brother.

All the Aretoli business partners would present themselves at the formal division of the *fraterna* in three days, but Niccolo suspected the distribution would be anything but fair. He needed to take steps now to secure contracts and relationships he could retain even if Flavio tried to undercut him.

The silk district was one of the most closely guarded areas of the city. Hundreds had attempted to steal the precious commodity. All had been put to death. As soon as Niccolo crossed the footbridge leading to the district, a pair of city guards approached, hands on the hilts of their swords. Only after he showed his gold senatorial ring did they bow and let him pass.

Finding his destination, Niccolo stepped through the door into a storefront. Unlike other craftsmen throughout the city, this weaver displayed very few samples of his work. A single mid-grade cloak sat behind the counter, out of reach. The real money was in the truly rare material, the high-grade silk that only Venice produced. The Senate forbade silk workers from ever leaving the city, a draconian measure that had successfully protected the republic's monopoly. Not until customers had demonstrated significant wealth would they be allowed to even see the fine fabric.

Discretely, he checked that the scrolls in the interior pocket of his coat had survived the mist.

A man with high cheekbones and powerful arms stepped through the curtain dividing the workroom from the storefront. "May I help you?"

Niccolo bowed as well as he could, considering the bulge of the scrolls within his cloak. "I am Niccolo Aretoli, here to speak with Master Weaver Di Natali."

"Signor Aretoli." Surprise gave way to a respectful bow. "I am Di Natali." He hesitated. "I was sorry to hear about your father. He was a noble man and a fair patron."

"I thank you for your words. My father highly valued your relationship with House Aretoli." He took a deep breath. "I've come today to determine whether that relationship will continue."

The weaver straightened and cocked his head. "Oh?" In addition to being a skilled weaver, he could obviously also recognize the start of a negotiation.

"Have you been satisfied with the terms of that agreement?"

"Yes. Did your father disagree?"

"On the contrary," Niccolo reassured. "I propose that we extend the term a further ten years."

Di Natali stroked the whiskers on his chin. "That's an interesting proposition."

Niccolo withdrew a scroll with a spherical knob on the end. They both instinctively approached the counter as Niccolo unfurled it. "Here are the current terms of the agreement."

The weaver surprised Niccolo by reading it for himself; he had been prepared to recite the terms aloud. The man looked up after finishing. "This contract has one weakness. The prices I could charge your father for my finished goods were fixed. When my costs increase, I suffer."

Niccolo grinned. "I agree. That's why this contract"—he withdrew the other scroll—"sets our buying price as a percentage of the going market rate."

Di Natali's eyebrows rose as he read. "Twenty percent below market value? That's steep."

"Not really. We purchase all the cloth you produce, no matter how much. You'll earn a guaranteed profit. Read the third condition."

Di Natali did as instructed. "No rent?"

"You've more than paid for the facility over the years. It would be rude to continue to charge a loyal partner, don't you agree?"

He scratched his chin. "You don't negotiate very well, young Aretoli," he finally pronounced. "I depend on you as my landlord and my buyer, but you've just given me more than your father ever did."

Niccolo shrugged. "I'll earn my profit. I want your loyalty, not just your business."

Having finished reading the new contract, the weaver curled it up and held it close. "This contract names you as my buyer, not the Aretoli. Why are you visiting me today instead of three days hence?"

Stiffening, Niccolo forced himself to answer casually. "The terms would be the same, and they're superior to your current contract."

Di Natali raised his hands. "I agree. I only wonder whether

you and your brothers agree on the *fraterna*." Before Niccolo could respond, the weaver added, "But a contract is a contract. I tend to stay out of other peoples' affairs, so long as I have a place to sell my silk."

"Then let's lodge this with the clerks."

As they settled in a gondola headed for St. Mark's Square, the weaver relaxed. "I was a boy when my family dealt with the Feratollos. I remember Giuseppe Feratollo and his thugs roughing up our shop when it was time to renegotiate." He met Niccolo's gaze. "Your father never did such a thing. He even helped to end to their visits after we reached an agreement."

Niccolo hadn't heard this story before. "I aim to continue my father's ways."

"And what happens when someone breaks their oath or wrongs you?"

He swallowed. "If I choose to destroy someone, it will be both swift and final."

Di Natali nodded. "As a loyal partner of the Aretoli, I'm glad to hear it." He leaned closer, so the gondolier couldn't overhear. "I hear Umberto Feratollo died last night."

"Is that so?" Niccolo answered a little too quickly to deflect suspicion.

"There weren't any witnesses. None of his valuables were stolen. The very silence of his death speaks volumes."

"Well," Niccolo replied. "It doesn't surprise me. But one shouldn't speak ill of the dead...or the mistakes that led them to that state." Niccolo would say no more, especially to a partner.

The clerks who lodged formal contracts, wills, marriage certificates, and court decisions had their own building in St. Mark's Square. Centuries ago, clerks had been forbidden from joining the Senate, but the system of bribes and patronage that had developed had destroyed their impartiality. The great houses no longer had a reason to miss out on the revenue—both official and otherwise—those positions enjoyed.

The official Niccolo wanted exclusively handled contracts. The office was often busy, and Niccolo could see a small line waiting nearby.

Senatorial status conferred the right to move to the front though, and while a few people grumbled behind him, they fell silent at a glare.

The young patrician clerk waved him over. "Name?"

"Senator Niccolo Aretoli, of House Aretoli." That quieted down the crowd behind him. He wished that they admired his senatorial oratory, but he suspected the tales Giovanni had spread about his service on Crete was a more likely source of their newfound respect. Could he do anything with the rest of his life to rival the reputation he'd gained as a war hero?

The clerk, too, looked at him with awe. "Signor, how may I be of service?"

"I wish to formally lodge this contract with your office."

The clerk looked it over, his gaze flickering back to Niccolo when he read the word *silk*. "Tiepo Di Natali hasn't signed it yet."

"We were waiting for you to serve as a witness. Quill and ink?"

To his right, Niccolo noticed a familiar face and muttered a silent curse. He had hoped to lodge this contract and a few others before anyone discovered his actions. Once they were official, no one could contest them.

The clerk fumbled to open the jar of ink. The stopper slipped out of his hand twice before he finally succeeded. Niccolo, out of patience, grabbed the quill and handed it to Di Natali. He threw another glance over Di Natali's shoulder as the weaver dipped the tip into the jar and signed his name: a large D and an irregular squiggle.

Breathing a sigh of relief, Niccolo handed the contract to the clerk as Antonio Galli slid up behind him.

"Ah, Signor Aretoli, what a pleasant surprise."

"Good day, councillor," he replied stiffly.

The clerk gasped upon seeing Galli at his booth. His gaze kept darting back and forth between the two senators. "Signor Aretoli, I acknowledge receipt of your contract with Master Di Natali."

"A contract? How extraordinary." He offered a twisted smile. "I thought you were a loyal son, not one to quibble over the *fraterna* so soon after your father's death."

Niccolo suppressed a groan. Galli would know his intentions now. Though he didn't wish to feign pleasantries with this murderer, he could not ignore this snake mentioning his father.

Beside him, Di Natali looked toward Niccolo for direction.

Niccolo shook the weaver's hand. "I'm glad we could reach a resolution, Di Natali." There was no point in subterfuge anymore. "I look forward to many years of continued cooperation."

The weaver gave a stiff bow. "I am at your service, Signor Aretoli. May God bless you."

Niccolo smiled, thankful for the man's deference as he withdrew. It would make the next few moments easier.

He rounded on Galli. "You are far too interested in my father's affairs. I would hate for your curiosity to lead you to harm."

"My, my!" He stepped back and raised his voice. "What have I done to warrant such abuse? Are we not both loyal friends to the doge?" He swept his gaze over those nearby, probably to gauge whether he was attracting enough attention.

Niccolo would lose this battle if he fought it. At least he hadn't made any specific accusations for Galli to use as a basis for slander.

He turned his back on the councillor and walked away. He needed to speak to more partners, not waste time arguing with one of his father's murderers.

When he hazarded a look behind, Galli had already departed. Time had turned against him.

FLAVIO

Flavio was breaking his fast at the long table in what had previously been his father's home when his steward announced a visitor. He had spent much of the night mulling over his brother's damnable stubbornness. Between Niccolo's volatility last night and Umberto's murder, sleep did not come easily.

From his steward's bewildered expression, Flavio suspected the doge was at his door again. Let him wait. The thought that perhaps Niccolo was right after all and he was simply being fattened up for slaughter returned unbidden. He tucked back one more fig and reached for the last of his wine.

Before it touched his lips, Antonio Galli stormed in, nostrils flaring. Flavio leaned back, leaving the goblet untouched.

"When I grace you with a visit, you will respond immediately."

"It's nice to see you." He took a bite from a chunk of bread on his plate. "How may I help such a polite ally?"

Galli started to pace in front of him. "First, we find Umberto dead, and now this."

"What are you talking about?" Belatedly, he dismissed the steward with a wave. The man had already heard too much.

"Guess who just formally lodged a new contract with a silk weaver, separating him from your father's *fraterna*?"

A chill ran down Flavio's back. He had intended to arrange a few discrete meetings with the most important Aretoli partners himself. How had Niccolo known?

"First your brother says he'll undermine our agreement, then Umberto winds up dead, and now he's filching your contracts. And silk, of all things." Galli halted and jabbed a finger toward him. "He's a threat to us."

Why didn't his brother understand? The doge was too powerful to antagonize. Everyone who had ever opposed a doge had fallen into infamy, except for those who had stopped Faliero, of course. And now, Niccolo had had violated all decorum by approaching the family partners before the division of the *fraterna*.

Flavio absently fingered his marriage ring. Rosalia. It had all started with Rosalia. He had done his duty for his family, and Niccolo had run away to Crete for two years like a spoiled brat. If Niccolo could still be angry enough to take revenge for losing Rosalia after two years, he wouldn't stop until he'd undermined everything Flavio intended to accomplish.

He inhaled a long breath. Now that he'd returned home, Niccolo would probably try to turn Rosalia against him, too. He had to keep them apart, no matter what it took.

Galli was staring at him in silence. Subverting the factors who represented the Aretoli in distant lands, the managers of the land they owned, and the business partners who produced or purchased their goods was one thing. But Niccolo had made the family look foolish in front of a councillor and the doge. He had made Flavio look foolish.

Perhaps his new allies could prove useful. "I will handle my brother. But first, I need to firm up the family partnerships. All of them."

"You can't officially deny Niccolo what's his," Galli insisted.

"Can't the doge do something? You're on the council. Can't you?"

Galli shook his head. "Meddling in an inheritance is going too far."

He bit his lip. "At least, if I control it, I can make sure the *fraterna* is distributed on my terms. I'll be damned if he gets anything I can't easily take away. I need a favor."

"With your brother?" Galli's grin made him look like a wolf ready to lunge.

Flavio swallowed at the implication of that expression. "No, I need men to carry letters for me. With your help, I can prevent him from influencing anyone else."

Galli considered, but Flavio knew he'd agree. Helping to divert assets from an unfriendly Aretoli to a friendly one benefited him. "Draft your message. My scribes will copy and deliver it."

"Your scribes?"

"Yes, the state scribes."

Flavio stiffened at the blatant corruption. The Senate retained scribes to copy its statutes and court decisions for general distribution, not for personal use. But he couldn't afford sanctimony now. And those scribes would be useful when he became a councillor.

"Let me prepare something."

"Copies will take time. How do you intend to delay Niccolo?" His tone carried a sinister edge. Flavio wondered if perhaps this man had first suggested murdering his father. Or had it been Lucia, the strange foreigner?

"Let me worry about that."

"You need my assistance, not the other way around," Galli reminded him.

Flavio scoffed. "I'm captain of the guards, aren't I?" This time, the power he was abusing was his own, but he saw no way to avoid it. He had no private guards and would have to detain Niccolo long enough to finish settling the family's contracts in his favor.

Galli grinned and patted Flavio on the shoulder. "What message do you want to send?"

CHAPTER NINE

NICCOLO

ONLY ONE OF the next four visits succeeded. The family partners weren't short-sighted enough to deny him entry, of course. But their refusal to even discuss their contracts sent a clear message: Flavio had gotten to them first.

As the sun began to set, Niccolo had to content himself with Di Natali, the blacksmith who had melted down his dagger, and the two relationships his father had granted him so many years ago. Flavio couldn't deny him a true third of their father's interests, but he would keep only what he could defend. He'd have to survive on silk for the next few years.

The sun had almost completely set by the time he returned to his neighborhood. He had wanted time to think, but his decision to walk rather than call for a gondola stemmed from fresh concerns about money, not a desire for solitude.

A feud would be expensive, as would maintaining Pietro's network of informants. And then there was Pietro himself, who deserved to live well after so many years of service.

The streets were nearly vacant when a figure approached. Niccolo's eyes hadn't yet adjusted to the encroaching darkness, so he didn't recognize the man until he came upon him.

"Pietro!"

A foul odor accompanied the steward. He kept his back rigidly stiff, a sharp contrast to his slumping posture the last time they'd spoken out here. He motioned for silence, waving his hands downward, and pulled Niccolo into the shadow of a nearby building.

"What is it?" Niccolo asked.

"Four men came to the house. City guards, I think. They're waiting there for you now. They want to ask you some questions."

"Are they armed?"

"Clubs. No swords or knives."

If they were investigating the murder of Feratollo, each would have been armed with both sword and dagger. At least they didn't mean to kill him in the act of escaping, like Alberto Brattori.

"They let you leave the house?" They would surely assume Pietro would warn his master.

"I escaped through the water entrance." That explained the smell: dried canal water. "What do you want me to do?"

Niccolo thought for a moment. "Nothing. Let them think I'm still coming. I'll spend the night at Asparia's. Treat them like my closest friends. Open up a few bottles of my wine." His thoughts turned to the disappointing results of the day. "Not the good stuff, mind you—'

"Say no more."

"You better return before they notice you've gone." Niccolo halted the old man before he could leave. "Thank you, Pietro."

He kept to the shadows as he crept toward the Sabarellis, even though he doubted anyone else was seeking him. Only one man had been directly affected by what Niccolo had done today. Flavio was, after all, a captain of the guards and could assign his most loyal men to a private matter.

Perhaps, Niccolo thought as he crossed the bridge leading out of his neighborhood, his brother had found his kind, after all. Flavio was proving to be more akin to Celsi and Galli than his own brothers and father. How wrong Niccolo had been to ever admire him.

The disappointment Niccolo had felt not ten minutes prior vanished, replaced by grim determination. He would have to bring down the doge, eliminate Galli's influence, overcome his brother's resistance, and protect his family. And he still needed to deal with Madina.

Those were lofty ambitions for a man who couldn't even enter his own house.

NICCOLO

A very startled Giovanni answered the door wearing a robe and an infinitely complicated *chaperon* atop his head. "Nico, what are you doing out at this hour?"

"Can I come in?" He surveyed the houses to either side. The streets were deserted. It must be later than he thought.

Giovanni stepped aside and placed a hand on Niccolo's shoulder as he passed. Once he was in, his friend poked his head out for a quick look, then latched the door.

Asparia descended, hair flowing freely behind her. "Nico, what's wrong?"

"Guards came to my home while I was out, seeking to question me."

His friend accepted Niccolo's coat and draped it over a nearby chair while Asparia ducked into the kitchens. "About Umberto?" he asked.

Niccolo shook his head. "They had cudgels, not swords."

Easing himself onto the chair, he let out a long sigh. Some of the tension drifted away.

Giovanni cocked his head. "Then why?"

Asparia returned with a glass of wine. With a reassuring smile, she pressed it into Niccolo's hand and returned to her husband's side.

A single sniff told him it wasn't watered. He smiled his appreciation.

He needed something to refresh him at such a late hour. "Flavio wanted to detain me."

His sister drew in a breath. "Flavio?"

"Galli or Celsi would have sent men with swords. They wouldn't have cared what mess the guards made of me." He took a long swig of the wine. The liquid struck the bottom of his stomach with a jolt. "Why would he want you out of the way?" she asked.

"It might have something to do with my meetings today," he replied. "Father's silk weaver, our Veneto factor, a few his more prominent craftsmen. For all the good those last few were."

She gave a quick nod. "I suppose it was only a matter of time."

It wasn't the response he expected.

"Flavio said he would honor this alliance, and he was never one to make idle comments." She shook her head. "I figured he'd try something like this. He's so stubborn."

He finished the contents of his glass. Unwatered, it started to warm his belly almost immediately.

"What are you going to do?" Giovanni asked.

He tossed his free hand in the air. "I have no idea." He amended his comment a moment later. "Flavio can't deny me my fair share, but I'll have a hell of a fight on my hands before the ink's dry on the settlement."

"What about Marco?" Asparia asked.

"If he keeps his head down, he should be fine."

She pursed her lips. "Are you sure?"

"My brother just tried to have me arrested, 'Ria." He gave a slow shrug. "I'm improvising."

"Guards, but no swords." Giovanni thumped one fist into his open palm. "He means to stop you from talking to any other partners."

"Who else is there for you to woo?" Asparia asked. "You said you already talked to those in Venice."

"The ones abroad, love," Giovanni explained to her. "Remember how I said I'd soon have to make a tour myself?"

Niccolo straightened. "Wait, when?" If Giovanni left the city, he'd be on his own.

"Now that my father is gone, I need to visit Sabarelli interests, make a good impression. It may be the only time some of them ever personally meet me."

He had forgotten Giovanni had lost a father recently, too. "Of course. I'm sorry."

His friend smiled. "That you don't see me as a source of profit is why I hold you so dear, Niccolo. Don't apologize for it now."

"Why…" Niccolo's eyes widened. "My God. I've been so worried about *what* happened to Father that I didn't stop to consider *why*. At first, I thought Madina and Feratollo wanted vengeance. But why would Celsi want Father dead?" Niccolo chewed on his lip. "Celsi opposed a Venetian army. Father, a minor senator, won his cause. But the doge seemed upset at the result. A few days later, he killed Father." He shook his head. "The two events must be related."

Venetians didn't resort to murder; they had plenty of alternatives for disposing of someone. Duels. Legal actions. Galli could have reported Angelo for treason. Even a false charge would have required investigation, and with Galli as a councillor, it would probably have involved torture. Murder suggested haste and improvisation.

"What are you suggesting?" Giovanni leaned forward.

"If Celsi was angry at the result, that means he wanted Father to fail. He wanted an army." He shook his head at the implications. "He must have a plan for using it, one so important that he'd be willing to kill a senator."

An uncomfortable silence descended upon them.

Treason. The last time a doge had murdered men, Marino Faliero had attempted to kill all the senators and establish himself as a prince of Venice.

"What threat did my father pose to the doge…or his plans?" Niccolo rubbed his eyes. "I'm sorry, these questions are too serious for so late at night."

"They're good ones, though," Giovanni said. "But you're right, we shouldn't—"

A series of thundering knocks at the front door interrupted him. "Are you expecting anyone else?"

Giovanni shook his head.

The guards. Not finding Niccolo at home, they must have begun searching for him elsewhere. Naturally, Flavio would assume he'd visit Giovanni. He had brought danger upon those closest to him despite his efforts to keep to the shadows. Feeling his hip, he wished he'd carried a sword during the day's errands.

Asparia recovered first and rushed up the stairs with surprising deftness given her condition. From upstairs, she shouted, "Just a moment!"

Giovanni rose silently and ushered Niccolo to his feet. Following his brother-in-law, they crept down the hall, passing Asparia as she returned. She carried young Alessandro in the arm closest to him and an unsheathed sword in the other.

Remembering the coat, he tapped her shoulder and pointed to it, resting over the chair. Setting the sword behind the door, she grabbed the coat and flung it at him.

At the end of the hall, Giovanni felt around until he released a hidden latch. The wall opened to reveal a smuggler's hole. He waved Niccolo forward.

Giovanni had a smuggler's hole!

The space was cramped but empty except for the two of them. Giovanni squeezed himself in and felt for the latch on the inside before closing the panel and sealing them up.

The muffled sound of his sister's footsteps penetrated the hiding spot. With luck, he would be able to hear their words.

The latch sounded. For a moment, Niccolo entertained the brief hope that this was all a silly mistake. It could just be Pietro reporting that the guards had left.

But then he heard metal strike metal.

"Lady, we seek your brother, Senator Aretoli."

"I suspect he can be found in his bed, sir. I've not seen him today," Asparia said.

"We checked there already." The words came quickly, impatient as if he spoke to a petulant child.

"And what did his wife say?" she asked.

"What?" came the startled reply.

"Well, if you checked his bed, I suspect his wife noticed you, what with that armor and those cudgels." That bit would be for his and Giovanni's benefit. She had specifically excluded swords.

"Lady, I mean your brother Niccolo, not your brother Flavio." Whoever this man was, he knew the names of the members of House Aretoli. "He didn't arrive home tonight, and we have reason to believe he's here."

"What reason?"

"Good reason. Is he here?"

"He is not," she answered in the same calm voice. "He is with my husband. He did come some time ago, and they decided—against my wishes, I can assure you—to spend the night out. Where they are, I cannot tell, but I suspect I will not be speaking to my husband when he returns."

Behind him, Giovanni shifted. Niccolo repressed the urge to laugh. *You chose her.* He patted his friend on the shoulder.

"We'll check for ourselves, if you don't mind." His voice had begun to lose its confidence.

"You will do no such thing!"

"We have our orders, lady. Stand aside."

At the shouting, Young Alessandro began to cry. Niccolo heard no further voices, but neither did he hear the shuffling of leather boots and flexing armor. After a moment, the baby quieted again, and he realized Asparia must have been soothing him.

When she did speak, she used a tone even Niccolo hadn't heard her use before.

"I, Asparia Sabarelli, have told you they are not here. My husband's father was very nearly your doge. He and my husband have served this republic faithfully and have defended it with their lives. I don't care one bit about your orders. The day that the Sabarelli let the city guard into their home without so much as a statement of the reason will be followed by a great number of executions. You have upset my son, and now you will leave."

"My lady." His voice faltered. "We were told not to leave without Senator Aretoli."

"By whom?" Her voice began to tremble with her flaring temper. "And for what reason?"

Her question produced only silence. Niccolo could just imagine the guard squirming. Flavio had the sense, at least, to choose a man capable of discretion.

Asparia continued, "Scour the city's brothels. If you find my husband as you search for my brother, perhaps you'd tell him not to bother coming home tonight? Good evening, gentlemen."

The door slammed. A few moments later, Niccolo heard the faint click of the lock.

Giovanni pulled the latch to open the smuggler's hole. As the light from the candles in the hallway poured in, the sword in the hall crashed to the ground. Giovanni twisted and leaped out, his arms in front of him defensively.

No guards remained, only Asparia slouched against the wall, trembling uncontrollably. Taking baby Alessandro out of her arms, Giovanni handed him to Niccolo and settled down next to his wife, cradling her head. "Hush now, 'Ria, it's all over."

She didn't speak for some time. Giovanni held her close.

She had been brilliant. They may have pushed past a senator, but even the hardest of men would hesitate to shove aside a pregnant woman with a small child. Yet, she'd had still needed to convince them, and that couldn't have been easy.

Watching his friend soothing his sister, Niccolo realized that

Giovanni had suffered in his own way, hiding while his wife had handled the delicate situation.

One of his sister's maids took the child from Niccolo and retreated back upstairs.

Asparia seemed to have recovered herself with several deep breaths. She turned to face him. "That bought you some time. But I won't do that again, Niccolo."

"'Ria!" Giovanni gasped.

"No, dear. My first duty is to the Sabarelli now. I will not risk my child or home to protect you from our brother." Her eyes held sympathy, but also resolve. "I'll help where I can, but I won't risk that."

"Asparia's right," Niccolo said. Her young son could have been harmed if the guards had decided to barge in. "And I can't keep dodging city guards, either for my health or as a strategy." He fell silent, willing himself to say what he now knew in his heart. "Flavio is one of them now."

"What will you do?" she asked.

"I need my own money, free from Flavio's influence. A silk weaver and a blacksmith aren't enough. The doge and the councillor are both fabulously wealthy, and I'll need resources to get to them. I can use Pietro's people, but that will involve money for bribes and informants."

"Pietro's people?" Giovanni asked.

Tonight's events had frightened them enough to eliminate their doubts. He could trust them to the end now. "Pietro didn't just manage Father's household. He also managed his network of informants and agents. I'll know everything that happens, no matter where I am."

"No matter where you are?" Asparia's eyes narrowed.

"If I remain in the city, Flavio will keep trying to arrest me. I need to leave."

"Why don't you come with me when I tour my holdings?" Giovanni asked. "I can advance my timing. I could make some introductions to help you circumvent the usual Aretoli partners."

"What did I just say about keeping us out of this?" Asparia asked. "What if Flavio sends someone after him?"

"He wouldn't go that far," Giovanni dismissed.

"Would you put anything past him?"

Giovanni cradled his wife's hand. "Dear, Niccolo and I have a bond. We saved each other's lives on Crete. I value him as I value you." As she started to protest, he cut her off. "No, it's true, 'Ria. You are my wife, and I love you. But Niccolo is my brother in every way that matters. I have to help him."

The simple honesty left Niccolo speechless. Tears begin to sting in his eyes. Before they could fall, he pulled Giovanni into a tight embrace. It was the only thanks he could offer. Though it lasted only a moment, he would treasure that moment alongside his father's last words.

"Do you have to go now?" Asparia cradled her belly. "Can't you wait even a few weeks?"

"I can only help Nico by going now. And if I wait, I may miss the birth." He placed his hand over hers on her belly.

"That's not so important. It's not like you would be in the room anyways," she said.

"It's important to me to be nearby."

The couple shared a meaningful glance, and Niccolo had the distinct impression all Giovanni's compliments couldn't touch Asparia as much as that tender admission. It bothered him that he didn't understand why.

"Tell Marco and Camilla what happened here today," Asparia instructed Niccolo, breaking the spell of the moment. "They deserve to know blood isn't enough to protect them. Marco's a legitimate target, and Camilla's vulnerable while she's living in the house the doge purchased."

"I don't know how I could get a message through; any sympathetic servants came over with Pietro." Marco was still in Father's—Flavio's—house, and Camilla couldn't possibly have moved yet. Only because Pietro had arranged it had Niccolo been able to move into a new home so quickly; that, and his father's final gesture of generosity. "Perhaps Petrarch? I doubt Flavio would open a guest's letters."

"Didn't you hear?" Asparia raised her eyebrows. "Flavio already kicked Petrarch out."

"Surely not!"

"He couched his words, of course. He said his staff could hardly do justice to their honored guest with all the changes and suggested he would find more comfort renting a home."

"Did he offer to pay for this rental?"

She snorted. "Of course not."

That was it, then. "Ink and parchment?"

Asparia went to fetch some.

Giovanni shook his head. "It still surprises me that all of you know how to write so well." Giovanni's father had always felt writing was for scribes, not merchants. He could read and write, but not with anything resembling Asparia's ease.

"It still surprises me you were four the first time you visited Alexandria."

His friend chuckled. "Different priorities, I suppose."

Asparia returned with two pieces of parchment, an inkpot, and a quill. "I brought two so you can also write to Camilla."

"I'm not writing to Camilla."

"You must. She's completely beholden to Flavio. She needs to know."

He thought back to her reaction when he'd reported Flavio's agreement with the doge. "Flavio will try to stop me if he realizes I'm leaving. I don't trust Camilla or my ability to persuade her."

He dipped the pen in the ink and expertly drained the excess off on the inside of the jar. Giovanni watched with an expression mixing delight and studious attention. Grinning, Niccolo scrawled Petrarch's name in calligraphy and began to write.

"How will we leave the city?" He wrote the first few words as he spoke. Even Asparia hadn't learned that trick.

"I'll charter a galley," Giovanni offered. At this time of year, the majority of the city's galleys weren't needed for trade convoys, and the republic would rather be paid for private use than let them rot.

"They may be watching you as well."

"That seems a little paranoid, Nico," Asparia said.

"They came here, didn't they? Plus, I'm not sure I trust the integrity of a galley captain who ostensibly works for the doge."

"Point taken," Giovanni conceded. "What do you suggest?"

Niccolo put the finishing touches to the parchment and turned to his sister. "Sand?"

"It's upstairs, and I'm not going up there again," she said with a hint of annoyance. "Let the ink dry naturally."

He turned back to Giovanni. "Pietro can arrange passage so it doesn't look like we're involved."

Giovanni shrugged. "Then let's make you comfortable. I'll send someone to collect Pietro. It's probably best we sneak you out in case the guards are waiting nearby."

Knowing his next move reassured Niccolo. "It seems like forever since we've been able to plan strategy. I almost forgot how exciting it is."

"I know!" Giovanni chirped.

Asparia snorted. "Men."

NICCOLO

Marco received the letter through the very excited intermediary of Petrarch. Niccolo suspected his Italian guest didn't get much opportunity to participate in intrigues anymore, though the stories about him hinted at a raucous and exciting youth.

Flavio's actions had disturbed the youngest Aretoli. Niccolo would have spared him this desolation if he could, but poor Marco simply didn't know how to deal with a hostile Flavio. In the end, he had agreed—with some gentle prodding from Petrarch—to study painting abroad. The poet had enjoyed the paintings Marco had shared and offered to make some introductions to master painters. They would leave together the same time Niccolo did, without informing Flavio.

Pietro arranged passage on a sloop leaving Venice just before midnight. It wasn't the most luxurious vessel, but it would ferry them to Modone quickly. Niccolo had to hurry to settle his affairs in Venice and pack the essentials, including his records and the few pagan scrolls he had managed to smuggle out of his father's house.

After a lengthy debate with Pietro, he decided to take only three sets of clothing: a basic brown and green doublet for everyday use, his formal blue and silver doublet ensemble, and a shirt-and-pants combination for aboard ship. His father's coat would have to remain in Pietro's custody. He insisted on bringing his sword, dagger, and crossbow, but Pietro had talked him into bringing only three bolts.

"If you need more than that, you weren't listening to my training."

"What if we're attacked from two directions at once?"

He answered as if to a child. "Then you run."

"A Venetian doesn't run."

"Dead men keep their honor," Pietro said. "Venetian noblemen got where they are by surviving." And from that position, he would not budge.

With time fleeting, Niccolo begrudgingly agreed. He may have been a battle veteran, but Pietro was a veteran of the alley fight. The rules were different.

While the steward attended to his trunk, Niccolo surveyed the contents of his chest: copies of contracts, his ledgers, plenty of extra paper, and his woefully limited cache of gold coins. This trip would be expensive. Either it would succeed quickly or not at all.

"Did you already send that transfer note?" he asked Pietro over his shoulder.

"Two hundred ducats will be waiting for you in the bank in Modone. If you aren't back by the time the *fraterna* settles, I'll send what I can."

His father had funds in the banks throughout the city and republic.

Flavio couldn't short-change him on that money, but he could arrange for Niccolo's portion to be spread throughout Italy. It might delay receipt by as much as a month.

Leaning against his *tavola*, he kicked the lid of the chest closed. "When I'm gone, hold onto as much of my *fraterna* as you can. Di Natali shouldn't be a problem, but the others may not be as agreeable. Negotiate as necessary."

"I will." The look he gave Niccolo reminded him so much of Angelo. "Take care, young man."

"I'll be fine. I'll write to you weekly, and you do the same." He offered a faint smile.

They carefully strapped the trunk and chest into the waiting gondola and seated themselves beside them.

The pilot had extinguished the lantern that normally hung from a tall pole for evening trips, guiding his craft only by the little natural light tonight. Clouds concealed the moon. "Let me worry about navigating, sir," the gondolier reassured. True to his word, he charted a straight and smooth course.

Pietro insisted upon at least accompanying him to the ship. Had Niccolo let him, the old steward would have followed all the way to the Hellespont. But he needed Pietro to report on his enemies, be they Madina, Galli, Celsi...or even Aretoli.

Niccolo found himself worrying not about enemy senators but about this woman near the doge, this Lucia. She had made his brother incredibly uncomfortable, and that spoke to impressive training. Where was she from?

They glided up to the private dock at Giovanni's home, and some Sabarelli men reached out for both ends of the boat.

Giovanni was waiting for them a few feet back from the water. "We'll stow these with my crates." He gestured to the chest and trunk. "I'll have my men stamp my house seal on it."

The trunk didn't bother him, but Niccolo had carried the chest since Crete. It didn't feel right defacing it with someone else's seal. "I can shift things around so I don't need to take the chest." After a few moments, he tossed the bag of gold, the ledgers, and half of the papers into the trunk and moved the crossbow to the chest. He also left his sample contracts behind since he could recreate them as needed.

The old steward nodded. "I'll accompany the trunk to the ship. Can we leave this chest here for now?"

Nodding, Giovanni directed his servants to stow it in a locked compartment of the dock. Once they'd loaded Giovanni's luggage, Pietro departed on the gondola toward the ship to Modone waiting in port.

"Did you hear the news today?" Giovanni led Niccolo into the house.

"No, what?"

"Carrara sent another delegation. They formally presented themselves to the doge today."

"Celsi?" Senators weren't comfortable with ambassadors speaking directly with the doge without supervision, particularly ambassadors for that deceitful duke.

"Matteo Dandolo visited today"—he cracked a smile—"but was more interested in Asparia's opinion. She knows more about the happenings in the Senate than I do." Such was the nature of politics: the Dandolos had been adversaries two weeks earlier, but they were now allies concerning Padua.

"Are you certain Celsi met with them first? The Council of Ten didn't greet them separately?"

"Matteo's father is on the council but only heard of it when he saw their pennants hanging from a palace balcony." Few pennants raised more suspicion than those of Padua, one of the republic's most mischievous adversaries. Niccolo recalled the gossiping couple at Easter.

It seemed foolish for the doge to flaunt the Senate's prerogative so brazenly, though. Was Celsi feeling confident after having Angelo murdered, or was it something else? Had he taken Flavio's capitulation to be the general sentiment in the city?

Several lamps filled Giovanni's reception room with pale orange light. Marco and Petrarch were both dressed for travel. Asparia was offering advice on how to stow their luggage more efficiently. She would be lonely after they all left. Normally, she would have Rosalia, but that seemed unlikely after her oath never to speak to Flavio again. Asparia did not take oaths lightly.

Whereas Marco would have eagerly rushed over to greet him a few days ago, now he simply clasped Niccolo about the shoulders. "Niccolo."

He had seen that sort of reaction before on Crete, usually accompanied by a tense 'sir'. Perhaps the comparison was apt, after all. He had become the commander of this little group.

"Marco."

"I was just telling Asparia. Camilla's gone. She moved into the house the doge purchased for her this morning."

"That didn't take long, did it? I didn't even know it was ready yet."

"It wasn't," Asparia said.

"I hope Flavio assigned a servant to keep an eye on her," Niccolo added.

"What do you mean?" Marco asked.

"A young, beautiful woman with a tendency toward drama living by herself? I can imagine all sorts of trouble, particularly if a dashing young man swoops by."

Marco glanced from brother to sister, shocked at the implication, but Asparia merely looked thoughtful.

Niccolo added, "And speaking of dashing, you cut quite the figure in a traveler's cloak, don't you?"

Indeed, the cloak filled out Marco's frame. He looked as if he were born to travel. Niccolo envisioned his brother and the poet adventuring across Europe, living by his brush and palette. Just a week ago, Marco had proposed the very thing to avoid a senatorial fate. Niccolo had opposed it then, but the situation had changed. The further away Marco was, the less he would be blamed for Niccolo's actions.

Marco beamed at the compliment. "Master Petrarch suggested a thick cloak, but since I don't have one, I had to borrow one of his."

"My thickest one, actually." Petrarch's voice piped with excitement. He was enjoying this. "In this cloak, I was welcomed into Naples as a conquering hero."

"When was this?" Marco caressed the fabric.

"Now, now, Master Petrarch, you know better than to expend your best tales before the journey begins," Niccolo said.

The poet, evidently aware he was being deflected, offered a wry grin.

Niccolo turned to his brother. "I expect you to become a brilliant artist."

"I'll do my best." They clasped each other's shoulders. "Take care of yourself, Niccolo."

"I will."

"I wish you didn't have to leave."

He squeezed his brother's shoulder once more. "I need to know why Celsi and Galli consented to our father's death. They had no special reason to hate him. It had to be part of some deeper purpose." Doges simply did not have men killed, not after Faliero. "But discovering what that might be will take money to buy men and information, and Flavio will almost certainly try to stop me. I'll look for Alvero in the East, but I'll also be setting up revenue outside my brother's influence."

"I can't believe it's come to this," he muttered.

"I felt the same way before Flavio tried to have me dragged into a holding cell."

Marco glanced away, but only for a moment.

Good man. "Please have a care for your safety."

Petrarch inserted, "I won't let anything happen to him, Senator Aretoli."

Niccolo smiled his thanks.

Asparia approached with crossed arms. "And you'll keep my husband safe, yes?"

"I promise." He smiled warmly until another thought came to him. "You'll have the hardest time of it, 'Ria. Marco and I will be out of the city, but you'll have to face awkward questions and act like nothing's wrong."

She stared hard at her brother, but after last night's events, she didn't object. "I'll do my part, and I'll write if anything important happens."

She then turned away from him and to her husband. "My love."

"I know." He kissed her forehead. "I promise I'll bring you a gift."

"No…" She rose onto her tiptoes. "I only want you back in one piece, understand me?" She kissed his lips, and he cradled her in an affectionate embrace. Abruptly, she pulled back and met his gaze. "But since you mention it, bring me back something unique."

Niccolo barked out a laugh that continued until the gondola arrived.

NICCOLO

Niccolo tried to burn the image of the canals of Venice into his mind during the ride to the port. "This may be the last time I ever see the city."

"Do you think it'll come to that?" Giovanni kept his gaze on the water sloshing into the boat. The unskilled gondolier kept jerking the vessel back and forth, letting a little more in each time. With each splash, Giovanni recoiled and pulled his cloak higher to keep it dry.

Niccolo shrugged. "It's possible. That's why I don't want the rest of you making yourselves targets."

"There are some things worth taking risks for, and friendship is one of them."

Niccolo squeezed his friend's shoulder. "I just don't want you to suffer the consequences if I fail."

Someone was waving his arms wildly in the air nearly three *ria* down the canal.

Pietro.

"Gondolier, berth near that man."

"Eh?"

Niccolo gestured to the waving arms in front of them.

"I'll have to cut it pretty hard."

"Do it!"

The man had been leading them at a good speed, expecting to have the time to slow before berthing. Quickly, he plunged his oar into the water on the left, forcing the gondola to turn toward shore. The aft began to creep forward, tilting the fore backward. He reversed the maneuver, straightening them out again much closer to the shore. He repeated the motion a few times, spilling their speed while maintaining their orientation.

Giovanni muttered a curse as water sloshed onto his boots. He instinctively jumped to his feet.

"Down in front!" The gondolier again swapped his oar from port to starboard.

Pietro stopped waving once he realized they had seen him. He grabbed the rope when the gondolier threw it to him. The ship pulled to a halt with a jolt as the slack tightened.

"I hope you had a good reason for flagging us down." The gondolier waved his oar angrily at the old man.

Pietro glared at him with his characteristic, unflinching gaze. Under the scrutiny, the gondolier subsided and seated himself.

"What is it?" Niccolo asked.

"The port is crawling with city guards, at least three units, all armed with swords. They say it's normal security, but they're definitely guarding your ship."

"How do you know?" Giovanni asked.

Pietro grinned. "I know."

Giovanni turned to Niccolo. "Swords."

"It must be Galli."

"Or the doge." He had hoped Flavio's attempt to catch him would be the only resistance he faced, but men with swords meant only one thing. Someone else—probably the doge—wanted him dead, just as he'd killed the assassin. This was no longer a trip to secure his finances; he was now fleeing for his life.

He couldn't return to Venice until he'd found a way to deal with them, or at least until enough time passed that they wouldn't risk blatant abuse of their authority to harm him.

Niccolo swallowed. "We need another way out of the city. Pietro, did they let you load our trunks, or did they stop you?"

He shook his head. "They didn't even question me."

"Good, good."

"Do you want me to retrieve them?"

"Not, but I do need you to go back." He lowered his voice so the gondolier couldn't overhear. "If they ask, tell them I'm face-down in someone's lap at one of the brothels. Say Gio can't get me up. Act annoyed, angry even. Say you have to cancel our transport, but once on board, tell the captain to take the trunks to Modone and deposit them in the merchant's bank owned by House Roscini."

"What about us?" Giovanni asked.

He eyed the gondola. "The salt workers go out at night, don't they?"

Giovanni shrugged. "The lagoon's too busy with fishermen and ships during the day. It's the only time they can sift through the... Oh, no, no, no." He waved his hands at Niccolo. "Hiding in the salt barges? Nico, this is a new cloak."

"Then it needs breaking in," he grinned.

"Not by smearing it with salt. I'm not made of money."

"Yes, you are!" He laughed. "You'll be fine."

"What will you do when you reach the mainland?" Pietro asked.

Where could he go, if his ultimate destination was Modone? One of his father's last letters mentioned a large number of soldiers near Padua, probably putting down another rebellion against Carrara rule. Niccolo didn't want to risk becoming a prisoner with only Flavio to ransom him. That left to the north—the wrong direction—or east. "Trieste. I have a contact there who might help."

Pietro nodded. "Then you better hurry. I'll arrange everything for you on Modone. You'll be a little late?"

"A week, probably." He turned to a sulking Giovanni, who was petting his cloak. "Are you still with me?"

Grumbling, he raised his hands in surrender. "Of course I am, damn it." He pointed at Niccolo. "But you'll buy me a new cloak, or I'll use some of the money I set aside for 'Ria's gift and send her to you for an explanation."

NICCOLO

When the salt barge pulled up to the mainland, Niccolo and Giovanni headed for a small building where dispatch riders could exchange their exhausted horses for fresh ones to continue their journey. A quick flash of his senatorial ring saw them properly outfitted with a pair of exquisite animals, tack, and dried rations for three days. If the Senate did nothing further for him, at least it could provide a good mount as compensation for his hardships.

Trieste lay on a patch of dirt on a peninsula that jutted into the gulf of the same name, where Venetian Istria met Italy. It had resisted efforts at Venetian annexation for nearly two centuries, so the doge likely wouldn't have spies in the city. Yet the many Venetian ex-patriots nonetheless gave it a familiar feel.

Niccolo knocked on a carved oak door in a district that featured fine torches affixed to high poles every hundred feet. As he waited for a response, a few people in brightly colored cotton and silk strolled down the street in either direction.

Streets. They reminded him of Candia.

The latch clicked, and the door opened a sliver. Inside, a young woman studied them. When her gaze rested on Niccolo's waist, her hazel eyes widened.

Embarrassed, he glanced down to find his silk tunic poking out from beneath his riding cloak.

"May I help you?" Her voice had a lovely lyrical quality to it.

"I am Niccolo Aretoli." He lifted the hand bearing his senatorial ring closer for her inspection. "I and my colleague have journeyed from Venice. I should like to speak with Guild Master Salvatore Neretti."

The woman studied him with the quick eyes of youth. What he could see of her skin seemed smooth and fair, far too delicate to belong to a slave or servant.

"One moment." She latched the door again.

Giovanni grunted. "Do you know this man well?"

He hadn't expected this kind of reception. "They've dealt with my family for years. Perhaps they've had recent robberies."

Giovanni scrubbed at the crusted salt and dried mud sticking to his cloak. "I don't blame her for being cautious."

"We do look fairly disreputable, don't we?"

"Please come in."

Niccolo hadn't heard the door open.

Their hostess was, indeed, a young woman, perhaps sixteen or seventeen, wearing a modest brown skirt and a bodice that rose much higher than the fashion in Venice. The style told him nothing of her station, which could be anything from the mistress of the house to the daughter of a free servant.

"I thank you for your hospitality," he replied.

"May I take your cloaks?" she asked after leading them into the reception room.

Giovanni quickly removed his. "Yes, thank you."

A few crumbs of dried dirt flaked to the floor as Niccolo removed his. "I'm afraid we've been traveling all day."

"If you don't object, I can have the servants beat them clean."

She wasn't a servant, then. Niccolo bowed his head. "Yes, thank you."

She jutted her chin forward. "If you'll wait in the salon, the guild master will be with you shortly." She offered a deep curtsey and marched off, draping the two cloaks over an arm and holding them at a distance.

As she departed, Niccolo noted the tell-tale signs of sophistication in the way she glided across the floor.

"Nico, look at this." Giovanni was studying a tapestry occupying the far wall.

He circled his friend for a better look. The panorama told the story of some sort of gathering. "You need to help me here, Gio. I'm the wrong Aretoli for an art assessment."

"Look what it's made of."

He leaned in for a closer look. The softness of the edge surprised him. He searched for the unique signs of the thread. "It can't be." Surprised, he moved to another spot on the tapestry, this time closer to the center. He found the same slight imperfections—but, oh, so few. "It's silk."

"It is indeed," a voice behind them confirmed.

Niccolo turned to see a man of around fifty with beady eyes and a short crop of gray hair. A large leather belt kept closed a robe of brown silk. Far from offended at his guests fingering his tapestry, he was grinning.

"Surely it's not pure silk," Giovanni said.

The man ran his hand over the material. "If not, I vastly overpaid."

"How is that possible? This is high-grade material, fit for kings and dukes. I could understand using low-grade—"

The guild master shook his head. "Low-grade was too thick. The pattern looked blotchy."

Niccolo gasped. "You mean to say you tried this design once before?" The staggering cost left him reeling. "I've never seen anything like it."

Neretti bowed, concealing a blush that told Niccolo much about their host. "Thank you, sir." He licked his lips. "Might I inquire as to which of you is Niccolo Aretoli?"

"I am."

He studied Niccolo for a time. "You have the look of your father in your eyes. I remember his negotiating skill well." The ambiguous phrasing did not reveal whether he knew Angelo had died.

Niccolo knew little of Salvatore Neretti other than what he'd just learned: he'd rather spend a considerable fortune on a high-grade silk tapestry than on expanding his business. Niccolo's father had never indicated the man had such wealth, though. If the Aretoli had a relationship with someone like Neretti, why did they need to keep the Cornaros solvent? "This is my brother-in-law, Giovanni Sabarelli, son of Emmanuel Sabarelli."

At mention of the name, Neretti offered an even deeper bow. "We were all saddened to hear of your father's passing, Signor Sabarelli. We remember his friendship during the last war."

Giovanni inclined his head again. "My father understood the delicate position of Trieste. If we didn't assist you, the Hungarians would have used you to stage attacks against us."

Neretti smiled in agreement. "What brings you so far from Venice, young Aretoli?"

His broad smile reminded Niccolo too much of Galli.

"I thought you would have heard. My father died recently."

Neretti opened his mouth in mock surprise, but the reaction didn't reach his eyes. He had already known. "I'm sorry to hear that. Signor Aretoli was a good man. He will be missed by many." As he spoke, his stony expression gave way to genuine regret. He hadn't wanted to reveal his knowledge of Angelo's death, but he genuinely mourned the loss. What did that mean?

"My daughter did not say the reason for your visit."

So, she was his daughter. She looked nothing like him; her mother must have been beautiful.

"You had a relationship with my father for years. I'd like to discuss us continuing it."

"I see." Neretti pressed his lips together. "Have you secured lodgings in Trieste yet?"

"We've only just arrived." In fact, they'd already booked passage on a Roman galley leaving the next morning, but the guild master didn't need to know that. Until Niccolo knew this man's intentions, he would reveal only what was necessary.

"Then you must stay here." He raised his chin. "We have the finest venison this side of the Adriatic."

NICCOLO

Neretti's servants set to work carrying heated water upstairs for Niccolo's use and bringing his clothes downstairs for a good scrubbing. Because of the distance involved, the water was only lukewarm by the time Niccolo submerged himself. He thanked them for their effort, nonetheless. Warm or hot, even offered by a man who concealed something, the water would wash away the grime of the long ride.

Even so, he kept his sword by the basin.

The water tickled his skin at the surface. He closed his eyes, letting the strain of three days of riding drift away with the grime.

When he opened them, Neretti's daughter stood above him. She had changed out of the tight bodice from before and into a flowing saffron garment thin enough to expose the contours of her nipples beneath, far thinner than was appropriate for entertaining a guest.

What was she doing in his chamber? He couldn't decide whether he should abandon the basin to cover himself or whether the water provided enough concealment. If he cried out, a servant would jump to conclusions about his nakedness and her presence.

"Can I help you?" he finally asked.

"Do you intend to ask my father for my hand?"

"What?"

"Did you come here to marry me?" she repeated.

"Where did you hear that?"

"The servants said your friend asked questions about me." Her words carried a tinge of pride. "Well?"

Damn Giovanni for his meddling! "My brother-in-law, not I, asked after you."

She tilted her head slightly. "Brother-in-law?"

"He's married to my sister."

"Ah, but *you* aren't married." She arched an eyebrow.

"No."

She lowered her gaze to the water, studying his body beneath it. "Do you normally interrupt your father's guests while they bathe?" She returned her attention to his face, but he held it only tenuously. "No." Her reply carried no remorse. "I've never had a suitor before. I was curious. I wanted to know what's so wrong with you."

"Wrong with me?"

"You must have some defect for my father to forbid me from coming to dinner tonight."

The back of his neck tingled, and not only because of the water dripping from his hair. A Venetian senator, particularly one who had just gained his inheritance, could protect against the day when Venice would again tried to seize the city. He doubted the master of the Trieste tailor's guild was so provincial as to think Flavio stood to inherit everything. Niccolo was assuredly among the finest possible matches for his daughter. Why would he reject the prospect? The possibilities were worrying.

But she was studying him intensely again. "You seem healthy enough. Is there something wrong..." She gestured toward the water.

"How would your father know one way or another?" Did young girls feel like objects for sale when their fathers decided on their marriages, too?

She frowned. "Are you poor?"

Patience fraying, he sought some way to end this interrogation before the servants returned with his clothing. Every second brought the chance of discovery.

Swallowing his embarrassment, he rose out of the basin. The breeze suddenly felt so much colder on his exposed skin. The tingling beginning in his groin brought a wave of panic. He wasn't ready to educate her on how everything worked.

Her lip quivered a little as she stared.

He twisted down to retrieve the robe folded nearby. By the time he turned back, she had gone, leaving the door open.

Reflecting on the conversation only increased his unease. When one of the servants entered a moment later with Niccolo's clean clothes, Niccolo instructed, "Please tell my companion I'd like a word with him."

Giovanni entered a few minutes later. "Niccolo, what is it?"

"I'm not sure, but we may have a problem."

NICCOLO

"Not only are you improperly dressed, but you're armed?" The steward's voice squeaked. "This is highly irregular!"

Niccolo rolled his eyes and continued down the stairs. His sword banged against the man's leg as he maneuvered past. "Men of rank have the honor of bearing arms in every court in Europe. I will do so here. As to my attire, I have no other clothing with me. And I would imagine a senator of Venice should be received gracefully regardless of how he's dressed. Is this not so?"

The steward licked his lips and looked helplessly down the stairs before bowing. "My apologies, signor."

The man's intransigence only deepened Niccolo's suspicions following his conversation with Neretti's daughter. Wearing their swords and riding cloaks might not have been the overreaction Giovanni believed. Niccolo had been betrayed too often recently not to prepare for the worst.

Giovanni was already in the dining hall. As the steward led Niccolo in, he announced, "I'm afraid Lady Magda will not attend tonight. She sends her warmest regards."

"A great pity." Giovanni's voice lacked his usual enthusiasm.

Neretti entered a moment later with outstretched arms and a broad smile. "Ah, I see my servants helped with your clothing. Good,

good." He chose not to mention that they looked prepared for the march. "Gustav, are we prepared?" His voice held an odd inflection.

The steward bowed. "Yes, Master. We shall be enjoying two courses,"—he dipped his head forward slightly at the number—"then the main course, then a pastry dessert, if that meets with your approval."

Niccolo judged the phrasing an odd way to describe a four-course meal.

"Excellent, excellent. Let us begin without delay." He gestured for Niccolo to assume the seat opposite him. "I suspect a hearty meal will lift our guests' spirits after their long journey."

"A good suggestion, Father."

Magda stood in the doorway. She had changed into a rich blue and red brocade gown with at least two underskirts since Niccolo had last seen her.

"I apologize for keeping everyone waiting."

Neretti's smile didn't reach his eyes. "I thought you weren't feeling well." He leaned toward her. "Shouldn't you be resting?"

"I feel quite well now." She pressed her lips together with a petulance that almost made Niccolo chuckle. She raised an eyebrow as she studied the fit of his clothing.

"You do us honor." Niccolo grinned openly at her brashness.

"Gustav," she said, "please tell the cook we will be one more for dinner."

As the steward left, Neretti pinned his daughter with a well-targeted scowl that Niccolo only noticed because he expected it.

Grandly, Niccolo slid her chair out for her. "My lady."

"Signor Aretoli." Her reaction carried the perfect measure of formality to convince anyone watching that she hadn't seen him naked less than an hour ago.

Neretti clapped his hands twice. Servants entered with plates of mixed greens, lentils, shaved onion, and tomatoes covered with olive oil. Niccolo waited until Neretti and his daughter began eating to taste some himself. After those fateful apple slices, he would carefully choose the food he ate going forward.

"This is a fine selection of vegetables," Giovanni said. "Do you sell such produce, as well?"

"No, my fortune rests in cloth."

Niccolo tried the lentils, which tasted bland. "Do you employ both weavers and tailors or do you simply craft the clothing?"

"Both." Neretti seemed to have more interest in food than conversation.

Niccolo frowned. "Do you also sell my father's cloth to your competitors?"

"Sometimes, yes." Over the rim of his glass, his gaze darted toward the doorway.

Niccolo looked questioningly at Giovanni. This was wrong. How could he convince Niccolo into offering better terms if he didn't talk up his importance? "I recently received a large quantity of silk. I'd like to offer you the first opportunity to purchase it."

The guild master waved his hand limply. "Let's not disrupt this fine meal with business."

The Aretoli partners in Venice had treated him the same way after Flavio had contacted them.

"Business is my purpose today, Master Neretti. With my father's recent death, I wish to re-affirm his contracts. I'm even prepared to extend them."

Neretti clapped his hands. The servants returned and removed the greens and lentils, replacing them with fresh plates containing clams. "Unfortunately, I recently signed a separate contract to provide for all my cloth needs, including silk. Only yesterday, in fact."

Niccolo's mind worked furiously. If he had already decided to end the partnership, why had he pretended not to know of Angelo's death? Why welcome Niccolo at all?

Few men could offer Venetian silk, and Angelo Aretoli had always been fair with his partners. He had intentionally structured his contracts so none but an Aretoli could offer equal value.

Eyes widening, Niccolo understood.

Catching Giovanni's attention, Niccolo set his left hand on the table and made a gesture for danger.

The steward had complained about them being armed and emphasized the first two courses, the second of which had already been served.

"May I compliment you, Master Neretti, on the beauty of your daughter?"

Neretti offered a strained smile. "Thank you, sir."

"Is she betrothed?" Niccolo feigned interest in the clams, forcing himself not to retch at the taste.

Neretti frowned. "Not presently."

"I suspect she has many suitors?"

"None at present, sir."

Cocking his head, Niccolo wiped his hands on the tablecloth. The juice from the clams had removed the oil from the first course. "If I told you I fell instantly in love with your daughter, would you consider my suit?"

Both Salvatore and Magda Neretti stopped eating and stared at him.

It was a cruel thing to do to the poor girl, but he needed to confirm his suspicions.

Neretti took a long swallow from his goblet and winced at the strength. Niccolo was thankful he hadn't touched his. "Pardon me?"

"Would you consent to my marrying your daughter?"

"This is quite sudden, Signor. I'm afraid it's out of the question."

"I'm an unmarried senator of Venice who has inherited a third of my father's *fraterna*, generating more than enough income to keep your daughter in a manner befitting her station. Why is it out of the question?"

"We would have to assess your suitability and confirm that all you say is true. That would take time."

"You said it's out of the question, not that it would take time. Why do you dismiss me out of hand?"

"It was a poor word choice."

"But you would consider my proposal?"

"Of course, Signor Aretoli."

"Then why did you forbid your daughter from attending tonight's dinner?"

Panic registered in the man's expression.

Giovanni nodded to indicate he saw it too.

Good. He understood my signal. Niccolo again wiped his hands on the tablecloth and slowly slid his chair back.

Niccolo turned to Magda. "I have an answer to your question from earlier, my lady. I apologize for my method of revealing it. You see, your father doesn't believe I'll be able to offer you anything after tonight."

Her gaze darted from father to suitor. "What do you mean?"

A galley could have brought a message from Venice in only a couple of hours. Flavio had reacted swiftly after learning about Di Natali; with the help of his new allies, he wouldn't have to limit his warnings to only his domestic partners. They could all be compromised.

Niccolo should have never come here.

"Your father and my deceitful brother are in collusion. Before I even arrived, he decided to betray me. He has also probably ordered my arrest."

Her father raised his hands to clap again. The end of the second course.

"Think before you unleash this in your own house!" Niccolo cried. "You offered us hospitality. You're about to violate that pledge."

Neretti glared at his daughter. "You had to defy me, didn't you?" He turned to Niccolo. "Your brother told me how you undermined him. He already offered me a steep discount on cloth. How much more will he give me when I return you to him?"

Niccolo would have clarified that he hadn't taken more than his share and that he did find Magda intriguing. Before he could do either, Neretti clapped his hands.

A pair of men burst through the rear door. Three more poured through the main archway, cutting off escape from that direction. Whirling out of their chairs, Giovanni and Niccolo stood back-to-back, their swords and daggers in their hands before their feet settled. Assessing their chances, Niccolo concluded there were probably too many of them.

Neretti stood and shuffled back against the far wall behind his chair, but Magda froze in place. Desperate, Niccolo grabbed her and pulled her toward him. Neretti cried out in protest but didn't move.

"I have no choice," he whispered to her.

The armed men began to advance.

"Stop where you are!" He held his sword in front of her neck with one hand and pressed her close to him with the other. He gestured to the corner with his head. "Over there. Move!"

They stopped and looked to Neretti for guidance before shuffling away from the main archway.

"Gio?" Niccolo asked over his shoulder.

"I'm here." He came up beside Niccolo, close to their exit. "I hope you understand, but I'm never dining with you again. It always ends in a quarrel."

"Fair enough." He inclined his head to the mercenaries. "Back off or the girl dies. I mean it."

She whimpered, and Niccolo squeezed her gently to reassure her.

"No, you don't." Neretti approached along the wall.

"Excuse me?"

"If you meant it, you would have slashed her dress or nicked her throat. But even if you had, I'd never believe a son of Angelo Aretoli could harm an innocent woman."

"How do I know she's innocent?" Niccolo asked. "She could be part of your treachery."

"A girl whose only mistake was disobeying her father?"

The men advanced slowly.

"Can you take that chance?"

They halted.

"Attack him," Neretti commanded.

Muttering a curse, Niccolo released the girl and rushed for Giovanni and the door as the attackers charged, slashing as the opportunity presented itself. Neretti reached out for him as he passed, but Niccolo ducked beneath his grasp.

As a consequence, the nearest mercenary's stab missed Niccolo but buried itself in Neretti's chest just below where Niccolo's head had been. The guild master screamed once before crumpling forward. His chin collided with the mercenary's knee in an audible crack that sent both of them tumbling in a heap.

The others halted as they saw their employer fall. Magda rushed over to cradle her father as he fell unconscious. But Salvatore Neretti's two guests were long gone, slipping into the concealing shadows of the darkening night.

NICCOLO

Their ship wouldn't be leaving for several hours yet, and remaining at the docks was far too risky. If the doge had thrown his support behind Flavio's letter, Trieste's guards would be locking down the city and searching all ships. Instead, Niccolo and Giovanni circled back to observe Neretti's house from a nearby stable.

A man who carried himself with the self-importance of a physician had entered almost immediately. A few minutes later, the servants emerged with a body.

"Neretti." Niccolo shook his head. "This was poorly done."

Giovanni patted him on the shoulder. "Would you rather one of us was on that litter?"

They continued to watch, but as time passed, no one else came or raised a general alarm. Perhaps Neretti had acted on his own initiative.

Niccolo had begun to relax when a thump sounded in a stall

behind them. He started to rise to soothe a restless horse when it happened again. And again.

Gesturing for Giovanni to circle around the other side, Niccolo leaned out for a closer look. Someone in a green velvet cloak, obviously of high quality, was preparing a mount. The figure moved like a woman, but he couldn't be certain in the dim light of a single lantern. He shuffled closer for a better look, and his feet scuffed against the straw littering the ground.

The figure turned at the sound. "Who is it?" a woman's voice asked.

"I might ask the same," Giovanni answered from the far side of the stable.

Niccolo wanted to risk a peek but feared that Giovanni's response hadn't drawn her full attention.

"Your voice sounds familiar," she said.

The additional words allowed Niccolo to identify her. "Magda?"

"How do you know my name?"

Wincing, he clenched his fists in frustration from behind the stall door. He shouldn't have said anything, but the damage had been done. If she feared robbers, she would call the watch. He had to speak to her, to try to allay her fears.

Taking a deep breath, Niccolo rose and stepped into the open.

She gasped but did not scream. Instead, she lowered her hood and met his gaze. "Niccolo Aretoli." Her voice contained neither bitterness nor friendship. "I'm surprised to find you here after the welcome you received last time."

"It seemed the best place to gauge how much danger we face." The light painted her in a yellow glow. Her eyes showed no puffiness from crying. "How is your father?"

"My father is dead."

"I'm very sorry." Though he attempted sympathy, his words rang hollow. The snake deserved his fate for betraying them.

"You damn well should be," she cried. "You used me as a shield and put a sword to my neck."

Glancing over at Giovanni, Niccolo saw the same look of befuddlement. "I thought you'd be angry about your father."

She crossed her arms. "He ordered his men to attack even though it could have killed me."

"I was the one holding the sword."

"Only because he tried to kill you." She tilted her head. "You knew what he had planned, didn't you?"

"How did you—"

"You were armed." She frowned. "Why did you stay?"

He sighed. "I didn't realize the true danger until we were eating. I never imagined how far my brother would go."

"I found a letter from your brother among my father's things. I wanted to see for myself what caused this." She took a step forward. "Your brother claims you violated the terms of your father's will. Did you?"

She could still call the guards. Niccolo stepped further into the light of her lantern so she could see his face. "In Venice, all sons share equally in an inheritance. I knew my brother would try to cut me out. So, I approached some of our partners before the formal division to protect my share." When she didn't respond, he said, "The doge and his men murdered my father. My brother allied with them. I stood against them."

"And, because of that, your brother involved my father in a family squabble that got him killed."

She had assessed the situation as his father might have. The comparison sent a chill up his spine.

"I'm sorry."

Sighing, she lowered her head enough to conceal it from the light. When she raised it again, her expression had softened. "What's done is done. At least I won't be used by anyone anymore." Her expression brightened. "I'm his sole heir, after all."

When his father had died, Niccolo hadn't understood how someone could be pleased by a parent's death. Here was that someone.

And yet, he could not blame her. Neretti had risked his own daughter's life; what other wrongs had he inflicted on her over the years?

"But…" Giovanni stepped forward. "Don't you worry about being ruined or exploited?"

She turned to face him. Though Niccolo couldn't see her expression, he saw his friend stiffen. "My father was a powerful guild master, but a terrible tailor and businessman. Who do you think oversees the workers?"

Niccolo asked, "But why the charade? Women can be craftsmen."

"Guild masters must practice their trade."

Her years of hard work had allowed her father to keep his position. For Neretti to discard her so casually now must have been intolerable.

"What will you do now?"

"I will do whatever I wish." She folded her arms, smiling. "And marry whomever I choose."

He shook his head. "I meant about my brother and me."

"Dealing with the Aretoli in any capacity seems to be unwise."

Niccolo nodded slowly. The family had lost a profitable partner, but at least he wouldn't have to flee Trieste as a fugitive.

As he turned to leave, Magda asked, "Did you mean what you said about being a suitor?"

The question hinted at a loneliness Niccolo could appreciate. But as a foreigner, she could never be his wife; their children could never join the Senate.

"If only it could be."

Two hours later, standing on the deck of the galley heading toward Modone under full sail, Niccolo imagined a life in which he had stayed in Trieste with Magda. He could have enjoyed a happy, quiet peace, close enough to keep in touch with his family without being bound to a murderous doge.

Had he made a mistake in leaving Magda alone in that dark barn? What was he sailing toward now? He was leaving behind everything he had ever cared for: his family, his country, and his position. Even Rosalia. It was all gone. With Magda, he could have built a new life.

Venice was lost to him, and the open ocean waves brought with them only uncertainty.

NICCOLO

During the next four days at sea, Giovanni befriended several of the sailors by losing a small fortune to them at dice. "It's always good to have some muscle on your side," he later explained. "Especially the way our luck's been going."

Niccolo couldn't argue with that assessment. Every town with an Aretoli partner might hold a potential ambush like in Trieste. He would have to avoid not only his brother but every contact his father had ever made for fear they might betray him.

Worst was the damage Flavio was doing to Aretoli credibility by using family partners to hunt him down. It was yet another of his brother's short-sighted decisions. As much as he didn't want to dwell on it, he could focus on nothing else.

At least in Modone, the Aretoli had no connections.

Ideally situated at the foot of the Peloponnese, the island welcomed ships sailing under any flag, including the smugglers and pirates who sailed under none. Venetians, protected in their fast ships, would accept payment from anyone seeking resupply or relief from pursuit.

The captain maneuvered neatly into a berth in the old town. As he descended the gangplank, Giovanni waved goodbye to his new friends. The sailors' winnings would let them afford a better class of women. One openly wept at the departure of such a bad gambler.

Niccolo and Giovanni walked the short distance to House Roscini's bank. The clerk eyed them suspiciously when they announced who they were, only confirming he had their crates when Giovanni presented his signet. Niccolo collected the two hundred ducats Pietro had arranged and a pair of letters from home. He read the longest one first, following Giovanni silently as his friend headed off to arrange the last leg of their voyage. A few words caught his attention, and he slowed his reading to absorb them fully:

> *The appointments occurred yesterday. Galli had to give up his seat as a councillor, of course, but Celsi immediately named him Avogadori of the Lagoon. A few in the Senate protested, saying only it had the authority to grant such an appointment, but they still accepted it. If only your father were alive, it wouldn't have passed.*

If his father were alive, Niccolo thought, a great many things wouldn't have happened. And, if wishes were horses, all men would ride.

Niccolo saw Giovanni's cloak sway as he turned a corner, so he obediently followed. They were backtracking toward the docks, cutting down a thin street jutting off along the waterline. The area contained several warehouses, some of which had private loading docks.

"Are we in the right place?"

"We can't use Venetians, so we have to go with someone else." Giovanni led them into a shipping office.

Niccolo nodded and returned to his letter.

> *Worth noting, none of the other councillors received new positions. I've never heard of some of the men who received appointments. I've attached a list. You may recognize more than I do.*

Studying the list, Niccolo had to agree with his steward. All the names came from new families, and quite a few disgraced ones at that. The Colezzi sons, for instance, had served as *condottiere* for Hungary against the republic during the last war.

> *Perhaps most surprising was the Council of Ten. The doge may have promised Flavio a position, but he evidently didn't*

mean this year. When they posted the rolls, you can imagine my
surprise to see his name missing.

Niccolo gave a cry of shock that interrupted Giovanni as he was
haggling with the ship owner. "My brother didn't get it!"

"What?"

"He isn't on the council," Niccolo said. "Listen to this: *Flavio spent*
all of yesterday trying to gain entrance to the ducal palace and then only
stayed for ten minutes. From the way he shoved a beggar out of his way
when he left, he wasn't pleased by his audience." Grinning, he lowered
the paper. "Serves the *pisello* right."

He looked up, inhaling a deep breath of the fresh sea air. He could
almost imagine the look on his brother's face when Celsi didn't deliver
his end of the bargain. Did the doge have someone more important
to pay off?

After refolding the letter, he turned his attention to the other one.
This paper was much thinner and bore his family seal, smudged and
hastily applied. It was from Marco.

His good humor faltered as he read the opening lines:

If you're reading this letter, my man reached a boat without
being intercepted. I couldn't escape the city, but neither were we
captured. Petrarch is bedridden and very near death, but Gian
Jacopo hopes he may yet recover.

Niccolo cursed softly. Yet if Marco could still access paper, at
least he was safe. He continued reading while Giovanni shook the
clerk's hand.

We almost escaped by boat, but a patrol intercepted us
and demanded that we submit to a search. Not knowing their
intentions, we jumped overboard and waded to shore. Half an
hour into our journey, Petrarch fell off his horse. He was as cold

HOUSE ARETOLI | 213

*as fresh snow and had a dangerous fever. I needed Gian Jacopo,
so we had to return home. Damn him for giving me his cloak!*
   *Flavio was more stunned than angry. He asked me why I
left in the middle of the night. He said Petrarch's death would
be my fault.*
   *Please, Niccolo, find some way to end this quickly. Too many
people have already been harmed.*

   He lowered the paper. *What do you think I'm trying to do?* Closing
his eyes, he took a few calming breaths. Marco wasn't really blaming
him, only voicing the frustration they all shared. First, Flavio had made
the family seem powerless, then he had lost them an ally in Neretti,
and now this.
   Of course, Flavio was worried about his future, not Petrarch's life.
It wouldn't do for a senator and prospective member of the Council of
Ten to have a great diplomat die under his inattentive eye.
   He folded the letter. They were back on the street again.
   Giovanni was studying him carefully. "Is it bad?"
   Sighing, Niccolo summarized the contents of Marco's letter.
"When are we leaving for Negroponte?"
   "There's a ship this afternoon, but I wanted to introduce you
to some of my contacts here first. I booked passage for a galley in
three days."
   Flavio's influence had reached Trieste, and Niccolo could almost
feel his brother's allies at his heels. While they could buy goods in
Modone, what he really needed was a market for Di Natale's silk. And
at Negroponte, he might catch Alvero.
   "Do you have any business here?"
   Giovanni shook his head. "I visited last year. That should cover
me for a while."
   "Then let's book today's galley. I need to end this before it gets
out of hand." He raised the letter and shook it. "At least more than
it already is."

214 | K.M. BUTLER

"Are you sure? The ship today is older, not quite as fast," Giovanni warned. A true Venetian, he only trusted vessels produced in the Arsenal.

Pirates were always a risk, but Flavio's influence was proving to be a greater one. What had Virgil written? *Fortune favors the bold.*

"We have to risk it. The sooner I return home, the better."

CHAPTER TEN

NICCOLO

WHEN THEIR CART reached the docks, the galley was already pulling away from its berth. The ship's owner had accompanied them and waved for the dockhands to re-tie the tow lines. They worked quickly, expertly knotting the ropes to the cleats as the ship's momentum pulled them taut. The hull groaned under the tension as the vessel came to a halt, then slowly drifted back toward the pier.

The captain ducked his head over the side. "What the hell?" Upon recognizing the owner, he limited himself to an angry glare and ordered his crew to help the men on the pier.

As Niccolo boarded, he shouted, "I appreciate your waiting for us, captain. If your men can stow our things, I'd like to repay them with a crate of wine. Let's consider it an advance payment for a speedy journey."

A cheer rose up as some of the crewmen repeated Niccolo's words to their friends. Satisfied, the captain slapped Niccolo on the back and craned his neck toward the owner. "Have any more like this for me?"

"I hope not," the owner shouted back, "or I'll have to fire the lot of you as drunkards!"

An hour later, they were sailing straight and true down the Greek coast. The voyage to Negroponte would take three days. The city sat along the trade routes to the east that would allow Niccolo to rebuild his fortunes, blessedly free of Flavio's influence.

He had made the first leg of this course before but had never been at leisure to really study the land they passed. The distant hills and cliffs were no more beautiful than the Veneto, but they were unknown. That fact alone exhilarated him.

The galley began rounding the Peloponnese at Cerigo early the next morning. Even from this distance, Niccolo could identify the lions of St. Mark on ships in the port. Billowing black smoke rose from a galley with a broken mast, an obvious victim of pirates. But it had reached port, probably due to its three rows of oars. Gnawing his lip, Niccolo hoped his own vessel's two rows would be enough.

Once they reached the open sea, the mood lightened. Ships faced a much higher risk of ambush closer to shore. Finding a ship in the vastness of the Mediterranean was much harder.

That second night, a pair of lanterns fore and aft provided the only break in the perfect darkness of the wide sea. The captain circulated Niccolo's wine, and the crew shouted themselves hoarse with celebration. Joining in a hopping dance he didn't know and whose name he couldn't remember, Niccolo let go of his tension. With a few of the officers, he drank to every god and saint they could name, forgetting no deity who might influence their journey.

Giovanni deferred with a look of practiced piety, causing Niccolo to laugh anew.

The next morning, a mild fog lingered. The captain insisted it didn't pose a hazard to navigation, and it lifted after an hour.

A little past noon, one of the crew noticed a silhouette following them in the distance.

The mood aboard darkened. Rowers took their seats. The crew checked and double-checked the rigging. At the captain's nod, the officers armed themselves, and the crew placed bundled crossbow bolts along the outer railing.

Niccolo, affixing his own sword belt, joined the captain as he watched their pursuer from the aft observation deck. "Well?"

"A sail two miles back. It rides high in the water." The captain rubbed his whiskered chin apprehensively.

"What does that mean?"

The officers shared a knowing glance but said nothing.

"It means one of two things," the captain said. "It could be going east without cargo for sale. That's not likely unless the ship's owner is a fool."

"Why's that?" The republic itself owned all Venetian galleys. He knew nothing about the business of shipping, only the merchants' costs.

"Putting a galley to sea is expensive. You want to sell goods at both ends."

"And the other possibility?"

"They're keeping their hold empty for our cargo."

"Pirates?" He had no sort of luck at all. "What do we do?"

"We row. If that doesn't work, we fight."

"Is that wise?" Giovanni had slid up during the conversation. "Won't we simply anger them by resisting?"

"Most raiders back off if you show some spirit," the captain said.

"Most?" Giovanni swallowed.

"Some decide to kill everyone. Others only dismember a few and let the rest spread the tale." The captain rang the bell at the front of the aft deck, the hollow sound of metal-on-metal signaling the crew to ready the ship for battle.

The other vessel had a shorter hull and a more pronounced keel. As it came within a mile, the most prominent difference became visible: an additional mast built into the deck. Naval warfare relied on maneuverability. An extra sail would give them a huge advantage.

The captain whistled. "That's not from any shipyard I know. He must have built it himself. We're dealing with a dangerous one here."

"Why do you say that?"

"Only a successful pirate has carpenters and shipwrights to build a custom ship." He ran his tongue along his teeth. "Not good."

The captain broke out the oars to augment wind power with sheer muscle. Even Niccolo and Giovanni took their turns. Despite their efforts, though, they only succeeded in keeping pace. The captain called off the labor after a few shifts to conserve his crew's strength.

Still, the pursuers raised no signal flags. That alone confirmed their intentions.

In the early afternoon, the trailing vessel unfurled its final sail and began its approach. The captain shouted for the men to come to attention as the pirate ship swung far to port, then swerved to starboard at a frightening speed. They were showing off.

Niccolo had sorely misjudged them. As the ship swung behind them, they lobbed what looked like small bottles of wine in a graceful arc at the galley. The first few harmlessly struck the water in their wake.

"What the devil?" the captain muttered.

They timed the second wave better. This volley sailed toward the upper deck. A fuse burned at one end. The first bottle slammed into the deck, sending liquid fire racing across the surface.

"Get down!"

The crew scuttled back from the blaze, staring in terror at the prospect of fire at sea. Abandoning their crossbows, they reached for anything that might douse the flames. Screams mixed with the acrid smell of burning oil.

Niccolo grabbed a nearby broom and rushed to the closest conflagration. "Stop it before it catches the wood!"

The crew set to work behind him as he brushed the oil over the side. After a couple passes, the broom itself caught fire. He flung it into the sea when the flames began to climb the shaft.

Someone shouted, "Move!"

He ducked and rolled forward, narrowly avoiding a bottle flying toward his head. When it struck where he'd been standing, it shattered in a spray of glass and burning oil.

"Niccolo!" Giovanni shouted with urgency but not panic.

He raced toward his brother-in-law, dodging sailors trying to clean up the burning mess. In several places, the flames had bitten in and burned hot. Before too long, the fire would be unstoppable.

"Look." Giovanni pointed over the aft railing.

Burning oil clung to a half dozen patches of the outer hull. The vessel would soon start to take on water. The pirates could sit back and let the flames finish the job for them.

The captain was fighting the flames alongside his crew. A few more bottles collided with the deck. Every second, the situation grew worse.

Niccolo had an idea. "Captain, forget the deck. Your aft quarter is on fire. We need to bank hard at full speed."

"Are you mad? We'll capsize!"

"If you don't, the flames will sink us."

The captain flicked his gaze from the aft quarter to the mid-deck. His crewmen were busily putting out the fires and hadn't fired a single crossbow bolt. What would happen if their attackers paired arrows with those bottles?

He pushed the pilot aside. "All hands, brace!"

The crew continued fighting the fires until the last possible moment. Only when the captain heaved his full weight into the rudder post and the ship groaned under the stress did they halt their efforts. The sudden shift in direction sent a few men careening into the starboard railing.

Giovanni grunted in distress as he started to lose his grip.

"Gio!"

Niccolo let go of the bell stand, sliding forward just as the wood slipped out of his friend's grasp. Grabbing hold of a railing, Niccolo extended his right foot. Giovanni clamped down on Niccolo's ankle. The force of the added weight wrenched Niccolo's shoulders, but his grip held.

The galley's bow kicked sharply to the left, forcing it headlong into a rush of water. A wave curled up and over the deck, slamming down and pummeling the ship just as the deck began to pitch forward with the ship's momentum. A hundred tons of wood collided with thousands of gallons of water in a colossal crack that prevented the ship from capsizing.

Niccolo rushed to survey the side again. He saw smoke but no orange flames.

It had worked.

"Starboard." Giovanni pointed to their attacker. The pirates had overshot but were circling back around.

"They didn't ram us," Niccolo said, surprised.

"Of course not." The captain rested against the rudder post, panting. "They want to capture us."

The other ship began a graceful arc to position itself behind them, but the captain turned as well, causing the two ships to circle each other warily. They were temporarily safe, but the merchantman fell behind the faster aggressor a little more with each rotation.

Instead of continuing their attack, the pirates hoisted a white flag that floated boldly in the breeze.

The captain met the gazes of his officers for a long while before finally nodding. A few of the men began to furl the sails.

The pirates steered themselves closer, and a man with a wrapped headscarf and a scar along his cheek stood at the railing of the aft deck. He cupped his hands and shouted in a surprisingly clear voice, "My captain congratulates you on your thrilling maneuver. It would be a shame to waste the lives of such skilled men. Surrender and he will spare you. Do it not, and we'll butcher you all."

The lack of a preamble made the simple statement all the more terrible.

"Just try it," the first mate shouted.

"Silence!" the captain demanded.

"It's too late," Giovanni warned.

The speaker stepped down to consult with some other men.

"You've killed us all!" The ship's carpenter brought his fist down on the first mate's cheek with a dull thud.

The captain and the rest of the officers separated them, albeit reluctantly. The first mate was bleeding from the nose and a cut below his eye by the time the furor died down.

When the pirate spoke again, it sounded eerily like a shouted sigh. He had the oratorical skill of a seasoned senator. "Think carefully. We have gallons of oil and can sink you without ever boarding. Enough of your cargo will float to turn a profit. This is your last chance." He stepped down again, replaced by several pirates carrying glass spheres in both hands.

"We must surrender," Niccolo said.

"Shut your mouth," the first mate grumbled. "You're not a part of this crew."

"If this ship goes down, I'll be just as dead as the rest of you, but I'll have paid for the privilege," Niccolo retorted.

"He's lying," the first mate cried. "He'll kill us all if we surrender."

"He can do that now with those bottles. They can throw them faster than we can put them out." Niccolo folded his arms. "Even if they ransom us, at least we're alive for another day."

The captain remained silent, darting his gaze from the blackened scorching of the deck to his exhausted men and finally to the pirates lining the railing of their ship.

Niccolo prayed he saw sense. They may kill a few pirates, but these sailors weren't a proper Venetian crew. They wouldn't be in this mess if they were.

"Strike the colors," the captain commanded.

The pirates cheered as they recognized the motions of surrender. Several grappling hooks sailed across and started bringing the ships together.

When they closed the distance, the pirates laid down gangplanks and began to pour across. A few archers positioned to the fore and aft provided surety against second thoughts.

Giovanni gestured for Niccolo to remove his sword belt as the marauders started to take up positions along the perimeter.

On the closest gangplank, a broad man with the smug, confident walk of a conqueror approached. "An unfortunate day to be on the seas, my good fellows."

Behind him, two pirates rushed to the rudder post and wedged it in place with large pieces of wood.

The broad man crossed his thick arms and jutted his chin forward as he boarded. The whiskers of his thick, coal-gray beard muffled the words a little as he spoke. "I am Captain Bolando Colmiera—Bolando the Brutal—and you are my prisoners."

His men shouted themselves hoarse and glared at the prisoners. A few sailors cowered under the noise, but the performance actually calmed Niccolo. One didn't take the time to intimidate dead men.

"Signor Col—" the merchant captain began.

The pirate raised a finger. "Captain Colmiera."

"My apologies, sir. Captain Colmiera. I only ask you to spare my crew," the captain said. "If you must kill someone, kill me."

The pirates started to whistle and stomp against the deck.

Colmiera simply widened his grin. "We've got ourselves a hero."

That set them off again, cheering and rapping their weapons on of railings, the deck, and the small shields some of them carried.

The pirate chuckled. "A captain who's willing to die for his men. I can respect that. What are you carrying?"

The captain bit his lip. Niccolo hoped he would answer honestly. "Half a hold of wool."

"And my men could use some new breeches. What perfect timing." He barked a laugh. "What else?"

"A few casks of wine."

"Looks to be a good night tonight, boys!" As they laughed, he asked, "What kind?"

The captain frowned. "Something from Tuscany, but I don't know the vintage."

Colmiera shrugged. "What else?"

"Nothing but the personal possessions of a few passengers."

"Passengers?" His eyebrows rose. "Anyone worth a ducat?"

"Captain Colmiera…" Niccolo approached with head bowed. He spread his arms out before him to show he was unarmed. If this man wanted theater, Niccolo would happily provide it. "May I address you, sir?"

Colmiera eyed him curiously, but the smile didn't fade. "Speak!"

"I hope you know what you're doing," Giovanni muttered.

Niccolo took another step forward. "First, let me congratulate you on the ease of your capture. You left us with no choice but to surrender or face a watery death." He suspected they would have stopped short of sinking the ship. Air could escape from a cargo hold more easily than casks of ruined goods. The salvage probably wouldn't outweigh the costs of those burning bottles. "All this, without risk of injury to even one of your men. I salute your skill, captain."

Niccolo eyed the other pirates as he bowed to his captor. Yes, they were listening. The more he could raise Colmiera in their estimation, the more receptive the man might be.

A measure of appreciation had crept into Colmiera's eyes. "If you think to sway me with fine words, lad, you'd do well to save them for your maker."

Having handled more than a few negotiations, Niccolo had expected this approach. "My intention is not to plea, sir. To do so would imply your decisions could be easily swayed. Our fate lies entirely in your hands. But skill is skill."

The captain pressed his lips together, a gesture that would have been difficult for anyone to see who wasn't directly facing him. "What's your name?"

"I am Niccolo Aretoli, merchant and senator of Venice."

The pirates fell silent. Men of position fetched a fine ransom.

"The passenger, eh?"

Niccolo bowed his head again.

"Niccolo Aretoli?" The captain tapped his finger on a tooth. "The same from Crete?"

Had he killed someone dear to this man on campaign, or had his reputation preceded him? All of Europe knew what had transpired on Crete, but he hadn't expected his name to be as well known among this company. Colmiera didn't look Cretan, and the Cretans hadn't used ships during the revolt. A lie could doom them, but telling the truth still carried risk.

"The same."

Colmiera nodded slowly. "Most senators don't announce their rank to pirates. It tends to lengthen their stay with us."

"I imagine most men desire to escape as quickly as possible."

"And, what, you plan to join my crew?" He barked another laugh. A few of his men joined him.

"That's not quite what I had in mind. But I do think you and your men could profit by hearing what I have to say." That brought forth a few murmurs from both the pirates and the captive sailors. "Might we speak in private?"

The captain ran his gaze up and down his prisoner. Colmiera was too large for Niccolo to overcome without a weapon. He hesitated for only a moment before shrugging. "Load the cargo, boys. I want everything buttoned up when I get back."

"Cap'n," one of the men asked, "What 'bout them?" He gestured to the prisoners being herded toward the front of the ship.

"As our friend here said, maybe I plan to tip them over the side, or maybe I'll let them live for surrendering." He glared at Niccolo. "If you waste my time, son, you'll find I can be swayed by your words, after all."

Niccolo followed the captain underneath the aft deck to the galley captain's private quarters. As Colmiera shut the door, Niccolo heard the pirates break into the cargo hold.

Colmiera swept his gaze over the room's contents before facing Niccolo and crossing his arms. Alone with the man, Niccolo could tell the captain was much younger than he seemed, but time had etched itself into the pirate's oft-burned skin and the crisscrossing scars that could only have been accumulated by multiple battles. He wore a dark red silk tunic left open at the chest with a baldric carrying a long, sharply curved scimitar that jutted out behind him as he walked. The silk seemed to be for show, though. Where it mattered, Colmiera preferred efficiency. His boots offered stable footing without adornment, thick gloves protected his hands from errant cuts, and the thick, plain breeches guarded his legs and thighs.

Colmiera began, "I may not be a captain in the Venetian fleet, but I understand the point of that grand speech." He paused, and his mouth folded into a smile. "As much as it pains me to admit it, I don't think it'll hurt your chances of a fair hearing."

"I meant what I said. Dukes and knights may call your tactics cowardice, but you're talking to a Venetian. It was brilliant."

The man chuckled and shook his head. "Venetians. You exist somewhere between nobles and thugs. I don't know whether to admire or hate you."

"I'll take that as a compliment."

"Take it as you like." Colmiera shrugged. "So, Senator Aretoli, why are we chatting?"

"House Aretoli is a merchant house. My father was respected but not wealthy. He was murdered just about two weeks ago now." He quickly recounted his father's death and Flavio's betrayal.

"Sad tale, but why should I care?" Colmiera asked before Niccolo could finish.

"One of the murderers, named Alvero Madina, left with a full cargo hold. I know where he's going. I'd be happy to tell you where he'll be, provided he doesn't survive the trip."

"So you want me to kill this man for you? In exchange for the cargo of that ship?"

"Exactly."

"Another senator, this one?"

Niccolo nodded.

Colmiera rubbed his beard. "I'm not some hired thug to do a senator's bidding. I'm my own man."

"I'd do it myself, but I can't reach that ship without you."

"You?" He studied Niccolo. "You don't have the look of a killer."

"I've done my share on Crete…and for less reason than this."

Colmiera shrugged. "It's one thing to slay a man in battle. It's anonymous. You don't have time to think. It's quite different to hunt a man down."

"Do you doubt I'm capable of it?" Niccolo asked.

"I'm only interested in whether you'll change your mind after I've committed resources to the act."

Would this man ever report this conversation to the Senate? Niccolo would have to take the risk to secure his cooperation and possibly their lives. "I've already executed another conspirator with my own two hands."

Colmiera's mouth fell open.

"He murdered my father."

"My father was murdered, too. He was a drunken lout who probably deserved it. You don't see me hunting down the man who did it."

"My father wasn't. I swore *vendetta* against those responsible."

"Now that"—Colmiera pointed a finger at him—"I understand."

"You recognized my name from Crete," Niccolo said. "Are you Cretan?"

"Hell, no." Colmiera spat on the floor. "Born and raised in Naples. But I knew a few of the men your Senate hired to sort out that mess."

Niccolo exhaled, pleased he wasn't facing lingering resentment. "Then you know about my reputation during the amnesty."

Colmiera crossed to the other side of the room. "And, what, you're a man of your word?" He sighed. "It seems to me you aren't the determining factor in this negotiation."

"What do you mean?"

Colmiera uncrossed his arms, dropping his hand to his sword. "What's to prevent me from ransoming you anyways? I wager a senator would fetch a few bags of ducats."

The hair on the back of Niccolo's neck stood up. "Who would pay?"

"You must have friends somewhere. No man is hated by everyone."

Niccolo smirked, tossing out the first of his lies. "Who? My brother decided it would be easier to work with the doge than oppose him. I'm an embarrassment and a liability. They wouldn't pay a ducat to see me again."

"And friends?"

He couldn't risk this man discovering that Giovanni was also a senator. "My lifelong friend sold me out to the doge for my old position on Crete." He shook his head. "I didn't find that one out until I very nearly walked into a dockyard full of guards."

"Ouch," Colmiera muttered. "What about the doge himself?"

Niccolo stiffened. "He'd probably pay. A day later, I'd be dead."

"But I'd be richer for the effort," Colmiera noted. "And I'd have an ally in the doge."

He pounced on the opportunity. "Trust me, Lorenzo Celsi is one man you don't want as an ally. My father died for the privilege." Suddenly, he thought of something else. "Besides, if he's willing to kill one of his senators, what would he do to a pirate with knowledge of his crimes? Very likely the only payment you'd get is the Venetian fleet bearing down on you."

Colmiera grinned. "So I may." He stroked his beard. "Tell me about this ship."

Though his pulse began to settle, Niccolo refused to let himself relax. He still had a long way to go in this negotiation. "It's a fully loaded Venetian galley. You can be certain it'll be worth the effort."

"Well, that settles it, doesn't it? My ship can't take down a Venetian galley." He gestured behind him. "She isn't fast enough, even with my extra sail."

"I can show you how. I know where our ships anchor, how they're defended, and where they're vulnerable."

"Venetian ships aren't vulnerable," he replied with more skepticism than before.

"Anything is vulnerable if you know where to strike."

"How do you take one down, then?" His voice sounded a little too eager.

"We can discuss that after we come to an agreement."

Colmiera flashed a grin. "If we take this ship, we'll plunder it. That's not negotiable."

Niccolo shrugged. "Of course."

"So we have an agreement?" Colmiera ventured. "This senator dies—I'll enjoy that—and you tell me how to take down Venetian galleys."

"I do have some conditions."

"Conditions!" He barked a laugh and grinned again. "Like what?"

"Obviously, no one dies today. Let the crew go on its way."

"Obviously." The speed of his assent suggested he had already intended to release them.

"Second, my friend and I can keep our goods."

He narrowed his eyes. "How much do you have?"

"A couple of crates with some clothes and papers, a little coin. No valuables, though. You can inspect them to confirm it."

He thought for a moment. "Agreed."

"Third, no one dies on the other galley except Alvero Madina."

"That's not up to me, now, is it?" Colmiera asked. "I won't ask my men to start a fight if they can't defend themselves."

Niccolo brought his hand up to his forehead, rubbing at his hairline absently. Innocent sailors could die. Could he live with that on his conscience?

But Alvero had already cast a long shadow. He and Umberto had killed his father. That single action had already led to the deaths of Neretti and Alberto Brattori. All the Aretoli, their partners, workers—the list of those affected was endless. Eliminating Alvero was worth a few sailors' lives.

"So be it."

Colmiera stroked his beard again. "Not good enough. I need more."

Terrible possibilities flashed through his mind: subverting the city, helping kidnap someone's daughter for ransom, selling a few men into slavery. Where would he draw the line?

"What do you propose?"

Colmiera seated himself on the map table. "You're a merchant, yes?"

"I am," Niccolo confirmed.

Colmiera gestured to the door. "That ship is just one of my vessels. I've accumulated plunder for many years. Gold and coins are easy to move, but the rest is just sitting in our base. If I sold it, I'd get a fraction of its value. On the other hand, you"—he gestured to Niccolo—"You're respectable-like. You can sell it for its true value."

Niccolo blinked, surprised at the simple request. "How much are you talking about?"

Colmiera shrugged and began to rattle off a list. "Two thousand bolts of cloth, some cotton, some silk. Two or three hundred crates of wine, five or six hundred bags of salt and spices, a few hundred planks of cut wood, several tons of granite, iron tools, weapons, and a few hundred suits of chain mail—"

"Stop, stop!" This was his chance! Though, he'd have to be careful when selling any unique items that might attract too much attention. "That's worth several hundred thousand ducats."

"Ho!" the captain chirped. "I'm glad I kept it all."

"For that much work, though, I'll need a cut."

"You don't seem to understand your predicament, lad."

"We're not talking about dumping it all on the first merchant I find. I'll need to make contacts, negotiate terms, and hire dock workers. I'll have to devote all my time to your goods and won't be able to make any contacts of my own. You can't expect me to do that when I have a father to avenge unless I'm being compensated." He added, "Besides, if you're giving me a cut, you can be damned sure I'll get you the best price."

"So, you'd delay avenging your father for profit, eh?"

Niccolo swallowed a sharp retort. "*Vendetta* costs money."

Colmiera shrugged, seeming to accept that. "How big of a commission?"

Niccolo shrugged. He couldn't estimate this man's intelligence. "You would clear perhaps eighty percent of the final take."

"Twenty for you? I don't think so." He crossed his arms. "I'll part with ten, but no more."

"Ten won't cover my expenses," Niccolo lied. "And if you'd found anyone else willing to take the risk of moving such a quantity of stolen goods, you'd have already done it."

The grin that reached Colmiera's eyes admitted the truth of that insight. "Fifteen and not a ducat more."

Niccolo moved his lips absently as if considering the offer. Of course, his decision was clear. He could buy a palace with that large of a commission. And a dukedom. And an army. "We have a deal."

Colmiera offered his hand, and Niccolo shook it heartily. The pirate studied Niccolo curiously. "What made you think I'd even listen to you?"

Niccolo shrugged. "You gave us a second chance to surrender and did all you could to avoid hard fighting. You had to be a different sort of pirate. A savvy one." He smirked. "Then there was the theater."

Colmiera barked out a laugh and slapped him on the back with so much force that Niccolo needed a moment to recover. "I thought it was a bit much, though the boys enjoy seeing folk squirm."

"I think a few of the sailors pissed themselves. But it also showed me you're intelligent." He gestured back to the door. "Speaking of them, I don't want the captain or crew to know about our arrangement. They'd ask too many questions, and that would damage my credibility in Constantinople. We wouldn't clear nearly as much profit."

The pirate asked, "What about the man who whispered to you when you approached me?"

"You caught that?"

Colmiera smirked.

"You'll let the ship go?"

He nodded. "We'll slash their sails but leave them their spares. If we reward this ship for surrendering, we'll have an easier time with the next one."

"Bolando the Brutal?"

"I've had ships surrender on the name alone," he piped proudly. "Chances are, they've never actually dealt with me. The name makes them think twice before resisting."

"I'd prefer that my friend stays here, then. I swore I'd watch out for him, and if this galley we're going to hunt down resists, he could be injured."

"We'll have to bring his cargo with us. It'd raise questions if his are the only trunks left in the hold."

"Then we take it with us."

Colmiera rubbed his chin. "Hundreds of thousands, you say?"

"Perhaps more, depending on the quality of the goods you mentioned."

The pirate stepped past him. "Then we better put on a good show for your shipmates." With that, he flung open the door and pushed Niccolo roughly through. The sunlight stung Niccolo's eyes after the darkened room.

The pirates had separated Giovanni from the rest of the crew as they awaited the results of Niccolo's conversation with their captain. He approached Niccolo as Colmiera began to give orders.

"You alright?"

"Yes," Niccolo whispered. "I'm going. You stay."

"Like hell—"

"I made a deal." He clenched Giovanni's arm. "It keeps you safe and gives me a ship."

Giovanni straightened. "The crew?"

"Released. He wants me to sell for him."

"How much?"

Niccolo shrugged. "Hundreds of thousands."

A whistle of surprise. "Rate?"

"Fifteen." He grinned triumphantly.

"Jesus." Envy flashed in Giovanni's widened eyes.

Niccolo didn't share any more with his friend. While Giovanni would happily trade with the devil himself, attacking a Venetian galley was another matter entirely. But this was his chance, and he refused to let Alvero escape again.

Colmiera interrupted them. "Bolando the Brutal rewards those who surrender. You may keep your lives and ship." He pointed to Niccolo. "But this man tried to sway me with pretty words. I'll teach him the cost of such an insult. Perhaps enough of him will even survive to be ransomed."

The captain of the merchantman was conspicuously silent now that his crew was safe.

At a gesture, some of his men seized Niccolo and separated him from Giovanni. One of them, a barrel-chested man with a full beard like Colmiera, bound his hands behind him with a gaudy knot designed more for appearance than effectiveness. The man bore a vicious scar on the left side of his neck. How did a man get a cut like that without it killing him?

Niccolo met Giovanni's gaze once more to reassure him.

They pushed him forward toward the gangplank. Giovanni shouted something Niccolo couldn't hear over the chatter of the pirates. As the vessel pulled away, Niccolo searched for his friend's face on the receding deck but could not find it.

He would either see Giovanni again in Constantinople or not at all. At least his brother-in-law would be safe.

CHAPTER ELEVEN

NICCOLO

FROM THE ROUGH way the pirates pushed him aboard, Niccolo briefly wondered if they might burn the ship and ransom him anyways. But a quick look back revealed that the merchant sailors were already replacing the ruined sails.

A pair of pirates jostled him but continued chatting about their good fortune as if they hadn't noticed. He'd have to get used to rough treatment until his real worth became known. Even then, some of these men might not pass on the chance to abuse a senator, regardless of what he might earn them.

Seemingly forgotten, Niccolo waited out of the way beside the stairs to the aft deck. A few men stowed the gangplanks by the railings in small slots made for the purpose. Half a dozen others loosened the rigging ropes, letting the sails sway a little more with the wind.

Niccolo shielded his eyes with his hand and craned his neck to study the extra mast. They had built it directly into the hull of the same type of wood as the rest of the ship, not retrofitted from a different design. The main mast even sat further back than on a typical galley to make room for it. Eyeing the stairs leading into the ship, he wondered whether the design was as perfect below deck.

Next to those stairs, an older pirate taught a young boy the proper to store the flammable bottles. Evidently, even pirates took apprentices.

Curious, Niccolo crept closer for a better look. Each glass bottle bore a strip of cloth stuffed into the top. The poor-quality glass contained imperfections that would make it dangerously fragile when heated. The craftsmen of Murano would have discarded them as flawed, but the bottles would serve well enough to create a flaming mess.

"It's called naphtha," Colmiera's voice boomed behind him. "The Arabs use it all the time. We figured it'd scare the hell out of our targets."

"To say the least. Your victims have to put fires out instead of attacking you." Niccolo shrugged. "But it's risky. Throw too many and fire consumes the ship. Too few and it doesn't do its job."

Colmiera grinned. "I see you understand."

When he returned home, he'd have to recommend extra barrels of water on every galley. These bottles posed a grave threat, one a galley wouldn't recognize until the first volley came arcing toward it.

"You have a fine ship."

"The best in my fleet." Colmiera crowed. "Now that you've had a chance to look it over, do you still think we can take down a Venetian galley?"

The reference to Venetians attracted the attention of a few nearby sailors. Self-conscious, Niccolo lowered his voice. "It depends on how accurate your men are with those bottles."

A brawl further down the deck interrupted whatever answer Colmiera may have given. The man with the beard and the scar on his neck punched another pirate, a lanky man with long arms. He connected squarely in the jaw, but the other man absorbed the blow and sprung up holding a knife. He raked it across the bearded man's forearm, sending a few drops of blood splattering against the deck.

The men around them gasped and separated the combatants. The bearded man gawked at his wound. The lanky pirate adjusted his grip on his blade. He shifted his gaze to the knife and swallowed, eyes widening.

Everyone around them seemed to be waiting for something, but it looked to Niccolo as if the situation had been resolved.

"Why is everyone nervous?" Niccolo asked.

Instead of answering, Colmiera shrugged at the bearded man. "It's up to you, Tiepo."

Without hesitating, Tiepo nodded.

One of the other pirates removed the knife from the other man's hand while the others formed a ring around them.

Niccolo recognized the configuration. "You can't let this happen, Bolando."

The captain pinned him with a cold stare.

Niccolo realized his mistake immediately. He may be a business partner in private, but he couldn't question a captain on the deck of his ship. "I'm sorry." Niccolo bowed his head. "Forgive me."

The crew backed off to either side, clearing almost the entire deck. A few latecomers were emerging from hatches.

Colmiera thundered, "Tiepo, Rolando, you know our law. A challenge was made and accepted. If any man here witnesses the drawing of additional weapons, the offender will be tossed overboard."

To the aft, a redheaded pirate brought the weapons.

Colmiera whispered to Niccolo, "They were ready for violence when we attacked you, and the resolution left them unsatisfied. So, they turn on each other. Without order, they'll tear each other to pieces."

Niccolo sighed. "It's damned inconvenient."

The captain raised an eyebrow. "You understand this is a duel to the death, yes?"

"Of course. They can't appeal to a judge, and if you decide their fates, their friends will hate you." Niccolo gestured toward the masts. "But we're wasting wind."

"It won't wait until we adjust the sails and set course. I can't let this spread."

Niccolo sighed, hoping Alvero wouldn't slip away because of the delay.

In the clearing, the combatants armed themselves and tested their blades. Tiepo carried a curved scimitar, while the other man, this Rolando, held a sword similar to those Niccolo had used on Crete.

"Nice sword," Niccolo observed.

"Tiepo's gonna win because of that blade," Colmiera said.

It took Niccolo a moment to realize Colmiera was referring to the scimitar. It looked more like a long, curved knife than a sword.

"Begin!"

Rolando lunged with a straight thrust. Tiepo quickly rolled to the side, letting the movement carry through into a stroke with the scimitar that missed his opponent's arm but traced across his thigh. Instead of continuing his attack, Tiepo withdrew.

Rolando raised his guard again. His free hand went to this thigh briefly and came back bloody.

They made a few passes. Rolando jabbed hesitantly while Tiepo probed his opponent's defenses, approaching as if ready to commit but always backing off at the last moment.

After the fifth pass, Niccolo discerned Tiepo's strategy. The straight sword was meant for thrusting, but with the curved scimitar, Tiepo could deflect an attack at a more natural angle and bring his scimitar around faster. Rolando was tiring.

Tiepo approached again, and Rolando finally reacted with a hard, downward slash. Deflecting the blade to the outside with his scimitar, Tiepo continued the motion with a stroke that raked the other man's chest.

Rolando screamed and recoiled, but the blade had severed his pectoral muscles. His own sword fell from his hand with an echoing rattle. Tiepo spun again, converting the momentum into a lateral strike that slid across Rolando's throat with a sickening squirt.

Niccolo could hardly believe how quickly it had ended. Never before had he witnessed a fighter manipulate an opponent with such skill.

Colmiera's eyes danced in satisfaction. Rolando had drawn a knife on a fellow crewman. His death would be a reminder of the consequences of violating his rules.

One of the crew said a few words over the corpse while others wrapped it in rough wool. They bowed their heads for a few seconds before tipping him over the side.

"Right, lads." Colmiera clapped his hands. "Let's go find our next victim."

NICCOLO

Niccolo had been so impressed with Tiepo's performance that he asked for lessons in wielding the curved blade. He spent his mornings with Tiepo and sparred with the other pirates in the evenings. Slowly, their attitude toward Niccolo softened. They engaged him in conversation more as the days went on and even taught him about sailing. He found their honesty refreshing. It felt strange to speak without guarding his words as he needed to with fellow senators.

Niccolo had no trouble identifying the best spot for an ambush on the set of remarkably precise maps Colmiera had taken from a Turkish sloop some months prior. The ship hid in a small cove along Alvero's most likely route to Constantinople. Colmiera stationed a pair of his men on a rocky overlook with orders to light a signal fire the moment they saw a sail.

Niccolo taught them the tell-tale signs of a Venetian galley, from the wake it would cut in the water to the shape of the sails. Catching Alvero depended upon them distinguishing his vessel from other ships. Attacking the wrong one would send warnings up and down the coast, and it could cost Niccolo his chance to put an end to another of his father's assassins.

Two days later, Colmiera interrupted Niccolo's lessons to invite him to his cabin. Inside were two carved oak chairs and the long table holding the Turkish maps. The pirate gestured for him to sit.

Easing into the other chair, Colmiera rubbed his knee. It obviously pained him, but Niccolo had never seen him favor it in front of the crew. "How are the lessons going?" he asked.

Niccolo relaxed, enjoying the chance to enjoy one of the only two chairs aboard the ship. The simple pleasure of a comfortable chair seemed precious after a week at sea. "Tiepo is a good teacher, if a little unforgiving."

Colmiera grunted. "You'll thank him for it one day. He says you have a strong arm."

"I spent some time on Crete," Niccolo reminded him.

"Yes, but noblemen usually sit around and feast."

He smiled. "Not in a republic, they don't."

"I suppose your republic suffers from too much initiative rather than not enough, eh?"

Niccolo supposed that summarized his current problems all too well.

Colmiera rose and crossed to a cupboard along the far wall. "Wine?"

"Please."

Releasing a complicated latch, the captain retrieved a bottle and a pair of goblets from a cabinet filled with straw. At first, Niccolo suspected such precautions jealously protected the captain's possessions. Only when a plank creaked beneath him did he recall the hazards of living on the ship. Without careful stowing, one nasty squall would reduce the bottle to a scattering of dangerous shards.

Drinks poured, the pirate sat back down and raised his in a silent toast. Niccolo did the same and sipped the liquid. It was a good, refreshing batch.

Colmiera timed his question for when his guest's mouth was full. "Why are you here?"

Niccolo swallowed too much too quickly. His mouth rebelled, overwhelmed by the flavor. "Pardon?"

The pirate swept his hand across the cabin. "Why are you leading a pirate ship to take down one of your own country's galleys?"

Niccolo balanced his glass on his knee. "My brother's idea of protecting our family was to ally with the very men who murdered my father." He stared into his glass. "But I knew that if we didn't respond, other houses would harangue our partners and steal our contracts. No one wants a weak ally. Even our friends might try to profit from our fall. I need to safeguard my family."

Colmiera leaned forward. "That's not what you said when we met."

Niccolo smiled weakly. "No, it wasn't."

"You told me it was about vengeance."

"That's an answer most people would understand."

"Most men don't consider piracy and murder legitimate ways to protect their family."

Niccolo gestured toward the vessel carrying Alvero somewhere on the sea. "The doge put that ship at risk when he protected murderers."

"Regardless…" Colmiera took another sip. "My point still holds."

"I tried appealing to Venetian law."

"Really?" He sat up. "How so?"

"I presented evidence. The doge killed the witness and threatened me with slander."

Bolando whistled and then downed the rest of his wine in a long swallow. "Your republic is rotten."

Niccolo couldn't argue with that assessment. "If it won't give me the protection I need, I'll make my own justice."

The pirate attempted to maintain his stoicism, but a grin eventually crept across his lips. "I'm glad to hear that. I was worried you were a blood-soaked loon."

Niccolo barked a laugh, spitting a little of his drink into the space between them.

Colmiera's grin widened. "Look at it from my point of view. A senatorial captive tells me, 'I'd like to help you kill someone.' Then, when he witnesses a duel to the death, his response is, 'We're wasting wind.' And then, he starts taking lessons from my men." He gestured up and down Niccolo. "Perhaps you're in the market for a new career."

"Piracy?" Niccolo could hardly imagine himself sailing the seas, attacking fellow merchants as a career.

Then again, he was planning to do exactly that.

"The men are impressed with you. For all I knew, you could have been a threat to me."

Niccolo supposed it did look suspicious. "I'm surprised you didn't skewer me as a rival."

The pirate shrugged. "The boys elect their captain. Mind you, things like that duel between Tiepo and Rolando tend to get rid of the opposition. All the same, I'm glad I don't have to plan ways of killing you."

"Me too."

"Besides…" Colmiera grinned. "I need a merchant, not a maniac."

Niccolo studied him. "So, I pass your test?"

The pirate nodded. "Yes, but do you mind some advice from someone who knows about *vendetta*?"

Sobering, Niccolo leaned forward.

The captain did the same. "Remember why you declared it. One of those men is already dead, and another will join him soon. You'll need to decide when it's time to stop. You don't want to become the monster you're trying to protect your family from."

He swallowed. "I'll remember that."

Colmiera rose and patted him on the shoulder. "See that you do." He crossed to a chest in the corner and rummaged through its contents. "Mind you, I only want to make sure you'll be able to honor your end of our deal. I've got something here to help with that." With a chirp of satisfaction, he withdrew a jeweled scimitar. "I took this off a Turkish captain. He reminded me much of you, actually. He didn't get spitting mad until I took this."

Colmiera presented an ivory hilt with sapphires encrusted on either side. Niccolo spent a moment admiring the craftsmanship of the slightly curved pommel. Wrapping his hand around it, Niccolo immediately felt the purpose. The sapphires, the shape, and the knob at the end all anchored his grip. It felt comfortable and well-balanced in his hand.

The sheath was made of well-sanded and lacquered wood. But the blade… The mottled pattern of Damascus steel awed him like a jeweled hilt never could. He had no idea how Easterners made these legendary swords, but they kept remarkably sharp edges.

"Beautiful."

"It's yours."

Niccolo almost dropped it in surprise, but his hand found a solid grip on the hilt before it hit the floor. The swords he had carried on Crete had been utilitarian. This scimitar was a treasure.

The pirate shrugged and backed away. "I don't have much use for a sword like that, and it's too long for use on a galley."

Niccolo ran his finger along the graceful, even curve of the back of the blade. "Nonetheless, you have my thanks. I won't let you down."

Niccolo wouldn't have expected a promise given to a pirate and a rogue to mean so much, but keeping it was the least he could do to repay Colmiera's advice and generosity.

NICCOLO

During the next session with Tiepo, Niccolo threw out his shoulder in a grapple. That same morning, Colmiera's watch on the mainland signaled an approaching ship. Rubbing his injured arm, Niccolo feared being put below deck while the pirates ran amok raiding fellow Venetians.

He wiped his hands on his sailcloth breeches as the ship pulled out of the cove and bore down on the galley. The loose pants—along with the simple shirt and bandana—were demonstrations of the pirates' own good faith. A silken senator couldn't be seen on the deck of a pirate galley.

His fellow Venetians would call him a traitor for his impending actions. Niccolo raised his chin, defying their unspoken protests. His republic, whether in the person of the doge or in the system that had allowed Alvero and Umberto to murder his father, had betrayed him first.

They cruised out of the cove and into open water on a direct course for the galley. The extra sail narrowed the distance quickly. Hoping to surrender only a single pass before escaping as the pirates circled back, the galley turned its prow to face them.

Niccolo grinned. "I told you they'd do that."

"They certainly aren't cowards," Colmiera shouted down. "But don't start preening. We need to stop them first." He turned to his men. "Furl the sails. Take positions."

On the masts, men began to loosen the sails, but they didn't tie them up as they normally would. Two groups of pirates gathered on either side of the ship. Each man carried a pair of naphtha bottles. Another contingent waited under cover at the rear. Smoldering matches burned slowly at positions every few feet.

The galley's three banks of oars were still down, stroking quickly to build as much speed as possible before withdrawing them for the pass. The Venetians were making no mistakes.

Moving much slower now, the pirate ship drifted closer until they were near enough to see Venetian marines crawling along the galley, readying their crossbows. They were preparing to pass on the left, squeezing a little extra speed out of their oars.

Colmiera shouted, "Now!"

At the command, the pirates tightened the sheets. The wind catapulted the ship forward in a sudden burst of speed. One man fell from the rigging and slammed into the deck hard, breaking his arm so completely that the bone poked through the skin.

Colmiera shoved the rudder post, turning the ship toward the galley. "Brace for impact!"

The Venetian captain shouted orders to his rowers, but they hadn't counted on the sudden burst of speed and had expected more time to withdraw the oars. When the vessels collided, a shower of snapped wood scattered in every direction.

A few pirates lost their grip and slid across the deck haphazardly, but none of their bottles broke, and no patches of *naphtha* blossomed. The others adjusted their stance to absorb the shock and cocked their arms, waiting for the order to attack.

The impact slowed the ships, but they continued to drag across each other. A few of the oars in the center of the ship shot inward instead of breaking as the rowers began to withdraw them. The rear rowers had managed to retract theirs by the time the pirates' prow reached them.

The vessels were fully abreast now.

Colmiera shouted, "Launch!"

Men were coming to their feet on both vessels as the first wave of bottles soared from ship to ship. The Venetians watched the odd projectiles without comprehension as they completed their graceful arcs.

The pirates' aim was good. The ship's pilot jumped out of the way, sliding forward down the deck as more than half of the bottles slammed into the galley's port side rudder and aft main rudder. A thick spray of burning liquid coated the back half of the aft deck, sending men scrambling for safety.

The pirates cheered while their target drifted forward aimlessly. The men along the port side turned their second volley toward the main masts. More erratic, it still caught the masts and sails on fire.

Colmiera turned to the men readying the third wave. "Hold. Don't waste it."

Niccolo relaxed. A few men on the other ship nursed burns, but perhaps no one had yet been killed.

The galley limped along under momentum as the sails burned to cinders. A few oars poked out as the crew began to transfer them from one side to the other, but achieving a balance would be slow work.

Colmiera piloted them in a graceful arc behind the galley as the pirates extinguished their matches and stowed the rest of the bottles below deck. At a signal, one of his men raised the white flag.

Niccolo held his breath. His countrymen were prone to occasional arrogance, particularly when on the sea. Hopefully, they would be sensible this time. Without a full complement of oars, any rudders, or functioning sails, the Venetians didn't stand a chance.

The galley raised its own white flag.

The pirate captain barked out a laugh. To match their target's speed, the pirates furled all but the smallest sail, and even that last one had to be loosened to spill the wind as they pulled alongside.

"Surrender and your lives will be spared," came the simple demand.

A few officers conferred on the foredeck while their men continued battling the flames engulfing the aft. From among the bodies fighting the fires, Alvero strode up angrily, pumping his fist at the ship's crew.

"That's him," Niccolo said to Colmiera.

"Where?"

"There, striding up to the front. See?"

The pirate leaned over the wheel. "Oh, he has the swagger of a senator." He whistled. "Dead?"

Alvero shouted something at the captain and gestured toward the deck. Niccolo could imagine that same imperious mouth curled smugly into a grin when he'd received news of Angelo's death.

"Yes."

"So be it." Colmiera shouted down to his herald, "I'm losing patience."

Cupping his hands, the herald repeated, "Surrender or we'll sink you and take what salvage we can from the wreck."

The Venetians returned to their deliberations. The captain pointed angrily at Alvero, then ordered the burned sails to be lowered and the oars withdrawn. Alvero tried to stop him, but the officers restrained him.

Niccolo couldn't help but smile. He turned to Colmiera. "Can some of your men tend to their injured?"

The pirate laughed. "How would we justify that?"

Niccolo pressed his lips together but remained silent. "Fair enough."

"Good." Colmiera turned toward the Venetian galley. "Now, stay here. If something happens to us, get the ship away and earn my crew its half-million ducats."

They had come far in the few days since that first conversation between captor and prisoner.

Colmiera adjusted the baldric holding his sword. "Let's go, boys!"

Niccolo and a few of the captain's men remained on the ship while the rest boarded, disarmed the sailors, and corralled the prisoners into small batches. Even from this distance, Niccolo could hear the same swaggering speech as before.

Near the end, Colmiera added a new twist. "I'm feeling generous and will reward your wisdom in surrendering. I understand you have a big shipment from some rich senator. That cargo's mine, but you can keep the rest."

"Agreed," the Venetian captain said immediately.

"What?"

Niccolo barked a sudden laugh as Alvero emerged from the crowd and descended the steps.

The assassin planted his feet and crossed his arms. "You'll not take my cargo, brigand. I challenge you for the right to it."

Strictly speaking, Niccolo doubted the pirate could best someone like Madina. But what would his men think if the captain declined?

Colmiera considered him for a moment in silence. "Yes, you have the look of a senator about you."

"And you, the look of an unwashed drunkard."

Laughter bubbled up from deep in the pirate's chest. Alvero actually smirked as Colmiera wiped a few tears from his eyes. "A challenge, eh?"

"Yes." Alvero tilted his proud chin.

Grinning, Colmiera turned to Tiepo. "Let me borrow your sword."

Tiepo handed him the scimitar he had used when sparring with

Niccolo. Both groups began to murmur. Nodding to himself, Alvero began to remove his outer coat to prepare for the duel.

He had only managed to fold up the cuff on one sleeve when the scimitar flashed across his throat. A spray of blood splashed across the Venetians.

Niccolo choked off a shocked cry.

The humor had left Colmiera's face. "This isn't your republic, dog. You insult a man at your own peril."

Alvero dropped to his knees, the life pouring out of him. Slowly, his color faded from a vibrant pink to a deathly white.

Niccolo swallowed a rush of bile. He looked much as Umberto had at the end.

As Alvero teetered, fighting a losing battle for balance, Colmiera leaned forward and whispered something in his ear. The assassin's eyes widened with shock and disbelief. He tried to lunge at the captain but succeeded only in falling to the deck.

Colmiera turned to the Venetians. "What could I possibly gain from dueling him?" The terrified men remained silent. "Your republic is better off without him."

The pirate kept his word. Despite Alvero's offensive bravado, the pirates unloaded only his goods. A few of the Venetians even joined in, eager to speed these brutes on their way. When ready to leave, the Venetian captain cheerfully pointed out one of Alvero's crates that they had missed.

The pirates returned to their vessel amid victory shouts and wild celebration. Colmiera gave the order to disengage.

After the ship had begun to pull away, the pirate captain approached Niccolo. "I made sure he knew why."

Niccolo drew in a breath. "Did anyone else hear?"

"I know better than that."

"Why?" Niccolo asked.

"I need your mind focused on my goods."

Colmiera's expression carried a sorrow that told Niccolo his explanation was a lie. If Colmiera truly understood *vendetta*, then he knew how important it was for the victim to understand the cause of his fate.

The pirates unfurled the sails and allowed a stiff wind to carry them toward Constantinople, the most important port in the world.

It was done. Niccolo had dealt with those responsible for murdering his father. The thought brought him little satisfaction, though. Before he could return home, he would also have to settle accounts with their conspirators, including a brother who had betrayed not only him but everything their father had ever believed in.

CHAPTER TWELVE

Two Months Later
June 21, 1365

Niccolo

NICCOLO SHIFTED HIS weight to alleviate the discomfort in his heels. Everything in Constantinople seemed to involve defined procedure, precedence, or behavior. So far, this feast had involved a lengthy presentation ceremony, little opportunity for introductions, and no food.

A couple strode past toward their seats at the head table. As he passed, the man lowered his gaze to Niccolo's waist and gave a look of surprise.

Giovanni insisted he needed to dress like the Byzantines at public events or lose the credibility as a successful merchant that he'd built over the previous two months. So, he had selected black hose and a dark blue cotehardie that hugged his chest and flared at the hips. The obligatory red sash at his waist had to hang below his waist, but he could be arrested for claiming descent from Byzantine nobility if it extended past his knee. His Venetian mind found such specific rules of fashion very strange.

While his clothing was appropriate for his station, his position in the hall had surprised the procession of other guests all night. While not seated as highly as an ambassador, he took precedence over a mere merchant because of his senatorial status. To a Byzantine eye, that would be noteworthy.

Some distance away, Giovanni chatted with the elderly widow of one of his Byzantine partners. Very quickly, he had learned that she—and not her sons—made the business decisions. Watching him charm her without appearing insincere was quite instructive.

The herald announced another couple, but Niccolo didn't catch their names. The length of his sash and the purple edging on his cape indicated the man had imperial blood. As she passed, the woman on his arm fixed him with a look that mingled seduction and disdain. The scent of her heavily oiled hair lingered long after she had reached the other side of the room.

At the main doors, the herald banged a scepter on the ground three times. "Romans, friends, and honored guests, I humbly present the curator of domestic affairs and the emperor's councillor, son of Alexander Melas, his grace, Tribounos Alexios Melas."

The guests lowered themselves as close to the floor as possible as a portly man with thick brown curls and an even thicker layer of cosmetics waddled in. His steps echoed off the white marble floor, accompanied by the dragging hiss of the long gold sash that hung from his waist and tangled with the bottom of his scarlet cape. Melas' red and white gown carried so many intricate folds that Niccolo could scarcely imagine how his tailor had designed the billowing garment.

As the man who maintained Constantinople's infrastructure, he could become Niccolo's most important customer.

He was glad Giovanni had convinced him to rub scented oil into his skin for tonight's dinner. The pungent odor indicated wealth in Constantinople as surely as a cellar of hundred-year-old wine or— utterly foreign to his Venetian mind—one's own shipping fleet.

The meal took the better part of two hours, during which Niccolo quickly exhausted his charm. To his left, a young woman who evidently saw Niccolo as her inferior responded to his efforts at conversation with a look of distaste he would only offer to Umberto Feratollo or Alvero Madina.

If they had still been alive, of course. That thought made him smile.

On his other side, the son of a lesser imperial functionary discussed only two topics: the movement of Turkish soldiers and the current contenders in the games. Niccolo would have happily engaged the cordial young man, but he knew little about either subject and had been unable to steer the conversation to other topics.

Surprisingly, the food was excellent and suited Niccolo's tastes. After a light salad of mixed greens covered in olive oil and fishy garum, he sampled a selection of bread liberally doused with garlic, cheese, and black pepper. Both dishes offered an explosion of overpowering tastes, but he could easily pick around the strongest concentrations of flavor.

Niccolo devoured the guinea hen that came next with true delight. Rather than dousing it with extravagant spices, Melas' cooks had restrained themselves to natural juices. He was still picking at the bones when the servants arrived to remove the dish.

A honey-glazed pork dish came next, but the cook had added extra sauce to hide the fact that he'd overcooked it. Likewise, Niccolo passed on the fish soup thickened with almond milk; the smell threatened to make him revisit the contents of his stomach.

An endless parade of fruits in a dazzling array of colors followed. Niccolo ate very little, though. The resemblance to the cinnamon apples that had killed his father was strong enough to ruin his appetite.

After the servants had removed the final course, some guests rose, while others remained in place in obvious discomfort. Niccolo caught one man surreptitiously stuffing loaves of the cheese bread into his wife's skirts.

One of the curator's house slaves approached and bowed. Eyes fixed on the floor, he said, "With respect, sir, Tribounos Melas wishes you to attend him."

Niccolo had been prepared to wait several hours for his meeting with the Greek. Wiping his mouth, he checked that no food particles had lodged themselves in the delicate embroidery of his cotehardie and followed the servant.

Melas rested on a couch atop a small dais. Guests of honor reclined on additional couches in a semi-circle on the raised platform. Though they dressed more plainly than Melas, their casual ease and grace hinted at nobility.

Even as he executed the formal Byzantine bow, Niccolo realized his mistakes in posture and angling. But as he straightened, his host was smiling. He must have performed well enough for a foreigner.

The curator spent several moments studying the length and knotting on his guest's waist sash, but Niccolo detected no hardening of his expression. "My agents tell me you've recently been selling a large quantity of goods," Melas said in a high-pitched, nasal voice.

The phrasing suggested the Byzantine had revealed a great secret, whereas Niccolo hadn't exactly been subtle. He had deliberately left a trail of starry-eyed merchants and giddy dockworkers in his wake to build his reputation these past few months. He had earned a hundred thousand ducats for himself, more than his father's entire portfolio would yield for ten years. Colmiera and his men had each earned more wealth than most senators could dream of.

Melas continued. "I understand that most merchants trade in only one industry."

"This is so, Excellency."

"How did you come to possess so many different goods?"

Because Colmiera's pirates have been robbing you for the past ten years. "As a boy, I watched my father cultivate relationships with agents in many cities."

Melas patted his stomach. "So you inherited your wealth?" His tone carried a hint of irritation.

Niccolo recognized his mistake. The clothing, the liveried slaves, and the way Melas had orchestrated his entrance to command attention all pointed to a self-made man. In closed Byzantine society, he would have had to face down his share of bias against a "new man".

"No, I don't have access to my father's wealth. But he did teach me the importance of diversification. As I rebuilt my fortune, I respected his advice."

The curator stroked his chin. "Your story pleases me." He lowered his voice, but the high pitch still carried easily. "I should like to discuss an arrangement."

Niccolo limited his reaction to a respectful bow, and Melas gestured for him to approach. Dutifully, Niccolo ascended the dais and seated himself on the couch the Byzantine had indicated.

Melas began to laugh. Between breaths, he said, "This isn't Italy, my boy!"

Niccolo glanced around. Everyone else was reclining on an elbow. Quickly, he twisted to mirror their posture, smiling despite its unfamiliar awkwardness.

Melas took a sip from a goblet held by a servant beside him. "I'm told you can be discreet."

Niccolo nodded. "I don't publicize my clients' business, unless they chose not to show me the same courtesy."

"Of course, of course." Melas took another sip before continuing in an even quieter voice. "I require cut stone, timber, and tools for construction. Can you fulfill this request?"

Niccolo mentally consulted both Colmiera's stock and what he could acquire with his new contacts. "The timber and equipment, yes. I have no access to stone, but I do have a small quantity of marble."

"What sort of marble?"

"As white as pure snow."

Melas' eyes widened. "That will be acceptable."

"I will need to know what sort of project you have in mind, so I can provide the right tools."

"There was some damage to the city's main aqueduct, and it falls to me to handle the repairs." He licked his lips. "I will require an inventory of what you provide to me for official recordkeeping." He waved a hand. "You need not list the marble, though."

No one would waste white marble on an aqueduct; Melas obviously intended to embezzle the cost from the Empire. That suited Niccolo well enough. He cared little where his money came from, provided it arrived promptly. He would have to transfer his accounts beyond the curator's reach, though, in case someone discovered Melas' theft. Foreigners were useful but could also become scapegoats. Since he could not trust fellow Venetians, he'd have to bank with Milan and Rome, perhaps Florence.

Melas waved a hand. "Of course, I expect a ten-percent discount off market price."

"Of course, Tribounos."

"Then we have a deal?"

Niccolo restrained his excitement enough to answer in an even tone. "We do."

Melas waved his hand again. "My man will see to all the details when you're ready to deliver."

Inclining his head in a silent farewell, Niccolo departed the dais.

Giovanni joined him as he returned to his seat. His friend looked striking in his burnt orange cotehardie that complimented his complexion and accented the rich, dark hair he'd slicked back with oil. "Well?"

"He's dipping from the imperial well. Who could he trust but a foreign merchant?"

Giovanni clapped him on the back. "That's good news. Now… since you're wearing my clothes, let's talk about my cut."

Niccolo laughed. "How about fifteen percent?"

"I'm serious." Giovanni had had poor luck these past two months. Two of his family's partners were wavering in their support, and a third had been feeling him up all night.

"So am I," Niccolo said. "If I'd dressed as I normally would have, I wouldn't have gotten past the front door. I owe you my thanks."

Giovanni offered a skeptical smile, evidently surprised at the lack of bargaining.

"But before you start charging by the hour," he added, "I want out of these clothes."

His friend barked a laugh that attracted attention. A young woman studied Niccolo from head to toe before offering a bashful smile.

"I imagine a great many young women in this city are interested in you," Giovanni said.

Niccolo's own gaze lingered on her long after she turned away. "Maybe they won't go home disappointed."

"Speak for yourself." Giovanni snorted.

"I was. I don't want to explain to Asparia why I didn't keep a better watch on you."

His friend smiled with a longing so intense that Niccolo immediately regretted broaching the subject. Giovanni had nearly finished his goodwill visits. While he could return home anytime, Niccolo still couldn't. What would he do without his friend's support?

He pushed the thought aside. "Are you making any progress?" He gestured to the widow.

Giovanni sighed. "I doubt the relationship will hold. She complains of joint pain and has no appetite. It won't be long until her sons succeed her, and they aren't fond of Venetians."

"What industry?"

"Jewelry."

Niccolo chewed his lip. "What if you could offer them free storage for their raw metal and finished products?"

He crossed his arms. "Sure, but we're talking hundreds of ducats."

"Not if you own the warehouse. In a few weeks, I won't need the one I bought for Colmiera's goods. You can have it."

"Have?" He narrowed his eyes.

"Consider it a wedding gift."

He gaped. "It cost you five hundred ducats."

"I'm only here because you helped me escape Venice. And I nearly got you killed in Trieste."

"That was a different Aretoli," he growled. Evidently, he hadn't yet forgiven Flavio.

"Nonetheless," Niccolo continued, "I want to make it up to you. You've been at my side since Crete. You saved me months of work here in Constantinople by letting me use your family's contacts. I'll always do all I can for you."

"Nico, I… Thank you. It'll make a world of difference."

"Then go tell your partner about your new offer while the vultures are close enough to overhear." He gestured to the sons surrounding her.

Niccolo snickered in delight as he watched Giovanni explain his offer. The slowest of them realized the advantage several seconds after the other two.

Sometimes, having money was truly delightful.

A voice called from behind, "Senator Aretoli?"

An elderly man wearing silk that matched his hair—a full, wavy head of silver with flecks of its original brown—had approached. Despite his age, he had lucid eyes and a face full of Venetian angles.

Then Niccolo realized this man had used his title.

The man executed a faint but formal bow. "I am Lodovico Contarini. I've lived within the Empire for the last several years, but I believe I am still a senator of Venice."

Niccolo offered a lower bow in honor of his advanced age. "Signor Contarini. Had I known any other senators were in the city, I'd have sought you out."

Contarini smiled. "I'm sure you understand my reluctance to announce myself. I'm told you've spoiled nearly every important market since you arrived a few months ago. Otherwise stoic buyers flutter with excitement at your name." He laid his hands over the folds of his long coat. "We must keep our most lucrative associations secret, mustn't we?"

Niccolo took a moment to digest his words before responding. He clearly had his suspicions about where Niccolo's goods came from. He had to be careful. This senator had a purpose in approaching him. "It would be foolish to do otherwise."

The crowd shifted, and a Byzantine jostled him. The man offered a quick apology before continuing on his way.

"Are the rumors of your sale of large lots of cloth and jewelry, wood and wine true?" Contarini had timed the question to catch Niccolo off his guard after the distraction.

"I've been fortunate."

"I've found that most Venetians who live here for any length of time left the Republic for a reason."

Niccolo shrugged with a casualness he did not feel. Contarini's question hit too close to the mark. "Few exiles arrive with galleys laden with marketable goods."

Contarini simply nodded and studied him in silence. Niccolo had grown used to this reaction over the past few months. "I wish to offer my condolences for the death of your father. From what I'm told, you are much like him. I suspect that affinity causes you to feel the loss terribly. My associates spoke very highly of him."

Niccolo smiled politely almost on instinct, but the pain had diminished, either from the passage of time or the punishment of those responsible. "I thank you, sir. I've sought to model my life on his example. I can think of no better way of honoring him."

"It would please any father hear that from a son. I'm sure he would be proud."

Niccolo inclined his head at the sentiment. He hoped Contarini was right. At the very least, he had earned a fortune. Any Venetian father would be proud of that, regardless of the methods employed.

In the corner of his eye, Niccolo saw Giovanni hovering nearby, waiting for a chance to approach.

"You seem to be an honorable gentleman, sir," Contarini said. "Could I persuade you to dine with my family tomorrow? I may have a proposal for you."

Niccolo hesitated to accept. The last thing he needed was to draw the attention of another Venetian senator. Yet declining might invite the wrong kind of attention.

"My son is only a few years younger than you. I imagine meeting the Cretan Fox would encourage him in the right direction." After the briefest hesitation, Contarini added, "I could also introduce you to my daughter, who will turn eighteen this winter. She is a stunning young woman."

A proposal, indeed.

The offer confirmed that the doge hadn't circulated the true reason for Niccolo's departure. If he had, a senator would have never countenanced the prospect of marriage. Even Neretti had refused to discuss the subject.

It seemed he still remained a senator and citizen. That piece of news alone deserved gratitude.

"I would be pleased to become better acquainted with you, Signor." Niccolo carefully avoided mentioning the daughter. "But I shall have to check my schedule. I believe I have another engagement tomorrow evening."

"Oh, of course." Contarini smiled. "If not tomorrow, I'm certain we can find another day." He shifted his gaze over Niccolo's shoulder. "I look forward to your visit."

Niccolo bowed. "Senator."

Contarini wove through the crowds until his speckled head stopped beside a beautiful woman of forty who lovingly caressed his arm.

Niccolo caught his breath. If that was Contarini's wife, Niccolo could only imagine how lovely his daughter must be.

Before he could contemplate the possibilities further, another father flanked by a pair of young women—all of whom eyed his silk with the calculation of the finest of merchant families—soon diverted his attention.

NICCOLO

"You should consider it," Giovanni said through a broad grin.

Niccolo removed his pouch and tossed it onto the table. It struck the wood with a tinkling thud. Both his worries and his money pouch had lightened since he had visited the Milanese bank. Within the week, they would see his gold distributed throughout Italy, protecting his finances from both siege and unfriendly governments.

He shrugged off his outer coat and sunk into the cushioned wooden chair nearest the door. "I didn't come here to find a wife."

"Nor did you plan to be accosted by pirates or make a fortune." Giovanni crossed to the window, picking a piece of fruit from a bowl balanced on the ledge. "Business partners and eligible daughters go hand in hand. You've been clinking together a lot of coins, Nico."

Still, he shrugged. "Compared to some of these Byzantines, we're both paupers. I've been selling a lot, but the buyers are the truly wealthy ones."

"I'm talking about Venetian daughters here," he reminded. "Byzantine nobles won't marry a foreign girl, so their prospects are limited. Plus, you're a ruggedly handsome young Venetian senator." Giovanni fluttered his eyes and pretended to swoon. Niccolo couldn't help but smile. "And you've already inherited your father's property."

"Such as it is." Despite his best efforts, Pietro hadn't been able to prevent Flavio from cutting Niccolo out of the *fraterna* over the last month. Only Di Natali had remained faithful, particularly after receiving Niccolo's letter that the emperor's tailor had wanted to buy his silk.

"Don't underestimate your desirability, Nico. You've made quite an impression."

"I wonder how much of the attention comes from your tales of the Cretan Fox." He glanced sidelong at his friend.

"I didn't say a word, I swear. You're here as a merchant, not a politician. You know my feelings about a martial reputation."

Niccolo shrugged. "Fair enough."

Giovanni pursed his lips. "Why not take a wife here in Constantinople?"

"It's too soon for that."

"I don't believe that." This time, he spoke with more certainty. Giovanni leaned forward to rest his elbows on his knees. "When Asparia started on you in her letters, maybe it was too soon. But now you're established with a sizeable fortune and a solid reputation."

"I never imagined the subject of my marriage mattered so much to you."

"It's not your marriage as much as what your refusal to consider the issue implies."

Niccolo stilled. "What does that mean?" Of course, he already knew.

"When are you going to move on with your life?"

He stormed to his feet and paced to the other end of the room. "You don't call this living? I've made over a hundred thousand ducats and connections my father could only dream about. I'd hardly consider that nothing."

"I agree. So why does it mean nothing to you?"

The change in tactics robbed Niccolo of his prepared responses. Giovanni had raised the topic of marriage before, but this approach was new.

"Nico, I don't understand you. I could work my entire life and never enjoy as much success as you've stumbled upon. But you look more miserable than ever. Look at this house you've bought." He gestured around them. "Yes, it's beautiful, but it's barely furnished. That says something."

"Is it a problem that I have simple tastes?"

"Not if it stands on its own, but it is if you're clinging to false hope."

He crossed his arms. "And what does *that* mean?"

"Don't you think you've taken enough vengeance?"

Niccolo fell still, except for his twitching fingers. "You know what my father said to me. I can't turn away from what needs to be done. Why do you question this now?"

"What else needs to be done? The doge had Alberto Brattori killed, and you took care of Umberto yourself. As far as Venice knows, Alvero met with an unfortunate accident at the hands of some pirates." His last comment contained a hint of lingering resentment. He had been furious when he'd learned about the galley attack. That the sailors hadn't come to harm mollified him, but only slightly. "What else remains?"

"The doge, Antonio Galli, and anyone else supporting them," Niccolo insisted.

"And how will you do it?" Giovanni interrupted. "Your father would have never expected you to destroy yourself, and I don't see any way to get to them without ruining your future. The doge could rally the city guards to his cause in a matter of hours. He's too well entrenched."

Niccolo's thoughts again turned to the problem that had occupied his every spare moment. Guards and officials, servants and slaves surrounded Celsi every moment. Niccolo could surely have him killed, but an assassin would be caught, and his own death would soon follow. Celsi was the doge. The state would punish any attack on him. "Do you propose that I write to tell him I've abandoned my promises?"

"Of course not, but don't put your life on hold." He licked his lips. "Celsi will be doge until he dies. What if he lives until he's ninety? His grandfather did. Are you going to wait to live your life until then? How is that different from Umberto Feratollo, who never married through his long feud with your father?"

Niccolo remained silent.

"Why did you break from your brother?" Giovanni asked. "Wasn't it because you feared the Aretoli being seen as weak? With Madina and Feratollo dead, you've dispelled those worries."

Yes, he had feared that the other families would sense weakness and begin clawing and scratching away at the Aretoli. That was how it worked. Cornaro had almost succumbed. But the deaths of Umberto and Alvero had sent as clear a message of Aretoli power as Flavio's marriage to Rosalia had of Cornaro's.

But though he couldn't reach Celsi or Galli, they could still harm him. He couldn't return to Venice. Besides, his contacts were here now. Venice had only a hostile doge and a brother who would undermine him at every turn. His family was safe; he had achieved his goal, even if it had cost him his ability to return home.

"Maybe you're right."

His friend rose and crossed to him. "I wouldn't be much of a friend if I didn't say something when I saw you going down a very dark road."

He pulled Giovanni into an embrace. "Thank you, Gio."

"So, can I arrange a dinner with Signor Contarini?"

The trivial matter had assumed vital importance. He could see Rosalia's face there, in the space before Giovanni. Memories came unbidden. The bridge before Crete. The few stolen moments at Easter. Her grief when Angelo had died. The feel of her skin. The warmth of her breath.

But that was all in the past. He would never hold her again. He willed himself to bury those feelings deep in his heart.

"Go ahead."

"Good!" More mischievously, Giovanni added, "We'd better get you some furniture if you plan on courting. A comfortable couch, a welcoming bed, perhaps…"

His brother-in-law's good spirits were starting to infect him. "As you say." He permitted a faint smile.

"Your sister will be delighted to hear how pliable you are these days."

He snorted, gesturing to the fresh pile of letters beside the inkpot on his *tavola*. "I can just imagine." He hadn't yet had the chance to read the latest from home. A missive from Asparia sat on top. He cracked the seal and began to read. It was dated two weeks prior, not a bad speed, given the distance.

Giovanni stretched his arms in triumph. "You know, she didn't think I could convince you." Preening, he folded his hands behind his head. "We wagered about it, you know. And I succeeded. She's working on Marco now. By Christmastime, both of you could be married." He clapped his hands as the grin stretched wider. "Oh, this is the most shocking thing she'll have heard in a long time."

Face ashen, Niccolo lowered the letter. "I doubt that very much."

Giovanni raised an eyebrow. "What do you mean?"

Niccolo shook the letter, filling the room with the sound of crinkling parchment. "Camilla's pregnant."

CHAPTER THIRTEEN

Two Weeks Earlier
June 8, 1365

FLAVIO

FLAVIO STARED AT his sisters across his father's *tavola*. His last question still hung in the air a full minute after he'd asked it. Only Camilla's occasional sobbing interrupted the perfect silence.

Asparia sat very still, glaring daggers at him. She had always been hardest on Camilla, yet now she defended a sister who had confirmed their worst fears. His attention dropped to Camilla's lap, where Asparia's hands clasped her sister's. Why was she being so supportive now?

"Well?" If his voice had halted conversation a moment earlier, it now rekindled it with the ferocity of an inferno.

"Flavio, you're incorrigible. Hasn't she been through enough?" Asparia asked.

"I'm a merchant at heart, 'Ria, much as Father made me."

She bit back her response, but her flaring nostrils suggested it would have been a good one.

"Camilla, I asked you a question."

His youngest sister's sobbing grew louder.

He scowled. "Did you at least charge a fee for your whoring?"

"Flavio..." Asparia warned.

He continued, undaunted. "You could have found yourself a husband worth at least five thousand ducats a year. I hope you sold your virtue for at least that much."

Hand flying to her mouth, Camilla rose and turned for the door.

"I have not dismissed you!" His voice reverberated off the walls. And Niccolo said he hadn't learned a thing from Father. "Sit down."

She sank back into the chair.

He began again in a softer voice. "Have you lain with a man before?"

Without raising her gaze, she shook her head.

"And no one would disagree with you on that?"

"She said no," Asparia said.

"Forgive me for seeking clarity, sister," he said without regret. "But I have recent cause to doubt Aretoli virtue."

Asparia set her jaw and gazed out the window.

He returned his attention to Camilla. "When did this happen?" He couldn't remember her ever slipping out of the family home unless accompanied by her servants. If they were her confederates, they would suffer greatly.

"Last month. It had to be." Her voice regained some of her confidence; she wasn't quite broken yet, after all.

"Last month? When exactly?"

"I...I don't remember."

"You don't remember the day you let another man enter you?"

Asparia gasped.

"Was it before or after you left this house?"

"After," she replied simply.

"After." Asparia raised her chin. "What do you intend to do about this?"

As much as he believed Camilla deserved ridicule, publicly shaming her would tarnish the Aretoli name. That had to be avoided at all costs.

"You said it was Valentino Erizzo. Do you mean the father or the son?" The elder had been widowed a few years prior, while the son, to his knowledge, had no prospects.

"The son!" Asparia spared Camilla the need to answer. "What will you do?"

Tears quietly dripped off Camilla's nose and chin and disappeared into her dress. Clearly, she understood the ostracism her future held.

"What choice do I have?" he growled. "I'll have to speak with this man, if I can keep from strangling him." More softly, he said, "Camilla, go and rest. You'll need your strength for what's coming. See if the kitchen can make you a nice stew." He offered her a small smile, a peace offering after his harsh questioning. Perhaps he had been a little too hard on her.

She shuffled off with her eyes downcast, probably not even having seen his effort.

Typical.

Almost the moment the door closed, Asparia rounded on him. Her words were both softer and briefer than expected. "This was badly done."

"You're not the one who has to confront young Erizzo."

"I wasn't talking about how you handled Camilla, brother. She shamed the family with her disgraceful behavior and deserves to be berated for it."

He nodded curtly, surprised at her agreement. "I handled it as you did her behavior at the funeral."

"But I'm not the head of our family now." She rose. "You should have sent servants to watch her, report on her. You know how she is." With a twirl of her dress, she strode toward the door.

"You're blaming me?" He rose with the volume of his voice. "No one could have foreseen this."

His sister turned with a victorious smirk. "Niccolo did."

FLAVIO

It was too warm for traveling. The formal doublet and thick outer coat the situation demanded clung to his neck and torso, threatening to suffocate him.

Flavio trudged down the street with Asparia's parting words still ringing in his ears. *Damn her.* If Niccolo had foreseen this, why hadn't she mentioned something earlier? How could he know his sister was too stupid to keep her legs together?

Remembering all the young women whose virtue he had once enjoyed, he regretted the thought immediately. At the very least, she should have been more careful. She could single-handedly destroy their reputation. Did no one think about the family but him?

Niccolo had wanted something like this to happen, just to embarrass him. What had he done to justify these constant attacks? First, Niccolo had made him out to be a fool in front of their new ally. Then had come that embarrassing withdrawal from the city—just how had he slipped past all those checkpoints?

He rubbed the tension out of his temples. Let him rot in the East, for all Flavio cared. If he ever did return, it'd take an army to keep them from settling this business. A rogue brother fouling up his relationship with the doge could turn everyone against them. That partnership had to be maintained, no matter the cost.

Having reached his destination, he sheltered in the shade of a large awning and knocked on the door. The sweat made his clothing cling to his chest and back. He tried to flutter his shirt, pulling cooler air into it, but after a few feeble tries, he gave up. Valentino would be the one to suffer, not him.

He deserved much worse for robbing Camilla of her honor.

A servant invited him into a reception room and accepted his coat. Erizzo emerged a few minutes later, sticking his head around the corner before presenting himself fully.

"May I help you?"

This man who had beguiled Camilla seemed too dainty, not quite manly enough. He wore his hair too long and pretty for Flavio's tastes. But he met Flavio's gaze with intelligent eyes.

Flavio raised his chin. "I am Flavio Aretoli, Camilla's brother and head of House Aretoli."

Valentino paled and entered further into the room with slow steps. He stopped just behind one of his chairs. "Ah." He licked his lips and gestured to a chair on the other side of the room. "Please sit."

"Thank you." Flavio approached the indicated chair. Only when Valentino had seated himself did Flavio cross to a chair uncomfortably close to his host.

Valentino squirmed but did not get up.

"You know why I'm here?"

"I can imagine, yes." As soon as he spoke, he bit his lip.

"I was none too pleased to learn about my sister's…" He restrained himself from using his chosen word. "Situation. Of course, we must arrange a quick marriage to avoid the appearance of impropriety."

"I suppose that makes sense." Valentino clasped his hands in his lap.

"I'm glad you agree."

"Do you know who the father is?"

The question froze Flavio's blood. "Excuse me?"

"I can only assume your sister is pregnant. Women tend not to produce such an effect on their brothers otherwise." Valentino grew more confident as he spoke. "You spoke of marriage, so I assume you know who the father is."

He should not have discussed this here; he should have invited this boy to his home. "You are. You knew why I was here."

"Me?" Valentino mustered a decent effort at surprise. "I imagined you wanted to discuss the issues before the Senate. I've been told you've sought meetings with several young senators."

Flavio clenched the arms of his chair. This was outrageous. But

Camilla had chosen this man; tactics that had worked on her would probably work on him.

He rose with such force that the chair careened backward, crashing into the wall behind it.

Valentino straightened but remained seated.

"So, you're a liar as well as a thief?" It wasn't enough. He needed more force. "And you take me for a fool?" He raised his shoulders and took a threatening step forward. "You will marry my sister and legitimatize her child."

Valentino offered no reaction beyond a narrowing of his eyes. "I took nothing that wasn't freely offered. And I'll not have you insulting my honor when you should look closer to home."

Did he know about his deal with the doge? "What does that mean?"

Valentino crossed his legs. "Your sister is not as pure as you may think."

Flavio let out a breath, relief washing over him.

"She did not bleed when we lay together. I have no reason to believe her child belongs to me. It could be anyone's bastard."

"You call my sister a whore?" Flavio's voice wavered.

"I simply state a fact that causes me to doubt her chastity."

This conversation was supposed to be so simple. He'd make a proposal for Camilla's dowry, and Valentino would accept out of decency and respect for a fellow patrician. Why did he so obviously reject the very idea of an alliance?

"I urge you to reconsider." Flavio took another step forward. He was looming over the boy now.

Valentino, though, remained defiant. "I will not sacrifice my chances of marrying into an influential family to cover your dishonor."

He felt Valentino's words like a physical blow. An influential family? He had the ear of the doge. In another six months, when he received his seat on the Council of Ten, Valentino would see how influential he was.

"And don't think you can intimidate me." Valentino crossed his arms. "The only Aretoli to accomplish anything was your father, and he died immediately afterward. Poison, I hear. If you didn't issue any challenges then, I very much doubt you'll do so for this."

For a moment, Flavio imagined it was Niccolo speaking the words, so prescient had been his brother's warnings. He had restrained himself from lashing out aimlessly at the doge to protect his family. The Aretoli would have been crushed; Celsi was too powerful.

But this arrogant man wasn't. Erizzo wanted him to react to attacks on his family? Then he would react.

With a quick movement, Flavio slammed his fist into Valentino's nose. A spray of blood squirted in a ragged arc. Valentino's eyes rolled back at the sudden impact. As the other man began to fall, Flavio grabbed him by the shirt.

"This is how I respond to insults."

Cocking his hand back, he launched another fist toward the man's jaw. The resounding crack was immensely satisfying. He struck again and again. Each punch added to his satisfaction. He forgot all about his purpose in visiting. The blood dripping down Valentino's face oozed between Flavio's fingers, and he lost his grip on the shirt. The other man fell awkwardly and lay still.

Chest heaving, Flavio glared at the man at his feet, wishing it had been someone else. This had all started with Niccolo. With his brother by his side, how could anyone have ever claimed weakness in the Aretoli? But Niccolo had chosen madness, and now it was all falling apart.

Valentino's leg shifted, and he moaned. His collar was almost entirely stained red.

My God, what have I done?

No one had yet come to check on them. There was still time to prevent this situation from spiraling out of control.

Turning his back on the unconscious man and forgetting about his cloak, Flavio rushed home to change.

FLAVIO

When Flavio finally received a private audience with the doge, Celsi wasn't alone. Galli and Celsi were standing by the doge's *tavola*, speaking to someone seated in one of the chairs. From Celsi's alarmed expression, Flavio already knew who that must be.

Valentino Erizzo, the elder.

Flavio offered a silent curse. He'd have gotten in first if he hadn't wasted time changing clothes.

The other figure turned toward the new arrival. Eyes widening, Erizzo scrambled to his feet and drew the dagger at his belt. Flavio slid a foot back into a defensive stance.

"Erizzo, stop!" The doge's face had turned red from the force of his shout.

The older man raised the weapon and managed a few steps before Galli restrained him. Once he'd prized the knife out of Erizzo's hand, Galli positioned himself between the combatants.

"I will see him dead for this!" Erizzo's complexion matched that of the doge.

"You will sit down," Celsi commanded. "Now."

The direct command compelled his obedience, but the rage in his eyes still smoldered. Erizzo perched on the edge of his chair. Beneath it, his foot fidgeted.

"Signor Aretoli…" The doge's formal tone made Flavio's skin tingle and presaged an unpleasant conversation. "Is it true that you severely beat a fellow senator?"

"When a man impregnates my sister and insults her honor, he should count himself lucky to receive only a bludgeoning."

"You don't deny it?" Celsi's voice contained surprise.

"Let this be a lesson to any who would challenge our honor."

Erizzo gestured to Flavio but responded to the doge. "What proof does this man have that his sister didn't spread her legs for the whole city? This nobody with a dead father and a paltry few years of service in the guards claims my son defiled his sister. I, Valentino Erizzo, former *podesta* of Parenzo, son of the former governor of Negroponte, deny this charge."

Flavio snorted. "*Podesta?* The Senate recalled you for embezzlement."

Erizzo started to advance again but subsided at a glance from Galli.

Celsi turned to Flavio with troubled eyes. "What proof can you offer?"

"The word of my sister."

"A known strumpet," Erizzo replied. "Her lack of chastity is already a point of fact. Are we now to trust her word?"

"What else?" the doge asked.

He bristled at the question. "My word. Is that not enough?"

"He admitted to nearly killing my son after being welcomed into our home," Erizzo said. "His word has no value."

Celsi exchanged a glance with Galli, but Flavio could not interpret its meaning. After a long moment, the doge cleared his throat. "This matter will not be made public knowledge." He jabbed a finger against the one spot of his *tavola* not covered in papers. "I will not have the ambassadors in residence reporting factional assaults to their governments."

"But, Your Excellency—" Valentino bristled.

"Nonetheless," Celsi continued, "punishment must be extracted. Flavio Aretoli, you will transfer assets yielding five hundred ducats a year as compensation for your assault on the younger Erizzo. That should teach you a lesson for engaging in arbitrary violence."

"Arbitrary?" Flavio scoffed. "I will do no such thing."

"Then you'll be tried in a private court. You'll be found guilty, be stripped of your citizenship, and forfeit your possessions to the Erizzo for your crimes."

Flavio's mouth fell open. Allies didn't behave like this.

Celsi turned to Erizzo. "Abandon all thought of vengeance, Valentino. This incident never occurred. Understood?"

"Money is a poor substitute for justice." Erizzo eyed Flavio critically. "But where the doge commands, the Erizzo obey." His lip curled up in a scowl. "Heed my warning, Aretoli. Next time, only your death will satisfy me."

He stomped toward the door. Galli, still holding Erizzo's dagger, pivoted to keep himself between the men until Erizzo reached the other side of the room.

Grasping the handle, Erizzo turned back. "I hope you treat the father of your sister's child with more decency than my son." He slammed the door as he departed.

Flavio rounded on the doge. "What value is your friendship if you abandon me at the first opportunity?"

"Abandon you?" Celsi gasped. "I saved you. God's wounds, man, what is wrong with you? Beating a senator half to death? Our alliance rests on political and economic cooperation, not me cleaning up your messes."

"We tire of these annoyances," Galli added. "First your brother, and now this."

"Exactly," the doge agreed. "You should be glad I stuck my neck out enough to keep this from going to trial. If that happens"—Flavio noted the present tense—"I will not endanger myself to protect your fortune."

Galli approached and squeezed his shoulder. His other hand still held the dagger's hilt, uncomfortably close. "You have to control yourself, Flavio. We need you to be at your sharpest for what's coming. We don't have time to waste on these distractions."

"Distractions?" Flavio pulled away. "My sister is pregnant by that man's son, and you just gave away my wealth."

"Then I imagine this lesson should make an impression, shouldn't it?" Celsi seated himself again. "Look at this as an opportunity."

"Opportunity?"

"An opportunity to divest yourself of disloyal partners, to consolidate Aretoli wealth," the doge explained.

"You chose to attack Erizzo," Galli said. "Our doge did not strip you of five hundred ducats a year. He saved the rest of your fortune."

Yes, he had attacked Valentino all on his own. Maybe he had overreacted. He had pledged to forgo vengeance and deliver the loyalty of the Aretoli, but his brother had refused to cooperate. Celsi was actually demonstrating considerable patience.

He sighed. "Very well." When he'd fled Erizzo's home, he had known there would be consequences. He turned to leave.

Behind him, the doge called out, "Flavio."

He turned back.

"I just preserved your honor and made this situation go away. Don't you want to thank me?"

When put like that, he did owe Celsi a debt of gratitude. "Thank you, Your Excellency."

As he walked home, he considered the doge's words. An opportunity to consolidate Aretoli wealth?

Yes, that was a grand idea. An opportunity, indeed.

MARCO

Marco was struggling to help Asparia and Rosalia calm Camilla when Flavio returned. Both of his sisters stood expectantly. While Asparia kept her composure, Camilla kept running her hands over her stomach.

"Flavio, what happened?" Asparia asked with growing concern.

He grunted and gestured to his study. "Marco, come with me."

"Flavio," Asparia repeated. "What happened with Valentino Erizzo?"

He managed a smile before grabbing his brother by the arm and ushering him into his study. "Too soon to tell." He closed the door on his sister's resurgent whimpering.

Bewildered, Marco sat in a chair while Flavio crossed to the window. "I take it things didn't go very well with Valentino."

"You could say that." Flavio rubbed his hands together. "I beat him nearly to death."

"What?" He bolted to his feet. "Why would you do such a thing?"

"He dishonored our family," came the quick response. "But, of course, you know nothing about that."

"Excuse me?"

"Why did you decide to leave the city when you did, in the middle of the night?"

That had been months ago. "Petrarch told me of an opportunity, and I decided to take it."

"And it was just a coincidence that you left the same day as Niccolo?"

Marco swallowed. "It was, actually."

A rainbow of emotion played across Flavio's face before it went blank. "You are a liar. You were in league with him."

Marco's breathing slowed. He had seen Flavio like this before. His outer calm belied a deep fury. "Next, you'll be saying Petrarch was involved, too. Don't be ridiculous."

Flavio shrugged. "Maybe he is. Is he my enemy too? Maybe I should find him and finish the job that fever began."

"You wouldn't do such a thing."

Smirking, Flavio shrugged. "No, I suppose not. But he doesn't bother me as much as your betrayal, brother."

"How long have I wanted to study art, Flavio? You know I hoped for this opportunity when Petrarch visited."

"Then why did you take such pains to avoid the patrols that night?"

Marco fell silent, even though he knew it damned him. Never before had Flavio admitted to abusing his position to arrest his brother. They had all known, of course. But speaking openly about it meant Flavio no longer cared whether they knew.

"You knew Niccolo's plans. Giovanni went with him, so I figured Asparia knew. But you, Marco?"

Flavio and Niccolo were politicians, but he had never felt

HOUSE ARETOLI | 275

comfortable lying. And it would be a lie to claim that he didn't oppose everything Flavio had done.

Raising his chin, Flavio announced, "Your secret flight from the city proves you're incapable of acting responsibly. You very nearly killed a man you consider a friend, perhaps even a mentor, and you lacked even the integrity to announce your intentions openly. I doubt our father expected this when he arranged for our *fraterna*."

An icy terror gripped Marco's chest. "What are you saying?"

"I can't let you squander the wealth our father struggled to build. You've shown you have no trust in your kin, so I have no trust in you. I am withdrawing your access to your assets."

Marco slumped into the chair. "You can't do that." This had to be illegal.

"I've already done it," Flavio announced. "One day, perhaps when your judgment improves, you can earn my trust." He gestured to the door. The conversation was over.

Niccolo had been right about everything.

Marco stumbled toward the door in disbelief. With the doge on his side, Flavio could do anything he liked. Despite Niccolo's warnings to attend to his finances, Marco had done nothing in these past few weeks to carve out an independent existence and was just as impotent against Flavio as when he'd tried to leave with Petrarch. He wasn't even a senator.

For several moments, he stood outside his brother's door, unable to face the women in the other room. They would ask what had happened with Valentino. Flavio had essentially assigned the task of telling them to him.

At least he didn't have a child to think of, like his sister. He took a deep breath to compose himself.

Rosalia was consoling Camilla when he rejoined them.

Asparia saw him first. "What is it, Marco?"

He swallowed. *Get it out quickly.* "Flavio nearly killed Valentino Erizzo during their meeting."

Camilla crumpled into Rosalia's lap and wailed. For her part, Rosalia kept her gaze firmly on Camilla, refusing to raise them in defense of her husband.

The despair and anger and pain on their faces threatened to overwhelm him. "I don't think he'll acknowledge Camilla's child."

"Merciful Lord," Asparia breathed.

"I'm sorry, Camilla," Marco said. "If I had any wealth left, I would do all I could for you."

Asparia's head snapped up. "What do you mean?"

"Flavio just cut me out of the *fraterna*. Said I showed a lack of responsibility for trying to leave the city with Petrarch."

"He did *what*?" Alarm filled Rosalia's voice.

"Why now, after all this time?" Asparia demanded, "What was his explanation?"

"I have no idea." He shook his head. "I need to get away from here. I'll take Camilla home."

"She'll need someone to tend to her from now on," Rosalia said quietly. "I'll send a few servants."

Asparia added, "And my maid."

"But what about you?" Rosalia asked. "You still need help, too."

She shrugged. "Then she can stay with me, and my maid can care for both of us. Marco, can you take her home to collect some things?"

"You aren't coming?"

She shook her head and ventured a glance at Rosalia. "Not yet."

Marco frowned. "'Ria…"

"Oh, he wouldn't listen to me anyways."

Marco didn't want to know what she had planned. He could do nothing to help, in any case.

Lifting Camilla into his arms, Marco carried her gently to the door. "Come, Camilla. I'm here. I'll take care of you."

He couldn't help with Valentino, but he could comfort his sister. It was the least—and the most—he could do.

ASPARIA

Once Marco and Camilla had departed, Asparia seated herself beside Rosalia. "Before Marco told us, did you know what Flavio had done to Valentino?"

Rosalia spread her hands over her lap. "I had some idea. His clothes were covered in blood."

Asparia nodded. "But you didn't say anything to us?"

Rosalia took some time to answer. It wasn't like her to keep things from them.

"You must understand, 'Ria. Flavio is my husband." She met Asparia's gaze. "I may not have wanted this marriage, but it's my responsibility to stand by him. Of course, I'd say something if one of you was in danger, but telling you about Valentino would have betrayed him without changing anything."

"No one can blame you for being a good wife, but this is wrong, Rosa. You know this."

"Yes." She eyed Flavio's door and bit her lip. "But if Flavio attacked Valentino, what can anyone do to convince him to accept Camilla?"

Asparia shook her head. "I fear it's too late for Camilla. But we can still help Marco. It's wrong of Flavio to rob him of his inheritance. He has as much right to it as Flavio does."

Rosalia's eyes widened. "What are you saying?"

"Rosa, only you can make him see reason. For God's sake, he disinherited his own brothers."

She shook her head. "I can't get involved in Aretoli matters."

"You are an Aretoli as much as I'm a Sabarelli. My brother chose you for a reason."

"Our fathers made this match."

Asparia offered a pained smile. "I wasn't talking about Flavio."

She blushed, a reaction Asparia hadn't anticipated.

She gasped. "Rosa, are you still in love with Nico?"

Rosalia jumped to her feet and flung a guilty look back toward

Flavio's door. She circled behind her chair and clenched its back with both hands.

Asparia nodded slowly. "I see." She released a long sigh. "Flavio won't listen to me, not after I harangued him about Trieste. There's no one else."

Without turning, Rosalia whispered, "You can't ask this of me."

"Look at all he's done, Rosa. He nearly got Gio and Nico killed. He nearly killed the father of Camilla's baby. And now, he dispossessed Marco. And let's not even mention undermining Niccolo's holdings."

Rosalia gasped. Asparia suspected she hadn't known about that last part.

"Please, Rosa."

Her sister-in-law's gaze focused on the space between them for a few frantic moments. "I don't have as much influence over him as you think."

Heart leaping, Asparia pounced on the opening. "Anything you can do would help. Marco deserves his inheritance. We can't solve the rest, but we can fix that." She shook her head. "Without the doge's backing, Flavio would never try something like this."

Rosalia returned to her chair and carefully lowered herself into it. "No, he wouldn't." She took a deep, cleansing breath. "He wanted to keep us safe with this deal. Maybe I can remind him of that."

ROSALIA

An hour after Asparia had gone home, Rosalia knocked on Flavio's door. She hadn't fully calmed the nervousness in her belly, but now was her best chance of convincing him to change his mind. Once Marco's income began flowing into his accounts, she suspected he'd find reasons for retaining it.

Admitting even that simple truth did not come easily.

When he invited her to enter, she pushed the door open while delicately balancing the goblet of wine and the plate of figs she had personally laid out.

He rubbed his eyes wearily. "Rosalia?" He sounded pleased and offered her a warm smile. She could hardly believe he had disinherited both of his brothers. There had to be some explanation.

She offered him a tender smile and gestured to the tray as she approached his *tavola*. "You've had a hard day. I know you've already been out, but I thought you might like something to eat."

His smile widened as he moved his ledger to make room for the tray.

She gestured to the papers. "Are we making money?"

He smiled but moved to conceal the open page. "We're doing quite well. I had to make some concessions to our partners when Father died, but none abandoned us for our enemies."

Of course not, now that Niccolo had permanently dealt with those enemies.

Where had that thought come from?

"I'm pleased. Just let me know if I need to reduce my household budget." His smile broadened, but before he could respond, she said, "It's harder than I predicted to keep this house in order. It's much larger than our old one."

He leaned back, popping a fig into his mouth. "I know you favored our old house, Rosa. Even though you never said anything, I always knew."

"Things have just gotten so complicated since Niccolo returned from Crete." She remembered the feel of his breath in her father's home that night.

Flavio nodded. "We were happy before he came back, weren't we?"

"Yes." She had never truly been happy, but she had been passably content. She forced a smile she did not feel. "So much has happened. Your father, Camilla expecting a child, and all the changes. I mean, Niccolo and Marco fleeing the city?"

He sighed and sipped the wine. "I expected that from Niccolo, but not Marco."

She cocked her head to the side. "I'm sure Marco didn't mean any harm by it, though. He was always such a nice boy."

He leaned back again. "Nice, yes. But he let Niccolo lead him astray."

"Do you really think Marco wanted to escape you?" She carefully avoided the appearance of defending Niccolo. That would ruin any chance of persuading her husband.

"How else can I take it, Rosa?" He popped another fig into his mouth. "He snuck through the marshes in the black of night. He obviously meant to avoid our checkpoints."

Her skin crawled at the word *our*. "How is Marco to prove himself without responsibilities?"

"I don't much care if he proves himself. He chose Niccolo over me."

"Please consider what you've done to poor Marco." Her instincts recognized his narrowed eyes as a warning, but she had come too far to stop now. "He's devastated. It's not about wealth with him, but the last link to his father."

"Maybe that's the problem. This isn't a game, and if he won't act like an adult, why should I waste money on him that I need for other purposes?"

The response surprised her. "What purposes?"

"Excuse me?"

It was too late to revoke the question now. "You said you need it for other purposes. What purposes?"

"That's none of your business."

She stiffened. "I have a right to know, if only to be prepared for the gossip I'll have to face." She already faced questions about Niccolo's absence. What other embarrassments would Flavio's plans bring her?

"The doge ensured there won't be gossip. It cost me five hundred ducats a year, but Erizzo won't breathe a word of this."

"Five hundred ducats!" Now she understood why he needed

Marco's holdings so badly. With that amount, they could have maintained their home for six months.

Her knees felt weak. She sank into the nearest chair. She could think of nothing more shameful than abusing family.

"He insulted our family, Rosa."

"How can you speak about protecting your family when you robbed your brother to pay for your mistakes?"

He scoffed. "I don't have to justify myself to you, of all people."

"I'm your wife."

"Are you?" he asked. "Right now, you sound like you married my brother Marco."

"That kind of reaction put Aretoli wealth into Erizzo coffers."

"Rosalia!"

She had even surprised herself. "Please, Flavio, look at what you're doing. Camilla is pregnant without hope of marriage, and you've robbed your brother of his inheritance. Your family loves you, but your actions are hurting them."

"Everything I've done is *for* them," he shouted. "So our family can rise."

"What's the point if you strip them of everything in the process?"

"That's not my fault, it's Niccolo's." A deep anguish gushed out with his words. "If you didn't care for him so much, you would see that."

She felt as if she'd been slapped. This was her reward for being faithful when her heart yearned to hold Niccolo again?

"See, you can't even deny it. I knew this would happen when he returned. You were in love with him before, and you're still in love with him." He jabbed his finger toward her. "That's why you refuse to see him for the coward and traitor he is." His voice grew louder with each word.

Unprepared for the accusation, she took an involuntary step back. She wanted to scream at Angelo Aretoli and her father for creating this hideous mess. She had tried so hard to make peace with her circumstances, but now she understood that she'd wasted her efforts on this jealous creature.

She wanted to hurt him, so he might feel some of what she had felt for the past two years. "Did Niccolo betray his father by befriending the man who had ordered his murder? Did he make you too naïve to send servants to keep an eye on your flighty sister? Did Niccolo make you nearly kill Camilla's lover during a marriage negotiation? And stealing your father's wealth from your brothers? Was that Niccolo's fault too?"

"See!" He extended his hands. "See the contempt you hold for me?"

"My contempt comes from your actions, not my feelings for Niccolo."

"What was that?" He leaned forward and smirked in triumph. "Your feelings for Niccolo?"

Her eyes widened. She had been so careful to resist the urge to fall into his arms only to let the terrible truth slip while he was hundreds of miles away.

Flavio's voice trembled with barely suppressed rage. "You do still love him, don't you?"

Balking, she shook her head. "He's my family now. Of course I love him."

"You know what I mean. You wish he was holding you when we lie together, don't you?"

It was true. It was all true. Now that the secret keeping her marriage together had escaped, did she dare admit to it? They could never return to the way things were. Perhaps she should put an end to this farce.

Perhaps she could be free.

"Yes," she whispered into the silence. "Yes, I do."

Liberated at last, she basked in the relief of honesty. She and Niccolo had shared too much in the years before his departure for Flavio to replace him in her heart. Had she known what her husband would become, she would have taken hold of Niccolo in that storage room and run away with him. Oh, if only she had that moment back.

Lost in thought, she missed the cold shift from disbelief to acceptance in Flavio's eyes. Something in them frightened her. Too late, she realized that she was a battlefield between the brothers, as well.

"Then, you can live without either of us," he pronounced. "To preserve your father's support, you will remain my wife. But you will never share my bed or my counsel. I won't dine with you. And I'll father bastards on every whore in the city, if only to announce how much more deserving they are than you."

No. He was supposed to throw her over, to give her the freedom she needed.

"I'll cuckold you with him, then."

He shrugged. "Do as you like. It'll only turn the city against you. Even your father will shun you. And Niccolo will grow to hate you for the terrible price he will pay for being with you. If anything, it'll give me an excuse to send you to a convent. I'll be rid of you just the same."

She had only wanted to help Marco. How had it come to this?

He headed for the door.

"Where are you going?"

Malice dripped from his lips. "To find a pretty girl to take the place of my shrew of a wife. When I make her moan, at least I'll know she's thinking of me."

"Assuming you can make her moan," she shouted, desperate to force him to throw her over once and for all. "You never could with me."

Blindingly fast, he knocked her down with the back of his hand. He reached back and brought his fist down against her cheek once, twice. A fold of her dress near her shoulder snagged on his family signet as he followed through after the blow, tearing the sleeve. She fell to the ground, sprawling in a pile of clothing and disbelief.

"You…you struck me!"

The sting spread across her face, followed by a warm flow. She raised her hand to her cheek. Two fingers came back bloody. She couldn't even feel the wound.

So, this was what it felt like to be beaten. The physical pain was momentary, but, staring up at him from her position on the floor, she felt small, defeated.

She had never before feared her husband, nor any other man. Her father wasn't like this. Niccolo wasn't like this.

She met the gaze of this terrifying stranger. "Look at what you've become."

Readjusting his clothing, he straightened his posture. The space between them grew even more distant. "I am what I am. Never presume to touch me again, woman." He grinned like a rabid animal. "When they point and laugh at you, maybe then you'll know how it feels to be humiliated, as you've humiliated me."

ROSALIA

She gave no thought to her appearance as she fled through the streets. The mid-afternoon crowds were heavy. The men ignored her, but more than a few women noticed the ripped sleeve, the bleeding cheek. Sympathy mingled with suspicion as if each one simultaneously pitied her and wondered what she had done to deserve a beating.

Damn her father for this wretched match! Had his circumstances truly been so bad that he needed to give her to a man like that as if she were a bolt of cloth?

She had been wrong, terribly wrong, to think she could reason with him. This Flavio was unrecognizable as the man she had married.

The numbness wore off almost immediately, replaced by a bone-jarring pain that turned into panic that he might have broken the bones under her cheek. Her eyes threatened to shed tears, but she willed herself to stay them. Tears would only sting where they touched the wounds.

Somehow, she found her way to her sister-in-law's door and drummed on it. Rosalia exhaled her relief that Asparia herself answered. At least she could avoid the indignity of the servants seeing her like this.

Surprise quickly gave way to anguish. The pity in her sister-in-law's eyes shattered Rosalia's tenuous control. Burying her head into her shoulder, she clung to the other woman and let the tears fall freely to soak into her sister-in-law's dress.

"Rosa, it's okay, it's okay." Asparia lifted a hand to cradle her head.

"He was so angry. He…he said terrible…he did…"

Asparia pulled away and studied the wound on her cheek. Upon seeing the tears in her dress, her eyes hardened. "He didn't…" she swallowed. "Did he force himself on you?"

"Good lord, no." She began to tremble anew as she realized how much worse it could have been. She imagined him forcing her down and had to press her hand to her throat to keep from vomiting. "He's off satisfying that urge on someone else."

"He threw you over?" She gasped. "Oh, Rosa, I'm so sorry. I put you up to this. I didn't know he would—"

"He didn't," she murmured. "That's the problem."

Asparia subsided. "I don't understand."

"If he had abandoned me, at least I'd be free." She would have been spared from his look of triumph, from feeling that humiliation. "He asked about Niccolo. I couldn't lie to him."

The other woman's gaze softened. "You'll stay with me."

"What?" She clung to the possibility, hungry for anything to help her escape him. "How will we explain?"

"He beats you, and you're worried about how you'll explain leaving him?"

Rosalia sighed and wiped her tears, being careful to avoid her wounds. "Lots of husbands beat their wives, 'Ria. You don't know because you have Giovanni." The city wouldn't gossip at yet another abused wife, but a wife who abandoned her senatorial husband would send even the Senate into a fit of apoplexy.

Frowning, Asparia subsided. "We'll say you're helping with the pregnancy, and Camilla's too, when people learn she's expecting."

"I'll need to go back sometime." A shiver consumed her as she remembered his grinning face looming over her. "Unless you and Camilla plan on being pregnant forever."

"My husband would have to be here long enough for that," she grumbled. Yet, her expression shifted to sympathy almost immediately. "Oh, Rosa, I'm sorry."

"It's fine," She mustered a faint smile despite the fresh pain.

"I have to write to Niccolo," Asparia said. "He needs to know what's happening with Camilla and Marco, and especially about this."

"Oh, merciful God. 'Ria, you can't tell him anything about me."

Her eyes grew wide. "Why not? He has a right to know his brother is abusing the woman he loves."

"No. I know him. He'll rush back before it's safe. If the doge or—God forbid!—Flavio harmed him because of this, I'd never forgive myself." She drew in a shaking breath. "I will deal with this."

Asparia frowned. "How?"

She shook her head. "I don't know. But I will handle it."

From that stance, she would not budge. Dutifully avoiding any reference to Flavio's behavior toward his wife, Asparia sat down to write her letter to Niccolo.

Two hours later, with her wounds having been treated by a tight-lipped Gian Jacopo, Rosalia fell into a troubled sleep.

FLAVIO

Still stinking of sex and desperation from the night before, Flavio pushed past Celsi's steward. As he knocked him aside, the scratches on his shoulders flared again, sending a burning pain down his back. He couldn't say whether they'd come from Rosalia or the woman whose face even now drifted beyond recollection. He just remembered rage and hatred.

Everything had gone wrong, and he could trace it all to Niccolo. He would be a giant among men but for his brother's meddling.

The doge's disdain at being interrupted faded almost immediately. "What happened? Did you attack Erizzo again?"

Images swirled in Flavio's mind. Rosalia and Niccolo locked in a passionate embrace. His brothers laughing about his failures. That impotent night when Niccolo had escaped. The argument about their father.

It took him some time to realize the doge had spoken. "Erizzo already cost me enough. Let my sister suffer the shame she deserves for rutting with an ingrate like that."

The doge's posture relaxed. "Then why are you here?"

His eyes began to tear. Niccolo had turned everyone he had ever loved against him, all because he had refused to involve himself in a fatal feud with the lifetime ruler of Venice. This was his thanks for making the prudent choice.

For each fond memory that came to mind unbidden, he reminded himself of his brother's crimes. Niccolo had turned against them all; why couldn't they see it?

Camilla. Asparia. Marco. Even Rosalia. He would save them from themselves. If he struck the shepherd, the sheep would scatter. His family would fall in line.

"Do whatever it takes to make sure Niccolo never returns to Venice."

CHAPTER FOURTEEN

NICCOLO

Eʏᴇꜱ ᴄʟᴏꜱᴇᴅ, Nɪᴄᴄᴏʟᴏ faced the sun, soaking up some of the day's first rays. He had celebrated the previous night's festival with the carpenter's guild into the early morning hours. Though he'd finally sold the last of Colmiera's excess lumber, he hadn't gotten home until after midnight. Even then, he hadn't slept well. More than a few bands of drunken revelers had caroused through the Venetian quarter, frustrating the guards and keeping Niccolo awake.

He inhaled deeply, searching for the moist scent of the nearby harbor, but the fetid fumes rising up from these docks burned his nostrils. All at once, he remembered he was halfway across the world. All his troubles came rushing back, from his sister's pregnancy to the doge to the brother who was ruining the family's reputation and finances.

Sobering, he leaned forward and returned his attention to the soup sitting before him on the table. He forced himself to swallow a few spoonfuls of the broth, telling himself he needed it even though he didn't feel like eating.

Stirring it absently, he wondered if he could ever reconcile himself to Constantinople, the city of Greek-speaking easterners where even the air smelled foul. He had bowed and scraped for favor from these

court officials enough to know he would never grow accustomed to
kneeling. He was a stranger without a home. Like this soup, his life
was growing cold.

"Captain Aretoli?"

It seemed like years since he'd heard that title.

Niccolo looked up to see a young man hovering nearby. He carried
himself like a soldier. Thick muscles filled out his shirt, but his gestures
were sluggish, not at all like other men of his stature. While he looked
familiar, Niccolo couldn't place the face.

"Eduardo Gallozi, sir. I served under you on Crete."

"Ah." Now Niccolo remembered the young man who had rushed
up to him at the docks, disoriented and apologetic. "The one from
the far side of the city. Yes, I remember."

Eduardo flinched.

That struck Niccolo as odd. He recalled thinking there was something strange about this man that night in Candia, as well. "I'm glad
you made it out alive. What brings you to Constantinople? I thought
most of the garrison longed for home."

"What was there to go back to?" A shadow crossed Eduardo's face.
"We returned in disgrace. We lost Crete. I couldn't bear the shame
of it."

"You didn't come back to Candia with me?"

"It was better for everyone that I wasn't there."

The force of Eduardo's answer took him by surprise. Niccolo had
seen the guilt of defeat before but never so powerfully. "Well, it's always
nice to see one of the old lads." He offered a quick smile and returned
his attention to his soup.

Eduardo shifted his weight. "Actually, sir, I hoped for a word
with you."

Raising an eyebrow, Niccolo studied him again.

"I made an appointment with your man for early next month, but
I saw you here, and, well…"

This was his only free time all day. God's blood, he had another one of those feasts tonight, didn't he? But Eduardo had served on Crete, the last time the world had made sense. Before Flavio and Rosalia. Before his father had died.

Niccolo gestured to an open seat in front of him. "What's on your mind?"

Eduardo perched on its edge. "A business proposition."

"Business?" Eduardo didn't look like a merchant.

The man bobbed his head up and down. "Mosaics. I think there's a huge market for Byzantine mosaics in the Veneto. I've lined up a few buyers. Signor Cornaro even expressed an interest in distributing them."

Niccolo restrained his alarm at the morsel. Perhaps Cornaro saw instability in Flavio, too, and wished to distance his interests from the Aretoli. "Have you lined up craftsmen?"

"Not yet, and that's the problem. A former soldier from a backwater assignment like Crete doesn't command much respect. I hoped…" He swallowed. "I hoped you could introduce me to some suppliers."

Niccolo leaned forward, surprised both at the nature of the request and at Eduardo's lack of acumen. He had revealed the name of at least one interested buyer and his difficulties. Had he approached any other Venetian, that man would have stolen the idea for himself.

Yet Niccolo detected no deception in this man's face. Perhaps it was their Cretan connection, but Niccolo wanted to help him. For all he knew, this is how one of his ancestors had begun House Aretoli hundreds of years earlier.

"I will help, on the following terms."

Eduardo leaned forward. The gesture told Niccolo he at least understood that introductions would tie Niccolo's reputation to his own and would come with conditions. He was bright, if untrained.

"I'll introduce you to the mosaicists themselves. Working with the merchants who sell the final product will only cut into your profits. You can use my warehouses here in the Empire when necessary. In exchange, I'll be entitled to five percent of your overall profit."

Eduardo's mouth fell open. "Five percent?"

Niccolo struggled to hide his amusement. Many merchants would have asked for half the profit. But even that amount would be insignificant compared to the massive fortune he'd built with Colmiera's goods. "I also insist that the contracts be placed in your name. I've already spread apprehension with the number of markets I've disrupted and don't want to make it any worse."

Eduardo's expression quickly shifted from disbelief to excitement. "I accept!" He narrowed his eyes. "But why?"

Niccolo shrugged. "Perhaps it's your lucky day, Master Gallozi."

"Thank you, Signor Aretoli."

A warm satisfaction spread through Niccolo's chest. Eduardo would have his work cut out, but perhaps this opportunity could help him put the trauma of Crete behind him. Everyone deserved that chance.

NICCOLO

Niccolo arranged a meeting with some mosaicists two days later. The arrival of the new Paduan embassy in Constantinople had clogged the streets and delayed him and Eduardo by a full quarter hour. The craftsmen's irritation at being kept waiting soon gave way to delight at the prospect of distributing their creations across the Mediterranean. Following a quick negotiation about terms, several signed exclusive Italian contracts. Eduardo was jubilant.

"Would you care to join me for a meal, signor?" Eduardo asked as they stepped back onto the street. He had been bouncing with excitement since his venture had begun to take shape.

"How many times must I tell you? I'm just your partner Niccolo." He gestured to the crowd, which had thickened since they'd entered their meeting. "Why don't we stop for something by the palace and see what all this fuss is about."

Eduardo shrugged. "You'd think they've never seen anything like this before."

They began to walk. "Perhaps it's the novelty of a large crowd being something other than an armed mob," he added, only half-jokingly. Unlike Venetians, Byzantines seemed to solve all their disagreements with rioting.

They weren't far from the center of the city, but traversing the few blocks to their destination took nearly half an hour. More than once, Eduardo walked ahead, forcing his way through. A few men offered glares, but soon even they subsided. The emperor often hid his guards in crowds to limit disturbances, and Eduardo was actively playing on that fear. Niccolo admired the tactic; this man definitely knew his adopted city.

The Paduan embassy had started at the port long before Niccolo had met up with Eduardo, but it was only now reaching the palace. They tossed copper coins before them to the crowd.

"Carrara's trying to buy them," Niccolo explained. That effort would fail, though. Even Milan could afford to distribute silver, at the very least.

The members of the embassy all rode white horses. The servants had ponies, while the ambassador and his close staff rode German war horses. Yet, for all the finery, the gold filigree on their livery, the pomp, and the showering of coins, Niccolo's gaze settled on the one individual he recognized.

"Good God."

Seated on one of the war horses was the redhead from the brothel in Venice.

What was she doing halfway across the world as part of the Paduan embassy? Had she ensnared one of the Paduans who had passed through Venice a few months earlier? She had left very early on the morning after their lovemaking. Perhaps she had already arranged to leave with them.

"What is it?" Eduardo asked with growing concern.

He pointed. "Last time I saw that woman was in a very dark room in a Venetian brothel. I never knew her name."

Eduardo sucked in a breath and backed away. He glared at Niccolo in abject horror. "Who told you?"

Niccolo turned away from the redhead to stare at his companion. "What are you talking about?"

Eduardo's gaze shifted from him to the courtesan as she distributed another handful of copper coins to a section of the cheering crowd.

"Do you know her?" The look in his eyes was one of fear, not hostility. "Eduardo, do you know her? Where does she come from? What's her name?"

By way of response, his companion staggered through the crowds, backtracking their route. Niccolo followed, initially thinking he didn't want to speak with so many people around. But after a couple sudden turns, he realized Eduardo was trying to elude him. As he ran, Eduardo glanced backward and picked up his pace.

Niccolo sprinted, catching him when Eduardo hesitated in choosing a course. He spun the other man around before he could escape again. Eduardo didn't even struggle.

"You do know her, don't you?" he panted, sucking in air.

The man looked at anything but Niccolo's eyes.

"I've been curious about her since she walked out on me. Who is she? Tell me."

"I can't, Signor Aretoli. It's...I can't, especially not to you, of all people."

Surprised, he stepped back. "Why not to me? I must know. She's unlike anyone I've ever met."

"Put her out of your head. I beg you."

Eyes widening, he understood. "I'm sorry. You desire her for yourself. Eduardo, forgive—"

"No!" he shouted. "Not after what she did to me...to us."

"What did she do to you?" As an afterthought, he added, "What did she do to me?"

Agony apparent on his face, he scowled. "She was the redhead we saw from the battlement the night of the rebellion on Crete."

Niccolo remembered the incident now. Swallowing, he placed his hands on Eduardo's shoulders. "What do you mean."

Eduardo met his gaze for the first time since seeing the redhead. "It was my fault on Crete. Everything was my fault."

He released him and took an involuntary step back. "What did you do?" Was this what Eduardo had carried around for all this time, what Niccolo had noticed back at the docks in Candia?

"I was supposed to be on guard at the wall." The words flowed in a jumble. "When I saw her down on the street, I just needed to have her. And that hair… She was so exotic. God forgive me, I went to her. And they attacked. They say the Cretans scaled the wall right by my post. If I'd been there, I might have…I could have…"

Niccolo exhaled the breath he had been holding. "You abandoned your post before the revolt?"

Eduardo nodded, letting tears begin to flow.

"After I told you not to."

He lowered his head into his hands, unable to meet Niccolo's gaze.

"And she was there, you say." He studied her among the procession, tossing coins to waiting children. She had lured Eduardo away from the wall deliberately. But what had she been doing on Crete in the first place?

"She said her name was Lucia."

"Lucia." Niccolo sucked in a breath. His legs weakened, and he clung to Eduardo for support.

His brother had mentioned a woman named Lucia counseling the doge. He had slept with her, pressed his skin against hers, shared a moment of complete vulnerability and passion with her. Had she already been plotting to murder his father when she'd seduced him?

If Eduardo remembered correctly—and Niccolo doubted he would forget the woman who had lured him away that terrible night—then this woman connected Crete, his father's death, the doge's schemes, and even Flavio's betrayal. And now Padua.

The implications chilled his blood.

"Signor Aretoli, I'm sorry," Eduardo squeaked in a voice stretched too thin. The poor man looked as if all his worst fears for this moment were coming true.

Niccolo needed this man who recognized Lucia and could place her on Crete. "It wasn't your fault." He placed a hand on Eduardo's shoulder. "They already had men in the city. Four of them attacked the governor well before the fighting started."

"I could have warned someone," he despaired.

"You would have been killed if you'd have raised an alarm."

His skepticism gave way to relief.

"If she helped Crete revolt, we must find out why," he muttered. "She was working with men who murdered my father. The doge was being advised by a woman named Lucia." Eduardo's eyes widened at that revelation. "The same woman, in all instances. Now, she's accompanying the Paduan ambassador." But the implications were far worse. "Why would the doge take counsel from a woman who had enabled a rebellion against Venice? Either he didn't know she was involved and is being led astray, or he has betrayed us all."

"Jesus Christ." Eduardo belatedly crossed himself and bowed his head.

Niccolo couldn't let this woman escape. He had to know how it all fitted together. The fate of the republic could very well be at stake.

He would need help. "We stood side by side on Crete." He extended his hand to Eduardo. "Will you help me once again?"

It must have been difficult for Eduardo to approach him knowing the memories it would recall. But Eduardo's expression no longer contained uncertainty. He grasped Niccolo's hand firmly. "Venice needs us. We can't let her down."

NICCOLO

A mixture of dew and slime seeped into his hair as Niccolo pressed the back of his head against the damp wall. The small group of guards moved on a few moments later, though, and he released a tense breath.

He studied the shadows of the alley across the street. He couldn't distinguish Eduardo's silhouette, but just knowing the other man was there made him feel better.

He wished Pietro were here.

A few raised voices bled through into his alley, soon followed by shouts of anger and surprise. That would be the muscle he had hired for this job. The sound of metal striking metal and footsteps on the brick echoed off the buildings. Lucia traveled with protection.

Licking his lips, Niccolo adjusted his grip on the club.

Two distinct sets of footsteps slapped against the puddles in the cobblestone street. Quickly, he drew his knife. Eduardo had probably heard, but Niccolo gave the signal anyways, tapping the blade once on the alley wall ahead of him.

The footsteps slowed, and one pair shuffled as if turning around. Into the silence, Niccolo heard the escalating struggle on the main road. She had skilled guards. Niccolo had expected his thugs to over-power them by now.

The footsteps drew closer, and the figure of a woman in a thick, fur-lined cloak came into view. A wisp of fire-red hair broke free when she spun. It was her. Lucia.

Flavio had said she was faster than lightning.

The next figure moved like a veteran soldier who could handle himself in a fight, not a ceremonial high-born escort. Niccolo was closer than Eduardo and would have to deal with this man. He wouldn't have much time, either. Surely, someone had alerted the city guards to the disturbance by now.

Releasing the club, Niccolo burst into the street and drew his sword. The space was narrow but still allowed room for them to slip by if he wasn't careful. They were only perhaps thirty feet from the main avenue.

The burly soldier drew his own sword without speaking. Lucia only gasped in surprise as she recognized the threat.

The Paduan lunged, but Niccolo parried to the side. He slashed, forcing the man to draw back.

His gaze fell to Niccolo's sword. Doubt flashed across his face at an Italian wielding a scimitar.

Niccolo offered three quick slashes. The Paduan's reactions slowed with each parry. He swung a desperate arc to stall the attack, but Niccolo jumped out of the way and, before his opponent could recover, brought his scimitar down on his neck. The guard crumpled from the killing blow.

Niccolo turned to Lucia. She covered the distance between them quickly. Even though he was prepared for her speed, he barely avoided the small dagger she drew from a concealed sheath.

He circled as she approached, carefully orienting her in the right direction. In a prolonged fight, she'd cut him to pieces with that quick knife.

But this wasn't meant to be a prolonged fight. Eduardo stepped out of the alley behind her and knocked her over the head with his club. With one last intentional movement, she sliced at Niccolo's sleeve with a final, desperate sweep of her dagger.

Lifting his right hand to the wound, he felt a dull sting and a drop of blood: a graze only.

She lay unconscious at his feet.

He exchanged a nod with Eduardo. "Good timing." He bent to pick her up. The back of her head felt sticky. "A bit hard, though."

"She circled into me." Eduardo cocked his head toward the main road. "I don't hear any more fighting."

"Go, go." Niccolo adjusted the weight of her body over his shoulder.

They withdrew down a side street toward the docks, disappearing into the night as the first Byzantine guards arrived.

NICCOLO

Lucia fluttered her eyes rapidly as she awoke. She tried to lift her hand to the wound on her head. When the ropes prevented her, cold comprehension replaced grogginess in her expression. "You've made a mistake, whoever you are. Release me, immediately."

Giovanni shifted his weight. Eduardo, standing behind Lucia, eyed the dress sitting on a nearby table, as well as the six knives they had found hidden within its folds.

Niccolo stepped into the candlelight. "Save your threats."

Her lips formed a faint smile. "So, this is where you ran when you fled Venice."

"Yes." His voice held neither embarrassment nor offense.

"I recall a more appropriate time for these." She gestured to the ropes binding her to the chair. "Are they really necessary?"

"A lot has changed since then. The ropes stay."

She looked around, first finding Giovanni then her dress on the table. She eyed the unfamiliar cotton shift she wore. "Perhaps not as much as you believe. I see you removed my clothes."

"I can't take credit for that. Eduardo helped."

Eduardo circled into view. She paled, attention shifting from him to Niccolo and back again.

Niccolo raised his chin. "Yes, we know."

A conspicuous swallow. "Know what?"

"Don't." He shook his head slowly.

She forced a smile. "I did nothing but—"

"Instigate a rebellion on Crete, subvert the republic, and kill a senator of Venice."

"I did not kill your father."

"But you were involved." His voice remained steady and deadly calm.

"I was present, but I swear to you, that was all." She licked her lips and fidgeted beneath the ropes. Evidently, she was beginning to understand the reason for her abduction. "Celsi wanted Angelo Aretoli dead, and he used Feratollo and Madina to do it."

"And you and Galli stood by and did nothing?"

"Are you going to let him do this?" she pleaded to Giovanni.

His friend grunted. "We all served on Crete. I suggested we kill you outright."

Niccolo dragged a chair in front of her. The scraping of the legs on the floor made her jump.

He sat down. "You are alive because I need answers. If you don't cooperate, you will suffer pain for a very long time. If you answer my questions, I'll release you." He inhaled slowly. "I've done many things to defend my family and my city. Never have I broken my oath." He allowed her to consider his words for a time. "Will you answer my questions?"

She remained silent long enough for Niccolo to lose patience.

"Eduardo, build a fire over there." He pointed to the hearth. "And get me a dull knife."

Her eyes widened as Eduardo laid the foundation of the logs. She held out until he lit a taper from the lantern and ignited the fire.

She sighed and nodded.

"Did the doge know of your efforts to subvert Crete when you advised him?"

"Yes."

"Did the doge plan the rebellion on Crete?" Giovanni asked, voice terse.

"No, but he didn't stop it, either."

Niccolo swallowed a lump. Treason, then. "Who planned it?"

"Francesco da Carrara."

The name fell like a lead weight. Niccolo rose and circled behind his chair involuntarily. This was far more than a simple insurrection if Venice's old enemy was involved.

"How?"

"He provided them with weapons, armor."

Dandolo had suspected a foreign power had supplied the Cretans. For Lucia's words to be true, Celsi and Carrara had to have been colluding for at least two years.

"They went to a lot of trouble, only to have you save Dandolo and thwart their plans," Lucia said.

"Is that why you seduced me in the brothel?"

Her cheeks dimpled into a grin devoid of embarrassment or shame. "That was just a bit of fun, a chance to enjoy the famous Hero of Crete firsthand."

Oddly, it comforted Niccolo that her only interest had been pleasure. He didn't know how he'd react if his failing to impress had invited the attack on his father. "What would Carrara and Celsi gain from a Cretan revolt?" Niccolo said.

"Imagine the consequences of the governor of Crete and the entire garrison—a militia garrison—being killed by a provincial revolt. Your Senate would lose its mind. Even with the doge condemning it, they would have authorized an army."

"The vote," Niccolo whispered.

"The vote."

"You're saying the doge wanted the Senate to authorize the army?" Giovanni asked.

"If he seriously wanted it defeated, why would he choose a minor senator to lead the opposition?"

Niccolo was too lost in thought to acknowledge the insult. Her testimony suggested subversion of the republic at the highest level. If he'd acquiesced to his brother, he'd be a party to that corruption right now.

"Is that why they killed my father?"

"When your father won the army vote, Celsi became angry," she continued. "He had to kill old Aretoli before he caused more trouble."

Giovanni pressed, "Why did he want the republic to have an army?"

Lucia scoffed. "You republicans understand nothing. Do you think a man with a modicum of pride would be content as a puppet duke?"

All the men reared back in horror.

"Faliero…" Giovanni whispered.

Yes, this was just like Marino Faliero a decade earlier. Only this time, the doge was conspiring not with a few irate *arsenalotti* but a foreign duke who could show him how to rule a city with an iron grip. The danger was greater than mere *vendetta*. He would brush away seven hundred years of republican rule.

How much had Flavio known when he'd partnered with the doge?

"Why would Carrara help Celsi?" Niccolo asked.

She shrugged. "He supported Hungary in the war that cost your republic Dalmatia. He knows Venice will punish him eventually."

Niccolo rubbed his cheeks as he reviewed this news. "If Celsi worried my father would cause more trouble, then he has further plans. What are they?"

She shook her head. "You're too late."

"Then you lose nothing by telling us."

"It's already started. You can't stop an army."

A chill passed over him. "An army?"

"I've said too much." She shook her head.

"Lucia…" He crouched before her. "What do you mean, an army?"

"I can't," she hissed.

"I will torture you if I must."

"Reporting what's already happened won't change anything, but this is different. If I betray my client's plans, no one will ever trust me again."

Client.

Niccolo reassessed her with that single word. "You aren't doing this out of loyalty. The Duke of Padua hired you, didn't he?"

She remained silent.

He nodded, understanding. "And because the Paduan embassy will have missed you by now, he'll know you told us."

"Even if I'm not killed, I'll still lose my reputation, everything I've built over the years."

His father's death hadn't been personal to her, not like it had been for Feratollo or Madina or even the doge. She'd simply been fulfilling an assignment. That, he understood. He had done the same in Crete. How many widows had he created?

"What if I could preserve your professional reputation?"

"How would you do that?" Though suspicious, her voice carried a hint of curiosity.

"I know a man with influence in Avignon. He can secure you a position with the church."

"Avignon?"

Niccolo nodded. "Serving the Holy Father would be a kind of penance for what you've done. God knows he needs people with your skills. I'm told the French are overbearing and he's considering returning to Rome. Have you heard of Francesco Petrarch?"

She nodded.

"He can arrange it, but you must swear never again to act against my family's interests."

"You would trust my oath?" she ventured.

"I would." After a moment, he added, "Mind you, we know what you did and who you are. And I've shown you that I won't hesitate to destroy my enemies. What I preserve today, I can destroy tomorrow."

She bit her lip. "You would really do this?"

"I swear it to you."

Her breathing had quickened.

"It's either this or death, Lucia. Decide." Without her cooperation, they would never understand her cryptic remark.

"You wouldn't kill a woman."

Niccolo shook his head once, slowly. "You invalidated that protection when you involved yourself in this conspiracy."

Eyes widening, she hesitated only a moment. "I swear, by Christ and all the saints, I'll never act against your interests."

Niccolo forced himself to inconspicuously release an indrawn breath. "Tell me about this army."

"A professional Venetian army would ultimately answer to Celsi, and he could misdirect it at the right moment, leaving the city exposed. But he never expected it to turn on its own people. Fortunately, your republic has plenty of enemies. Two Hungarian armies are on the move. The first left Buda two days ago, and the second departed Györ two days before that. When they reach the Veneto, they'll join five thousand Paduans and besiege Venice itself."

Eduardo stumbled back against the far wall.

Celsi had learned the lesson of Faliero's failure all too well, it seemed, and was determined not to make the same mistakes. He didn't intend to subvert the republic. He intended to conquer it.

Giovanni and Niccolo met each other's gaze. Crete had been years past, but they still remembered how to handle such a crisis.

"How many?" Niccolo asked.

"Thirteen thousand."

"Composition?"

"A third is mercenary cavalry. The rest are men-at-arms and peasants."

The cavalry would be the most dangerous element. "When will they arrive?"

"Three weeks, no more."

He grimaced. That was no time at all. "How do they plan to cross from the mainland to the city?"

"A fleet of transports will shadow the Paduan army along the coast."

Niccolo fought the panic beginning to rise within him. The republic's galleys were protecting the convoys from the east. The city itself would be relatively undefended. How had Venice heard nothing about this? Of course. Celsi and his supporters likely buried any reports that may have arrived.

He should have killed Celsi, no matter the personal cost.

"Why Hungary?" Giovanni asked.

Niccolo already knew that answer. "Istria, of course. They got Dalmatia from us, now they want the whole coast."

Lucia smirked. "As you say."

"I don't understand something." Niccolo frowned. "You say you were the Duke of Padua's personal envoy to the doge."

She raised her chin proudly. "I was."

"Then why are you here now?"

"My employer needed the Byzantines to maintain their treaties with Venice afterward."

Beside him, Giovanni wrinkled his nose. "Genoa and Milan didn't renegotiate after they had their uprisings. All the agreements with the republic would remain in force, even with the doge as a king."

"Unless Carrara doesn't intend on giving up control once he has the city," Niccolo supplied, beginning to understand the Paduan duke's intentions. The Arsenal, the Venetian glassworks, the silk industry. No one would surrender those prizes. "Only by controlling Venice does he believe he will be safe from our reprisals."

Lucia met his gaze in silent confirmation.

"What did he offer the Empire?" Giovanni asked.

"Crete."

It made sense; the island had gotten the taste for rebellion, and Carrara would be busy with Venice herself. The Byzantines had long hungered for the return of all the Mediterranean islands.

Niccolo never expected that investigating his father's death would lead to something so large and terrifying. The anticipation of learning the truth had been replaced by despair and the destruction of everything he knew.

He had made a fortune in the Byzantine Venetian quarter; he could always stay and marry Signor Contarini's daughter. Theirs was a good family, and she was a charming woman, seductive in her way. He could build a fine life here, separate from Venice.

What had the republic really done for him? It had killed his father and corrupted his brother. He couldn't simply blame Celsi or Carrara. They weren't responsible for creating Alvero or Umberto or the constant bickering in the Senate.

That sort of political wrangling had cost him the love of his life.

Rosalia. What would happen to her? The city wouldn't surrender easily. The people would fight over every bridge. Carrara would be forced to execute the entire Senate. Her father would die, as would Flavio.

He imagined the flames from a siege licking the tops of the roofs all along the Rialto. Carrara could burn the neighborhoods without damaging the Arsenal or trade districts.

A sack was a terrible thing. The Paduans and Hungarians would loot the whole city. How many of the senators' wives and daughters would their soldiers rape? Anyone who objected would be murdered. Asparia. Camilla.

Rosalia.

He had come to Constantinople to gain the strength to protect them. Now that he had it, he would see that responsibility through, even if it cost him his life. It would mean returning to a hostile city with nothing but a known acquaintance of Carrara as his proof of the doge's complicity. It meant confronting his brother and possibly walking into a prison cell.

Niccolo straightened as he inhaled a long breath. "Eighteen thousand men are marching on Venice. We need to stop it. Eduardo, when you first introduced yourself, you said many men from Crete came here. How many?"

Eduardo considered. "A few hundred."

"And do they keep up with the militia drills the Senate mandated?"

"Of course. Twice a month. Crossbows and swords. And pikes every other muster."

"Good, good." Several thousand Venetian citizens lived here, more than enough for a respectable force.

"You mean to use the Venetian quarter to relieve the city?" Giovanni asked.

He nodded. "The musters ensure everyone knows how to fight. They already have their leadership structures and own their own weapons. And I'll convince Colmiera to transport us."

"I can't imagine they all have battle-ready weapons and armor," Giovanni warned.

Niccolo turned to Eduardo. "Talk to the blacksmiths. Buy everything they have. We need swords, breastplates, greaves, crossbow bolts." Remembering the Hungarian cavalry, he added, "And pikes. Something manageable, but larger than what we used on Crete. But we need it fast."

The former sentry nodded. "What should I tell them?"

Niccolo frowned. "What do you mean?"

"About payment. If we say the republic will pay, it'll start rumors. I doubt the Byzantines would let so many foreigners assemble in their city, particularly if they hope to profit from Padua's invasion."

He hadn't thought of that. "Say I'm planning to start my own mercenary company and will pay them in coin before I take possession of the goods."

Lucia gasped. "That'll cost a fortune."

"Then I'm glad I have a fortune." He turned to Giovanni. "Someone will have to warn Venice. I doubt the doge would raise the alarm about his own coup."

"We don't know how many senators Celsi bought," Giovanni added. "We'll need to alert the entire Senate at once." He swallowed. "I'm not sure either of us has the clout to do that."

Niccolo considered. "We could use Contarini. His family helped to found the republic. With him on our side, there won't be any doubt." He doubted Contarini would object; he'd be a hero if they survived this.

Giovanni frowned. "What should we do first?"

"First we talk to the guild masters and leaders of the quarter. They can help with mobilizing our people."

"If we can convince them. We don't exactly have proof."

"I know." Niccolo gnawed on his lip. "I'll have to use a trick I learned from our pirate friend."

Giovanni raised a questioning eyebrow.

He grinned. "Theater."

NICCOLO

Later that evening, he gathered the leaders of the Venetian community in Constantinople in his dining hall. He had neglected no one who might contribute men or money, so his servants had to disassemble and remove his dining table.

A sea of expectant faces glanced alternatively at him and their companions. The crowd was so dense that Niccolo couldn't identify even a sliver of the carved design running along the walls at waist level.

He hadn't made make the mistake of believing he commanded such respect. They came because his missive had been direct in its urgency. *Venice faces destruction. By St. Mark and God Almighty, I beg you to immediately accompany the servant who carries this message to Senator Niccolo Aretoli's home.*

He met Giovanni's sympathetic eyes. His friend nodded grimly. He hadn't smiled since hearing Lucia's words three hours earlier.

Contarini stood beside him with a sour expression. The news had hit him harder than Niccolo had expected. Whether it came from worry about the republic or dismay that the leading candidate for his daughter's hand was an enemy of a corrupt doge, Niccolo couldn't say. Regardless, questioning Lucia himself had banished Contarini's lingering doubts about the authenticity of the danger.

"Gentlemen," Niccolo began simply. "Thank you for coming. I understand I've summoned many of you from bed, so I'll be brief. Our republic is under threat. Eighteen thousand Paduans and Hungarians led by Francesco da Carrara are descending upon Venice. They'll arrive in three weeks."

Pandemonium.

Shouts of alarm and anger competed with cries of disbelief. Most of them had left family and friends in Venice when they had come east to make their fortunes. Good Venetians all, more than a few probably worried about losing their trade partners.

One of the elder guild masters managed to shout down the others.

"What you propose is impossible, Senator. We've had no word of this. No one prepares and marches an army in silence."

Niccolo shrugged. "And yet, they have. Whether anyone in Venice observed these preparations, I can't say." He had chosen not to mention the doge's treason for fear of dividing their loyalty; the Celsis and Gallis were both influential families.

"How did you discover this?"

"Last night, Senator Sabarelli and I captured and interrogated one of Carrara's agents. This agent also verified that the Paduan duke supported the rebels during the Cretan revolt."

That quieted them, but Niccolo wasn't finished. "If Carrara takes Venice, our homes will be ravaged and plundered. His men will rape our wives and daughters and sell them to the highest bidder. He'll melt down the lions of St. Mark and form the gold into a crown to anoint himself as King of Venice. Those of our relatives who survive will populate Carrara's brothels and toil away in the salt works. The dead will choke the Grand Canal until the gulls pick them clean."

He had intentionally inflected his voice as Colmiera had done to recreate the same sense of inevitability. From the silence that followed, he supposed the old pirate would have been proud.

Contarini raised his voice. "Carrara has wanted Venice ever since his first war with us. We must stop this catastrophe." He gestured to Niccolo. "This man saved the lives of our governor and the hundreds of men under his command on Crete. He can save our home."

A few men in the room fell silent at the mention of Niccolo's reputation. Evidently, Giovanni's rumor-mongering about the Cretan Fox had spread all the way here. It had even been his idea for Contarini to exaggerate Niccolo's role in the escape from the island.

"What do you propose?" a young man in the back asked.

Niccolo pitched his voice for all to hear. "I will muster as many volunteers as I can and sail to the city's relief. There are many former soldiers in the city, and I understand you've all kept up with your militia training." His father's proposal to increase the militia training had given him this chance. Even in death, Angelo Aretoli still protected his homeland. "I'm still a newcomer here. You know the men of the Venetian quarter. I need your help."

The shouting began anew. One man said it'd be cheaper to ransom their relatives back, but several others jostled him back.

Finally, one of the guild masters waved his hands back and forth to silence the crowd. "What if you're wrong?"

Niccolo shrugged. "Then every man who goes with me gets a free trip home, passage back, and a set of arms and armor if he doesn't already have it."

They gasped in disbelief at the announcement. It was a fortune in equipment.

The room fell silent as an old man dressed in thick silk rose. He was the *podesta*, a governor in all but name of the Venetian residents here.

"I lived through the terrible events a decade ago. My family was targeted by Faliero's minions. We cannot allow that to happen again." He squinted as if he could barely see. "If Venice is in need, it is our duty to respond. Senator Aretoli, Senator Sabarelli, Senator Contarini"—he emphasized their titles—"the militia is at your disposal."

In the Senate, Niccolo had argued that the militia was the only defense the republic needed. Now, its survival relied upon his being correct.

CHAPTER FIFTEEN

NICCOLO

WHILE THE *PODESTA* and guild masters called up the citizens of Constantinople's Venetian quarter, Niccolo spoke with Colmiera. The pirate was in the city, excitedly counting his profits. Though Niccolo had worried he might hesitate at the dangerous prospect of transporting an army, those fears proved unnecessary. Colmiera had even agreed to spread the word to several of his fellow captains, who would, of course, demand payment.

"What would I do without Venice's trade? You make me wealthy." Niccolo merely offered a sidelong glance and politely thanked him.

Less than six hours after Niccolo had explained the situation, Senator Contarini had already boarded Colmiera's fastest sloop, waiting to depart. Giovanni, on the other hand, arrived only as the sailors were unfurling their sails. Nor did he come empty-handed.

"What's in the crate?" Niccolo pointed to the small parcel with circular holes at strategic intervals.

"A gift for Asparia. We all know how she reacts when she isn't plied with presents." He grinned.

"If that's a hint, it's not a very subtle one. I bought her a very fine scarf, and I already sent a carved oak cradle for your little one."

"Praise to God for that much, at least." He scrupulously avoided Niccolo's gaze as he studied the pirates loading crates onto the ship. "What do you think of our odds?"

Niccolo shrugged. "Your odds, you mean. You'll need to convince the Senate and people to take this threat seriously. Nor will you have much time to mobilize the militia. Their commanders need to drill relentlessly."

Giovanni nodded. "What do you want me to say about the doge?"

"Nothing, yet."

"Nico, he's a traitor."

Niccolo pulled Giovanni aside as a few of Colmiera's pirates passed on their way up the gangplank. "We only have the word of a spy. No one will believe us."

"Even a wild accusation should stop the Senate from involving Celsi in our defense."

"That would also reveal to Celsi what evidence we have," Niccolo reminded. "We have to make sure he feels he has no choice but to follow through with his plan, or he'll wiggle out of this. This is our one chance to expose him."

Giovanni frowned. "We're risking the republic."

"We are," Niccolo admitted. "But we know about this conspiracy. We may not get a warning about the next one."

"Do you want me to take Lucia with me? Maybe seeing her will validate his fears."

He considered the possibility for a time before shaking his head. "I won't have her go the way of Alberto Brattori. I'll ask Colmiera to keep her with him while I take care of a few things. If he didn't betray me to the doge, he won't hand Lucia over either."

"You aren't going directly to Venice?"

Niccolo shook his head. "Two armies are coming from Hungary. The first one is coming from the north and will probably pass over the mountains from Győr. We can't reach them. But the army from Buda will cut through the Istrian forests and hug the coast. Colmiera has better maps than I've ever seen. We can get there first. I'll try to slow them down."

"It makes you wonder how the Turks drew such precise maps of our shores."

"One battle at a time," Niccolo said.

"Of course." Giovanni ran a hand through his hair. "How many recruits do you have?"

Niccolo grimaced. "The convoys already left for the Levant, and many went with them. I hoped for three thousand, but we'll be lucky to get half that."

He appreciated that Giovanni chose not to mention that he hadn't commanded anywhere near that number of soldiers before.

On the ship, one of the sailors waved his hands to attract Giovanni's attention.

"It's time, I suppose."

"I suppose so," Niccolo agreed sadly.

"I bet you never thought heading east with me would bring us to this point, did you?"

Niccolo had hoped only to establish himself where Flavio couldn't touch him. "To say the least."

Giovanni embraced him tightly. "Take care of yourself, Nico. Don't be a hero, just keep it simple."

This parting wasn't the same as on the galley; they both faced genuine danger this time. "I will, but don't wish me luck, Gio. I'd rather you use it to convince the Senate." He pulled back and met his friend's gaze. "When I reach the Veneto safely, we'll command these lads together."

Giovanni smiled. Unshed tears glistened at the corners of his eyes. "I'll hold you to that."

Niccolo knew he wasn't speaking about the joint command.

GIOVANNI

Niccolo was right about the maps. Ten days after setting out from Constantinople, Colmiera's ship cruised into the lagoon. After months away, Giovanni felt none of the joy he had expected upon returning. For an instant, he imagined that the glint of sunlight off St. Mark's was actually flame, filling the sky. But it was just a trick of the light reflecting off the golden domes.

Upon docking, Colmiera's men doubled as town criers, raising the alarm about the imminent danger. Contarini went straight to the Senate chamber, but Giovanni made his way to St. Mark's Basilica. The bishop and a few shocked penitents turned in surprise. "By authority of the Senate, sound the bells." Ashen-faced, the poor man kicked a nearby servant to pass the order along.

Once they recognized the traditional alarm and not the sounding of the hour, the men of the city took to the streets, congregating in the square for instructions. The militia hadn't been called up in decades, but regular training had ensured that everyone understood his duty.

The Senate was already half-full when Giovanni arrived.

"We were fortunate in our timing," Contarini explained. "A meeting is about to begin."

Giovanni pulled him aside. "Say nothing of the doge's involvement. Niccolo has something planned to draw him out. But be careful. Celsi may try to derail us."

The Council of Ten sat beside the empty ducal seat, but no one made a move to formally convene once the chamber was full.

Contarini raised his hands to let the sleeves of his ragged travel cloak fall down his arms. "Senators, I will make this brief. The armies of Hungary and Padua are marching to lay siege to Venice in less than a fortnight. We must raise the militia to our defense."

The pronouncement produced a silence so profound that Giovanni could hear the murmurings of the crowd outside.

"For God's sake," Contarini cried, "we need action!"

Marco Cornaro stood. "How did you hear of this?"

"Niccolo Aretoli discovered a Paduan spy in Constantinople whose mission was to secure Byzantine approval for the conquest. This spy offered Crete as a bribe." That produced several murmurs. "Our source also confirmed that Padua aided the Cretans in their rebellion."

Men shouted to each other along faction lines. Those who advocated punishing Padua for its role in the last war were bragging about their foresight, while the anti-war camp decried the news as ridiculous. It was the usual indicator of an impending, lengthy debate.

Doge Celsi chose that moment to enter, sliding up to his seat unobtrusively. Giovanni noted his alarm at the passionate shouting.

"This is not the worst of it." Once the noise died down, Giovanni continued, "We have also learned that in both this crisis and the Cretan rebellion, the Paduan duke coordinated his actions with someone within this very body."

"Who? Who?"

A few senators jumped to their feet in alarm, but the rest remained silent, glancing suspiciously at their neighbors. Galli simply watched the scene with apparent disinterest. He was a calm one.

Giovanni's lips tightened. "Niccolo Aretoli will reveal that information."

"And where is he?" This question came from the doge.

"He's returning at the head of fifteen hundred men of the Venetian quarter of Constantinople who volunteered to defend our city." Before they could respond, Giovanni added, "Will our citizens in Constantinople defend our republic alone, or will we call up the militia?"

"This is ridiculous." Celsi rose. "We have no evidence. For all we know, this Aretoli brat is coming to conquer us for himself."

Flavio stood, and though it had been mere months since Giovanni had last seen him, he looked wilder, with dark circles surrounding his eyes. "When he left, my brother was distraught by our father's death. He is capable of anything."

"See?" the doge pointed. "We should trust nothing this man, one of Aretoli's minions, has to say."

Giovanni stepped forward. "You almost sound like you have something to hide, Celsi."

The casual comment, lacking any title of respect, drew the attention of the senators. More than a few whispers wondered at its meaning.

"Whether I speak the truth or Aretoli intends to seize the government, your course is the same," Giovanni said. "Call up the militia. If there is no threat, call it a training muster. The Aretoli and Sabarelli will even pay for it if this is a lie."

"And the Contarini," Lodovico added.

The senators began to shift nervously. It was unheard of for three senatorial families to back such a claim with their own fortunes. The charges had to be true.

"This is our one chance to save our city. I leave the matter to you. I'm going to prepare for the arrival of men who have proven their loyalty." Giovanni turned and marched out of the room.

Two minutes later, the Senate voted overwhelmingly to muster the militia.

GIOVANNI

At first, Giovanni didn't believe his eyes. When he stopped before his front door and saw Asparia watching the gathering crowds from a second-story window, he thought she was a figment of his longing. But when her gaze drifted down to him, her expression melted into relief.

That was his Asparia. She had to be real.

One of their servants too old for militia duty answered the door. "Master Sabarelli is home!"

Giovanni smiled politely but sidestepped the old man as Asparia began to descend the stairs. She had swelled since he had last seen her, much like when she had been pregnant with young Alessandro. God be praised, he hadn't missed the birth.

Face beaming, Giovanni met her halfway and wrapped her in his arms.

"It's really you." Her voice cracked.

He kissed her cheeks and wiped the tears from her eyes. "Come on." He helped her down the stairs. Once she was safely ensconced on a chair, he brushed her cheek with his hand. "There were nights when I could almost see your face in the stars, my dear."

"Lonely nights?"

The gentle vulnerability in that jealous question set his heart leaping. "Very lonely nights," he reassured. "Lonely enough to make me never want to leave you again."

She closed her eyes and smiled softly, nestling herself against his chest.

"More than once, I seriously considered abandoning everything I have in the empire and rushing home to you."

"I know you, my dear. You'd never be content to be outdone by my brother."

"So you got my letters?"

"Not nearly often enough."

He laughed. "I brought you something."

She pulled back, curious. "Oh?"

He narrowed his eyes. "Something no one else in the city has, correct?"

She perked up, giddy now. "Oh, good husband."

Grinning, Giovanni rose and retrieved a crate from the door. He lifted it into view with a broad grin.

Asparia studied it carefully before lifting the lid with hands shaking with excitement. A furry white cat, licking its paw with disinterest, nestled in the middle of a wool blanket. It was fluffier than the cats in the city, and its face looked flattened.

She blinked and glanced at her husband.

"It's a cat," he said.

"Yes, I see that," she said patiently.

"The breed comes from the Muslim lands. They call it a 'Persian'. Very rare."

She grunted, turning the crate to study it from different angles. "When I said something no one else had, I meant an emerald the size of my head." The cat raised its head and gave her a curious look. "It is cute, though."

With a little trill, the animal rolled onto its back and kicked its feet up. Asparia reached out to rub her hand across its face. It rewarded her with a soft, rolling purr.

Behind her, Giovanni grinned.

"Gio…" Her tone hardened.

"Yes?"

"Were there other cats on the ship?"

He wrinkled his brow. "Of course. The sailors use them to kill rats."

"Yes, well, evidently, they impregnate their passenger's gifts, too." She pointed to the animal's belly.

"What?" He peered closely at the mass of fur. Unconvinced, he eyed his wife's belly for comparison.

"Gio!"

He dodged her slap and grinned.

"The last thing this house needs is another pregnant woman."

"Well," he added in his most cheerful tone, "comfort yourself with the knowledge that I'll buy you an emerald the size of your head after I sell these kittens. At least I'll get my money's worth."

"Oh, no," she warned, "this is my gift. And you know what's going to happen, don't you?"

His nascent dreams of profit dissolved. "I'm going to have a house full of cats, aren't I?"

"Yes, yes you are," she confirmed.

"Emerald, you say?" He motioned to take the crate back.

She slapped his hand. Laughing, she pulled him close and held him tightly.

It was good to be home.

The moment passed as Rosalia emerged from the hallway leading to the guest quarters. "Giovanni, it's good to see you." She searched the room before returning her gaze to him.

"It's good to see you too." He glanced from his sister-in-law to his wife. "But what are you doing here?"

Rosalia's eyes widened. Beside him, Asparia sat in uncharacteristic silence.

Then, he noticed the slight discoloration of bruises nearly healed. Those marks, unnoticeable until he really studied her face, did not come from an accident.

"Flavio?" he asked tensely.

Rosalia lowered her gaze.

"Niccolo doesn't know, does he?"

His wife shook her head. "She did not wish it."

He frowned before nodding slowly. The matter was between her and Flavio, and the consequences of telling this secret would be dire. "I will say nothing, then."

"Thank you." Rosalia's gaze shifted to the sword hanging from his belt. "The bells were ringing." She drew in a breath. "Giovanni, where's Niccolo?"

Giovanni recounted what they had discovered and what Niccolo planned. Asparia bristled when he explained that Niccolo promised Lucia her freedom but subsided when he explained the necessity.

"You took a terrible risk in capturing her," she chastised.

He squeezed her hand. "I didn't. Niccolo did that with a man who was on Crete with us."

"Where is he now?" Rosalia demanded.

"Returning with a company of Byzantine Venetians."

"Dear," Asparia said, "He's never led an army like that. Is he up to it?"

He hesitated. She would appreciate this next revelation the least. "He won't be doing it alone."

Though her eyes widened, she did not protest. "I suppose every man must do his part. I'd rather you be at his side than in the ranks of the militia."

He wrapped his arms around her again, offering silent thanks that his friend had such a wonderful sister.

"Keep him safe," Rosalia pleaded softly. "Please, Gio. Keep him safe."

"I will, Rosa. I swear it."

"Giovanni…" She stared ahead for some time. "Did my husband know the doge planned treason when he allied with him?"

He swallowed. He hadn't considered that question. "I honestly don't know. Lucia didn't say one way or the other."

Rosalia nodded slowly, but her gaze remained vacant. Giovanni could not read her thoughts in her shadowed expression.

NICCOLO

The Hungarian column snaked its way along the plains north of Istria, content with the scouts' reports that no armies lay between them and the Veneto. A few patrols were overdue, but no one paid much attention to the delay. Last night, their scouts had stumbled upon a merchant with a cartful of wine casks and had returned very late. The riders this morning no doubt hoped for similar fortune.

The sun was beginning its slow descent, and the invigorating cool of the early morning had long since vanished. The mercenary cavalry at the front of the column trudged onward through fields of tall grass, foot after foot. Behind them, the stamping of nearly seven thousand pairs of feet thundered like waves crashing on the shore.

"Present!" came a shout from ahead.

A wall of pikes burst out of the grass and charged forward, jabbing a row of spears at the surprised horsemen. The mercenary captain screamed as one of the blades embedded itself into his side.

Men and animals shouted in panic and rushed to escape the sudden assault. The ranks behind them, unable to see past the larger frames of the cavalrymen, continued to march forward, compressing the vanguard that was trying to withdraw.

As the pikemen surged forward, they kept their order. Fresh casualties went down among the Hungarian ranks every few steps, only to be trampled by the relentless surge. The horsemen routed in all directions, opening up enough space for the first rank of Hungarian infantry to recognize the threat. They began to form up in a desperate attempt to halt the advance of these pikemen, whose numbers continued to swell as men converged on the column from all directions.

As the archers behind them bent down to string their bows, a score of horsemen charged from the woods to the left. At first, they took little notice of a few more mounted men. After all, they wore the same livery as the scattering cavalry.

Only after they had sliced through the vulnerable archers did anyone pay them any attention. By that point, swords and hooves were chopping downwards, setting the lightly armed bowmen running for their lives.

Isolated now, the men-at-arms tried to extricate themselves. But as their progress halted, they fell into panic. Attackers were still streaming in from the woods with apparently no end in sight. The Hungarians fled in the wake of their routing cavalrymen.

Word of the attack spread quickly, not as much by report as by the steady stream of terrified men fleeing down the column, kicking up dust and debris as they ran. As screams and the sounds of panic reached a unit, it too joined the flight. No one really knew who was attacking or how many there were. They only cared that their fellow soldiers were running away.

Half an hour later, Niccolo surveyed the scene from his new horse, courtesy of a scout his men had killed the night before. All along the winding path lay a trail of bodies following the rout.

Eduardo rode up on his own horse. "Several hundred dead, general, maybe a thousand. We've captured several who had been trampled by their fellow soldiers."

"How many did we lose?" Niccolo asked, dreading the answer. Each one would never see his family again, all because of him.

Eduardo grinned. "From the main attack, only injuries. The pikes kept them at a distance, and panic prevented their archers from forming. We lost a couple men when the mercenaries fought to recover the body of their captain."

"A couple?" Niccolo could scarcely believe the report. He hadn't dreamed of such a success.

Eduardo nodded. "What should we do with those we've captured?"

He didn't have the time or men to manage prisoners. Besides, now that the battle had died down and the dust was settling, those prisoners would know their strength. If the survivors realized they faced such a small number, they would reform and join the other half of their army.

You will choose the necessary thing, even knowing the cost.

He swallowed. "Separate them into small groups and execute them. Leave their bodies out in the open. I want the survivors to find them. I want them to be terrified."

It was a terrible order to receive, and an even harder one to give.

But Eduardo only nodded. "I heard the men talking. They say you outsmarted the Hungarians. They say no one can beat the Cretan Fox."

His strategy wasn't that innovative; he had used the same maneuver in Crete. How much of what had happened over the last couple of weeks—the volunteers, the grueling training schedule, the seasickness, and even their confidence leading up to this surprise attack—would have been possible without Giovanni's rumors of his prowess?

"We're off as soon as we secure the spoils. Each man will get his share, plus a cup of unwatered wine if they finish within the hour."

The Venetians were on the move within half an hour. If they walked a little unsteadily the rest of the way to Venice, their general chose not to comment. They had earned their reward.

CHAPTER SIXTEEN

NICCOLO

THE QUARTER FOXES, as they had begun to call themselves, reached the plains of the Veneto opposite the Venetian archipelago three days later as the sun was setting. A loud cheer erupted as they recognized the lion pennants adorning the encampment on the plain.

Niccolo sighed with relief as he surveyed the mustered militia. "Giovanni did it."

Eduardo nodded. "Where should we set up camp?"

Whether Eduardo's industry had come from guilt over Crete or love of Venice, Niccolo appreciated his presence. The men loved him, and he had organized the army incredibly well.

"Wherever you think is best."

Eduardo nodded and shouted orders to the senior officers, most of who had been with them on Crete. These fortifications would be more permanent than the quick camps on the march, lasting until Venetian outriders found the enemy.

Sooner or later, they would come. This time, Niccolo wouldn't have surprise on his side.

Assuming a normal number of men in each tent, Venice had mustered perhaps six thousand. Niccolo's heart sank. He had hoped for more, given the prospect of facing an army of eighteen thousand. They couldn't possibly know Niccolo had scattered half the Hungarians. Celsi must have muted the response. No part of the doge's plans involved the Venetians winning this battle.

Word of his victory against the southern half of the Hungarian army finally spread when messengers exchanged news between the two camps. Matteo Vellini, the militia commander and former finance minister, fell to his knees and gave thanks to God upon hearing of the rout. Most of the soldiers had grown up with stories of the loss of Dalmatia. The prospect of revenge against the Hungarians boosted morale.

As Niccolo made his way to the center of the city's militia camp, his spirits improved. They were few but determined. Most joyful of all was the surprise when he reached his command tent.

"Gio!"

His friend greeted him with an embrace. "Niccolo, the victorious."

"We hid a pike wall in the grass and collapsed on the column, just like on Crete." He glanced nervously at the door, where Eduardo stood guard. "I'm amazed it worked."

"Sometimes, it's that easy, particularly if your enemy has been marching for several days without resistance."

"How are things in the city?"

Giovanni sighed and crossed his arms. "The doge acts like he has nothing to hide."

"Did you tell the Senate everything we talked about?"

He nodded. "Vellini may have the official command, but he has thirty senators advising him."

"Vellini? There has to be a better man for the job."

"No fear of him being corrupted. I doubt he's ever met a foreign prince or ambassador."

"Ah."

"Nico, the doge brought hired help."

"Mercenaries?"

"I know." Giovanni raised his hands defensively. "He claims they responded to couriers he sent after we began mustering. One company of foot and one of cavalry. He paid for them himself."

"He had them ready all the while." He blew out a breath. "That's how he'll do it."

"Flank attack, for certain," Giovanni agreed. With cavalry, the doge could attack their rear while the Hungarians and Paduans pinned them in place.

Niccolo rubbed his temples. "What can we do?"

Giovanni shrugged. "What equipment did you bring?"

"Swords, crossbows, pikes. We even took a few horses in our ambush."

"How many of those?"

"Don't know." He craned his neck toward the entrance. "Eduardo?"

His lieutenant ducked his head in.

"How many mounts did we take?"

"About fifty, sir."

"Thanks, my friend."

Eduardo ducked back outside.

"Fifty," Giovanni repeated. "We'll need to keep them in reserve."

"If at all possible, yes," Niccolo agreed.

Raised voices attracted their attention and drew them outside. Antonio Galli was standing in the clearing with fists on his hips, flanked by two pairs of soldiers. Hands on the hilts of their swords, Eduardo and a couple of the other officers from Constantinople surrounded the group.

"Niccolo Aretoli, Giovanni Sabarelli, you are ordered to surrender your command to me," Galli bellowed.

"Is Vellini aware of this?" Giovanni asked.

"My appointment comes from the doge himself."

Eduardo burst into laughter that lasted several seconds. Niccolo grinned as his lieutenant replied, "I think you're sniffing around the wrong army. I know your master betrayed us, and I refuse to take orders from his tame *castrati*."

"Are you refusing the doge's command?" Galli feigned disbelief in a repetition of his performance at the records office.

Unfortunately for him, the circumstances weren't the same.

"Let's ask the men." Eduardo shouted, "Men of Constantinople, who commands us?"

The shouts came from every direction. "The Cretan Fox!"

"There you have it." Niccolo turned back to his tent. "Boys, show him out."

"You'll regret this, Aretoli."

"No!" Niccolo rounded on him with a flash of anger that caused Galli's guards to take a step back. He considered stabbing the man right here but restrained the urge. Then, he would be a murderer.

He had a better idea.

"It's over, Galli. We both know you're a traitor. You made your choice, and I'm going to ram it down your throat when I show the Senate my proof."

Instead of responding, Galli stormed back toward Vellini's camp.

Giovanni watched him go. "I think I'd prefer him to threaten us again."

"I know what you mean."

"Was it wise to bait him like that?"

"He and Celsi have been planning this for at least two years. I want him to feel trapped. The doge's best option has to be to make his move during the battle." Then, another thought struck him. "Eduardo, organize four squads of horsemen. Send groups to the north, the west, and the east. I want to know the minute they spot the enemy."

"And the fourth?" Eduardo asked.

"Have them watch the doge's mercenaries. Stop anyone who sneaks out."

"Stop them?"

Niccolo nodded. "Celsi knows from which direction the Paduans are coming, so he'll leave scouting to the militia. But he may try to warn our visitors of our strength. We have to prevent that."

Eduardo departed to carry out the orders.

"I wouldn't be surprised if Celsi's supporters join his mercenaries by dawn," Giovanni said. "He'll want to have men he can trust near him."

Niccolo sighed. "Then there's a chance I'll have to fight my own brother."

Giovanni said nothing further.

NICCOLO

Late the next day, one of Niccolo's scouting parties returned with news of the Paduan arrival to the west. They were hugging the coast, accompanied by a fleet of transports and galleys, just as Lucia had predicted. They had halted six miles from the Venetian encampment.

Vellini sent his cavalry to harass their efforts at fortifying. At the same time, Niccolo's second and third scouting parties arrived with news that more than seven thousand Hungarians, including some who had recovered from Niccolo's earlier rout, were approaching. Niccolo urgently dispatched a man to tell Vellini to halt his attack on the Paduans, but they arrived too late.

The Paduans had evidently received the same reports. Instead of fortifying, they abandoned their half-finished camp to join with their allies. The Venetian horsemen harassed their flank with a charge. Though desperately outnumbered, they rode down more than eight hundred Paduan archers. But they remained too long, and the Paduan cavalry arrived to turn the successful sally into a desperate fight for survival. While some managed to escape, Venice lost almost all of its mounted soldiers.

Disgusted, Vellini transferred the survivors to a grateful Niccolo to augment his cavalry. "What can I do with only two dozen horses?"

Niccolo chose not to educate his general on their value for fear of losing the gift.

As they were discussing possible strategies, one of his scouts stepped through Vellini's tent, breathing heavily and sporting a gash over his ear. "Sir, I have news."

Niccolo recognized him as the leader of his last scouting party. "Speak freely." He gestured toward Vellini.

"We waited just inside a patch of woods between Celsi's mercenaries and the Paduans. We intercepted a messenger trying to cross from one to the other."

Niccolo simply nodded. "From Celsi, or from Carrara?"

"From Carrara to the doge."

Niccolo sighed; Celsi had managed to get word to the Paduans, after all.

Vellini rose, shooting a hard gaze at Niccolo. "What's the meaning of this?"

"I suspected the doge might try to signal the Paduans. I had my men watch his camp."

"Why would you be spying on the doge?"

Niccolo patiently stared at him.

It didn't take Vellini long to make the connection. "The doge is the traitor?" He choked back a cry. "I want to speak with this messenger."

"That won't be possible, if you get my meaning, sirs."

"Why not?" After a moment, the general sighed. "Oh."

The scout explained, "Slippery one, that. He broke past us, and we had to shoot him down. Dead by the time we reached him."

"So, we have no idea what Carrara wanted to say to the doge?" Vellini summarized. "You have no proof of collusion."

"I wouldn't say that." The man grinned. "The messenger we killed was Antonio Galli."

Vellini stared in horror.

Niccolo, on the other hand, grinned. "Antonio Galli." He didn't regret the toad's fate, only that he hadn't witnessed his death. But Galli's treason was far worse than simple murder. Perhaps it was best that Venice had dispensed the justice.

"Galli was communicating with the enemy," Vellini repeated, as if he needed to hear the words aloud to truly accept them. "Why?"

"I suspect he informed the duke of changes to the doge's plans on account of the militia."

"I don't even accept that you're right about all this, Aretoli."

Niccolo sighed. "The Paduans and Hungarians expected no resistance. Celsi would have to inform them about your army. But he may only get one chance. Before mustering, he couldn't be certain of the militia's strength. He wouldn't want to call off the attack if you didn't muster in time or mustered too few men. But now that they're here, it's a small matter to ride the couple miles to their camp."

"How did you know to send your men?"

"Galli tried to take command of my troops."

"I never ordered him to do that," Vellini cried.

"He wasn't following your orders. The doge knows I wouldn't come this far without proof of his guilt." He dared not reveal how little evidence he had. "He has to act before I present it to the Senate."

Vellini raised his hands to halt him. "What are you saying?"

"Celsi had to reassure Carrara by sending someone the duke would trust. Galli."

"Reassure him about what?"

Niccolo crossed his arms. "I'm guessing he'll turn his mercenaries on us during the battle. The Paduans, the Hungarians, and his mercenaries will surround us from three sides."

Vellini lowered himself into his chair, clenching its arms for support. "My God, not another traitorous doge..."

Niccolo took the opportunity to nod a dismissal to his scout. He would pay that man something extra for ridding him of Galli.

"We very nearly left a portion of our forces in the city to guard against sea invasion," Vellini explained. "The doge's idea."

"I'm sure Celsi did everything he could to discourage recruitment, too."

"I would have drawn his *condottiere* up on our left flank," Vellini explained. "If I had, they'd have obliterated us." He licked his lips and met Niccolo's gaze.

"It's still a good plan," Niccolo offered.

"Are you mad? We can't let him be with the army if he's a traitor."

Without proof, he needed the doge to commit overt treason, but Vellini would need another explanation. "If we change the plan and separate him from us, he'll know you suspect him. He'll turn his men on us immediately. Into the confusion, the Paduans and Hungarians will attack. We won't be ready, and we'll be destroyed."

"But we'll be undone if the doge turns on us during the battle."

"Not necessarily," Niccolo said. "Carrara intends to keep the city once he has it." He let Vellini digest the implications of a Paduan occupation for a moment. "He'll need his army intact for that, so he'll wait as long as possible before engaging. That gives us an opportunity."

The general rubbed his chin. "If you're wrong, I suppose we'll know it before the Paduans engage."

"And Celsi can reinforce you," Niccolo finished. "But if I'm right, we save Venice from annihilation."

Vellini swallowed.

Leaning over, Niccolo pointed to the general's map. "Let me show you what I propose."

ROSALIA

All the canals and causeways were empty except those leading to the city's churches and cathedrals. Even the pickpockets that populated the city at night were quiet. Many of them were with the militia.

The buildings lining each *ria* and canal cast long shadows in the moonless darkness. Rosalia had to navigate by the lanterns above the doors to the various homes. Their light was faint, but it was enough for her to make her way.

The faint haze of the fires in the Venetian camp rose up from the plain of the Veneto. Niccolo was somewhere amid that tent city.

Giovanni seemed certain it would come to battle. She prayed Signor Sabarelli would honor his pledge to her—both of his pledges.

Her battle would be tonight.

After Giovanni had announced the doge's treachery, her thoughts had dwelled on her husband's possible complicity. Had Flavio betrayed their city, too? She was too much of a Cornaro to ignore the possibility, and he was no longer enough of an Aretoli to be above suspicion.

And so, she would go home, back to the man who had beaten and discarded her, to discover the truth.

She hesitated at the locked door.

This was still her house. He had insisted on that point. She drew in a fortifying breath and knocked.

Her maid's son opened the door and regarded her with wide eyes. "My lady?"

Chin held high, Rosalia stepped inside. "Is Master Aretoli at home?" she asked with more confidence than she felt.

"He…he isn't, my lady. I'm sorry."

She wasn't. Relief washed over her.

"He left some time ago but did not say where he was going."

"How was he dressed?" It figured he'd go whoring even with the city under threat of invasion.

"A dark cloak and plain clothes, my lady."

She wrinkled her nose. It wasn't like Flavio to dress so unfashionably. What could he be doing? "I came to collect some items. Please do not report my presence to the other servants. Do you understand?"

The boy nodded and lowered his gaze. She hadn't been home in weeks; hopefully, he'd at least wait until she left before spreading this bit of gossip.

"Off you go, then." She offered a conciliatory smile.

She had planned to confront Flavio directly and gauge the truth from his reaction. But she now realized how foolish that plan had been. She remembered that look terrible in his eye. He was capable of anything. Confronting him would have been dangerous.

She rubbed some warmth into her arms. Simply being in this house felt threatening. But she needed to know the truth.

The great carved door that had led to Angelo's refuge was unlocked. Rosalia slipped in quietly. Flavio's *tavola* stood where it always had. Any evidence in the house would be there. She spared one more glance down the hall before quietly closing the door.

A stack of papers sat on the corner of the *tavola*. Most were Flavio's copies of contracts signed following his father's death. After reading a few of them, Rosalia learned how deep a discount he had offered to retain the loyalty of his family partners. They weren't as eager to isolate Niccolo as Flavio had led her to believe.

There were invitations to dinner, reports from factors abroad about market conditions in their cities, and supply estimates from his partners. But none of it connected him to the doge.

Sighing, she studied the room. It was empty except for a pair of chairs and a small table that held a decanter of wine and four goblets.

But in the corner sat the great chest where Angelo had kept his forbidden scrolls. She knelt before it. It had a latch but no lock. She grunted as she raised the heavy lid. Looking inside, she gasped.

All of Angelo's precious scrolls were gone.

The Aretoli patriarch had spent a fortune painstakingly gathering them over the years. He had paid his factors and partners a bounty for each scroll they acquired. That collection had been the effort of a lifetime.

Flavio had probably sold them for a pittance or burned them in frustration. Niccolo would be furious when he found out.

Only a few creased pages remained within the chest. She brushed aside the old contracts and correspondence, whose broken seals made lumpy bulges at the bottom, after reading the first few words.

A crisp piece of paper with Flavio's signature rested off to the side. It bore no creases. She quickly read the short letter.

Your Excellency, Doge Lorenzo Celsi,

When will you deliver the Council of Ten seat you promised? I've isolated my brother and prevented him from harming you. I've supported you in the Senate, even though you still withhold your intentions and plans from me. And yet, you did not support my candidacy during the last election.

I have fulfilled my obligations to you, and I now expect you to do the same. I need your support to win my seat.

Flavio Aretoli

She set the paper down. He had known nothing of the doge's plans. Relief that she wouldn't be tainted by treason battled with a crushing disappointment. If he had been a traitor, he'd have been executed, their marriage would have been annulled, and she would have been free to marry again.

But there was something more. She re-read the missive with growing revulsion at the way he had pleaded for the support of such a vile man. He wrote as a supplicant dragging his name into the mud of beggary.

This was the man who had struck her to the ground a mere few feet away from here? He was contemptible in so many ways.

But, unfortunately, he was no traitor, just a sad, jealous man.

Outside, the door to the house opened, and she heard voices. Men's voices. Most of Giovanni's male servants had presented themselves for militia duty, and Flavio's household had likely done the same.

It had to be Flavio.

Eyes widening, she looked around for an escape. Where could she go? He could see the door to the study from the entryway; she could never slip out unnoticed.

The footsteps were coming closer.

The chest. She remembered Niccolo hiding in it when they had played together as children, and with Angelo's scrolls gone, perhaps she could fit.

She stepped inside and bunched up the folds of her skirts. There would just be enough room, and only because of the curved lid. Footsteps were approaching the study. Quickly, she checked again to make sure her dress wasn't poking out and closed the lid.

It was stiflingly hot and dark inside. But she could still hear the large carved door open.

"Quickly now." The hushed voice sounded like Flavio's. The door shut again. "I've not done this before. How do we proceed?"

Another voice, deeper and steadier, replied, "Tell me what you need."

"I want him dead. Make him suffer if you can."

She pressed a hand to her mouth, suppressing a gasp.

"Poison?"

"Too slow," Flavio replied. "He must die before he can report to the Senate."

"Where can I find him?"

"He's with the militia now." The militia? Her hands began to shake as a dreadful fear grew.

"…impossible to reach. I must wait until he returns."

"Fine, fine."

"If he dies in battle, I still expect to be paid."

"Yes, yes, whatever." After a pause, "Do you need a contract? I have paper."

Paper she was kneeling on!

Footsteps approached the chest. She was trapped in this room with a murderer and a man who had beaten her once already. If they found her…

"Absolutely not. Write nothing down." The footsteps stopped.

"You're a trusting sort."

"Not at all. If you betray me, I will kill you too."

The pause was longer. "I will pay you after."

"Half now, half after." Footsteps approached the door. "Is there any message you wish me to convey?"

"Message?" Flavio asked.

"Sometimes, a client wishes the victim to know the reason for his death."

"Ah, yes." A faint laugh that barely reached her inside the chest broke the silence. "Tell him, 'I'll treat Rosalia like she deserves, brother.' I want his last moments to be agony."

Rosalia shut her eyes, holding back the scream begging to be released. He was ordering his own brother's murder! Niccolo, her sweet Niccolo.

"So be it," the second voice agreed. "Payment?"

"Yes, of course." The door opened. The footsteps retreated down the hall, through the main entrance, and out onto the street.

Rosalia couldn't muster the courage to raise the lid and emerge from the chest until long after the door had closed. Her breath came in ragged gasps, and not only because of the heat of the chest. Sweat beaded on her forehead. Her heartbeat thundered in her ears; how hadn't they heard it?

Even when he had disinherited his brothers and betrayed his father, she hadn't believed Flavio capable of this.

But then she remembered the frenzied delight in his eyes when he'd looked down on her and the blood dripping down her cheek. That was who her husband was. And he intended to murder the man she loved, the man she would always love.

She could not let that happen.

NICCOLO

Shortly after midnight, Vellini announced they would give battle on the morrow. Not only would further delay cause more damage to the surrounding land, but it would give the Hungarians Niccolo had scattered more time to arrive.

As discreetly as possible, Niccolo's men worked through the night to position the equipment for his plan.

When the sun crested the hills to the east, the Venetians drew up their battle lines with the sun at their backs. They were mortgaging visibility in the afternoon, but if the battle lasted that long, their gambit would have failed and no one would be alive to complain about squinting at the evening sun.

Niccolo and his Quarter Foxes formed the right flank. He stretched his pikemen thinner than usual and placed his cavalry in front to let them maneuver. The Venetian militia arrayed itself in the center, with the crossbowmen behind and the doge's *condottiere* on the left.

As soon as the Hungarians and Paduans recognized the invitation to battle, they also assembled. Hungarian mercenary cavalry opposed Niccolo's battalion, and the infantry faced the Venetian militia. The Paduans formed up opposite Celsi's mercenaries.

Perhaps eager to begin looting the city before they lost the light, the Hungarians dispensed with the usual skirmishing and sent their infantry forward.

The sudden movement sent a murmur down the Venetian line. Crossbowmen launched a volley over the backs of their pikemen into the advancing line, then quickly reloaded behind their free-standing, man-sized *pavise* shields. The bolts cut a shallow course, slamming into the front ranks of the Hungarian flanks. Men went down in screaming heaps that tangled the feet of their brethren. Frantic for secure footing, many drifted toward the center, creating a compacted mass that crashed into the Venetian pike militia with an audible crack.

But the pikes held, and the Hungarians recoiled before forming up to charge again.

Niccolo scanned the enemy rear for signs of the mercenary cavalry, but the thick dust thrown up by their movements drifted across the field and obscured his view of the Hungarian horsemen. It was the perfect cover for a surprise charge, though.

Niccolo, trusting his instincts, raised his hand and gave the order.

His herald sounded a long-short-long pattern on his horn. The Quarter Fox pikemen sidestepped, forming into companies separated by thin corridors. At the next horn—this one three short puffs—Niccolo's cavalry pulled their horses around and rushed through the open paths, reforming in the rear near himself and Giovanni.

His timing was uncanny. Just as the last of his horsemen had withdrawn, the Hungarian cavalry emerged through the dust at full tilt with lances lowered. But instead of soft, mounted targets, they confronted segmented walls of pikes. Some riders reared back, while a few navigated through the corridors between companies only to be attacked on all sides as they ran the gauntlet. The rest impacted the jagged hedges in a screeching collision.

Niccolo shouted out encouragement to his militiamen.

The pike wall collapsed almost immediately under the tremendous pressure, but not without achieving its purpose. Flung forward, dozens of horses and riders impaled themselves on the militia's rows of spears. Wooden shafts snapped, sending splinters flying in all directions. Most fell to the Foxes' thirsty blades. A handful managed to escape through the militia ranks only for Niccolo's cavalry to dispatch them.

With the right flank firmly in hand, Niccolo spared a glance at the center. The militia was holding under the onslaught of the Hungarian infantry. Though thinned to match the Hungarians' greater width, they fought like the lions on their pennants, keeping the swordsmen at bay with their longer pikes.

On the other flank, separated from Niccolo by six thousand pikemen and several tons of airborne dust, the doge's mercenaries began to advance. They marched in formation toward the Paduans but were still behind the Venetian line.

And then, Lorenzo Celsi made his decision.

Just before their front ranks pulled even with the Venetian rear, the mercenaries halted, wheeled to the right, and marched into the Venetian flank. At the same command, the doge's cavalry charged toward the defenseless crossbowmen in the Venetian rear.

There would be no evidence or lengthy investigation into his dealings; the doge intended to destroy the only army between him and the throne of Venice.

But Vellini and Niccolo had prepared well. Niccolo ordered the final horn, a sequence of three long blows, and his cavalry broke off from their attacks to form ranks.

While the doge's mercenaries surged forward, Vellini's heralds sounded two short notes. The rear rank of the Venetian line peeled off to the left, dangerously depleting the militia's depth but presenting an ever-thickening hedge of leveled pikes at the mercenaries running toward them.

Meeting with unexpected resistance, Celsi's mercenary infantry halted, pinned in place.

A moment before Celsi's cavalry struck them, Vellini's crossbowmen lifted the pikes Niccolo's men had distributed during the night. But the *condottiere* weren't hindered by dust and were more experienced than the Hungarians. Pulling up short, they hedged the crossbowmen in on all sides, probing them for weaknesses. The doge pulled back with a small bodyguard and directed the attack on the island of Venetian crossbowmen, at whose center stood a furious Vellini.

Gradually, Celsi's cavalry opened up a small hole in Vellini's pikemen and began to surge into it. Vellini's crossbowmen lacked the experience with the large spears to work as a unit and were starting to panic. But with nowhere to go, they fought on, even as their companions next to them began to fall under the merciless hacking of mercenary swords.

The Paduans chose that moment to begin their march toward the Venetian center.

Astride his horse, the doge turned, intending to order a rider to re-direct the Paduans behind the Hungarian rear to attack Niccolo's militia.

Instead, he turned to see Niccolo Aretoli and seventy Venetian riders bearing down on him in complete silence. Not for his men. For him. They muttered no battle cry meant to strike terror in the hearts of their opponents.

For a brief moment before they collided, Niccolo met Celsi's gaze. The doge's panicked eyes filled Niccolo with a terrifying thrill.

I've come for you, Celsi. You're the last one, and I've come for you. Vendetta.

The Quarter Foxes crashed into his mercenaries with a crack like thunder. They collapsed into a frenzied hand-to-hand battle. Niccolo fought his way to Celsi, but before he could close the distance, a sword came down on Celsi's neck, shattering bone and sinew as it lodged itself in its target.

Though denied the chance to kill Celsi with his own hands, Niccolo nonetheless basked in the satisfaction of the moment.

Celsi tottered for a time and released a dull moan. The mercenaries nearby broke off their attack, watching in stunned silence as Celsi listed in his saddle before finally falling to the ground. After a few moments of stillness, they sounded a retreat.

A very few—those senators and Venetians who had participated in Celsi's conspiracy—continued to fight. Niccolo's men, in no mood for mercy, cut them down to the last man.

Niccolo's riders gave a cheer that was soon picked up by Vellini's crossbowmen. Slowly, word of Celsi's death and the defeat of the mercenaries spread.

The Paduans halted and withdrew from the battlefield without having ever engaged. Evidently, Carrara didn't intend to ruin his army with this enterprise.

Left alone without cavalry support, the Hungarians broke off their attack soon after.

The Venetian militiamen, battered and bloodied, watched the professional armies of its enemies flee the field in a mix of elation and disbelief. Only when the dust from galloping horses and shuffling boots began to clear did the cheering begin. The plain filled with the clamoring of swords on shields, crossbows on *pavises,* and pikes on breastplates.

They had won. The republic had survived.

CHAPTER SEVENTEEN

NICCOLO

NICCOLO HAD HOPED to visit Marco before returning home, but cleaning up the battlefield took longer than expected.

They had found the doge immediately. Niccolo, Giovanni, Vellini, and the rest of the senators advising the general took special note of the ordinary sword still sticking out of him. Instigating a murmur of surprise, Niccolo calmly retrieved it from the body and returned it to Eduardo, his eyes alight with wry satisfaction. This had started with Eduardo on Crete, and it had ended with him in the Veneto.

Vellini, cautious since his reckless cavalry charge, ordered a thorough search of the surrounding countryside for further threats. But by the end of the day, patrols returned with the news that the Hungarians and Paduans had both gone home. Satisfied, the general dismissed the militia.

Niccolo returned to the city with the last of his men. He didn't reach his door until early evening.

Pietro wrapped his arms around Niccolo when he opened the door. "Praise to God, you're safe!"

"I've missed you, my friend," he said between reassuring laughter. "There were times I could have used your help."

Pietro eyed the man next to him. "Who's this?"

Niccolo gestured to Eduardo. "A dear friend, and now a war hero." Eduardo broke into a proud smile.

"He was with me in Constantinople," Niccolo continued. "I've invited him to stay here since he's so far from home."

Pietro eyed the newcomer with unfriendly eyes. "You say he's been with you for some time?"

Niccolo nodded. "About a month, and I've known him for two years."

"And you trust him?" Pietro demanded.

"I do." Niccolo narrowed his eyes. "Why?"

The steward ushered them inside and shut the door. "There's someone here you should speak to."

The steward led them to one of the servant's rooms and knocked softly.

"Come in."

Niccolo's pulse raced. He knew that voice!

Pushing the door open, he leaped inside and searched the room's contents until he found her. She was straightening her hair with her back turned to him, but he would recognize her from any angle at any time. He had pictured her a thousand times, and never did he imagine she would be standing in his house like this.

"Rosalia!"

"Nico?" She turned. "Oh, thank God you're safe." Her words carried no longing or desire, only relief. Nor did her eyes well with tears at a loving reunion. They carried only determination and worry.

He didn't care; he had wasted too many chances to tell her how he felt. He would not waste another. "Every day while I was gone, I've missed you—"

And then he saw the bruises, and his heart broke. Only one thing could have caused such wounds on a patrician woman.

"He did that to you?"

"What?" Frowning, she brought a hand up to her cheek. Her eyes widened. "Oh, yes. But we have larger concerns."

He was about to protest that nothing mattered more than her safety, but her next words halted his every thought.

"Your brother is going to kill you."

NICCOLO

He hadn't believed her at first. It just didn't made sense for Flavio to want him dead after so many months. This was the man who had protected him against the neighborhood boys, the brother who had gotten into trouble with him as children.

But as she had described what she had heard, he realized the last few months hadn't changed his brother; the seeds of his descent had always been there. In Constantinople, Niccolo hadn't seen what his brother had become. Marco, Camilla, and Rosalia had, and they had suffered for it. Flavio was a stranger, capable of anything.

The bruises on Rosalia's face proved that.

The Senate meeting was the next morning. If Flavio truly meant to do this thing, it would have to occur tonight. So Niccolo sat in the darkness of his room with a loaded crossbow and his scimitar across his lap, waiting to learn if his brother had fallen so far that he could not be saved.

A faint click sounded in the distance, followed by the slow sliding of the front door.

A tear spilled from Niccolo's eye. By God, Flavio had hired an assassin, after all. To kill his own brother.

Niccolo heard no footfalls on the stairs. Only when the door slowly slid open did he realize the intruder had already reached his room. It was dark, but Niccolo could discern the faint outline of a wiry man creeping toward the bed.

It was the assassin. A robber would have stolen whatever he could downstairs.

The man ripped the covers back and stabbed downward. "Your brother says he'll treat—" He stopped and felt at the covers. "Huh?"

Niccolo thumped the floor with his foot. Pietro rushed inside, uncovering the lantern in his hand and casting an orange glow on the attacker. Eduardo followed a moment later, wielding his sword.

"Halt."

The assassin turned to attack, but upon seeing Niccolo's crossbow pointed at him, he froze, recognition dawning.

"Drop the knife," Niccolo commanded. "If you pull that hand back to throw it, you'll be dead before you release it."

The man studied him, searching his target for injuries or weaknesses. Niccolo couldn't help but smile as he stood perfectly still, holding the crossbow motionless before him.

The assassin's knife clattered to the floor.

Eduardo kicked it away while Pietro placed the lantern on a table and quickly bound the intruder's hands. The old steward discovered a sheath up the man's sleeve and took it. He studied it with interest once he withdrew to lean against the wall.

Niccolo remained still with his crossbow trained on its target. "You've come to kill a senator of Venice. Your life is now mine." He swallowed. "Who hired you?"

In spite of everything, he prayed the answer was not what he feared, that this was all some sort of mistake.

The assassin's attention shifted between the crossbow and Eduardo's sword. "Flavio Aretoli."

An ache settled in the pit of Niccolo's stomach. There could be no negotiating, no reasoning, with a man who would murder his own family. He would need to deal with his brother, once and for all.

This was the price he would always have to pay, the price his father had predicted.

"I'm told he still owes you half of your payment. How was he supposed to deliver it?"

The assassin stared at Niccolo's crossbow. "I'd send a courier to report that the deed was done."

"How?"

"He would say, 'It is done.'"

Niccolo frowned. "That's it?" He had expected a secret word or gesture, something more complex.

"He'd understand its meaning."

Niccolo turned to Pietro. "Send one of your men with the message. Someone Flavio doesn't recognize."

"What should I do with him when it's done?" Pietro glared at the assassin.

"If he speaks the truth, I'll release him when I get back."

Pietro gasped. "You can't be serious."

"You'd let me go?" Even the assassin sounded astonished. "I tried to kill you."

"I've recently become acquainted with people like you." Niccolo lowered the crossbow as he recalled Lucia, whom Colmiera was keeping under guard pending news from Venice. "All of my enemies are already dead, and killing you would solve nothing." He sighed. "Besides, by the time you're free, there won't be any profit in trying again."

"I could have my man handle Flavio," Pietro began.

"No. He's still an Aretoli, even if he doesn't act like one."

In Pietro's eyes, relief vied for control with sorrow. The old man knew what Niccolo intended and that his master was sparing him the responsibility of doing it.

Niccolo owed it to his father to handle this himself.

FLAVIO

Dawn was still two hours away when Flavio received the assassin's message indicating success. He rushed off to the docks to meet the assassin with a skip in his step. Just in case the man intended to betray him, Flavio strapped on his sword.

The Senate was staying tight-lipped about the result of the battle, but some of his guard contacts revealed that the doge was dead and the Senate was rounding up his remaining allies. While Flavio had been as shocked as anyone to learn of Celsi's plans to overthrow the republic, who would believe his protestations of innocence? He had moved against Niccolo just in time. Now, no one would ever know about his relationship with the doge.

Flavio Aretoli, not Lorenzo Celsi, stood triumphant. Niccolo had had his revenge, but so had he. The troublesome brother who had caused all his problems was dead.

He savored the thought of telling Rosalia he had made her dear lover into a corpse. He would show her his body, so the image of Niccolo lying cold would sear itself into her memory. The more blood, the better. Never again would she imagine the wrong Aretoli brother when he bedded her. And bed her he would, just often enough to remind her he still owned her.

The meeting spot was concealed behind a maze of crates waiting for shipment. Celsi had claimed they were standard gifts from one head of state to another. Now, Flavio understood that they were bribes due to ship the next day to princes and despots throughout Europe. Once he'd finished here, he'd have to look through those shipments. Celsi had mentioned something about a fine oak table. It would look perfect in his dining room.

A slapping sound came from the left. He picked his way around a few crates to investigate but only found water lapping against the pier.

The muted shouts of celebration sounded in the distance. He grinned. They had no idea their great hero was dead.

The scrapping of boots on the deck paneling signaled that his agent had arrived.

"My friend, you have made me a very happy man!" He turned to face the triumphant assassin.

And stopped cold.

Niccolo stood hauntingly still in the middle of the clearing, blocking the only exit.

At first, Flavio thought he had simply imagined the subject of his idle thoughts on the assassin's face. After all, Niccolo was hardly a dangerous man with a blade; he would have been an easy target.

"It's time to answer for your crimes, Flavio."

This was no figment of his imagination.

NICCOLO

"I thought you were dead," Flavio muttered.

Niccolo stared unblinkingly. "As I intended."

"What are you—"

"I didn't want to believe it." His quiet voice rasped. "You robbed Marco of his birthright. Your temper denied Camilla a decent marriage. You collaborated with the men who murdered our father. Your orders almost killed Giovanni in Trieste. You brutally beat your wife—"

"She was an adulteress. She deserved what I gave her."

Niccolo ignored him. "This can't continue."

"What are you going to do, report me to the Senate?" Flavio scoffed. "You wouldn't do that to your own brother."

"No, I wouldn't." He drew his scimitar from its sheath with a smooth hiss.

Flavio gawked for a moment. "You want to fight me?" He barked out a laugh. "My little brother wants to fight me?" He drew his sword. "Then have at it. I'm glad I get the chance to do this myself, actually."

Niccolo intentionally slipped into a classic Italian combat pose wholly unsuited to his curved weapon. "You stood by while, all this time, the doge was forging a collar around our necks. Didn't you realize what was happening, or have you become so corrupt that you didn't care?"

Flavio circled his brother, offering an occasional feigned thrust. "I did what was necessary to protect my family."

"The only abuse they suffered was at your hands."

Flavio cocked his sword back and released a broad overhead swing at Niccolo. The shifting of his brother's weight, the wide movement of his arm—Niccolo had plenty of time to simply step out of the way.

Niccolo offered a quick thrust, an intentionally awkward motion with the curved scimitar. Flavio deflected it easily but slowly. He was faster than this. They were both toying with each other, just as Pietro had taught them.

Flavio lunged, and Niccolo parried as he would have six months earlier. Abandoning his previous lethargy, Flavio responded with a lightning jab. Niccolo narrowly avoided it, only for Flavio to twirl his wrist and come back at him overhead at blistering speed.

Niccolo made his move. Shifting out of his awkward stance, he deflected the attack with a circular motion. His brother's sword slid right off the edge of his scimitar. As Niccolo spun out of his brother's range, he slashed sideways and caught Flavio on the right thigh. The leg, bracing his weight after the downward strike, buckled, and he fell to the ground.

Niccolo brought his scimitar down, but Flavio rolled out of the way and kicked up with his good leg. Niccolo stumbled backward, hand snapping up to the sharp pain in his side.

As the distance opened up between them, Niccolo scowled. He'd probably broken a rib, while his subterfuge had resulted in Flavio taking only in a light graze.

Rising, Flavio recovered his posture. "You've improved since you left."

Niccolo remained silent, refusing to be baited. This wasn't like Flavio's other duels. Only one of them would survive.

When Flavio took a step with his injured leg and stumbled, Niccolo slashed at him. But his brother spun aside and sliced along his left shoulder, sending searing pain down Niccolo's back. He lashed out blindly and caught the meat of Flavio's upper arm.

Flavio scampered away, clutching his bleeding arm. The injury must have been much deeper than the first scratch. From the blood darkening his tunic, he would be sluggish for the rest of the fight.

But Niccolo was preoccupied with the blistering pain running down his left side. His back felt damp. Raising his left arm was becoming more difficult by the moment. His fatigue was mounting, and he couldn't take many more of these cuts. While Niccolo's eastern training had helped, Flavio was still the better duelist. He had to settle this quickly or Flavio would simply outlast him.

As his brother circled, Niccolo searched for anything that might give him an edge. An old plank warped upwards by age? An exposed knot of rope to deflect his brother's sword? Even a puddle of water he might slip on.

But then Flavio charged and heaved his sword down in a vicious chop.

Surprised, Niccolo instinctively raised his left hand to bat his brother's sword out of the way. The blade dug into the side of his hand with a sickening squish and a searing pain. Blood splashed against his face as Flavio's sword reeled off to the side, out of control.

Flavio's momentum forced him forward. Seeing the opening, Niccolo struck. With a crunch and a grinding, Niccolo's blade dug deeply into Flavio's ribs, sawing its way across his midsection. Flavio's sword fell to the ground with a clamor, followed by the thump of his brother's body.

As Niccolo reared back, blood slid down his blade and moistened his grip on the hilt.

Flavio's blood.

Aretoli blood.

Blood he had drawn.

The pain pulsed again. Holding his scimitar beneath his armpit, he ripped at his left sleeve until it came free and wrapped it around his badly mangled hand. He couldn't move his fingers. Whether that was from the injury or pressure from his makeshift tourniquet, he didn't know.

Flavio was struggling to recover. He looked almost pathetic now.

Niccolo approached carefully, his eyes watering from the searing pain of his wounds. Squinting, he cleared his vision enough to see his brother's sword lying some distance out of reach.

Niccolo remembered the brother who had soothed him when Father would punish them, the brother who had comforted him when their mother died.

Flavio fumbled to withdraw a knife from his boot. He rose to his knees, feebly holding the weapon before him. "Okay, you've made your point, Nico," Flavio even managed a smile. The bottom half of his tunic was stained a dark red. "Now call Gian Jacopo so we can clean me up." He convulsed when a fresh spasm of pain lanced across his face.

"I can't do that, Flavio."

Flavio's eyes widened. "I'm your brother."

He recalled Flavio's vulnerable relief upon hearing Niccolo hadn't blamed him for his marriage. But that relief had been a lie, masking the jealousy and anger that had led them here.

"Not after you tried to murder your own blood."

"You can't let me die. You're too good of a man to do that. That's what Rosalia loves about you." He licked his lips. "You want her? Take her."

Even now, Flavio still believed Niccolo had done all this for her. As if the love of a woman could justify the murder of a brother.

He was a good man. He knew that now. Despite what his brother thought, he had resisted his feelings for Rosalia. He had aided his friends and family and had punished those who had threatened them. He had risked his life and his fortune to protect the republic that had raised him.

But his father was right, as well. He would do what he must and bear the burden, good man or not. And Flavio would never stop. He had proven that.

"I'm sorry, Flavio. I love you."

Rage twisted his brother's face. "I hate you! You're just like fath—"

Niccolo's slash to Flavio's throat offered as quick of a death as he could provide.

His brother gaped at Niccolo for a few heartbeats with the same expression Umberto had worn. And Alvero. The similarity brought the taste of bile to Niccolo's throat.

The knife fell from Flavio's hand as he fell backward. Kneeling, Niccolo slid it and his scimitar out of reach and placed his injured hand on Flavio's chest. Even Flavio didn't deserve to die alone.

They met each other's gaze at the last moment.

"Sleep, brother."

Whether he heard him, Niccolo would never know. Tears of regret splashed onto Flavio's face as the last hint of light faded from his eyes.

Niccolo sat with his brother for a long while. Only when his injured hand went numb did he finally recover his scimitar and rise to search for Gian Jacopo.

NICCOLO

It took a week for his injuries to heal enough that movement wouldn't open them again. Though his hand would eventually heal outwardly, he had severed the tendons of his two outside fingers. Despite Gian Jacopo's skill, Niccolo knew the truth: he would never use those fingers again.

Pietro chided him for the foolishness of blocking with his bare hand until a stern glance silenced him. His duel with Flavio was not a subject for discussion.

There were a dozen things that needed urgent attention, from the mess Flavio had made of the Aretoli name to the consequences of the doge's fall from power. But one stood out above all the others. With a weary, broken voice, Niccolo ordered a litter to carry him to the Aretoli home.

The trip took less time than he expected. As the Venetians on the streets realized who was approaching, they cleared a path, reverently touching the wood of his litter as if he were the pope. They must have heard about his role in recent events.

If they only knew the cost.

Flavio's steward opened the door. "May I help you, sir?"

With surprise, Niccolo realized he had never visited Flavio's home.

Naturally, his brother's steward wouldn't recognize him. "I wish to speak to your mistress."

The man eyed him, noting his bandages and the sling. "And you are?"

"Niccolo Aretoli."

Eyes widening, the steward ushered him into the reception room that had been his father's.

This had been where he'd first seen Rosalia and his brother together after he'd returned from Crete.

He heard her approach—the creaking of weight on the steps— long before he saw her. She wore a modest black dress with a surprising amount of fringe. As she entered, she met his gaze briefly before lowering it again.

"Rosa..." They hadn't spoken since she'd told him of Flavio's plans. "You saved my life. If not for you, I would be dead."

She raised her gaze. The terror and anguish in her eyes nearly broke his heart. He had stolen her husband from her. Regardless of what he'd done to her, that had to be painful.

"I couldn't let you die." She swallowed. "He meant to kill you, Nico. Kill you. I couldn't let him." The tears fell.

"I'm sorry for all this, Rosa. I'm so sorry, but I had no other choice. He was unstable, a danger to us all. I couldn't let him hurt the people I care about."

"It's not your fault," she insisted. "It's mine. I told him. He wanted to kill you because I told him."

"Told him what?"

She wiped the tears from her eyes. "I let slip how I felt about you. How I still feel. I remember the look on his face, the fury..." She touched the healing bruises on her cheek. "I didn't realize it then, but that's the moment he decided to kill you."

Niccolo heard only one of those sentences. "How you still feel?" He swallowed. "Even after...after I killed your husband?" Hope sparked. He'd thought she'd be furious with him.

"Oh, Nico, you are a fool. I knew what you would do. I know you better than you know yourself." Rising, Rosalia circled behind a chair, putting distance between them. "I had to choose one of you. Of course I chose you. It was always you." She shook her head. "But now you know. You know I put you in that position. When you look at me, all you'll ever see is your brother's death."

That was her worry? "That look you saw in his eyes? I saw it too when we fought. He lost his way. He made his choice." Careful to keep his left hand and arm still, he slowly circled the chair to stand beside her. "I could never blame you, Rosa. I love you. I always have. I always will."

Tentatively, he raised his good hand and caressed her cheek. She wrapped her arms around him. He grunted when she hit his shoulder, but the tender warmth of her body pressed against his was worth the fleeting pain.

NICCOLO

The Senate worked with unusual alacrity to put the Celsi situation behind them. The torture of some of Celsi's remaining supporters revealed the extent of the conspiracy.

In the end, Lucia did not need to give evidence. At first, Petrarch refused to recommend her to the pope on account of some old quarrel with the pontiff involving his sister. Only when Niccolo mentioned her nocturnal talents did the old poet agree.

"She'll fit right in."

With the danger thwarted, the Senate turned to preserving its reputation. Stability kept interest rates low and eased the difficulty of renegotiating treaties. Before that esteemed body degenerated into squabbling over who should fill the vacant ducal post, it sent riders to deliver two messages.

The first reminded Francesco da Carrara that Venice's victorious army was less than two days' march from his city. However, the republic was prepared to pretend nothing whatsoever had happened on the plain of the Veneto if he would do the same. The other letter offered a similar proposal to the King of Hungary, with the addendum that he wouldn't want the legacy of his rule to be an embarrassing loss to a week-old militia.

The Senate's next decree caught Niccolo by surprise, authorizing the payment of stipends to every volunteer who had been wounded or killed. Niccolo only learned of it when an *avogadori* arrived at his front door to reimburse him for two-thirds of the cost he had incurred for his army. Evidently, the Council of Ten had found a curiously overlooked copy of the doge's will that listed as his heirs all the men who had volunteered for militia service for the year. Celsi died a very rich man, and more than a few senators winked slyly as they praised the old doge's generosity.

To ensure that no future doge would be inspired to overthrow the republic by the example of Marino Faliero, as Lorenzo Celsi had, the Senate ordered the name of that first ducal traitor erased from the official records and his portrait removed from the council chamber.

No one would ever know how close Venice had come to hailing Celsi as prince. The appearance of weakness had to be avoided at all costs. As it had done in the past, the Council of Ten ordered all charges against Celsi destroyed after hanging the few remaining conspirators in St. Mark's Square. Official documents would record the death of their doge in his bed and the loss of a Venetian galley bearing a dozen senators, including Antonio Galli, to a storm.

But most importantly to Niccolo, the declaration settled all matters even incidentally related to the conspiracy. While it prevented him from revealing the true cause of his father's death, it also absolved him of any future blame for the fates of Umberto Feratollo and Flavio Aretoli. If anyone discovered his involvement in Alvero Madina's death, that too would be forgiven. And the Cretan revolt would be known merely as a disagreement among Venetian subjects.

With a simple matter of administrative manipulation, the official record would report that absolutely nothing of interest happened on the plain of the Veneto that warm summer day.

NICCOLO

Niccolo had been mulling over how to convince Valentino Erizzo to reconsider Camilla's suitability when Pietro announced that the young man had arrived to speak with him. Intrigued, Niccolo beckoned him in.

Not one Erizzo but two entered after a short while. The younger Erizzo still bore the scars of half-healed injuries. Much like Rosalia's, his wounds hinted at a savage beating.

Niccolo, still recovering from his own confrontation with Flavio, rose from the chair behind his *tavola* to greet them. "Gentlemen. Please forgive me for not bowing in respect for men of your stature."

"Of course, Signor Aretoli." The elder Erizzo gestured to the chairs. "May we sit?"

The deference only increased his curiosity. "By all means, sirs." As they all settled, Niccolo asked, "How may I help you?"

Young Erizzo glanced at his father, who began, "First, we wish to welcome you home. I'm pleased to hear your travels were so profi… productive."

Niccolo suppressed a smile. Old Erizzo had sniffed a change in the wind. "Indeed. The East had its opportunities for growth, where a hundred thousand ducats are valued as a mere trifle."

Old Erizzo's pupils dilated. "Also, I am sorry for your brother's tragic accident." The sentiment lacked sincerity, but Niccolo could hardly blame him.

Having determined the reason for their visit, Niccolo relaxed. "I appreciate your sentiment. What brings you to my home?"

Erizzo gestured limply. "We wished to discuss an unresolved matter."

"Oh?" Niccolo feigned ignorance.

"The matter of marriage between your sister and my son."

"I see." Niccolo leaned forward slightly. "I understood the matter to be resolved when you declared your hatred of my family and your son suggested my sister was a whore."

Erizzo grimaced. "You are well informed, Signor Aretoli."

Niccolo refused to release the squirming old man from his piercing gaze. "Extremely so."

Young Valentino fidgeted in his chair. "Perhaps your brother and I each spoke precipitously. Recent events have shown us how important courtesy and respect should be among senators."

Recent events, indeed. Rumors of a trail of sapphires from Byzantium to the battlefield likely had more to do with it.

"What do you propose?"

"Propose?" Erizzo briefly looked to his son. "I propose marriage between your sister and my son and legitimacy to their child."

"I understand that," Niccolo added, "and I agree it's a good goal. But what of the related issues?"

"Related issues?"

"To start, am I to ignore your slander against my sister? If I agreed to your proposal as it stands, it would appear as if House Aretoli had bowed to House Erizzo." He lowered his voice. "It should be obvious to you by now that submission is not an option I will ever entertain."

Erizzo leaned back, speechless.

Into the silence, Niccolo explained, "I'll tell you what's happening here, senator. You've heard rumors about my wealth and my role in…recent matters. Allow me to set them to rest. Yes, I've acquired a massive fortune. And my *vendetta* against the doge and his allies resulted in a vacant ducal seat and a dozen dead traitors."

Confusion washed across Erizzo's face. He'd probably expected Niccolo to happily accept whatever he had offered. "What are your terms?"

"Your argument was with my brother, wasn't it? He treated you disrespectfully. In return, you received a sizeable portion of his holdings."

"Yes?" This came from the young Erizzo.

"I can think of no better sign of reconciliation than the return of those holdings. After that, I see no impediment to the marriage you suggest." He quickly added, "You will, of course, receive a proper dowry."

Valentino's head snapped toward his father, but old Erizzo remained unconvinced. "And what of Flavio's attack. It must be answered."

Niccolo shrugged. "What about a public announcement, perhaps at the wedding, during which I express my respect and admiration for your family?"

He gasped. "You would do that?" A political endorsement from a man who had so recently saved the republic held incalculable value.

"To see my sister properly wed, yes."

"Father…" Valentino urged.

Niccolo turned to the son. "You need to answer to me for your treatment of my sister, young Erizzo." They were very much of the same age, but this man seemed like a babe in swaddling clothes. "Why did you insult her?"

Instead of a measured response, he answered in a jumble. "I'm so sorry. Your brother…he was looming over me. I couldn't help it. I thought if I acted confident, maybe he would just leave."

Niccolo sighed. Had he ever been this young and foolish? "I hope you show more caution in the future." Yet, Camilla had chosen this man, and that counted for something. "If you ever mistreat her, you will answer to me." He had given enough evidence recently as to the form of that reckoning.

"I won't. I swear."

Leaning back in his chair sent a stinging pain through Niccolo's back. These Erizzo were untrustworthy allies, but he couldn't bear to see Camilla raise an Aretoli child alone. Her happiness was worth the risk, even if it brought a man like old Erizzo into the family.

"No one had the heart to tell Camilla what you said about her. Be sure she never finds out."

The younger Erizzo nodded quickly.

Niccolo turned to the father. "Do you agree to my terms?"

The first time an Aretoli had discussed this marriage, the family had appeared weak. Now, they were wealthy, a rising power.

Erizzo extended his hand without hesitation. "Most heartily."

NICCOLO

With contracts and deeds in hand, Niccolo visited Flavio's home a day later and knocked on Marco's door.

When his brother answered, he lowered his gaze to Niccolo's sling and swallowed. "Niccolo."

Though he hadn't expected Marco to understand, the pain in his eyes made Niccolo question whether that night had cost him two brothers. He handed Marco the bundle of papers. "I came to give you these."

Unprepared for the topic, Marco shuffled through them. "These are the contracts Flavio surrendered to Erizzo." He gasped. "How did you manage this?"

Niccolo shrugged. "Evidently, saving the republic makes a person popular. I've come to terms with Erizzo. His son should be asking Camilla to marry him as we speak."

Marco smiled faintly. "Thank you, Nico."

They were back to *Nico*. That was progress.

"I've also included two new contracts." He gestured to a wide sheet in the middle. "The first one settles the division of father's *fraterna* between us. It is fully and truly divided, and I cannot act on your behalf without explicit permission." He pointed to another document. "The second is a stewardship contract for your consideration. Essentially, you would hire me to manage your holdings. I would be obliged to deliver certain amounts of profit each year."

With such protection, Niccolo couldn't follow in his elder brother's footsteps, even if he wanted to.

Marco looked up. "I could paint."

"My thoughts exactly. Your income would be assured, and you would have full legal recourse if I failed to deliver on my obligations."

Marco offered a brief smile. "Here, sit down." He helped Niccolo to a chair before taking one himself. Hesitantly, he gestured to Niccolo's bandaged hand. "Is it bad?"

"Bad enough, yes." He flexed it, demonstrating the two fingers that remained frustratingly immobile. "But I'll survive."

Marco nodded absently and fell silent again. He had come a long way from the young man who would spew his thoughts freely. The realization saddened Niccolo, though he couldn't decide why.

He lowered his hand. "I suppose I'll carry this reminder with me for the rest of my life."

"Reminder?" Marco asked.

He suddenly felt so weary. "A reminder of how great pains spring from minor hurts, I suppose. A nudge here, a nudge there, until all that's left are two terrible choices."

"What choices?" His voice had quieted.

"The easy, wrong path and the difficult, right one. And the wish that things could have been different." He sighed. "Even when what you must do and what you can't bear to do are the same thing."

Marco pressed his lips together but still didn't share his thoughts.

Niccolo could no longer endure the silence. "Marco, I'm sorry this happened."

But his brother raised a hand, an eerily calm gesture from a young man. "I keep asking myself what would have happened next. With what he did to Rosalia, what he tried to do to you…" He shook his head and wiped an eye. "I should have done something."

Niccolo leaned forward. "What I did, none of us should have had to do. I'm glad you don't have to live with it."

He would, though. And he could. His father had understood that when he lay on his deathbed. Niccolo would carry that regret with him for the rest of his life, the agony over the decision his brother's actions had forced him to make.

Yet, given a second chance, even knowing the injuries and the memory of the life draining out of his brother's eyes, he would do it again. Only he could have summoned the will to face that terrible choice and endure it, because it would keep his family safe.

And that thought, somehow, made it bearable.

CHAPTER EIGHTEEN

SEPTEMBER 14, 1365

NICCOLO

THE NEW DOGE invited the entire Senate, every guildsman, and all the *arsenalotti* to celebrate his investiture. The ceremony was a long one, and the celebration seemed certain to last through to the early morning.

Niccolo found Giovanni and Asparia relatively quickly despite the thick crowd. Newly churched after the safe delivery of her child, Asparia had steered her husband toward the nearest libations.

Giovanni met Niccolo halfway, embracing him and planting a kiss on both cheeks. As Niccolo clasped his friend's shoulders, his limp fingers got tangled in his sleeve. While his wounds had healed over the prior two months, his coordination would never recover.

"A bit long-winded, wasn't it?" Giovanni asked cheerfully.

Niccolo shrugged, gesturing outside. "From noon until dark? I suppose you can't blame him for wanting everything to go right, considering all that's happened." Asparia slid up next to them. She still looked a little flushed, but she had recovered nicely. "How are the little monsters?" he asked her.

She brightened. "Blessedly driving someone else mad at the moment. Between chasing them and a house full of kittens, at least I'll have my old figure back in no time."

"You'll do no such thing," Giovanni cried. "I love your curves."

She crossed her arms. "I thought you loved my figure before children."

Without missing a beat, he raised his chin. "I didn't want to say anything, but you were gangly. If you insist upon losing weight, we'll have to see about another child right away."

She jabbed him in the ribs. The gesture drew the attention of a few of the other guests, but they quickly averted their gaze.

While useful, the newfound respect with which their peers now viewed the Aretoli still felt strange. Niccolo doubted he'd ever grow accustomed to it.

"Look." He pointed. "Camilla and Valentino."

"Call them over," Asparia suggested.

Giovanni shook his head. "They're too far. They'll never hear us."

"I'm sure they'll see us," Niccolo said.

Asparia snorted. "The way they fawn over each other, I doubt it. But they do make quite a pair."

"Marco sent me his latest painting," Niccolo said.

"How many is that now?" Giovanni asked. "Ten, eleven?"

"Only six," Asparia corrected. "Is he improving?"

"I honestly can't say, but he's proud of them. So is Petrarch, apparently." Niccolo flexed his left arm. The muscles of his shoulder still felt stiff, but they were healing. "If Marco's happy, that's good enough for me."

"Best behavior," Giovanni warned. "Here comes the new doge."

Marco Cornaro, adorned in the gold and white ducal robes, approached with his brother Emilio at his side. Though nearly eighty, he glided across the floor with the grace of a man half his age. Giovanni and Niccolo bowed, but Asparia offered an elegant curtsey that outshone them all.

362 | K.M. BUTLER

"Your Excellency," Giovanni greeted him.

Leaning close, Doge Cornaro whispered in a voice meant only for them. "Giovanni, Niccolo, I would not be here today without your loyalty to Venice." He turned to Niccolo, "And to your father's loyalty in our time of need. I will not forget your actions, I swear to you."

Niccolo bowed again. "He would have loved this moment. Congratulations on your election."

Marco Cornaro smiled. "I trust we can continue our close alliance?" The doge offered a knowing grin before moving on to the next group of senators.

As he left, Emilio Cornaro patted Niccolo on the shoulder.

"He probably says that to all the senators," Giovanni said lightly. But they both knew they'd been catapulted into a new tier since Constantinople. Things would never be the same.

Asparia responded to her husband, but Niccolo wasn't paying attention anymore. He met Rosalia's gaze from across the room. She had been in mourning since that day in her home. But today, she had abandoned black for a blue, high-waisted dress like the other widows.

When she turned to withdraw from the room, Niccolo muttered a quick apology to his sister and plunged through the crowd after her.

NICCOLO

He found her on a terrace overlooking the Grand Canal. He was shivering despite the warm September air. Slowly, furtively, he crossed the distance and rested his hands on the railing beside hers. "You were staring at me."

She smiled faintly without turning. For a time, they simply watched the city arrayed beneath them. An occasional bubble of laughter from the party interrupted the otherwise calm sound of water lapping against the edge of the canal. This far from the celebration, they could barely hear the music.

Finally, she asked, "Do you remember the last time we stood like this?"

How could he forget?

"It was a calm, cool night," she said. "Just the two of us."

"And our entire lives ahead of us."

She offered a faint laugh. "If only we knew."

He turned to face her. "Then I'd have taken you to the farthest corner of the world and never come back."

She met his gaze then. So much had happened since that moment almost three years past. His heart soared as her lips parted a fraction. "How about now?"

He raised his good hand but hesitated. This was his brother's wife. The church would object because she had lain with his brother.

He no longer cared. He would happily sacrifice his newly acquired renown for Rosalia.

He ran his fingers through her hair. He couldn't stop himself. He had no reason to stop himself.

She gasped at the delicacy of his touch.

"I won't let you go," he whispered. "If the church won't sanction it, then we can go to the Empire."

She pulled away, but her eyes were sparkling. "Oh, Nico. We're staying right here."

"But—"

She placed a finger on his lips. She was smiling now. "Oh, you fool, you're the hero of Venice, and my uncle is the doge."

He blinked, suddenly understanding her father's earlier wink. The pope could grant a dispensation for the right price...and for the right people.

"You already talked to him?"

"Of course I have," she laughed. "I love you. I always have. And they want you as an ally more now than ever." Beaming, she brushed a lock of his hair back into place. "Nothing, not even ecclesiastical law, will stand in the way of what I want."

Cradling her in his arms, he leaned down to meet her lips. As he kissed her, tears ran down both of their cheeks. The tension and the torment binding his heart for so long uncoiled and faded.

"I love you, Rosa. I only want to be with you and make you happy."

She brushed a stray lock of hair from his forehead and laughed. The sound soothed his wounded soul. "It's about time, you fool!"

MAJOR CHARACTERS

ARETOLI

Angelo Aretoli, patriarch of House Aretoli

Flavio Aretoli, eldest Aretoli son and senator

Niccolo Aretoli, middle Aretoli son, senator, and captain of the Venetian garrison on Crete

Asparia Aretoli, eldest Aretoli daughter

Marco Aretoli, youngest Aretoli son and aspiring painter

Camilla Aretoli, youngest Aretoli child

Pietro Corsici, trusted steward of House Aretoli

Lucia Dandolo, deceased matriarch of House Aretoli

VENETIANS

Giovanni Sabarelli, a wealthy senator and Niccolo Aretoli's friend and fellow captain

Marco Cornaro, venerable senator and close ally of House Aretoli

Rosalia Cornaro, daughter of Marco and Niccolo's beloved

Leonardo Dandolo, governor of Crete and senator of a famous family

Lorenzo Celsi, current Doge of Venice, the ceremonial head of the Venetian government

Umberto Feratollo, senator and sworn enemy of House Aretoli

Alvero Madina, senator and sworn enemy of House Aretoli

Marino Faliero, executed former doge who attempted a coup against the republic

ITALIANS

Francesco Petrarch, world-renowned poet and diplomat

Francesco da Carrara, Duke of Padua and rival of Venice

Bolando Colmiera, dreaded pirate admiral

Lucia, a mysterious foreign spy

HISTORICAL NOTE

House Aretoli incorporates many real historical figures. The Contarini, Dandolos, Celsi, Orseolos, and Cornaros were all powerful senatorial families. As governor of Crete, Leonardo Dandolo very nearly died in the Revolt of St. Tito depicted in the novel. Duke Francesco da Carrara of Padua battled with and schemed against Venice his entire life. Francesco Petrarch did visit Venice during the events of *House Aretoli*. During his lifetime, he was celebrated more for his diplomatic ability than his poetry.

Likewise, Lorenzo Celsi was a historical figure, but the circumstances of his death are a mystery. The Council of Ten investigated the events leading to his downfall, but the Senate ordered the destruction of all records of their findings and all open accusations against him. Considering that they didn't repress knowledge of Marino Faliero's amateurish coup ten years earlier, what could Celsi have done that was bad enough for the Senate to erase it from history? That mystery begged to be explored.

The fictional characters—including the Aretoli themselves—are nonetheless historically authentic. Each represents a different aspect of the mercantile, maritime, and largely literate Venetian republic of their time.

For instance, Niccolo Aretoli encapsulates the tension at the heart of Medieval Venice. As Colmiera says in the novel, Venetians behave like something "between nobleman and thug". They appreciated and exerted power like any noblemen, but their veneer of sophistication was utilitarian. First and foremost, Venetians were merchants. When the need arose, they would bribe, negotiate, fight, or rob their way out of any situation. Men like Eduardo who lacked family connections would often travel to Venice's colonies, their merchant quarters in large cities, and entirely new markets to make their fortunes. Like Marco Polo, another famous Venetian, they would follow opportunity anywhere, no matter how sordid.

As Niccolo considered long-term relationships with men like Di Natali and Neretti, so did Venetians tend to consider the "long game". They judged the value of territory by its resources, potential profits, and the costs of defending it. Venice often preferred establishing merchant quarters in other cities instead of owning land outright. Merchant quarters were profit centers; occupation and conquest involved significant costs.

This long view also caused them to take *vendetta* very seriously. Ignoring a slight would signal weakness and invite attacks on a Venetian family's holdings, business relationships, and ability to conclude strong marriages. Large problems grew from tiny causes. Venetians would happily commit a little evil for practical gain, then do penance later.

Flavio depicts the darker side of this holistic Venetian view of business. Rather than achieving feudal titles, which didn't exist in Venice, marriage enabled new markets and partners. In times of emergency, they could occur quickly, regardless of the feelings of those involved. Such marriages didn't always go smoothly, with dire consequences for those involved.

Not every Venetian was cut out for the family business, though. Many second or third sons would enter the clergy, while others with the talent would devote themselves to art, like Marco Aretoli. Though this period saw the Italian republics falling to despotism one by one, those despots created a demand for skilled sculptors, painters, and architects to create masterpieces to legitimatize their reigns.

Compared to other European powers, Venetian women had few rights. In England and France, wives were often responsible for managing estates and widows could own businesses. Not so in Venice. Economically minded, few senatorial fathers believed educating their daughters was worth the investment. The Aretoli attitude on this topic both serves story purposes and accents their outsider status. Women in abusive situations, like Rosalia's, had few options for redress. More often than not, they would be told to submit to their husbands no matter the treatment they received. Outside of the nobility, educated women became far more common. Many, like Magda, actively helped with family businesses.

On the other hand, Venetian women did have ways to contribute to family success and accumulate considerable influence. Rosalia's Easter celebration, Asparia's gossip circle, and Asparia's valiant stand against the city guards accurately reflect ways women expanded their family's influence, defended them, and opened additional opportunities.

Of course, despite deep faith and omnipresent preaching, the guy down the street was sometimes too irresistible. Camilla's all-to-familiar story shows how individual decisions were inseparable from a family's fortunes. Paternity tests didn't exist, and unmarried men were under no obligation to claim a child. In such situations, a woman's fate depended on whether her ancestors had laid a strong foundation of good decisions to earn wealth, fame, and a history of honorable service. If they had, that family could pay or persuade the father to legitimatize a child with a hasty marriage. As with everything in Venice, families rose and fell together. A pregnancy could ruin an entire family, but a famous and wealthy family had the influence necessary to avoid scandal from those inevitable accidents.

While Christian faith was omnipresent, it didn't restrict Venetians' actions concerning brothels. Venice became well known for its brothels and the alluring companions within them. Both married and unmarried men regularly frequented them, and doing so wasn't considered shameful. Brothels offered more than prostitution, including games, performances, and musical entertainment. Men would discuss the issues of the day, and the women who worked there, like Lucia, would hear private information unattainable elsewhere.

As a maritime republic, Venice relied upon the sea for wealth and its fleet for its survival. Convoys traversed the Mediterranean and Black Seas twice a year. The massive Arsenal shipyard produced every Venetian galley that existed. When operating at full capacity, its assembly line could launch a new galley every couple of hours.

Pirates were omnipresent and could range from individual ships to coordinated fleets like Colmiera's. The republic had a mixed attitude toward these pirates. While Venice's ships were generally the fastest—they were manned by professional rowers who drilled relentlessly—pirates could still pick off individual exhausted or damaged ships. On the other hand, Venetians also viewed pirates as both potential customers and sources of cheap goods. As long as those pirates hadn't attacked their vessels, Venetians would welcome them into their ports and resupply them. Venetians were still merchants, after all.

I'd like to say a word about dialogue. I've chosen to use modern language to make the characters relatable to my audience. Since my characters would have spoken Tuscan, Venetian, or Greek anyways, I saw no harm in conveying the concepts my characters would have perceived rather than the words their ears would have heard. For a similar reason, I refer to the *Byzantine Empire*, even though that term wasn't invented until long after it fell to Mehmet II.

To those interested in learning more about Venice, I highly recommend John Julius Norwich's *History of Venice.* It is both informative and highly entertaining.

I hope the characters and story provided a sufficiently entertaining read to justify any liberties I've taken. Thank you for reading!

ABOUT THE AUTHOR

 K.M. Butler studied literature at Carnegie Mellon University and has always had an avid interest in history. His writing influences are *The Lions of al-Rassan* by Guy Gavriel Kay and Colleen McCullough's *Masters of Rome* series.

He lives in Philadelphia with his wife and two daughters. His wife is his first and harshest editor, while his daughters always want his stories to feature more blood and talking animals, but never at the same time.

Contact K.M. Butler at kmbutlerauthor@yahoo.com or on Twitter at @kmbutlerauthor.

ALSO AVAILABLE FROM
K.M. BUTLER

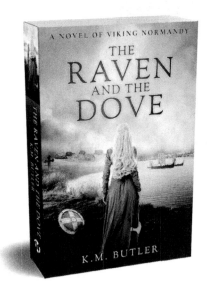

THE RAVEN AND THE DOVE

At the end of the Viking Age, Norse shieldmaiden Halla and Frankish landowner Taurin must overcome their hatred to bring their peoples together. Failure means seeing their family, their homes, and their futures fall to ruin.

Historical Novel Society's Editor's Choice Winner

ALSO AVAILABLE FROM
K.M. BUTLER

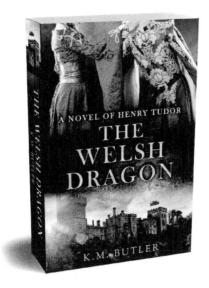

THE WELSH DRAGON

Amid the Wars of the Roses, Henry Tudor struggles to build a humble life in exile despite being relentlessly pursued by enemies jealous of his single drop of royal blood.

Bosworth awaits, promising either a crown or his doom.

Long-listed for the 2020 Chaucer Book Awards

Printed in Great Britain
by Amazon

39878279R00219